Praise for Lois Richer
and her novels

"Baby on the Way by Lois Richer is a delightful gem that sparkles with tender poignancy."
—*Romantic Times BOOKreviews*

"His Answered Prayer is another winner and will please readers who love traditional story lines with new twists and terrific characters."
—*Romantic Times BOOKreviews*

"Mother's Day Miracle by Lois Richer is quite possibly her finest book!...The only problem with this heartwarming story about blossoming love is that it ends too soon."
—*Romantic Times BOOKreviews*

D0206820

LOIS RICHER

Baby on the Way

Wedding on the Way

Steeple
Hill®

Published by Steeple Hill Books™

STEEPLE HILL BOOKS

Steeple
Hill®

ISBN-13: 978-0-373-65200-6
ISBN-10: 0-373-65200-3

BABY ON THE WAY AND WEDDING ON THE WAY

BABY ON THE WAY
Copyright © 1999 by Lois M. Richer

WEDDING ON THE WAY
Copyright © 1999 by Lois M. Richer

www.SteepleHill.com

Printed in U.S.A.

CONTENTS

Books by Lois Richer

LOIS RICHER

Sneaking a flashlight under the blankets, hiding in a thicket of Caragana bushes where no one could see, pushing books into socks to take to camp—those are just some of the things Lois Richer freely admits to in her pursuit of the written word. "I'm a book-a-holic. I can't do without stories," she confesses. "It's always been that way." Her love of language evolved into writing her own stories. Today her passion is to create tales of personal struggle that lead to triumph over life's rocky road. For Lois, a happy ending is essential. "In my stories, as in my own life, God has a way of making all things beautiful. Writing a love story is my way of reinforcing my faith in His ultimate goodness toward us—His precious children."

BABY ON THE WAY

People are not cast off by the Lord forever.
Though He brings grief, He will show compassion,
so great is His unfailing love.

—*Lamentations* 3:31–32

For Robynne Rogers-Healey, Ph.D.
You make me laugh, and cry, shake my head and nod in agreement, but always, always, I appreciate what a gold mine of blessing you are to my spirit. Thanks for being the one I can run to, whine beside, cry on, tease, giggle over and drink gallons of coffee with no matter how far away we live or how many changes God sends into our lives.
You are my friend.
I love you.

Chapter One

❧

"It must be terribly difficult for poor Caitlin without her husband. And her being eight months pregnant." The whispered remark of the nurse carried clearly into the hallway.

Caitlin Andrews lifted her face as she slipped around the side of the receptionist's desk and into the foyer, refusing to acknowledge the commiserating look she knew she'd see on the nurses' faces. Pity was the one emotion she couldn't afford right now. She tugged her coat from the rack and slung it over her shoulders before walking outside.

I'll manage, she decided fiercely, braving the gusting wind. She lifted her chin, allowing the watery afternoon sun to warm her. *I always have.*

Of course pregnancy *would* be infinitely more enjoyable with a husband in the picture. She'd never even considered life as a widow, and certainly not before she'd welcomed her first child into the world. This was *not* part of her plan.

"Unfortunately, my plans don't count for much," Caitlin Andrews acknowledged tiredly, thoroughly out of sorts after an hour spent in the doctor's office where she'd watched the scale move further upward.

She crossed the street and moved toward the nearby coffee shop. Pushing the door open, she breathed in the wonderful aroma of freshly brewed coffee.

"You and I are just going to have to make do with what we've got, Junior." The baby kicked her in the ribs to indicate his feelings in the matter.

"And may I remind you that we've only got each other?"

He thumped again, hard and strong. She smiled at the strength of that jab.

The restaurant was filled with people and Caitlin had to wait a few minutes for a place to sit. Finally a mother and her two small children got up and went outside while the father paid the bill.

A family, whole and complete. The picture emphasized her own lonely state and Caitlin made herself look away.

Just get yourself into the booth. Smile. Take off your coat. Pretend everything's fine. Be strong.

"Hi, sweetie. Still growing I see." The teasing waitress winked and plopped down Caitlin's usual order of a pot of tea and a fat bran muffin.

"Hi, Ruth." Caitlin dipped the tea bag into the water, her voice low and controlled. "You're not going to lecture about eating for two again, are you?"

Caitlin had walked miles along the riverbank and faithfully counted every calorie that passed her lips for the past six months. And for all her efforts she'd just increased another two pounds! That wasn't in the plan, either.

"Weight up? It's only natural when...well, you know!" Ruth held out another bran muffin, her smile wicked.

"That is not funny!" Caitlin looked at the friendly woman. "And you should know that someone in my condition is not to be trifled with."

Ruth's hearty chuckle ignored Caitlin's chiding look.

"Someone in your condition shouldn't be out in this weather," she advised lightly. Her long vivid fingernails tapped the table. "Don't you know there's a storm warning out for tonight? Snow and blowing snow."

"It's only the first of October, Ruth. Winter can't come yet." Caitlin smiled placidly, well used to the vagaries of Minnesota weather. "It's just a threat weathermen use to warn us of what's to come. The sun's still shining."

"If that isn't positive thinking, I don't know what is. Honey, you just keep that chin up. You're going to need it." Shaking her head, Ruth glanced down pityingly. "Drink your tea, Mrs. Andrews. You'll feel better."

"I hate tea." Caitlin made a face at the white china pot. "Coffee is the beverage for any hour of the day or night,'' she informed the older woman, noting the sparkle of amusement in Ruth's laughing eyes.

''I've heard. In fact, I think it was the last time you were here. Unfortunately for you,'' the waitress eyed her protruding stomach, ''Andrews Junior doesn't like the stuff. So you get tea.''

''I know,'' Caitlin said. ''And what Junior wants, Junior gets. This kid is going to be a real tyrant.''

The waitress, a slim, youthful mother of five chuckled and turned away to take another order. Caitlin poured out a cup of the steaming liquid, allowing the fresh clean scent of peppermint to soothe her jangled nerves.

For the umpteenth time that day she wished Michael were here to talk to, to lean against, to hold her. And for the umpteenth time she told herself to get on with her life. Michael wasn't ever going to be there anymore. He was dead. There were only her and the baby now.

''Lyn?''

Caitlin was so engrossed in her thoughts of the past that she jumped in surprise. Only one person used that shortened version of her name.

''Jordan.'' She peered up through her lashes, hoping she was wrong.

Oh no, she groaned. Not now. Not today!

''Caitlin. I thought it was you. Your hair is different.''

Her brother-in-law's voice boomed in that deep bass tone she could have recognized from several blocks away. She knew the sound well, heard it in her dreams sometimes. She'd never been able to forget Jordan.

His curious glance moved from her face to the obvious mound of her stomach. She watched his gold eyes widen in surprise.

"Uh, that is, oh." The craggy face, so unlike Michael's, drooped in shock.

She smiled. "Yes, oh. A master of understatement as usual, Jordan."

Not now, she begged silently to the God she hadn't prayed to since that awful night seven months ago.

Please don't do this to me now. Not while my emotions are doing these ridiculous prenatal flip-flops. Not when I've almost made it through this on my own. Not now, when I'd almost convinced myself that I don't need Michael's family.

She opened her eyes but Jordan was still standing there, gawking at her.

"How are you?" Caitlin couldn't help but ask, despite the lump in her throat. Her question was polite, perfunctory, that of one stranger to another.

He didn't pretend civility. Instead he folded his muscle-honed body onto the bench seat opposite hers. As he leaned forward, his face mere inches from her own, she caught a whiff of his tangy lime-scented aftershave.

"I'm just absolutely fantastic now that I know I'm going to be an uncle, Lyn." His tanned face clenched in a rigid mask, his words icy chips of mockery.

The sting of his glittering eyes ate at her, cutting through her carefully preserved mask of control.

Hadn't it always been that way? Hadn't Jordan always cut right to the heart of things?

"Good grief, Lyn, why didn't you tell me? Or Mom and Dad? Someone!"

She watched as he visibly fought to control his temper and that irritated her.

"You weren't here, remember? And your parents have been away on that trip to Europe for the past three months. Remember?"

Caitlin swallowed. He wasn't buying it. Jordan mad was infinitely worse than Jordan bossy.

"What about before they left? Why couldn't you have told my parents you were expecting Michael's baby then?" A muscle twitched at the corner of his mouth, testament to his anger. "It would have meant the world to them."

"I had to get used to the idea first myself. I wasn't exactly expecting it, you know." She glared at him. "By then they were planning their trip to get away, to try to put Michael's loss behind them. It just wasn't the right time." Caitlin flushed.

He *would* put her in the wrong. It was just like old times, she fumed. Unbidden, Jordan's scathing remarks about her elopement with Michael flew across her brain. *She* should have known better, waited a while, stopped to think.

Caitlin had felt like a helpless ninny then, worried that Jordan would think she was marrying Michael on the rebound from him. Stupidly she'd kept quiet, waited for Michael to take charge of the situation, needing his protection against Jordan's pushiness.

Now she was alone. And *she* was in charge.

"Eventually they will know," she explained, easing her aching back against the seat. "Now that they're back, I'll tell them soon."

She shrugged, striving for nonchalance. Jordan Andrews prided himself on his ability to look inside people. It was a trait most folks didn't expect to find in a man obsessed with the intricacies of high-tech computer systems.

"When?"

"This is my situation to deal with, Jordan. Mine. I'll handle it in my own way."

He watched her. Caitlin knew those assessing, calculating eyes could see clear through to the fear that filled her soul. Fear that he'd see how scared she was, fear that he'd seen how easy it would be to give up her staunch determination to manage her life alone.

"It's still the same old story, isn't it, Lyn? You're determined not to let anyone past those steel bars and into your heart."

"Hardly anything that melodramatic, Jordan." She forced a note of calm reason into her voice. If he couldn't be mature about the past, she would.

"I simply felt there was no need to worry your mother and father ahead of time. I've spoken with them once or twice, of course, but I didn't want to disturb them, especially when they were still mourning Michael."

She flushed under his condemning look, her chin thrust out defiantly. "I never meant to *not* tell them!'

"Yeah, right." The exasperation in his voice

mocked her. "And when is the blessed event? By the looks of you, it can't be long now."

Jordan had always been able to get to her weakest spot without really trying. Just a few well-chosen words and Michael's brother could score a direct hit on her most vulnerable area. Right now that happened to be her shape, or rather, the lack of it.

He was the quintessential male, always right, always in control. Once she'd loved that about him, that calm assuredness, that certainty, as if he knew exactly what he was doing with his life. Once she'd thought Jordan would be the man she would marry.

Once she'd been stupid, childish, trusting and he'd pushed her away like an annoying pest.

Well, she wasn't buying into his world again. She was an adult now, in charge of her own life. Not some insecure young girl to be manipulated by the crazy dreams and impossible wishes she'd held ten years ago.

Caitlin couldn't afford to live in make-believe any more. Happily ever after was a nice dream, but it wasn't very realistic. Not for her. She'd figured that out after Michael died.

She reined in her fluctuating emotions with an effort, trying to remember her positive self-talk. It would be a relief if she could vent this building frustration, but this wasn't the time or the place. She decided to try a different tactic, turn the tables on him, smother him with kindness.

"Thank you, Jordan," she offered sweetly. "I feel fine."

He grinned unrepentantly, the light of understanding dawning. Caitlin had to admit, he wasn't slow on the uptake. Never had been.

"You're worried about your looks?" He crowed with uncanny perception. "You were beautiful before. Pregnant, you're the most gorgeous woman in the place. You should know that by now."

A little bubble of mirth tickled inside her at his familiar phrasing. Caitlin shrugged. She had never been able to stay mad at Jordan for long. Perhaps he hadn't forgiven her for marrying Michael, but at least he was willing to put it behind them. For now.

"Look, Jordan, I've had a lot to deal with. And time sort of slipped away."

His stare was relentless. Caitlin knew she'd have to elaborate but opening up her heart wasn't easy.

"I'm an adult, Jordan. I am capable of running my own life. And that means *without* your interference. I'm not trying to keep your parents away. They're the baby's grandparents, they deserve to know." She swallowed the lump of fear that clogged her throat and continued, trying to explain why this was so important.

"When I tell your mother and father about this child, it will be because I want them to be happy and share it with me, so we can remember Michael together." Using her eyes, she implored him to, just this once, understand.

"I didn't want them to come racing home, cancel their plans, just to worry. I don't want them to hang around just because they think I can't handle having a baby on my own. I don't want them to think that because I was married to Michael, they have to stand in for him.'' She sipped her tea. ''They have their own lives to lead. I'm perfectly capable of managing my life without anyone's interference.''

It was a long speech and Caitlin wasn't sure even now that it made a lot of sense to him. It was hard to explain that she just knew she was supposed to do this on her own. It was her job. That's why God always took away the people she loved. So she would be strong.

''Lyn, I wasn't trying to interfere. I was just surprised.'' He looked up at her sheepishly. ''Okay...and angry.''

She stared him down.

''All right! And upset.'' He still sounded mad as he cleared his throat. ''I had hoped...'' his voice died away. ''Never mind. I just thought that this one time you might accept some help,'' he muttered, staring at his hands.

Caitlin frowned at him. ''Next time, please wait until I ask for help.''

''Which you never will,'' he grumbled, echoing her inmost thoughts. It was proof positive that Jordan knew far too much about the way her mind worked.

''I am going to do this my way, Jordan. In my own time, depending on myself.'' Her eyes held his as she reiterated her plan of action in the back of her mind. ''It's just the way it has to be.''

''No, it isn't the way it has to be at all.'' His accusing stare glowed hot behind the round lenses of his wire-rimmed glasses. ''It's the way you want it. It's the way you think your life has to be. Fine. Be alone. Refuse to accept anyone's help. But just remember one thing.''

''And what is that?'' She didn't have to ask. She knew what he'd say even before he said the words.

''Someday you're going to have to depend on someone else. And when you do—'' he paused ''—when that day comes, remember that you have people who are just waiting to be asked to help.''

''Fine.'' She nodded her head. ''And you understand that I want to have Michael's baby my way, the way I've planned.'' At his reluctant nod, Caitlin gathered her belongings. ''I have to go. The next bus will be along in a minute.''

She slipped her shoes on, ignoring the pinch against her toes. Taking a deep breath, she heaved herself up from the low booth.

Caitlin wasn't surprised to see him slide out or to feel Jordan's strong hand beneath her elbow, taking some of her weight as he gently assisted her. He'd always been there, making his presence felt.

''Why aren't you driving?'' Concern wrinkled his forehead. ''Lyn, did you have an accident?''

She grimaced. As usual, Jordan was jumping to conclusions about her. *Poor little Lyn couldn't manage.* Caitlin fidgeted, as frustrated by his consideration as she was touched. It would have been nice not to have to explain this particular weakness.

Summoning all her nerve, she met his puzzled glance.

''No, not an accident. It's just that, well, um…''

She lowered her voice and spoke the truth. "The car's not really built for pregnant women."

He burst out laughing then, great boisterous chuckles that had the other patrons smiling benignly at them.

"It's not that funny," she complained.

"Yes, Caitlin, it is very funny. You continue to hang on to that decrepit heap of rusting metal regardless of its impracticality and all advice to the contrary. That dinky little two-seater has been around for ages." He shook his head, his mouth creased in a grin.

"I've told you before what I think of a ragtop with our frigid winters. Now you're stuck without wheels because you can't fit into the thing." His broad shoulders shook with renewed laughter, his eyes twinkling down at her. "Priceless!"

"I love Bertha!" She defended her car staunchly. "And when that baby comes, we'll take rides in her together."

"No doubt! At twenty below, with the top stuck down, I suppose, and just to prove you can do it."

There was no point in telling Jordan that she kept the car because it was her one and only link with the woman who'd cared for her since her parents had been killed in a car accident when she was ten. He'd probably deride her for being too sentimental about a woman who'd never shown the least bit of affection for her.

Caitlin sighed. Maybe she was being silly. In actual fact, the car wasn't really a gift, it was hers simply because she was next of kin. At least Aunt Lucy had admitted that much about her. And even that one familial link had been taken away.

Jordan lifted her coat from the seat and helped her into it with that special brand of care he always conferred on a woman. It was the sort of attentive thoughtfulness that made her feel special.

Caitlin supposed she should have felt flattered by his concern, but as she straightened her bulging sweater, she grimaced ruefully. She didn't feel flattered or feminine. Actually, she felt more like a Mack truck, one that was about to burst at the seams.

"How much longer?"

The low voice was just behind her shoulder. She could feel the heat of his body radiating against her as his big frame shielded her from the jostle of other customers filling the small coffee shop.

"Not long," she told him. "I can hardly wait."

"How long, exactly?" he demanded, turning her to face him.

Caitlin sighed. She'd have to tell him. She wouldn't put it past Jordan to phone the doctor himself. None of the Andrews family were exactly reticent when it came to getting exactly what they wanted.

"Six weeks from today is *supposed* to be my due date," she informed him. "But babies don't always arrive on time. I could go up to two weeks longer."

"Or you could go into labor right now." His voice was low and concerned as he searched her tired face. "You look beat."

He grinned that slow, lazy smile that spread to a

warm glow and mesmerized her into agreeing to whatever he said. Caitlin blinked, trying to reassert herself.

"Come on, I'll give you a lift home. I'm not sure bus drivers know the latest in Lamaze techniques."

Caitlin smiled, softly rubbing her aching back with one hand, hoping to ease the momentary discomfort.

"Oh, right! And I suppose you do?"

Just then her abdomen hardened with a contraction. She sucked in her breath as Jordan's hands lifted her long hair free and spread it down her back.

Whew, this was a strong one. She concentrated on breathing through it, immersed in the sensation.

As he pulled her coat together in front, Jordan's hand accidentally brushed against her rock-hard midsection. Shock, mixed with sheer panic washed over his tanned face, draining it of all color.

His wide eyes stared into hers and Caitlin noted the white lines of strain creasing his face. She breathed steadily, waiting for the end of the false contraction. When it came, she drew a calming breath and moved toward the door.

Within seconds Jordan had paid the bill, rushed her out the door and propelled her over to a full-size silver-gray sedan. Moments later Caitlin was sinking back gratefully, appreciating the smooth comfortable leather interior as it curved around her tired body. Junior was settling down now, thank goodness.

She breathed a sigh of relief which turned into a startled gasp as Jordan slammed all two hundred pounds of his muscular frame into his bucket seat and tore away from the curb with a squeal of tires that would do a rowdy teenager proud.

"See an old girlfriend?" she teased, glancing at him.

He returned her look with an uptilted eyebrow that reminded her *she* was one of Jordan's old girlfriends. The one that had married his brother.

The deep groove beside his mouth kept his features frozen in a mask as his fingers clenched the leather wheel. Caitlin frowned at the obvious signs of stress. She pressed her hand on his muscled forearm.

"Jordan, what's wrong?"

"Which hospital?" he growled.

"I'm not going to the hospital," she told him in confusion. "I'm going to Wintergreen."

"Wintergreen?"

"It's the old Cardmore house. I bought it. I'm fixing it up. It's going to be a new start for the baby and me." A place where she could forget the memories and move on.

"You're going to have the baby at home?" He squeaked the words out, risking a wide-eyed glance of horror over his shoulder.

Caitlin sighed. "Pull over, Jordan."

When he kept going Caitlin cleared her throat. "Jordan. Pull over. Now!"

"What?" His strong tanned fingers still gripped the steering wheel.

"Jordan, I am not going to the hospital. I am not, repeat *not*, in labor." She kept her lips from twitching only by using the utmost restraint.

"But...but...I..." His voice died away in embarrassment.

Caitlin took compassion on his obvious distress and explained. "That was a sort of fake contraction," she murmured, conscious of his gaze on her stomach. "It happens more and more lately."

His dark eyebrows rose in disbelief.

"Scout's honor," she promised. "Doctors call them Braxton-Hicks contractions." She grinned at his skeptical face.

"Trust me," she told him in an echo of his own tone. "I do know what I'm talking about. They've gone now."

Jordan looked less than convinced, but when she nodded again, he seemed slightly relieved.

"It doesn't mean I'm going to give birth in your car." Caitlin smiled, struggling to maintain the look of solemn assurance. "Promise."

When his eyebrows quirked and his eyes opened wide, she couldn't hold on any longer. Her giggles finally erupted at the look of patent relief on his face.

He breathed at last, eyes closed, head bowed. Color began to return to his chiseled profile. "Sorry," he said as, one by one, his fingers released their death grip on the wheel. "Robyn pulled a 'not my time' one on me last summer."

His high cheekbones tinged a bright pink. "She had her baby in the back seat of my car at the hospital doors. Talk about procrastination!"

Robyn, Jordan's older sister, was famous for postponing things until the last possible moment. Apparently she'd done it once too often.

Caitlin laughed out loud at the chagrin that contorted his handsome features into a mask of dismay. It felt good to laugh again.

"It's not funny," he told her, his face mournful. "I loved that car, but I had to sell it. I could never drive it afterward without hearing her calling me names and carrying on. I felt totally helpless." He huffed, obviously affronted at the indignity he'd suffered.

"She even had the nerve to say it was my fault for not getting to her house earlier! How did I know she'd decide to get things moving just before I showed up? I only went over in the first place to visit Glen. You remember her husband?" He rolled his eyes. "I don't know how he stands her."

It wasn't easy to ignore his wounded look, but she just managed to stifle the laugh that threatened to spill out. This was something to remember, Jordan Andrews completely out of his depth.

"I promise not to do that," Caitlin told him solemnly. "Can I go home now?"

Jordan drove her home all right, at a sedate twenty miles an hour through the streets of a town in the throes of rush hour. He wasn't doing anything that would start labor he told her frankly, correctly interpreting her impatient glance at the speedometer.

"It sure is cold here," he muttered finally, cranking up the heater. "I can't seem to get warm lately."

"Yes, well, life in the tropics will do that to you.

Wasn't Tahiti where you were heading after the funeral?''

"Yep, the sunny South Pacific."

"Must have been nice."

If her voice betrayed just a hint of envy at his ability to escape the mean existence of those dreadful months after Michael's death, Jordan didn't comment on it. He also never mentioned the reason he'd decided to leave so abruptly the day following the funeral. She'd never understood that, but she'd accepted it.

"So how long have you been back?"

"Actually—" he snorted in amusement "—I should be used to this weather. I've been back for a month. In the country, that is. I had a little business in New York first. I flew into Oakburn yesterday."

Caitlin pretended to study the curving riverbank. Only a few of the brilliant red and gold leaves still hung on the trees. Hikers and joggers walked through the crisp crackling carpet underfoot. And the carefully tended pathways bulged with outdoor enthusiasts taking advantage of the sunny fall weather.

Her nose caught just a hint of wood smoke in the air as up ahead a family gathered around a fire pit. A wiener roast in the park. She smiled at the memory that flickered across her mind.

"How is Robyn?" Caitlin asked.

Michael's sister had announced her pregnancy just after Caitlin had decided she was in love with Michael. Everyone in the Andrews family had been thrilled at the thought of a new baby. Caitlin knew they'd welcome Junior with open arms simply because this was

Michael's child. Maybe they'd even try to take him away from her. Then she'd really have no one.

Caitlin shoved the ugly thought away with grim determination.

Jordan frowned, obviously organizing his thoughts.

"Robyn? Oh, you mean with the baby. She's fine. I still can't believe she called the kid Eudora. I called her Huey for a while. It seemed fitting—she was totally bald."

Jordan's strong fingers jerked the wheel suddenly, twisting out of the path of an oncoming motorist in the wrong lane. There was no lull in his conversation which seemed remarkable.

There wasn't a lot that fazed Jordan. Apparently births outranked everything else. She grinned again, cherishing the greenish-tinged look she'd seen on his face.

"I didn't like the other option much. Anyway, I always remember Mrs. Hatchet calling people 'dumb Doras' when they didn't catch on to her algebra lesson."

Caitlin grinned. Everyone who had been under the malevolent thumb of Agatha Hatchet had been called that at one time or another in their high school years.

"Seems too bad to saddle a kid with that kind of negative self-image label from day one." He shrugged helplessly.

Caitlin smiled. If she remembered correctly, Jordan himself had acquired a few rather interesting tags in high school.

"There are worse things to be saddled with," she

murmured. "Wasn't *Jordan the man, who rolled the van,* one of yours? And how about *Heartthrob Andrews?*"

"Well, if that isn't the pot talking to the kettle!" Those glowing eyes glittered with good humor. "I seem to remember *Cait the Great* when it came to chemistry. And *Dim Lyn* in, let's see, wasn't it history and phys ed?" A smug little smile tilted his lips.

"You tell me, Jordan Andrews...just how many of those seventeenth-century dates can you still remember?" She flushed at the old nickname, the familiar tide of indignation surging upward with the memories of those unhappy years.

He held up a hand. "Truce." He called out, grinning. "Let's just admit that neither one of us has done too badly. Especially you." He whistled at the metal name tag she'd forgotten to remove from the tip of her collar. "Doing some teaching now, huh? Do I call you *Professor* Lyn?"

Caitlin lifted her chin. She ignored the question and the reference to her newly acquired job. That had been her dream, hers and Michael's. While she'd dreamed of completing her doctoral studies as a nutrition and dietetic counselor, he had finally decided to complete his own education. More dreams that had died with him.

"You can call me whatever you want." She grinned.

There were a lot of things she preferred to forget about the old days. Her painful crush on Jordan during those high school years was only one of them. She was about to change the subject when he interrupted her thoughts.

"Well, here we are, safe at home with nary a scratch."

Caitlin glanced around, surprised at how quickly the time had gone. She hadn't even noticed they were near her home.

"I wasn't actually coming here," she muttered. "I told you I want to go to Wintergreen. I've got to get it ready."

"That old barn? Ready for what?" He frowned.

Caitlin was sure he was about to offer some unwanted advice about purchasing a huge, rambling Victorian mansion to live in, so she hurried into speech.

"I've invited some friends to live there with me. We're going to share the place. Do you remember Maryann MacGregor? She married Terrence Arnold, that lawyer from New York. Anyway, he died a while ago and she came back home to raise her daughter."

"Shy, quiet little Maryann married a hotshot, eh? Who'd have thought she'd become famous. And now she's going to live with *you*, the person who always has to be alone?"

Caitlin stuck her tongue out at him and then flushed in embarrassment. Why did she let him get to her like this? She was acting like a bratty kid.

"Not exactly live with. We each have our own suites. Beth Ainslow and I share the first two floors and Maryann has the top floor. Beth and her sister Veronica are already living at Wintergreen."

"Sounds like fun. At least you'll have help nearby

if you need it. Though, I'm not sure you should be doing much. As I recall, that place needs a lot of work. Are you sure it's safe?'' Jordan fiddled with his jacket, avoiding her eyes.

''Not so much work is left now. Most of the big stuff is already done. That's partly what's been keeping me so busy. I've had walls removed and new ones put in, carpets and flooring, cabinets, the entire thing looks totally different inside.''

Caitlin ignored his skeptical look. She *had* been busy. On purpose. It left less time to think.

''All we have to do is a little decorating. I'm looking forward to it.''

''Well, I'm not taking you there now, Lyn. It's late and you need to put your feet up and relax.'' He swung open his door, his mouth set in a determined line as he strode around the car he'd illegally parked in the No Parking zone in front of her condo.

Caitlin sighed with resignation. No one could change Jordan's mind once he'd set it on something and there wasn't any point trying. Besides, she did want to get these shoes off.

He opened the door and Caitlin swung her feet out tiredly, accepting his helping hand as she stood.

''Beth's a widow, too. Her husband was killed in an accident.''

Jordan didn't reply. Instead he escorted her into the house through the sporadically swirling autumn leaves before returning with her packages.

''I think that's all you had.'' He set the bag down

inside the door and then straightened, his eyes studying her.

"Thanks, Jordan. I appreciate the lift." She stood there, not knowing what else to say. What *did* one say to an old boyfriend who was also your brother-in-law?

"You're welcome. I've gotta go. I have to pick up some parts for my modem at the airport. I'm working on something new." Jordan bent over to brush his lips against her cheek.

"See ya, little mama," he murmured. His face peered down at her. "Take it easy. If you need anything, I mean anything," he emphasized, "just call."

She accepted his admonition and his card, and bid him good-night without promising anything. That was Jordan, she reflected with a grin, always dashing off on the trail of a new computer gizmo. It was good to know some things never changed.

She closed the door of her condo and sighed. "Pack," she ordered her tired brain. "Pack or you'll never get moved."

Hours later, after the newscast, Caitlin forced herself to bank the fire, refold her afghan and shut off the lights before awkwardly climbing the stairs to bed. Only once she was tucked up in the big four-poster with a thick comforter to shield against the north wind howling outside her window, did she allow herself to think about meeting Jordan again.

He hadn't changed much. But somehow, today Jordan had seemed more human. Less bossy than usual. Less angry. He hadn't laughed at her, not really. He'd even seemed to understand.

And he had said he would be there if she needed him.

Caitlin tugged the thick softness around her ears, allowing a smile to curve her tired mouth. It would be nice to have a friend to call on if she needed one. Even if that friend was a know-it-all, Type A personality like Jordan Andrews.

She lay there a long time, thinking about him, remembering. The rugged, jutting angles of his handsome face filled her mind's eye. A girl could get used to those strong arms and broad shoulders. Once, a long time ago, she'd even wanted to stay there and hide. But that was then and Jordan had never returned her foolish affections, not the way she wanted.

Caitlin mocked her wayward thoughts. She wasn't a little girl any more. She knew all about life. Just as you got used to having that shoulder to lean on, it would disappear and you'd have to start on your own all over again. She knew that better than anyone. It had happened too many times to count and Caitlin wasn't a slow learner.

But she was in control of her own life now, looking out for herself. It was the way the world was. She was an orphan and a widow, on her own, expecting a baby. Her husband was gone. God expected her to grow up, dig her heels in, and manage her life as best she could.

She couldn't depend on anyone else. And especially not Jordan.

She had only herself.

"It will be enough," she told herself, thrusting away the memory of those glowing gold eyes. It had to be.

Chapter Two

"I'm completely settled in at the house, Caitlin. It's great!" Beth's enthusiasm was contagious, even over the phone line. "You call me when you're ready to move anything, okay? I know lots of people who'd be happy to help an attractive pregnant little widow like you."

"Oh, brother!" Caitlin yawned, delighted to be able to relax on a Friday evening, knowing she didn't have to get up early tomorrow.

"After all," Beth added, "it'll be easier for the old poker faces uptown to keep track of us brazen hussies once we're all in the same place."

Caitlin giggled, snuggling her mug of tea against her cheek as she slouched in her favorite chair. She ignored the packing boxes scattered about her apartment.

"I know what you mean. They call us the Widows of Wintergreen. Isn't it awful?"

Beth sniffed. "At least they're leaving someone else alone when they gossip about us. That's good. Isn't it?"

Caitlin knew everyone in town expected fireworks when Garrett Winthrop finally met up with Beth, his high school fiancée. She could just imagine that the hottest topic on coffee row had reached Beth's ears days ago. She sympathized with the frustration in her friend's voice.

"They'll find someone else pretty soon, Beth. How'd your first week of business go?"

"It's been a smashing success." Beth's voice brightened. "Veronica came after school today and we unpacked those Christmas things. I can hardly wait to open officially. As soon as I get some fresh stock, that is." She giggled.

"I'm like a little kid! I've never wanted to celebrate Thanksgiving and Jesus' birth as much as I do this year. I can hardly wait. I feel as if I'm going to do really well in my first year of business."

"Good for you. Just keep that attitude, kiddo. You'll show 'em!"

Beth's flower shop was the new love of her life and she gladly shared it with anyone who listened. The fact that her sister had willingly pitched in to help get things ready was a big weight off Beth's shoulders.

"How was your day?" Beth's voice softened.

It had been twelve hours to forget, Caitlin conceded privately. Nothing had gone right. Her alarm clock declined to ring at the appointed hour, allowing little time for Caitlin's usually prolonged morning routine and no time at all to relax and contemplate her future life at Wintergreen or the advent of Jordan Andrews.

"You don't want to know, Beth. Pregnancy might increase your waist, but it does not increase your ability to tolerate certain stubborn people." She launched into an account of a client at the counseling place where she worked.

"So you didn't advise him to go back and ask Mommy for her fat-laden recipe for fried green tomatoes?" Beth giggled at the telling silence, then switched topics. "I heard you had a visitor."

The town gossips. Privacy in Oakburn was an almost impossible feat. Which was why, up until now, Caitlin had always kept mostly to herself. In Oakburn, most of the women her age had husbands and a family to keep them busy. She had friends at work certainly, but they had never become very close.

It had been relatively easy to stay a loner with Michael's parents on an extended holiday overseas, but they were back now. In fact, she'd received a call only this morning. Caitlin pushed aside the guilty reminder that she still hadn't told them about the baby. They just wanted to see her, they said. Caitlin knew it was time to tell them herself, before someone else did.

Her high school friends Maryann and Beth had come back to Oakburn within weeks of each other, and with them, Caitlin had felt as if an old connection was restored. They didn't ask a lot of questions, but she knew they were there and that they cared. It helped.

"You've been visiting the cronies on coffee row, I

see, Beth. Yes, my brother-in-law Jordan is back. He drove me home last night.'' And stirred up a few unhappy memories while he was at it.

"Good! He can help you move your stuff tomorrow. It's time you got settled in here before the snow flies for good. That baby isn't going to wait forever.''

"I know." Caitlin yawned again. "I keep meaning to do it, but something else always gets in the way.''

"Procrastination is no excuse. Ask him. Right away!''

"I don't want to ask him. He'll bulldoze his way in here and take over everything. I want my move to Wintergreen to be happy, not frustrating. Jordan is just too bossy.''

"Caitlin, you can do this. And from what I hear, your Jordan has a good strong back and great strong arms, which are exactly what you need.''

"I don't need him, Beth,'' she insisted stubbornly. "I can manage.''

"How?''

A long, drawn out pause hung between them.

"You find someone and find them quickly. You should have been moved and settled in weeks ago. You know Maryann and I can be over there in two minutes to help.'' Beth waited a moment. "Do you hear me, Caitlin Andrews?''

"Yes, mother.'' Caitlin hung up the phone with a smile, knowing her old friend was only trying to help. And help wasn't a bad thing right now, she decided, glancing around the messy room.

Boxes littered the worn gray carpet. Some would go

to Wintergreen, some would go to Goodwill. It was time to part with Michael's stuff, to give it to someone who could use it. It was time to move on. Embrace the future.

Why did that thought fill her with terror?

The doorbell rang. When her caller wouldn't let up on the annoying chimes, Caitlin yanked the door open, knowing from the sinking feeling in her stomach, exactly who would be standing there.

"What do you want, Jordan?" She hadn't meant to sound so cranky and immediately regretted her harsh tone.

He lounged in the doorway, a wounded look on his face. Her eyes widened at the two brown paper bags he pulled from behind his back.

"Try to do someone a favor and that's the thanks you get! I brought you dinner. Chinese food."

"I already have something on for dinner," she said even as her mouth watered at the spicy smells of egg roll and something else. Shrimp?

"Yeah, right. And I'm a monkey's uncle."

She had to smile at that. It was too good an opportunity.

"I am not carrying a monkey," she protested, knowing full well it would do little good to argue with her brother-in-law in his current mood.

"But thank you very much for the food. I'll enjoy it." Gently she eased the door closed in his startled face. His booted foot barely stopped it from clicking shut.

"Hey," he hollered. "That's not nice."

"Oh, all right. I suppose there's enough for two. Or three. Come on in," she relented, smiling as she flung the door wide.

He smiled and walked in, closing the door behind him. She knew he was ready with a smart repartee, but the words died as his mouth dropped open and he blinked while the smoke alarm began its shrill summons.

Caitlin hurried toward the kitchen. The acrid odor of burning cheese and clouds of thick smoke rendered the kitchen atmosphere blue.

'I told you I had something on," she reminded Jordan as she heaved open the window to let in some fresh air. When the noise didn't stop, she grabbed a knife and attempted to force the toaster oven to yield its charred remains of what had been her cheese sandwich. It wouldn't budge.

Jordan flicked the alarm off, waved a dish towel back and forth and then reset the unit. It immediately started its high-pitched whine again.

After dumping the smoking bits of charcoal into the garbage, Caitlin pivoted to face him. The alarm had finally stopped but left behind an aching in her temples that she didn't need. The emotions of the day rose to the fore and there was no way she could stifle her bad mood.

"I have been making myself dinner for quite some time now," she told him. "I don't need a nursemaid."

"Toast is not dinner," he returned calmly, stepping around her to put his bags on the table. He pulled several different cartons from the bags and set them carefully on the table. "And I know very well that Chinese is your favorite, so forget the furious rebuttal." He grinned that wide boyish smile that would make a weaker woman swoon at his feet.

"I don't listen to it anyway," he reminded her, his lopsided smirk firmly in place.

"That, my dear Jordan, is at the very root of our problems."

He ignored her frown, flopping down onto one of her kitchen chairs. "It's just dinner, Lyn. Don't make such a big deal of it."

Yeah, just dinner! Caitlin pressed a hand to her stomach, wondering how her traitorous body would react to this feast. She was starving, but had no desire to repeat lunchtime's woes. Especially not in front of him.

Morning sickness was supposed to be over months ago, wasn't it? So how come she still had it at noon when a colleague unwrapped an egg salad sandwich? Or in the evening after she'd finished a bowl of hot buttery popcorn? Why didn't anything in her life go according to plan?

She couldn't help lifting the lids, just to see what he'd brought.

"I'll just have some of the chop suey," she decided eventually, spooning the brightly colored vegetables onto her plate. "And a bit of rice."

Surely rice would settle her stomach.

Her senses caught the vinegary-sweet fragrance of sweet-and-sour sauce as she lifted the other lids. When her tummy growled again, she gave in and ladled out three slivers of beef nestled in a glistening orange-red sauce.

"Just a little," she declared as he inspected her dish, grinning as it grew fuller by the moment. Caitlin ignored his smug look and sat down, mouth watering at the feast before her.

Jordan's murmured words of thanks to God for His goodness irritated her unreasonably. She supposed it was because she felt so tired, so abandoned. Where was God when she needed Him most? Certainly not anywhere that Caitlin had been able to find Him lately.

They ate silently together, enjoying the freshly steamed vegetables and succulent bits of pork and beef. She wasn't surprised to see there was no chicken. Jordan hated chicken in any way, shape or form.

Partway through the meal, Caitlin set up the coffee-pot, giving in to a day-long craving for caffeine. More than anything she wanted a cup of coffee right now, and she wanted it to stay put in her stomach, where it was supposed to be. Perhaps then she would have enough energy to handle Jordan's bossiness.

"Do you think that's a good idea?" he asked idly from his perch on the other side of her kitchen.

All her magnanimous goodwill vanished at the peremptory remark. The stress of pretending they were good friends, that there was nothing between them, that he was just a friend, made Caitlin's blood begin to boil. It was the proverbial last straw in a day full of frustration and she whirled around.

"Yes, Jordan, I think coffee is a very good idea right now."

He opened his mouth to say something, but she cut him off before he got started on his lecture.

"Do you have any idea what it's like to be stretched so far your stomach has no room to hold your meal? To have someone constantly kicking you from the inside? To be nauseated by the very food that attracted you only moments ago?"

She clapped her hands on her hips, eyes narrowing at the amusement on his face. "Well, do you?"

Caitlin Andrews was quite a sight when she got mad, Jordan decided, admiring the sparkling green eyes and reddish flash of color in the fall of curling chestnut-brown hair. He smiled to himself, thankful to see her old spirit return.

"Of course you don't know," she raged at him. "How could you? You're a man!"

Jordan winced at the particularly nasty ring she gave to the last word. Caitlin was tired and out of sorts, that was for sure. He was glad he hadn't told his parents anything about seeing her yesterday. She was too bushed right now to handle any more than a phone call from them. He got up and walked across the kitchen, taking her arm in his and escorting her back to her chair.

She sank into it after a moment of consideration. He knew it was because she was too tired to stand. One long fingernail shook in the air at him, emphasizing her annoyance.

"Well, let me tell you, buster. I know. And I'm sick and tired of it!"

Big shiny tears welled in her turbulent green eyes.

She stared at her hands, refusing to look at him. Jordan watched the tiredness swamp her body, leaving her slumped and vulnerable.

He felt like a heel for laughing at her. It couldn't be easy, having a baby. And if anyone knew all the rules to follow, it was his sister-in-law. She was a nutritionist, for Pete's sake! Jordan lambasted himself for saying anything. She hardly required him to tell her what her body needed.

He moved quickly to wrap one long arm around her shoulders.

"It's okay, Lyn. Cry it out. Soon the baby will be here and you'll be back to your old self. Everything will be…"

"Awful," she wailed, setting him back on his heels.

He shook his head in disbelief. It was amazing. Strong, capable, fiercely independent Lyn now dissolved into a soft mound of whimpers and tears. How had this happened? What was he doing wrong?

"Nothing's going the way I thought it would, Jordan. I don't know anything about having a baby, let alone raising a child." She gulped, her face pinched. "I'm scared witless at the thought of it. I grew up with Aunt Lucy after my parents died. How do I know what to say when my child asks me questions I can't answer."

Her big green eyes begged him to help. Jordan had never felt so totally useless in his life. He didn't know how to comfort her, didn't know the words to say to help her through this.

Please, God, show me what to do. Help me now, he pleaded silently.

"I'm so tired, Jordan," she continued. "Right now all I want is to be able to walk without lumbering around like an elephant. I want to do up the buttons on my clothes and not see gaps in between."

Her sad face squinted up at him. "I want to be able to sleep more than two hours at a time. Isn't that selfish?"

He patted her shoulder awkwardly, searching for something, anything, to comfort her.

"I want Michael."

Pain, sharp, sweet and condemning hit him. Jordan ignored it, as he had in the past, focusing his attention on the weeping young woman before him. He hadn't done anything wrong then. He wouldn't now. She was his brother's wife.

"Lyn, I know what you've been going through," he offered quietly, trying to calm her.

It was the wrong thing to say.

"Ooh, you are so frustrating, Jordan Andrews!" She yanked her shoulder away from his touch, eyes blazing. "You always think you know everything. Well you don't know what I'm going through at all!"

She jerked to her feet, her chair falling sideways, stopped only by his knee. He winced at the impact, brushed the heavy oak chair aside and then winced again as the chair hit the floor.

Hard and loud, the sound reverberated through the quiet room emphasizing the tension that strung out between them. He could feel the heat radiating across his knee from the old football injury. He absently rubbed his hand against the stinging flesh.

It was actually kind of funny. He'd gotten that injury because he'd been watching Caitlin instead of the offensive end headed his way. Now he'd been broadsided again.

"Oh, dear! It's your bad knee, isn't it? I'm sorry, Jordan," she groaned. "I'm really sorry." She set the chair back in place and sat down on it.

He smiled at her contrite face. "It's okay. And you're right, Lyn. I don't know how you're feeling right now. Why don't you tell me about it?"

He resumed eating. Without looking at her, he pushed the rice to one side, then spooned several more beef strips onto his plate in an attempt to avoid her eyes, waiting to see if she would open up.

"I really am sorry. I had no right to take out my bad humor on you. I should have been more careful." Her small hand reached out to cover his in a soft touch.

"It doesn't matter." Jordan sat there, feeling like a lump of putty, mesmerized by the plucky little smile that tipped up her mouth.

"Yes, it does matter. My only excuse is that I'm not very good at managing everything yet," she explained with a tremulous smile. "But I will be. I just have to rely on myself and do the best I can." Her shoulders pressed back as she said it, as if she were drawing on a cloak of armor.

Irritation chafed him. Jordan snapped his fork against the plate with an audible *ping*.

"Lyn, there's no way you have to go through all this yourself. I'm here. Mom and Dad would love to see you. There's Robyn and the other girls. Lots of people are there, just aching for a chance to help you out. But they won't offer again. You'll have to ask."

He stopped when she shook her head.

Caitlin didn't say the words but Jordan could almost hear them in the silence of the kitchen. He knew what she was thinking, could read the words in her expressive eyes.

I've gone through that too many times. And everybody always goes away when I need them. Just like my parents, just like Michael, just like you did.

What Caitlin did say didn't make him feel any better.

"I've got to face life on my own terms and learn to handle what comes along. I can't afford to depend on other people all the time. Besides," she squared her shoulders. "I should be really good at it by now."

Jordan flinched at the misery underlying those words. He watched her push her plate away before ambling slowly to the living room. He followed silently, standing by helplessly until she sank onto the soft cushions of the sofa, her sigh piercing his heart.

"Caitlin, honey, I wish Mike was here for you. I'd give anything if he could be here to help you through this." He took a deep breath. "But since he isn't, I'd like to help. Sort of a stand-in. If you'll let me." His dark eyes met hers seriously. "Whatever you need, Lyn, you just tell me."

"I know you'd like to help." Caitlin closed her

eyes, her wistful face pinched and tired. "And I know you're there, Jordan. Thanks."

But it wasn't the same thing and they both knew it.

"I know everyone thought we were foolish to marry like that, that it was too fast. I knew people thought Michael wasn't very responsible about a lot of things. That was okay, I was responsible enough for both of us." She fiddled with her hands, twisting one inside the other.

"I knew he was a terrible driver and took too many chances. But I never took any chances! Michael bubbled with life, he could hardly wait to dig in and sample everything." Her voice clouded with emotion and he watched her struggle to keep herself under control.

"But I loved him, Jordan! And I didn't care about any of that. I don't understand why he had to die. Where was God when Michael needed him?"

The tears came then, rolling down her cheeks in rivulets of emotion.

"You tell me, Jordan. Why couldn't God have left Michael to watch his baby being born, taking the first step, growing up? Why?"

Jordan sat silent, helpless, and watched her weep. Then when he could be silent no longer, he sank onto the cushion beside her and wrapped his arms around her shaking shoulders. Ignoring his own aching heart, he cradled her head against his chest.

"Caitlin, I loved him, too. He was my brother." He let his fingers stroke over her dark curls as he tried to express himself clearly. "And I don't pretend to comprehend the way the universe works. How could I, a mere human, ever grasp something so complicated?''

She peered up at him through her swollen, red-rimmed eyes and Jordan felt his heart bump in the old familiar way. Gently he pressed her back against the sofa, away from him. He searched for the words to adequately explain his faith.

''I think that life holds something wonderful for each one of us if we look for it. And that's true for you, too, if you'll only look ahead. You're doing work that interests you. You're moving into a new home. You're going to have a baby!''

He lifted her chin, coaxing her to look at him. ''Yes, you've had some rough times. And there may be more to come. But you've got to believe that God loves you and cares for you enough to be there whenever you need Him. You have to trust that He will do the best for you, even if we can't understand right now.''

''And you think I should *trust* someone who took away the one thing I loved most in this world?'' Caitlin watched him, her eyes vicious shards of jade. ''You think I should just shrug it off and move on?''

Jordan groaned inwardly as he listened to her tirade. *The one thing she loved most.* It hurt to hear her say that about Mike and not him. But it hurt more that she was still bitter and full of anger against God.

''How can I believe in something so vengeful?''

He shook his head. ''No, Lyn. He is never like that. There was a reason Michael had to die. I don't know what it was. You and I will probably never know what he might have had to face if he had lived. But God knew and decided it was time for him to leave. And because He's God, He did what was best."

Caitlin shuffled a little, pulling herself up and forward. Jordan let his hand fall away.

"I know what's right, Jordan. I know all the appropriate words, all the correct phrases." She peered at him from under her lashes. "I know I should have shared the baby with your parents. Michael would have loved that."

He nodded.

"It's just that I can't seem to get there. Can you understand that? I made the choice, I put everything I had into that marriage. And He took it away. Why?"

Jordan patted her hair awkwardly, searching for the right words. "I don't know, sweetheart. But He didn't take everything. He gave you something, too, Lyn. A brand-new baby. A living memory of Michael. You owe it to Michael and his child to go on with your life. That baby is going to need its grandma and grandpa."

"Junior's got me." She hugged her mounded stomach protectively.

"And he's a lucky baby to have you. But children need families. Friends. Uncles." He smiled, praying desperately for the right words. "You've grieved a long time, Caitlin. It's time to live. Will you let us in now? Let us share some of the good times and the bad with you?"

She didn't say anything, just sat there, peering at him, thinking it all over. Jordan knew she would need time to adapt, change gears. He was more than willing to give it to her if it meant she would allow him back into her life.

Maybe if he went now and let her think about it, she'd realize how much she needed him. He stood. "One of these days it's going to start snowing and it won't stop. You need to focus on the future, get ready for this baby. You're moving soon, right?"

He pulled his leather jacket from a nearby chair and tugged it over his shirt, studying her wan face seriously. "I'll come over tomorrow and we'll get things organized."

She smiled, her voice softly accusing. "You always were the organizer, Jordan. That much hasn't changed."

"Can I get the family to help?" He held his breath, waiting for her answer. Surely she wouldn't deny them this little bit of sharing, not when she was so worn-out.

He pushed it just a tad further. "You're tired, Lyn. You need to rest. Let us help. Just this once. No strings, I promise."

She smiled but there was no bitterness in those jade depths. She seemed to have accepted that it was time to lean on someone else. Or maybe she was just too tired to argue.

"It won't be this once and you know it, Jordan Andrews." Her mouth slashed in a teasing grin. "Your mother will have everyone marching to her tune within five minutes of her arrival. The two of you are like peas in a pod in that respect."

Jordan arched one eyebrow teasingly. "And that's bad?"

"That's Andrews." She sighed, but he heard laughter hidden in the depths. "All right! I'll do it your way. Just this once."

"And can I tell them about the baby?" He wanted her to do that herself, but maybe it was asking too much.

"If you want to." She shrugged, lurching to her feet.

She pretended it didn't matter, but he knew better. Still, this one relenting bit was a step forward. And that one step was better than none at all.

"All right! What time is good? Ten?"

Caitlin nodded tiredly, one hand massaging her hip. "I suppose. I'll be awake no matter what time they come." She followed him to the door, slopping along in her floppy slippers. "I'm always awake."

"I'm sorry, honey." He stood there for a moment, staring down at her, aching to hold her, ease her burden.

"No, I'm sorry I'm so cranky. Thanks for everything, Jordan." She offered a tremulous smile that tore at his heart.

"It's okay, Lyn. You can tell me anything, you know. It won't make any difference." He picked up her hand and held it between both of his.

Her fingers curved soft and delicate in his. Jordan glanced up, searching her tired face. A pain tightened his chest as he noted the lines around her mouth, the blue tinge under her eyes.

"Don't let the past be only sadness, Lyn. Michael loved life and he went all out for whatever he wanted. Be happy. That's what he would have wanted for you."

The rest could wait. They had time. *Please, God, give her time to accept me.*

"Remember to call if you want me. I left my number by your phone. I can be here in five minutes. Okay?"

Caitlin nodded, although Jordan wasn't sure what she was agreeing to. Perhaps she only meant she understood about the phone call. Feelings of helplessness washed through him as he closed the door softly behind him, waited for her to lock up and then got into his car and drove away in the chilly fall evening.

His heart ached to hold and comfort the young woman he'd seen peering out from those weary worn eyes. He wished he could take away some of her pain. He wanted her to trust him. He wanted to be there for her, to share part of the burden.

He wanted to go back in time, back to a past when he should have grabbed at the childish adoration she'd so innocently offered.

Instead he'd run away, cleared the field because he'd known his younger brother was in love with Caitlin. And he'd watched while Michael had claimed her. Caitlin was Michael's wife and now she carried Michael's child.

In her current state, Caitlin wasn't ready to hear anything about Jordan's regrets. Maybe she never would be. And he could deal with that. He'd have to.

But what he wouldn't accept was that wall of distance she projected, the refusal to find the good things God had given her. Life wasn't all bad. He could show her some beautiful parts of it, parts that were bright and happy and filled with promise.

He itched to order her to relax and let someone else be at the helm for a while. He wanted to coddle her, make her feel safe. He wanted to be the one she put in charge.

Jordan mocked this ridiculous notion. He'd wager his new high-tech digital scanner that Caitlin Andrews would find it awfully difficult to let go of the controls. And he knew she'd bat his ears if she ever caught him trying to coddle her from anything. But he would be there anyway. Just in case she wanted him.

For something. For anything.

Jordan breathed a silent prayer for Caitlin as he wove his car through the streets toward his lonely apartment. She was beautiful in a way that no other woman had ever been to him and her pain stabbed him deep in his heart.

"Help her, Lord. And help me. I can't give up on her."

Chapter Three

Caitlin opened the door the next morning to the boisterous crowd outside with a reminiscent smile. "Come on in!"

It was just like old times. Except that, back then, she and Michael had usually gone to the Andrewses'. Their sprawling split-level housed assorted numbers of Michael's family at any given time and one more was always welcome. She had often arrived for dinner uninvited and Eliza, Michael's mother, had always been just as gracious as she was now.

"Caitlin, my dear. How are you?"

Caitlin found herself enveloped by soft round arms in a loving hug that warmed her tired soul. Eliza's periwinkle eyes searched her face.

"Oh, honey, I'm so happy for you, so happy about the baby!"

Tears welled in Caitlin's eyes, her heart blooming with relief. She should have known she could trust

Michael's mother. Not a word of recrimination, no demands to know why she hadn't told them. Just friendly care and concern.

Why hadn't she told them sooner? Why was she so scared of allowing them in?

She thrilled as the trickle of warmth in Eliza's smile stimulated a ray of warmth in her frozen heart. "Thank you, Eliza. I'm sorry I didn't tell you sooner."

"There's nothing at all to be sorry for. I'm just so thankful the Lord has brought you back to us." Eliza hugged her again, her eyes tender, her arms welcoming.

There wasn't time for much else. Stan Andrews insisted on his turn at hugging *little Caity* as he'd always called her.

"I'm not so little anymore, Stan." She glanced down at her protruding stomach.

He laughed, but deep in his eyes Caitlin could see the flash of pain. It was gone as quickly as it appeared.

"All the more to love," he whispered in her ear, bringing a glow of happiness to her world. Here again, unconditional love.

She had missed them, Caitlin realized. More than she would have thought possible. But she had to be careful. No matter how friendly they were now, they would eventually leave, go on with their own lives, and she'd be left behind. After all, she wasn't Michael's wife anymore.

"Do you mind?" Jordan's distressed voice boomed behind them. "You're blocking the doorway, little mama." He had a load of empty boxes in his arms.

"If my brother starts making those gross mother-to-be jokes, just let me know." It was Robyn, trim and fit, elbowing her brother out of the doorway, a little blond girl on her hip.

"I'll straighten him out posthaste." Robyn held up a hand and waved it threateningly around his ears. "I'm allowing no talk about weight gain today."

"All right, already. I'm going." Jordan moved out of the way to put his load down in the living room.

Olivia came behind her sister, imitating Robyn's wild hand movements. Both of them converged on Caitlin, hugging her while they proclaimed their congratulations. For her part, Caitlin exclaimed over the baby as she coaxed the little girl into her arms.

While the dear, noisy, garrulous family gathered together in her tiny little living room, Caitlin let her eyes wander round. Just for a moment she allowed the joy and pleasure of it all to flow into her, rejuvenate her. She considered what she had been willing to give up and called herself a fool. This could have been hers all along.

Of course, it would be all the harder to manage alone now, having experienced the warm sense of belonging once more. But even if it was only temporary, it was worth it to have them all here again.

They were a family. Happy, loving, enjoying each other's company. And, for now, they wanted her to be a part of it. Why couldn't she just accept that and join in? Why did she feel so lost, out of place, like an interloper?

Jordan's fingers squeezed hers as the tears welled

in her eyes. He alone seemed to realize how much this moment meant to her and she hadn't even heard him come close. She turned to glance at him and saw his encouraging smile.

"They just want to help," he murmured in her ear. "We just want to love you."

"Okay, children. This is the way we're going to do this."

Within minutes Eliza had everyone organized. After an inspection of her puffy ankles, Caitlin was dispatched to her bedroom to rest on the bed, feet up, while her sisters-in-law packed up her wardrobe.

"You know I've got two or three outfits left over from Eudora's premiere," Robyn offered thoughtfully. "You're welcome to them if you want a change. Although I'm certain I was ten sizes bigger than you before I delivered." She twisted and turned in front of the mirror, checking her trim figure.

"Don't worry. You've still got some left." Olivia teased her sister with a grin of commiseration as she emptied drawers. "Mom said you keep a little with each baby."

"Not me. I'm not keeping any of it," Robyn assured them both. "Next time I'm going to be extra careful about what I eat."

"I've been careful," Caitlin murmured, staring at her huge tummy. "I've done everything by the book, including exercise. At my last checkup I'd gained twenty-nine pounds. That was not the plan."

"You're kidding! Twenty-nine?" Robyn pulled

herself out of the closet to take a second look. "You don't look that big."

Olivia groaned and shook her head at her sister, grinning when she noticed Caitlin watching her in the big mirror. "Robyn always blurts out whatever she's thinking. I have to watch her."

"I heard about some things she said to Jordan." Caitlin giggled, remembering her brother-in-law's face the day he'd described his niece's debut. "He seems traumatized by your daughter's arrival." She burst out in delighted laughter at Robyn's exasperated snort.

"That man doesn't have the sense of a pea when it comes to having babies!" Red spots of indignant color glowed brightly on Robyn's cheekbones. "I feel sorry for any woman my brother marries. And woe betide her if they ever decide to have children. She'll probably knock him out before it's over. And he'll deserve it!"

Caitlin glanced at Olivia, who rolled her eyes and shrugged.

"What happened?" Caitlin finally asked, smothering her giggles with great difficulty.

"He told me to stop being such a wimp! Can you believe it? As if that great lummox could even imagine pushing a nine-pound watermelon out of his body! The man has no compassion."

"None at all," Olivia agreed, smirking at Caitlin behind her sister's back. She leaned down to whisper. "He told her that having a baby was a perfectly normal, natural thing for a woman to do."

"Well, I suppose it is," Caitlin murmured, frowning. She wouldn't have said it, but she couldn't argue with his logic.

"Maybe. But no one in their right mind tells a woman doing hard labor that women in some countries have their babies and then go immediately back to the field and finish their work. Not if you value your life."

"And not if that woman is Robyn," Caitlin agreed, remembering that Michael's sister was particularly sensitive to pain. "We'll have to give him the benefit of the doubt then. Jordan wasn't in his right mind."

Olivia burst out laughing, then clapped a hand over her mouth. Caitlin knew exactly what she meant. She could picture the two of them, brother and sister nattering at each other as a baby waited to be born. It was something she could only dream about.

"She called him names," Olivia said, loudly enough for her sister to hear. Her eyes still sparkled in merriment.

"And he deserved every one of them." Robyn was stout in her own defense, her voice emerging muffled from inside the closet. "Control myself indeed! As if I had any *control* over Eudora's arrival!"

Caitlin couldn't help it. She let the laughter break free. Just then Jordan's curious face peeked around the door and she giggled all the harder, tears rolling down her face as he frowned at them.

"Is everything all right?" he asked Caitlin, ignoring the other two women. "You're not in pain or anything?"

"You mean pain, as in labor?" Robyn's snarl was

only half pretend. "And what would you do if she was?"

When Jordan's face blanched, Caitlin burst into renewed gales of laughter, joined seconds later by Olivia. It was evident he didn't relish the prospect.

"I'll get Mom." He gulped.

"Don't bother. Caitlin is fine. *I* at least, know how to treat pregnant women," Robyn informed him smartly. She smacked a group of hangers together and laid them in a box. "Go and do some wonderful hulking-man thing like tossing around furniture, Jordan. You're not needed here."

"What did I do to you?" He scratched his head, peering at his sister through lenses that were smudged and dirty. "You think you'd appreciate me a little more since I assisted your daughter into the world."

"You what?" Robyn pushed her way free of the clothes, hands on her hips as she glared at her brother. "I dare you to say that again."

Olivia rushed to the rescue, tugging her brother's arm to get him to move out the door. "Uh, this isn't a good time to bring that up, Jordy. Come back later. Or better yet, wait till we call you. Don't call us. Okay?" When he frowned at her, Olivia stood on tiptoe and pressed a kiss against his cheek. "I love you, big brother, but you're not doing yourself any good here. Go away!"

The order was just audible enough that Caitlin heard every word. She saw Jordan shake his head, obviously confused.

"Okay, if you think so."

"We think so!" Robyn added her two cents' worth.

Jordan frowned and then retreated, his golden eyes puzzled at her sour tone. "I'll see you later, Caitlin. Alone." He glanced from her to the other two, then left, muttering to himself.

"He's impossible once he gets an idea in his head." Robyn rolled her eyes, her tone confidential. "As if he helped! I don't know where he gets this stubbornness from. None of the rest of the family is like that."

Those words were so far from the truth, Caitlin burst into renewed chuckles, her heart warming to these wonderful women. How had she stayed away so long?

More important, what would she do when the novelty wore off and they left her on her own?

Olivia and Robyn arranged her jewelry, clothes, lingerie, socks and shoes in several boxes and then urged her to move from the bed.

"We've got to get this bedding off before they come for the mattress. Dad rented a trailer and he and Jordy are going to load everything onto it and haul it over when Glen comes this afternoon. Then we'll get you settled in. Wintergreen, Jordan said?"

Olivia's eyes glowed, begging for information. "I heard there are going to be three of you. It sounds like such fun. Can I come once in a while for some girl talk?"

Caitlin nodded slowly. "Sure, Olivia. Anytime. But I'm hoping it won't be just us girls for long." She saw Robyn's head jerk back at the same time that Olivia flopped on the bed beside her.

"Why? What's going on?"

"I'm going to try my hand at matchmaking," Caitlin told them smugly. "But you can't say a word to anyone. If the old gossips on coffee row get hold of this plan, they'll spoil everything."

Eliza wandered in, a list in her hand which she consulted after a glance around the room. Olivia beckoned her over.

"Listen to this, Mom. Caitlin's got a plan to match up her roommates with husbands. You're good at that, you can help."

"Of course I can help," Eliza agreed smugly. "I got Robyn married off, didn't I?" She preened a little in front of the mirror. "That was my biggest coup so far."

"Hey!" Robyn half frowned, half laughed. "I didn't need your help to marry Glen."

"Of course you did. You just didn't *know* I was helping you. If it wasn't for me, the two of you would still be arguing over who has the better job, reads the most books, and things like that." She ignored Robyn's gasp of outrage.

"Now, what's your idea, Caitlin?" Eliza's eyes opened wide, innocently.

Caitlin quickly explained about Beth's husband, the man she'd married on the rebound. "Then he was killed and Beth and Veronica had to move out of the company house. Beth was left with a mound of debts, it's a miracle she can still smile. It's a terribly sad story. And Beth's had such an awful life anyway."

"What do you mean?" The women were all ears.

"She doesn't talk about it and the only thing I know is from when we were in school together. I got the impression that Beth and her sister didn't have the happiest home life. She was always afraid to go home when we were out with youth group, and if she was late she'd get all shaky."

Caitlin stopped, remembering her own youth with an aunt who had never cared when she came or went as long as it didn't cost money and there wasn't any noise. She and Beth made good soul mates, she decided grimly.

"The poor dear. Of course, I barely remember the family. I was so busy with the children in those days. Five children were enough to keep anyone busy." Eliza shook her head. "We'll be happy to help you however we can, Caitlin. Certainly Beth needs to find someone who can love her the way God meant."

"Oh, b-but, I didn't mean for you all to get involved," Caitlin stuttered, aghast at the thought of these managing-Andrews meddling in the delicate affairs of the heart.

"Of course we want to be involved! I can't stand to see anyone unhappy. Now what about the other girl? Mary something, isn't it?"

"Maryann." Caitlin gulped. What had she unleashed with her careless tongue? "Maryann MacGregor. But she's not, I mean, I don't want, that is, she's already in love with someone."

Oh, no! Now she'd blurted out Maryann's most private secret. And she didn't know it for certain. Not really. It was just that a funny soft look came over the woman's face whenever she saw Clayton Matthews. That plus the fact that they'd been really close ten years ago made Caitlin suspect an ember still burned. All she wanted to do was fan it a little.

"Well, that's just wonderful, dear! How kind of you to help things along." Eliza held out one hand and helped Caitlin off the bed. She pulled a chair forward and pressed her into that while still speaking.

"But first things first. We can't possibly help out with someone's love life until we get *you* settled in your new home. You just sit there and relax, dear. Olivia, I want you to start on the kitchen. Robyn, you finish packing the books in the living room. Then we'll have lunch."

Caitlin sat where she was told, stunned and filled with disbelief.

What had she gotten herself into? She'd meant to get her friends together in the nicest possibly way. A hint, a few words to the right man. Maybe a chance encounter that wasn't so chance. Just a few little things to encourage her widowed friends to reconsider a couple of men she happened to know were interested.

But this! This would turn into an all-out assault campaign, not unlike guerilla warfare. In spite of her protestations, she knew it was snowballing out of control even now. That was the way Eliza did things. Stan claimed that her brain concocted schemes even though her body was sleeping like a log.

It was true! At this very moment Caitlin could feel Eliza's mind whirling as she turned from the doorway, her eyes intensely scrutinizing Caitlin's burgeoning body.

"Hmm," the older woman murmured, her pen tapping against the pad. "Widows. Right. Three of you. I'll have to think about that."

Fear and trepidation filled Caitlin's mind. She would probably ruin the only friendships she had left. Then she'd be well and truly alone in a house that was far too big for one woman and one tiny baby. While everyone bustled out with a box, she sat there brooding.

"Caitlin?" Jordan flicked on the overhead light. "What are you doing just sitting here? Is something wrong?"

"Everything," she whispered, clenching her fist at her side. "Absolutely everything."

"What do you mean?" His face blanched. "What's wrong? Is it the baby?" He waited, shifting impatiently from one foot to the other as he waited for her to answer. "Caitlin?"

She glanced up dazedly, an idea forming in the back of her mind. "It's your fault, Jordan," she whispered. "You're the one who insisted I have them over here. You're the one who said I needed their help."

"And?" He frowned. "What's wrong with that? Honestly, sometimes you make no sense, Lyn. The moving is going really well."

"That's nice," she murmured, nodding absently. "It's a good idea to get it down to a science."

"It is?"

"Yes, it is. Because unless you help me get out of

this mess, I'll be moving back here in a matter of days.''

He slid his hand along her forehead, checking the temperature. ''Caitlin, are you feeling all right? Can I help?''

''Oh, yes,'' she asserted, lurching unsteadily to her feet, her fingers tightening around his helping hand. ''You offered and I'm taking you up on that. You're going to help, Jordan. You're going to end up helping me a lot.''

''Help you do what?''

He didn't pull away, but Caitlin could feel him flex his fingers in her tight grasp. She didn't loosen her grip in the slightest.

''I've opened a Pandora's box, Jordan. And now you've got to help me get the lid back on before your family ruins everything. What you're going to do is keep your mother away from Wintergreen. If that means you have to come over every day, so be it.'' Caitlin tumbled it around in her mind as the plan evolved. ''She won't bother me nearly as much if she thinks you're filling in for her.''

''Huh?'' He stood where he was, shaking his head. ''I don't get it.''

''Oh, you will,'' she assured him, a tiny smile lifting the edges of her lips. ''You most certainly will.''

Chapter Four

"**Y**ou're late, Lyn," Jordan chided Friday night, almost a week later. He straightened from his leaning position against his car and took her arm to walk her to the front door of her new home.

"I know. Two clients showed up after their scheduled times." She opened the door and ushered him into the foyer. "I just want to change and then we can leave. Where are we having dinner?" she called over her shoulder.

It took only a moment to unlock the door and then they were inside. In the days since Jordan had reentered her life, eating together had become a ritual. He would either show up on her doorstep with take-out food or insist on escorting her to a restaurant. He claimed it was because of his mother. He'd even shown up once for lunch, drawing surprised stares from her co-workers. Now her friends Beth and Maryann were full of questions.

"Have a seat. I'll be down in a few minutes." She scooted up the stairs to change clothes.

In some ways Caitlin was grateful for Jordan's attentions. She hated cooking after a long day at work and would have happily settled for hot buttered toast and tea even though she knew the folly of such a diet. Under Jordan's insistence she ate a nutritious dinner without all the work of preparing it and none of the tedium of cleaning up afterward.

Then too, there was Eliza. As long as Jordan kept coming over, his mother seemed perfectly happy working on the Thanksgiving decorations for the annual fellowship supper. Caitlin felt confident that if she could only keep abreast of Eliza's doings, as reported by Jordan, and keep herself out of her mother-in-law's path, she couldn't possibly divulge any more secrets. The fact that Eliza sent Jordan over to Wintergreen on the most minor of things didn't bother Caitlin at all. In fact, it was nice to have him to talk to.

But some evenings, like tonight, Caitlin would have preferred to stay at home and read a book in front of the roaring fire in Wintergreen. The old house seemed to wrap its arms around her and she'd felt comfortable there from the first night.

"Lyn? Hey, did you hear anything I just said?"

Jordan's voice from the bottom of the steps pulled her from her musings and Caitlin tugged on her maternity pants, sweater and sneakers without further hesitation.

"Be there in a minute."

"How about Giorgio's?" he called up the stairs.

"Sounds fine to me." She took a deep breath and let the busyness of work drain away. "I'm ready."

An hour later, she stared at him across the table in a low-lit family restaurant. It was comfortable but not intimidating and she loved the wonderful pasta dishes Giorgio's served.

"What did you do today?" she asked, curious about his work. Since he had bounded back into her life, his days seemed to be full of plans for bigger and better computer systems.

"Let's see. We got that contract in London for the security order, so I've been trying to map out exactly how soon we can fill those needs."

A tremor of fear coursed through her veins. "Does that mean you're going overseas again?" she queried softly, half afraid to hear his answer.

"Nope." He grinned that boyish smirk that made him look younger than his twenty-nine years. "Bank securities are my partner Devon's specialty. When the times comes, he'll go."

Caitlin relaxed and then realized that what she really felt was relief. It wasn't a good sign. She couldn't allow herself to rely on Jordan. Or anyone else. God intended for her to manage things herself.

"I've got a deal pending in Banff that could be a biggie if I can land it," he told her as they discussed the computer firm Jordan and his friend had built up from scratch.

Caitlin listened as he described a satellite system that would monitor vast areas of the mountainous terrain enabling park rangers to uncover potential forest fires and tourists lost in remote terrain, in record time.

After several minutes, she was lost in the intricacies of engineering such complex equipment. She sat, dreamy eyed, content to let him ramble on, basking in the warm pungent aromas of garlic, tangy tomato sauce, baking cheese and yeasty bread sticks.

It was several seconds before she realized Jordan had stopped speaking. Instead he was peering at her with a look of concern on his face.

"Are you okay?" His voice was soft. "Having more of those hiccup things?"

Caitlin smiled. "No, I'm fine. And they're Braxton-Hicks contractions, not hiccups."

She waved a hand at the groups of families scattered through the busy restaurant, their happy chatter a hum of noise in the bustling restaurant.

"I was just thinking of a girl I've been counseling. She would give almost anything to be here, with her father, having dinner." Caitlin fingered the water glass on her place mat. "Actually, Addie reminds me a little of myself at her age," she admitted.

Jordan grinned. "Oh? She's stubborn, too?"

"No. It's because she's an oddball. Like me."

His gold-flecked eyes studied her seriously. "Caitlin, you are not an oddball."

"Yes, I am. Or at least I was. I never fit into the high school cliques. Now I just plain don't fit into anything." She giggled at the silly joke, pushing a length of her hair behind her ear as she eyed her bulging tummy, but Jordan didn't laugh.

Her brow furrowed in concentration as she chewed on her bottom lip, striving to clarify her meaning. "I was different, you see. And nobody had to tell me that. It was something I knew. I didn't have a family like the other kids, I was just staying with my aunt because there wasn't anybody else who wanted me. After school, when the others dumped their homework and went out for a shake, I toddled off to my job."

"Lots of kids have jobs, Caitlin." Jordan countered.

"Yes, they do," she agreed. "And many enjoy them. That's not what I mean."

He shrugged. "I don't get it."

"Not every kid feels they have to contribute something or they'll lose their home, Jordan." Caitlin shrugged avoiding his eyes. "I felt I had to earn that money so Aunt Lucy would keep me, so I wouldn't be a burden. In some sort of weird logic I figured if I made my own money, bought my clothes, looked after things, she wouldn't mind having me there so much."

She watched the furrow on his forehead deepen as he considered her words.

"I'm sure your aunt was happy to have you there, Lyn. She was a lot older, I know. But I don't believe she ever meant to make you feel beholden or unwelcome. You probably imagined that. She just wasn't used to having a child around."

Caitlin nodded thoughtfully. "Could be," she admitted. "Things get skewed when you're a kid. I withdrew because I didn't like my own reality. I didn't think much about her side of it, I guess." She munched on her bread stick for a few minutes, trying to discern reality from her memories.

"Addie's like that, too. When we discuss her food choices from the week before, it's simple to see she's camouflaging her feelings by overeating."

"I suppose everyone does that."

"Maybe. For a time. But when it goes on long-term, it's denial. That gets serious." Caitlin threaded her fingers together and then, when she realized what she was doing, laid them in her lap.

"I recognize it because I did the same with my aunt. Lucy wanted a calm, quiet retirement, and I tried to give her that. I didn't feel comfortable inviting anyone over, and I sure wasn't in with the group who held sleep-overs. I used my books to escape." She smiled softly, remembering those fantasy stories.

Jordan stared perplexedly at her. "Used your books?"

Caitlin realized he wasn't following her meaning. How could he? Jordan had a big, loving family. He was far too involved with his life to need the illusions fairy stories would provide. Besides, Jordan always dealt in the here and now, in reality.

"When people, teenagers especially, don't have a real sense of security, they often move into a fantasy life. Mine was in books. And food." There was no way to describe those deep, secret longing for happiness, she decided.

"But Lyn," he protested. "You were smarter than anyone else in school. You were years ahead in most subjects."

"Yes. But that wasn't as great as it seemed. When you add to my insecurities the fact that I was two grades ahead of my peers, had nothing in common with my classmates and that I was overweight to boot, well—" she grimaced "—it wasn't a solution for successfully handling what life throws at you. I ended up hiding the real me and falling miles behind my peers in developing my own personality."

"How did you figure all this out?"

"I talked to a counselor back in my undergrad days. She helped me see that I was compensating for losing my parents. Her words, not mine."

Jordan shook his head. "I can't believe I didn't see anything," he muttered. "I was in the same school. I even worked on the same newspaper."

Caitlin grinned. "And all you saw was *the brain,* right?" It was reassuring to see the glint of teasing in his dark eyes. She brushed his arm with her hand.

"Don't worry about it, Jordan. You were a teenager, not my adviser. You had your own problems." She wished she hadn't let it all out, let him see how insecure she'd been. It was time to lighten up. She peered up through her lashes. "I can't seem to remember you suffering from anything other than girl problems!"

His face grew darker then and she laughed at his chagrin.

"Ten years later and you're still embarrassed about being the school heartthrob?"

"Listen. I had problems like everyone else. But I sought my counsel in the Bible."

"Oh, please. I do *not* want to hear about that!"

Jordan removed his glasses, wiping the lenses with his napkin as he glared at her, golden eyes filled with warning. "Fine. But I think," he said firmly, "that's enough talk about me. Let's hear how things are going at the house. Did you get the baby's room finished?"

"Nag, nag, nag. No, I did not. I've been busy."

"Doing what?"

"I'm helping out a friend." She avoided his eyes.

"Not Clayton Matthews?" He frowned when she nodded. "Again? What is it that the two of you are doing, anyway?"

"Oh, I'm just showing him a few things."

Caitlin had no desire to explain how totally clueless the farmer was when it came to matters of the heart. Not that she had any great knowledge! But anyone could learn to dance and socialize and Clayton did seem desperate to gain the attention of Maryann. He just hadn't had much success in relaxing in her company.

"*Showing* him?" Jordan's eyes darkened. "What do *you* need to show a man like him?"

"He's very shy. I'm just trying to help him get over that so he can ask someone out." Caitlin glanced around the room, hoping he'd drop the subject.

"Maybe I should talk to Clayton. Give him another man's perspective."

"No!" Caitlin immediately lowered her voice, fully aware of the interested stares from the other patrons. "Clay would never forgive me if he thought I'd told anyone about this!"

Jordan put his fork down and studied her face intently. His forehead furrowed in a frown. "I don't like any of this, Lyn. You insisted I help you, and I've tried to keep my family out of the way. But my mother's been asking a lot of questions and it's getting harder to put her off. She keeps wanting to know if you're going out with anyone, if you're having dinner alone, if you need some odd job done. That kind of thing."

"You have to put her off. If she finds out about Clayton and me she'll get involved and that would ruin everything." The very thought of Eliza jumping in to match up two reticent people like Clayton and Maryann made her cringe.

"Mom might be able to help."

Caitlin shook her head firmly. "Uh-uh. No offense, Jordan, but your mother couldn't keep a secret if her lips were taped shut and her hands were tied behind her back." She smiled to show she wasn't serious, not completely anyway. "It's important to me."

"Important to you?" Jordan's glowering face was full of questions. "Just what is this man to you, Caitlin?" The chill in his voice set her hackles raising.

"Oh, for Pete's sake! Not you, too." She whooshed out a breath of disgust and straightened. "I've already got half the town plotting to match the Widows of Wintergreen up with some unsuspecting male. If they guess why Clayton..." She shook her head, her imagination taking over.

"I'm not trying to match anyone up," Jordan

growled. "But you spend hours with the man. Good grief, what are we supposed to think?"

"You're supposed to think that I'm trying to help him get up enough nerve to ask out the woman he's loved for years! That woman is Maryann MacGregor, not me. And you're supposed to believe it because that's what I told you." Caitlin tamped down her indignation.

Small towns, she thought with disgust. Everybody was always trying to make something out of nothing. It was so frustrating. If they kept this up, Maryann would soon notice Clayton's comings and goings! Caitlin suspected her friend wouldn't appreciate her efforts, no matter how kindly they were meant.

Maryann had been in the limelight too long. She'd returned to Oakburn with the intention of leaving the cameras behind. Caitlin shuddered to think how upset the shy, reserved woman would be if she knew people had been talking about her.

"I suppose the next thing will be finding someone for Beth Ainslow?" Jordan pushed his plate away, his eyebrows drawn together.

Caitlin took a sip of water, unsure whether to tell him her thoughts or not. He didn't seem very sympathetic. And besides, what did he care if she was busy the rest of her life?

"I don't know if there's a lot I can do for Beth. She's very kind, very bouncy, very..." she searched for the right word "...up. But she's hiding behind that. It's not easy to get her to talk about personal things."

"Sounds like normal reserve to me."

She ignored that. "Besides, Garrett Winthrop is still nursing a grudge. It's not going to be easy to get him to forgive and forget."

Jordan's gaze settled on her, something glinting in their depths. When he finally spoke his voice seemed faraway. "Sometimes it's just not that easy to forget the past." One hand reached out to brush a lock of hair away from his eye. "Sometimes the past looks a whole lot better than the future."

Caitlin frowned, wondering what he was talking about. Did he mean Garrett and Beth, or was he talking about the two of them and the fact that when she'd needed him, he'd sent Michael to her.

"Jordan, I..." She didn't know how to tell him what was in her heart, didn't know whether he regretted his actions or not. Maybe it was best to leave things be.

"Sorry." His voice was low and apologetic. "Let's change the subject. What are you planning for tomorrow? You don't have weekend clients, do you?"

"No." She shook her head and then waited while their server set down the steaming platters of lasagna. "Oh, this is great. I'm starving!"

He grinned. "So what's new? What about this girl you mentioned earlier?"

"Addie. She's making progress but it's slow. She doesn't feel very secure in herself and that causes a lot of problems."

"I thought you said her father was some wealthy businessman? She doesn't have to worry about money or security." He frowned. "What does bother her?"

"It's complicated, Jordan." She shrugged, neglecting to mention that Addie's problems made her reflect on her own. "I'm still studying her, but basically she just doesn't feel loved and she's trying to get her father to prove he does."

"Ah." He nodded with understanding then sprinkled Parmesan cheese liberally over his pasta. "Her father's away a lot, I suppose?"

"A whole lot. He tends to use his secretary as Addie's mother and she, of course, feels abandoned so she tries to prove that she's worth loving." Ouch, this was getting too close to home. Caitlin clamped her lips closed and concentrated on her food.

Jordan was silent for a long time, picking at his lasagna absently as he considered her words. When he finally looked up there was a softness about the chiseled features.

"You know, I grew up in a home where my parents treated us as people, a part of the circle of their love in spite of our faults. Somehow I never felt I had to measure up to anyone. I always felt they just wanted me to be the best me I could be. They seemed happy with that."

His eyes stared ahead unseeingly. "I realize now just how much of a gift that acceptance was when I hear you talk about this Addie." His glance shifted to Caitlin.

She could almost hear him say "and you."

"But I can't help feelings that Addie needs someone to rely on. Someone who will be there for her when she runs out of her own power. I think she needs to find someone to put her trust in. Someone who won't let her down. I think she needs God.''

"I don't think religion is going to solve all of Addie's problems, Jordan.'' Caitlin heard the skeptical tones in her own voice and mentally winced. There was no point in offending him just because *she* had a problem with God.

"No, not a religion. A relationship with God. And I'm not saying all her problems will disappear. But when you look at it, none of us are really great human beings. We need someone to depend on. Everybody has some little flaw they try to hide from other people.''

Caitlin grinned. Opportunities like these weren't to be passed up. "Even you?''

"Yes, even me, I suppose. Though I don't have many and most of them have already been corrected.''

She chuckled, enjoying the repartee she'd missed for so long. "Your sisters think there's work to be done.''

He sniffed. "They should take care of their own colossal imperfections before looking at my few faults.'' He slid a hand onto the table, his face growing serious. "Everyone needs to know that there is someone there, to trust in and to believe that they'll come through.''

"That's what I just said. You've learned to deal with life.'' Caitlin savored the rich tomato flavor, happy that she'd given in to his persuasion and come along. This was very relaxing.

"No, Caitlin, it's more than just 'dealing with

life.'"' Jordan hunched over the table, his fingers entwining together as he tried to make her see his point.

"I don't have to worry about pleasing someone else all the time, trying to fit his or her mold, because I've already learned that I am important to God. That's the first big hurdle to acceptance."

He ignored her arched eyebrow. "The difference is that this Addie sounds like she's trying to get through everything on her own. She can't do it. Or if she can, it will only last for a while. People need God and other Christians in their lives to help validate them and the choices they make."

"And what about when those Christians fail?" Caitlin wasn't talking about Addie's father now. This issue was a little too close to home. She had a feeling Jordan knew it, too.

"Everyone fails now and then. It's called being human. You get up and move on."

Caitlin bristled, realizing he was directing some of his comments at her. It was so easy for him. He didn't have to worry about being alone, depending on himself, making mistakes. There was always a crowd of people hovering around in the Andrewses' household.

"Not everyone has dependable people in their lives, Jordan. And sometimes the people you do depend on leave you high and dry."

Jordan nodded. "Quite often, in fact. That's the beauty of having faith. Things will work out. You just have to be patient and trust that God has something special for you. You have to *trust* Him."

Caitlin paused before she said anything. She didn't

want to hurt his feelings, but neither could she just let this pass. "Jordan, I don't think I believe that any-more. Michael's gone. It's not going to get better." She sipped her ice water in an effort to control the frustration that whirled within.

"God let me down with Michael, just like He did with my parents all those years ago. They died, my aunt died, and Michael died. God could have stopped it, but He didn't. And no amount of faith is going to bring them back. Now I've got to learn to stand on my own two feet."

Jordan was silent for a few minutes, obviously deep in thought. She reared in surprise when his next words came.

"Caitlin, would you believe God hadn't let you down if Michael had survived the crash and was lying in the hospital in a coma?"

"It's hypothetical," she murmured. "But at least there might be some hope."

"Even if the doctors said he would never regain consciousness?"

Caitlin shuddered. "No, I wouldn't want him to just lie there, with no possibility of ever waking up."

Jordan nodded. "Would you feel better if Michael had lived but been paralyzed, then?"

She hated this. "I don't know."

"What if he was in constant agony, but still alive?"

"I've said I don't know," she replied tersely, laying her fork on the table. "Why do you keep asking me these awful questions?"

"Because we can't second-guess life, Lyn. And, no

matter how much we want it, we will never know why Michael died. No explanations, just reality.''

"It's awfully hard to accept that.'' She bit her lip.

"Yes, it is hard,'' he agreed. "But we can get through it. With God's help. And friends.'' He cleared his throat. "I miss my brother every day. But I know that where he is has to be a far better place. I have to let God take care of him and get on with my life. Someday I'll see him again in heaven.''

His smile lit up his eyes as he spoke and Caitlin found herself mesmerized by the lilt in his voice.

"You see, Lyn, the difference is where we put our faith. You want to put yours in yourself. You think if you do enough, be enough, work hard enough, you'll be okay. But if something knocks you down, your house of cards tumbles and it takes a long time to rebuild.''

"And?'' She avoided his eyes.

"I put my faith in God. He's all powerful, all knowing, all seeing. We make a strong team. What I can't handle, He does. And He gives me faith in myself and my friends.'' His hand covered hers. "When I get bowled over by life, He's still there, waiting to help me up.''

Caitlin reconsidered Jordan's words as they finished dinner and then during the short silent car ride home. She continued to think about things long after he'd brushed her cheek with a friendly kiss and left her inside her door.

Was she really strong enough to be everything to her child when she herself felt so needy?

The answer was simple. She had to be.

But how?

Caitlin brushed the problem away, unwilling to probe that question too deeply. Grabbing a nearby pad of paper, she began to list the essentials that had to be completed before the baby arrived. This, at least, she could get a grip on, she told herself. *This* was under her control.

Chapter Five

Saturday morning dawned bright and clear. It would be the last really good day of autumn, Caitlin decided, eyeing the baby's nursery with dismay,.

Where had the time gone? She had intended to have Wintergreen, her apartment, and especially the baby's room, ready at least a month ago. With a little more than a month before her due date, it was high past time to get the painting done. And the weather had provided the perfect opportunity to do so. The unseasonably sunny, clear day meant she could open the windows and allow the nontoxic paint fumes to escape while she worked.

But before she could even begin, she was interrupted by a knock on the front door.

Jordan asked her as he stepped inside, "What are you going to do this fine day, Mrs. Andrews?"

"I'm painting the baby's room." She ignored his

gasp and stepped around his big frame to walk toward the nursery.

"Caitlin, you can't paint a room in your condition," he admonished her loudly, following behind.

"I can paint if I want to! I have to get it done before the baby arrives." There he was, bossing her around again.

"Yes, but breathing paint fumes isn't—"

"Mr. Becker at the hardware store said the paint I chose doesn't have that problem." She glared at him furiously. "I'm not totally helpless, Jordan. Good grief, even I can paint a room."

"Can I help?"

"Jordan, I'm not helpless. I can do this." She stopped when his head started shaking.

"Yeah, I know that," he told her, staring down at his shoes. "It's just that, well, uh…" he cleared his husky voice.

Caitlin stared, unsure of this new side of him. She had never seen Jordan so at a loss for words before.

"I just thought, maybe I could be, well, part of the preparations? You know? Help get things ready for my new little niece or nephew."

His eyes had melted to a deep bronze. They were soft and molten like liquid gold. She saw tenderness but no pity.

"Kind of, well, step in for Mike."

The softly spoken pledge tugged at her heart. Jordan wasn't bullying or ordering now. He just wanted to be a part of things. Against her better judgment, she gave in.

"Okay," she agreed finally. "But no telling me how to do things. I have something in mind and you're not changing it, Jordan. Not one little bit!"

He acceded easily enough, the twinkle of mischief back in his eyes. And to his credit he said nothing when she teetered on the rungs of the ladder, reaching for the crease along the stippled ceiling. He merely stood below, his lips pursed in a tight, straight line, holding the ladder. Nor did he comment when she dripped paint into his hair. Or when she wavered with dizziness on the second from the top rung.

But when she finally came down off the ladder, he was there with a cold glass of water.

"Sit down and drink this," he ordered.

As she watched, his face assumed that tight mask of control, devoid of any visible emotion. She hated that look.

"I'll take my turn now." He took the roller from her without asking and climbed the ladder, his lips pinched together.

Caitlin drank the cool refreshing water thankfully. And when it became clear that Jordan had no intention of relinquishing his hold on the roller or the ladder, she took the brush to the corners, filling the seamed areas his roller didn't cover.

They worked in silence as the fresh autumn breeze blew in the windows. It helped carry away some of the nontoxic paint smell and Caitlin was grateful.

But eventually she had to get out of the room. Her aching head and queasy stomach refused to subside and since Jordan had insisted the bedroom door remain closed to seal off the rest of the house, it was impossible to get totally away from the odor as long as she remained in the room.

"I think I'll go make some tea." She left with an admonition for him to call her when he needed help. Once downstairs, Caitlin headed for the front door to check the mailbox.

"Hi. What's up?" Maryann stood in the front hall, the area that divided their apartments. "Got company?"

"Jordan." Caitlin made a face. "I'm trying to paint the nursery and he insists I leave it to him. That man is so bossy." She grinned. "But to tell you the truth, I don't know what I'd do without him. At the moment I've got a splitting headache."

"There's nothing wrong with having someone care about you, Caitlin," Maryann murmured.

"Yes, I know. It's just that Jordan sort of bulldozes me into things. And I don't even realize it until he's left." She frowned. "I've got an idea for that room and I intend to carry it out."

The doorbell rang then, cutting into their conversation.

"That's for me," Maryann said. "Amy and I are going out."

"Oh." Caitlin's interest perked at the mention of Maryann's daughter. "Going with anyone I know?"

"Everybody seems to know everything around here," Maryann chuckled as she tugged open the front door. "Come on in, Peter. I'll just get Amy. Peter's Amy's skating coach for ringette."

"Okay. Hello, Mrs. Andrews." Peter Bloomfield stepped into the hall, his smile white and gleaming.

Caitlin nodded absently, wished him a good day and then turned back into her apartment. She closed the door carefully, her mind busy. Seconds later she had the phone next to her ear.

"Clayton? Maryann and Amy are going out with Peter Bloomfield. I thought we agreed that you would ask her out. Dancing, you said."

The bachelor's quiet tones rumbled down the phone line. "Oh. Yeah. Well, I tried. But I just couldn't do it, Caitlin. Maybe after a few more practice sessions."

All that time she'd spent encouraging him and he *still* wasn't sure? "All right, Clayton. If you're certain?"

"Yes. Yes, I am. Can I come over for lessons again?"

"Yes, all right. Monday night. Bye, Clayton." Caitlin hung up the phone with another sigh.

"He's coming over *again?*" Jordan stood frowning at the bottom of the stairs. "What's it for this time?"

"He's not quite confident yet. He feels he needs a few more sessions before he makes a move."

"What kind of sessions?" Jordan's face was dark. "Are you counseling this guy or something, Lyn?"

"No. If you must know, I'm trying to teach him to dance." She held up a hand. "Please, Jordan, I can't say any more. He made me promise, so don't ask. Just make sure your mother doesn't happen to drop over for coffee on Monday evening, okay?"

Jordan didn't say yes. But then he didn't say no,

either. He just stood there, glaring at her, before he turned and went back up the stairs.

"Did you want something?" she called.

"Yes," she heard him mutter, his voice grumpy. "But I don't think I'm going to get it." Seconds later the nursery door slammed shut.

Caitlin shrugged and walked out into her tiny kitchen. She watered the herbs that had started to sprout in the windowsill planter and realized her headache was easing.

Some time out of that room was all she needed she told herself, ignoring the muscles that protested from the effort of too much unaccustomed reaching.

Time out and some time away from Jordan Andrews was the best possible solution to her problems. Lately he had a way of looking at her that made her strangely nervous. A quiver would start in her tummy and zap to her brain, rendering her mental functions virtually useless.

It was a schoolgirl reaction and she ordered herself to get over it. Jordan was handsome and kind and sweet. He'd help out anyone in her predicament. And, after all, she *was* his sister-in-law.

At twelve she went to call him for the small lunch she had prepared. She found Jordan whistling as he rolled on the last few strokes.

"You're finished, already?" she said, amazed at the difference a paint job could make. The walls glowed smooth and creamy in their new coats of velvet gloss.

"It's not that big an area and the surface is in good shape."

''It should be. I paid a small fortune for a plasterer.''

He avoided her eyes as he covered an area she'd already painted earlier. His smooth even strokes blended out the lines left by her hurried determination to do it herself.

''This is where I'm going to put the duck decals,'' she told him happily, holding up her hands to frame the area.

It was amazing how quickly the feature wall evolved after that. Jordan suggested a light-blue background for the space behind Mrs. Puddleduck.

They walked downstairs, still discussing the nursery.

''She needs a pond,'' he told her seriously, his eyes gleaming through the paint-spattered metal rims of his glasses as he stood in the kitchen. He washed out the roller while she served the soup.

A pond sounded reasonable.

''Okay,'' she acquiesced. ''But that's all. No more frills. I want to do ruffly curtains and with the border I bought today, that should be enough accents. The furniture I ordered will complete it.''

They ate without speaking, enjoying the relative calm of their lunchtime, munching on the cold cuts and rolls she served.

They sat for a while and then Caitlin moved to the sofa where she could feel herself drifting to sleep. When she awoke, she realized Jordan had covered her with the teal afghan from the living room.

The dishes lay stacked neatly in the kitchen sink.

And there was a faint sound of whistling from upstairs. She followed that sound and found Jordan in the nursery, surrounded by small colored cans of paint. She also saw that the mural had expanded from a simple pond to include three white, puffy clouds floating in a pale blue sky.

"Atmosphere," he told her. His eyes were fixed on the wall, studying it as if something were about to emerge.

Shaking her head, Caitlin went to get him some coffee. When she returned, an array of bright-yellow daffodils waved on thin green stalks from a clump of warm-brown dirt on the edge of the lake.

She hadn't finished admiring those when he added two thick green trees and a patch of high reedy grass. She called a halt then.

"Jordan, you can't put on any more. There won't be room for Jemima Puddleduck or her brood!"

His eyes were glazed as he stood back, studying his efforts, paintbrush in hand. "A boat," he murmured. "A little sailboat with a bright-red sail, maybe."

"No, no more. It looks wonderful just as it is."

He didn't appear to hear her. "I think if I..."

Caitlin took the brush from his hand and tossed it into the garbage bag. "If you've got so much energy, you can help me put up the border along the ceiling edge," she muttered. He agreed readily enough and once he'd finished his coffee, they began pasting the bands of color onto the newly painted walls.

"Are you sure we shouldn't wait before doing this?" she asked him for the sixth time. Her hand swept over the wall, assessing its condition. "This paint does seem dry enough."

"It was dry ages ago," he reassured her. "Otherwise I wouldn't have started that." One long finger pointed to the scene he'd created.

"Here's another one. We're almost done," she cried exultantly as he placed the last bit carefully against the wall.

They picked up the bits of paper and glue that clung here and there to the pale-gray carpet. Finally Jordan went to wash while she called the baby store to request a rush delivery of the furniture. It suddenly seemed urgent to get the room finished.

To her surprise, the store manager said they could bring everything within the hour. Caitlin could hardly control her anticipation as she surveyed the room, mentally placing the items she had chosen earlier in the week.

When she couldn't wait any longer and Jordan had returned, she insisted that the walls were dry enough. They lifted up the sticky characters and applied them, using great care to avoid smudging the freshly painted mural. Jordan continued to speculate.

"Perhaps a beach ball," he deliberated. "And a pail and shovel."

"No, Jordan."

"But Lyn, if it's a boy, he'll want some boy toys."

Caitlin was losing her patience. "Jordan, we're talking about a newborn baby here. Toys will come a little later, okay?"

He nodded absently, his mind obviously somewhere else. "I really think a boat…"

"Jordan," Caitlin muttered, tugging the change table Robyn had given her through the door to its place under the wall lamp. "Jordan?"

He was on his hands and knees staring at the bottom of the grass. "You know—" his dark eyes beamed up at her "—if we just put a little garter snake here…"

"No," she bellowed, repulsed by the very idea of a snake in her baby's room. "No reptiles!"

His merry chuckles made her flush with embarrassment.

"I was only teasing," he muttered, unabashed when she fired off a glare.

They worked together with the delivery man, her directing and the men lifting as they moved the oak crib and an antique rocking chair Caitlin had purchased to just the right place and then moved them again because the ambience wasn't quite right.

The chair she finally placed near the window so she could see outside. A tall bureau found its home strategically situated near the change table to allow her handy diaper swaps.

At last everything was where she wanted it. Caitlin gazed round the room with satisfaction. It was a beautiful room. And it had taken half the time she had expected to ready the nursery. Thanks to Jordan. She turned to meet his dark gaze.

"Thank you." She felt as if her whole body was smiling with the relief of having this job done. "I appreciate the time you've spent here, helping me."

She smiled softly. "You've made this room very special. I value your help."

He grinned back, bowing at the waist. "My pleasure, Caitlin. I enjoyed every minute."

His face grew more serious as he studied her through his spattered lenses. "I think you're going to enjoy sitting in here. And the baby will love it."

A wistful look covered his face. Then, like a cloud, darkness flooded his eyes. "I just wish you would consider allowing the rest of the family to help a little more. Mom and Dad would love to be on call for whatever you need."

The goodwill and harmony they had just shared evaporated now like the sun behind those dark wintry clouds that had started blowing in from the north. Caitlin turned to leave, tugging the black garbage bag behind her. When Jordan took it from her, she let him, not saying a word. Her footsteps were weary as she plodded slowly down the stairs. He followed silently.

But Jordan wouldn't leave it alone. She knew him well enough to know that he was like a dog with a bone once he got hold of an idea. And right now, the last thing she needed was more tension. Life already seemed like she was walking a tightrope. Quarreling with Jordan would only make it worse.

"I promise, I'll involve them in the baby's life. They'll be so tired of me, they'll beg off. But not right now, okay?"

"But Lyn, they'd love to..." He took a second look at her face and stopped talking.

As she sank into the big armchair, Caitlin's brain

searched for a way out of her dilemma. She did not want to have this discussion again. How could she tactfully explain that she was afraid their interest wouldn't last, that she'd become a burden on them, that they reminded her of what she'd lost?

Nothing momentous occurred to her by the time he broke the silence.

"Why don't you come over to Mom and Dad's for supper tonight? The girls are planning Dad's birthday on Sunday. They'd love to see you again."

Caitlin recognized the veiled reference to the fact that she had studiously avoided his family. Jordan, it seemed, was intent on making up for lost time. Two visits in one week?

"I know they're a bit talkative and my mother does have a slight tendency to stride in where angels fear to tread." Jordan winked. "But if it gets to be too much, I promise I'll take you straight home. Inquisition or not."

"Okay," she agreed softly after several moments of rapid thought, eventually admitting the real reason for agreeing to his plans. She wanted to see them again, revel in the love and caring. "But only if you phone your mother first and tell her I'm coming."

"Fine," Jordan grunted, obviously satisfied if not mystified by her sudden capitulation. "I'll phone her, but you know perfectly well that she loves company. The more the merrier."

"And tell her we'll bring over some chicken, too."

Jordan groaned his dismay, his face curled up in disgust.

A scant hour later they were waiting at a local fast-food establishment to pick up the fried chicken Caitlin insisted on ordering. Jordan climbed out of his car with reluctance, only to poke his head back in at her.

"I hate chicken, you know," he muttered, his wide mouth curving down in distaste.

"I do know, Jordan." Caitlin grinned at him without apology. "And even if I didn't, you've reminded me at least six times since we left home."

"Why couldn't we just pick up some steaks and barbecue?"

"Because I feel like eating fried chicken. I'm sure your dad will have something else, just in case. He doesn't seem to enjoy this particular delicacy any more than you do."

"That's what I'm afraid of," he groaned. "Dad likes some really wild things. What if it's bear sausage?"

She grinned. "Maybe it will be roasted pelican or unruffled duck. Will you stop wasting time and just get the chicken?"

"Fine. I'll go, but I don't like it." He shoved his hands in his pockets, his hair flopping down over one quirked eyebrow. "How come you don't eat pickles and ice cream like the books say?"

"You read books about pregnancy?" The very idea sent her eyes winging to his.

"I'm interested. Okay?" Jordan flushed a deep, dark, embarrassed red. He sauntered into the store, mumbling to himself all the way.

Caitlin sat in his car and considered this newfound

knowledge. Jordan was reading up on pregnancy. It was…endearing. Imagine taking the time to study her condition! The knowing warmed her inside until she considered the folly of what she was doing.

She was letting them in. Little by little Jordan and his family were eating away at the protective wall she'd built around her heart.

"But it's only temporary," she assured her nagging conscience. "Just till after I get settled with the baby. Surely it's not wrong to be friends with Jordan. Is it?"

But is it friendship you want from him? Or are you looking for a replacement for Michael? Is Jordan just a way of avoiding the truth?

"I know I'm alone here, God," she muttered, dashing the tears from her eyes. "You don't have to hit me over the head. I know that there's only me I can count on."

I'm here.

The words resounded through her head like a train whistle in a tunnel.

You can depend on me, Caitlin.

"No, I can't," she whispered, twisting her hands miserably.

I will never leave you. I'm always here.

Could she believe that?

Chapter Six

A half hour later, ensconced in his mother's front room, Jordan allowed his eyes to rest on Caitlin once more. Her hair curled down her back in a riot of dark russet that refused to be confined. Her clear profile was both elegant and arresting. She was as beautiful as she had ever been.

Caitlin's eyes, dark and mossy, almost hid the fears and secrets she never talked about. He'd been acquainted with her for years and yet Jordan realized he had never really known her at all. When she was hurt or worried, Caitlin pulled inside herself. That was exactly what had happened when Mike died. She had closed herself off to everyone.

Those same eyes seemed duller now. The dimples remained though, hidden away at the corner of her mouth until she grinned that impishly heartrending smile that stretched her wide full mouth and tore at his heart.

Jordan turned away, calling himself a prize fool. Caitlin was his brother's widow. She was lost and alone because his brother had died while driving Jordan's car.

Rationally, in some part of his brain, Jordan knew it wasn't his fault. Michael had always driven fast. And the terribly cold conditions last winter made black ice a sure thing. But nothing he told himself, and nothing anyone else could ever say, took away that niggling bit of doubt at the back of his mind.

Should he have died in his brother's place?

He was brought out of his introspection by the slap of his father's hand on his shoulder.

"Come on, son. We've got to get those buffalo steaks seasoned and on the grill if we're going to eat tonight." He chuckled at Jordan's quick look toward the kitchen. "I, for one, refuse to eat chicken."

The hint was subtle, and Jordan surged to his feet as Stan had known he would. "Chicken, yuck. Those are the magic words, Dad," he whispered conspiratorially. They sneaked out while the women chatted and admired the newest antics of Robyn's daughter Eudora.

As they sat out on the deck, watching the northern lights wave and flicker in the black autumn sky, Stan questioned his son's sudden silence. "What happened to the life of the party?"

"I don't know," Jordan replied, then teasingly turned the question around. "Are you tired or something?" He grinned at his father's smug look. "Maybe your age is catching up with you. Or maybe it's the peculiar food you eat. Has Mom been feeding you Scottish haggis again?'' He ducked to avoid the swat Stan directed at his head.

They shared sympathetic male glances of commiseration.

''She looks good, doesn't she Jordy?'' They both knew who Stan was talking about.

''Yeah. Better than she did this afternoon, anyway.'' Jordan filled his father in on the now ready nursery.

''Why'd she keep away for so long, do you think?'' Stan asked, his lined brow creased in thought. ''Michael's death should have drawn us closer.''

''I know, Dad. But Lyn's always been a loner. Remember that her folks died when she was little and she was left with that old aunt of hers for company. I guess all that kind of built up over the years and she feels isolated.'' Jordan followed the white ribbon of light as it folded and rolled across the dark sky, turning green, then fading away.

''When Lucy died, she left everything to her next of kin, that is, Caitlin. Never even named her. Not a very loving gesture to the girl who lived with her for so long. I suspect Caitlin doesn't really understand the bond between families.''

Stan nodded, his voice soft with affection. ''At least she's got the baby, son. That'll help her.''

Jordan shook his head. ''I'm not so sure the baby's a good thing for Caitlin right now, Dad. I'm not even sure she's really over losing Michael.''

When Stan's white head reared back in surprise,

Jordan tried to explain himself. "It's not that I'm not happy about Michael's child being born. I think it's great." He stared into the night trying to organize his thoughts. "It's just that Lyn's going to bank everything on this child, you know. He or she is all Lyn has left and her emotions are all wound up in that responsibility, in proving herself."

He took in a lungful of the cool, fresh air and tried to explain more clearly. When the harvest moon slid out from behind a cloud, Jordan could see leaves floating down to earth.

"Lyn is going to have to be both mother and father to this child and the idea scares her. I think that's why she's backed away from you and Mom. She's afraid she won't measure up or something. She hasn't had a role model for a long time, remember?"

His father studied him wordlessly, his look thoughtful.

"Since her parents' death, Caitlin never had anyone who made her feel extra special. Then Mike came along to look after her, be her protector. Now she's lost him and gained the responsibility of a new life. I'm not sure that what she needs are more worries. I think what she really needs is a childhood." Jordan grimaced at his father. "Twenty-six is awfully young to take on all those burdens alone."

"It's awfully young to die, too, Jordy," Stan murmured softly, reminding him of Michael's youth so quickly gone. "But we can't question God. If He's going to be in control, we have to let go and trust Him to work everything together for good."

"I know, Dad, I know." It wasn't anything Jordan hadn't been telling himself for months now. "I don't understand, but I'll try to trust."

Stan straightened from his position with a groan, kneading the small of his back. "You know, son, if Caity never had a real loving home, then she's never had the security of love that comes from a family like you and Mike had. She probably never found someone who cared about her until you guys came along. You two must have been like some kind of knights to her back then."

Jordan broke in with his own thoughts, his face heating with embarrassment. "I wasn't that, Dad. She just had a crush on me. It was Mike she really loved. In fact, other than that short time she shared with him, I think she's spent most of her life on the outside, looking in."

"So you've said before. But, Jordan, the thing is..." Stan stopped and stared up at the stars that glittered above. "Maybe the purpose of us in all of this is to make sure Caitlin finds out what it's like to have love backing her all the way. Maybe if she feels she can rely on the rest of us, she'll be able to let Michael go."

Stan met his son's clear gaze head-on. "I think Caitlin is going to need us now more than ever. She's a strong young woman, but nobody can do it all. Only God can do that." His father grinned slyly. "Maybe you'll be the one Caitlin will lean on again. That should please you."

Jordan thought about his father's advice as they

pulled the buffalo steaks off the grill and took them inside. He thought about it as the family ate dinner. He considered every aspect of having Caitlin lean on him, allowing much of the conversation to ebb and flow around him.

A faint smile curved his mouth as he considered the likelihood of feisty, determined Caitlin Andrews leaning on his shoulder. It wasn't apt to happen anytime soon, but he couldn't think of anything he would like better.

Caitlin perched on the corner of the huge double bed Stan and Eliza shared, admiring the quilt they'd come up to see. She'd been aware of what was coming when Robyn offered to load the dishwasher so they could "talk." Now Eliza's hand folded around hers.

"Honey," the older woman's soft voice comforted. "I'm not complaining, but I wish you had told us sooner. So we could have helped you. It must be difficult for you."

"I'm sorry," Caitlin apologized, feeling silly for doubting their warm reception and yet still needing to hold on to her reserve. "I should have. I just wanted to make sure I could do this on my own, I guess." She met Eliza's probing blue eyes. "I feel I have to stand alone, be strong. Besides, you were busy."

"Not that busy! And you are strong, dear. The strongest young woman I've ever met. But sometimes it's okay to lean on other people, too. At least we're here now and you won't be able to push us away. We're going to keep you really close."

There wasn't a hint of censure in Eliza's smooth voice as she hugged her daughter-in-law, just a wealth of warm, unconditional love. She held no grudges.

"Now tell me," the older woman commanded, smiling. "Did you have a lot of morning sickness?"

"No, thank goodness. I was never really sick, just sort of woozy some mornings. The oddest thing still sets me off." Caitlin rolled her eyes back in her head. "Of course, some foods have the power to make my insides flip," she acknowledged with a grin.

Eliza nodded. "I know exactly what you mean. I craved onion rings with Robyn, but one taste and that was it."

Caitlin giggled. "I just get the slightest whiff and whoosh...there goes my stomach. Hamburgers do it every time."

They laughed together at the vagaries of pregnancy and Eliza still held her hand as they wandered back downstairs.

"I love having you here," she whispered, a tear in the corner of her eye. "It's like having my other daughter home after a long absence." She tucked a strand of hair behind Caitlin's ear and smiled. "Shall we see what Jordan's up to?"

As they walked through her home, Eliza related a few stories about her five attempts at motherhood, including Jordan's unexpected arrival.

"He was early, you know. Almost a month." Eliza winked as they returned to the kitchen to find the two men playing chess and sipping coffee at the kitchen table. "But then, Jordan's always been pushy," his mother teased. "Never could wait his turn."

"I've noticed," Caitlin replied tongue in cheek as she watched her brother-in-law sprawl across the table, reaching for his king. With a wing of dark hair dropped over one eye, Jordan resembled a mischievous little boy. He stared up at them through his lenses, one hand dangling over the chessboard.

"Were you two talking about me all this time?" he speculated, puffing his chest out. "Of course, there is a lot to say."

He assumed a wounded look when they burst out laughing, but bore their teasing with reluctant good grace. He offered a few choice witticisms of his own that had them clutching their sides just as Natasha, the youngest of the Andrewses' daughters, stuck her head through the kitchen door, closely followed by Olivia.

"Caitlin," Natasha squealed, enveloping her in a hug before standing back to survey her sister-in-law. "You look great. Big, but great."

Robyn groaned. "I've just cured Jordan of foot-in-mouth disease, Nat, and now you start. Olivia, feed her a cookie, so she'll stop embarrassing us."

Everyone began chatting at once and Caitlin sank into a nearby chair, enjoying it all.

A few moments later Eliza questioned her daughter. "What have you been up to tonight? You look like the cat that swallowed the canary."

Natasha grinned her big toothy smile and shrugged her elegant shoulders, dislodging her white wool cape. She hung it on a nearby peg then smoothed a hand over her suede pants. As buyer for a women's boutique in nearby Minneapolis, Nat always wore perfectly coordinated outfits in the latest styles. Caitlin envied her chic look.

"Oh, just trying to get the rest of my Christmas shopping done," she said, plugging her ears when the entire room began to protest.

"Good grief," Stan grumped, using his son's favorite expression. "It's barely the end of October. What's the rush?"

"Oh, you know Nat. Always be prepared. Good thing she's going out with a Boy Scout." Jordan put in his two cents' worth with a smug look. He clutched his chest in pretended pain when his sister glared at him, her eyes daring him to continue.

"Ow, that look hurt!" He burst out laughing when she ignored him. "You're such a bully, Nat."

"Just because you never get around to doing any shopping until four o'clock on the twenty-fourth," she reminded him with a sniff, "is no reason to make fun of everyone else, brother dear. Some of us are organized." Her wide eyes beseeched Caitlin's in mock despair.

Caitlin couldn't suppress a grin. They were like little kids.

"You know, Caitlin, the man is almost thirty years old. You'd think he would have figured out by now that Christmas comes on the same day every year."

"What day is that, Nat?" Jordan kept his tone perfectly serious as he moved his knight one step closer to Stan's king.

''See what I mean,'' she wailed to Caitlin, eyes sparkling.

I see, Caitlin thought to herself. I see that you love Jordan as much as he loves you.

That thought started a little ache in her heart. There was so much love here, she could feel it surrounding her, nestling her inside its warmth and protection.

''Checkmate!'' Jordan snapped his piece onto the board, then crowed with delight, rubbing his hands together with glee while his father sat frowning and confused.

Stan protested, glowering as he studied the board. His eyes searched for some devious means that would explain his son's sudden success.

''You cheated Jordan. I don't know how, but you did. There's no way you could have pulled that off!''

''Cheated?'' Jordan's big grin drooped. He thumped a fist to his chest. ''You wound me to the quick!''

''If you mean your heart, it's on the other side,'' Robyn chastised, but her lips twitched. ''And you did take advantage of Dad. We just don't know how. I think you should get closed-circuit TV, Stan.''

''As if you know anything about chess,'' Jordan sniffed disparagingly.

''Children,'' Eliza pleaded, although her face was wreathed in smiles. ''No fighting when company is here.''

''Caitlin's not company,'' Jordan denied. His big grin warmed her chilled heart. ''Caitlin is family.''

''That she is, son,'' Stan agreed. He pushed the board away, then stood to press a light kiss against his daughter-in-law's cheek. "That she is. As my daughter she should learn how to play chess, don't you think, Eliza?"

Eliza nodded absently. "I suppose so. Though it's a rather boring game, I always think."

When Stan and Jordan would have protested at such heresy, she cut across their objections by urging everyone into the family room. Minutes later she and Robyn passed around her special blueberry pie and ice cream. As they ate, they talked, one voice over another, changing subjects faster than lightning. At one point Caitlin found herself involved in three separate conversations. She couldn't help but grin when Stan got so involved in Olivia's story to her that he ignored Jordan's diatribe completely.

"Yes, but you don't understand politics," he chided his daughter, a twinkle at the back of his eyes. "Women always take it too seriously."

"It is only our country, after all," Caitlin teased, watching Olivia's eyes. "No point in getting all hot and bothered about a little thing like that." She burst out laughing at Stan's guffaw of disgust.

"Where's Glen when I need him anyway?" Stan grumbled, searching the room for his son-in-law.

"He's working late so he can take the weekend off," Robyn informed him. "And you two don't agree on politics anyway."

"We'd agree about this," Stan blustered.

As the controversy raged, the entire family got into the act. There was no acrimony, no hard feelings, no overruling of one by the other. They bickered and squabbled good-naturedly while the last of the pie magically disappeared off Jordan's plate.

"I saw that," Caitlin whispered.

He nodded. "I know. And you're not going to tell a single soul. Particularly not my dad. Right?"

"Or?" For the first time in a long while Caitlin felt really alive, a part of something. She narrowed her gaze. "What will you do?"

He thought about it for a few moments, his forehead pleated in a frown.

"Well?"

"I don't know yet." He licked his fork clean, then slipped his empty plate behind him on the bottom shelf of the nearby coffee table. "But it's going to be really, really bad."

"Oh, no! Now I'm *really* scared," she giggled, feeling the years roll away as she teased him.

"Good." His fingers laced through hers and he leaned back on the sofa, pulling her against the cushiony softness, his shoulder touching hers. "I suppose I'll have to keep you here beside me, just to make sure you don't blab."

"I suppose." She relaxed, content to be quiet and observe the give-and-take of love that flowed so easily in this family.

"Hey, Caitlin, are you awake?" Robyn turned the focus on her.

Jordan shook his head, watching Caitlin smother a yawn. In seconds he was on his feet, reaching out a hand to pull her upright. "Right now Caitlin's too tired to listen to you silly girls any longer."

The female contingent rose en masse in protest.

He blithely ignored them all, tugging Caitlin toward the front door. Once there he dug in the closet, found what he wanted, then placed Caitlin's thick coat over her shoulders.

"Time to get the little mommy home," he whispered for her ears alone.

She frowned at him, knowing it would be absolutely no good whatsoever to rant at him for his bossiness. Who said she wanted to leave? What she wouldn't give for a little more height and a really authoritative tone right now. Unfortunately she was just too tired to argue. Instead she accepted his outstretched hand that held her gloves, tugged them on and walked obediently to the door.

"I always said he was pushy," Robyn muttered to her mother as they gathered around.

"It was a lovely evening," Caitlin murmured, hugging her mother-in-law goodbye. "I'm glad I came."

"I'm glad, too," Eliza whispered back. "I just wish I had some free time to discuss that girl with you. Mary something, isn't it?" She frowned. "We need to get cracking on some plans for her and that shy young man. It's just that I've been so busy lately. Jordan's looking after you, isn't he?"

There was an odd look on Eliza's face that Caitlin didn't understand. But there wasn't a lot of time to think about it and she brushed the nagging questions aside. Eliza was involved in her own life. Wasn't that what she'd wanted?

"I've tried to make sure he gets over there every

day to check up on you. It gives him something to do and then we know you're okay. Otherwise he'd come over here and eat all my pie.'' Eliza's bland smile made Caitlin giggle.

"He thinks no one noticed," she whispered.

"Of course he does. But mothers always notice." Robyn hugged her too.

"If you need me, you just call, Caitlin. I'd come over more often myself, but I just can't spare the time right now. Besides, you've got Jordan." Eliza said it triumphantly, as if the very idea thrilled her. "Since he's home, he can lend a hand. I know he doesn't mind and there's so much to do in the church. It'll soon be Thanksgiving!"

"Don't forget, Mom, I'm doing the pumpkin pies for our dinner," Robyn announced, her eyes glinting with mischief.

"That's nice, dear. Don't forget to put the spices in this year, will you?" Eliza glanced over her shoulder to be sure her daughter heard, then turned back to Caitlin.

"Of course, Caitlin, if you need something moved or rearranged, Jordan can help with that, too. He has plenty of muscles and they need a good workout now and then. He does far too much sitting around, staring at those computers of his. It's not healthy."

"I do work out!" Jordan frowned, affronted by this slur against his physique. "And I'm very healthy. Aren't I, Dad?"

Stan shrugged. "I don't think it's healthy to eat so much pie that you try to hide the dishes," he quipped as he leaned down to kiss Caitlin's cheek. "Bye, dear. Don't feed Jordan, okay? He's getting a pot belly."

"I am not." But he couldn't resist checking his midsection in the hall mirror in spite of the smothered laughter. "You guys, I am perfectly healthy!"

"If you say so, dear." Eliza ignored his grumpy tones. Instead she focused on Caitlin, wrapping a scarf around her throat. She buttoned the top button firmly and then stood back to admire her work.

"There, now. At the first sign of labor, you call *me*, Caitlin. Jordan will be no help at all. He's not good at handling pain." She winked a big blue eye at the officious hand her son had wrapped beneath Caitlin's elbow. She didn't lower her voice at all. "But don't tell him I said that."

"No." Caitlin agreed with a smug little smile. "It wouldn't be fair to let Jordan know he's not great at everything." She smiled at his snort of disgust.

The girls all wished her goodbye. As Natasha hugged her, she whispered, "We didn't overwhelm you, did we?"

So that's why she and Olivia had come later than the others. They'd been worried about her. Caitlin felt a nice steady glow of love inside.

They left the house with good wishes and demands for a return engagement ringing in their ears.

"I hope they didn't wear you out," Jordan's deep voice broke into her musings as they walked to the car.

Caitlin rubbed her abdomen absently, wondering why the baby always chose late at night to exercise.

Jordan held open the door and she climbed inside, glad to relax against the seat. "Of course not. I like your family, Jordan. I've missed Robyn and Natasha and Olivia."

His dark eyes studied her solemnly, his voice softly mocking. "They've been there all along, Lyn. All you had to do was phone."

There was no condemnation. He simply closed her door, walked around and climbed inside as if nothing untoward had happened. The engine started on the first try and soon they were moving, slipping into traffic without difficulty.

"I know it." She threaded her fingers together. "It's my own fault I've been alone. I guess I thought I deserved it." As she said the words, Caitlin realized how lonely she had been for the friendly banter and warm friendship that was so much a part of the Andrews family.

They both fell silent as Jordan negotiated the car through the busy streets. It wasn't an uncomfortable silence, though. More of a companionable pause in the conversation. A short time later they were pulling into the driveway of her home.

Once inside, she slipped her feet into a pair of soft terry slippers, enjoying the snug feel of the soft fabric against her cold toes. Tomorrow she'd buy a new pair of warm, sturdy winter boots, she decided, hanging up her coat and closing the closet door as a waft of fresh cedar filled the hall.

"I'll light a fire, shall I?" Jordan stood inside her living room, patiently waiting for her answer.

"Yes, please." She smiled as he walked over to the big stone fireplace and removed the wrought iron screen. "I like having a fire."

Caitlin glanced around the room, admiring the hominess. There was something about coming back to Wintergreen that cheered her up, warmed her soul. Was it because she knew the others were here, that she wouldn't be alone? Or was it, she wondered guiltily, because she'd run away from the place where Michael had lived, laughed and loved? Was she trying to escape her past?

Sinking gratefully into the comforting depths of the sofa, Caitlin lifted her legs onto a nearby hassock. She sighed with relief.

"Problem?" Jordan turned from his kneeling position in front of her fireplace. The flames licked at the paper and kindling he'd laid.

"Just calisthenics time." She smiled. "This kid always chooses the evening to start bouncing around. I hope it's not a precursor of things to come."

She glanced back at him shyly only to find Jordan's dark gaze fixed on the tiny movements outlined on her abdomen by the thin fabric of her top. As he stared, Caitlin thought she detected a flicker of something in his eyes. Longing?

"Do you want to feel him?" she asked without thinking, totally unprepared for his immediate response.

"Yes," he agreed rapidly, sliding the grate into place before striding over to where she sat. He squatted down beside her, his face telegraphing his discomfiture, letting her know he wasn't quite sure of the next move.

Caitlin grasped his big hand in hers and placed it over the rise of her tummy while her eyes remained glued to his face. The baby chose that precise moment to deliver a walloping belt.

Jordan sucked in his breath, his eyes swiveling to hers. Caitlin couldn't help but grin at the wonder on his face.

"That's just a warm-up," she told him solemnly.

"Does it hurt?" His dark head tilted to one side as he stared at her through the clear lenses of his wire-rimmed glasses.

"Uh-uh," she denied, sucking in a breath as her abdomen contracted into a hard lump. She closed her eyes to concentrate on the feeling, breathing in and out rhythmically. "Just kind of like a cramp."

Jordan's hand moved in a gentle circle. His voice was so soft, so gentle and full of love, Caitlin barely heard the words as he spoke to his niece or nephew. The voice was mesmerizing and hypnotic, brimming with compassion. She closed her eyes and let it wash over her.

"Whoa, there, tiger. Your mama has had a long day. Take it easy now and get some sleep." His hand kept up the gentle, soothing stroke until the contraction had vanished. The baby gave one more vigorous poke before settling down.

"That's the way. Sleepy time. Good baby." His deep voice died away.

Caitlin opened her eyes to find his face peering into

hers, his lips mere inches away. A look of stunned wonder held his dark eyes wide.

''It's a tiny little miracle,'' he whispered. ''Too fantastic to understand. Thank you for sharing it with me.'' His lips grazed her cheek for just a second before he moved away, surging to his feet with leashed energy.

Caitlin sat frozen, afraid to move. Afraid that if she did, she would fling her arms around Jordan's wide shoulders and bawl her heart out.

It hurt, it hurt so much. To know that if he'd offered just then, she'd have let Jordan into her life, no questions asked. What was wrong with her? How could she betray Michael and his memory like this? How could she even think of Jordan as this baby's father? Was she so weak, she'd lean on anyone, rather than get through this herself?

The questions bit at her like condemning ice pellets, demanding that she face the broil of emotions inside. Caitlin refused to listen any longer. She needed a diversion. When Jordan offered to make tea, she agreed. As he walked toward the kitchen, she got up to listen to the answering machine and hopefully regain some control.

''Caitlin, it's Garrett Winthrop. I'd like to speak to you. In private, if you can manage it. Call me, please?''

''Caitlin, it's Beth. He called again and he's really upset. Oh, Cait, what am I going to do?''

One more beep.

''Mrs. Andrews? This is Ferd's Music. Uh, it's

about those songs you asked for, the ones your aunt had. The only way we can get those songs anymore is on some old, secondhand records. Not too many people want CDs of that stuff and, like I told you before, we're not up on that old time music.'' A pause. ''So do you think you want old records or what? Should I keep on looking?''

By the sound of his voice, Ferd Weatherby thought he was dealing with a woman two bricks short of a load. And maybe he was. What made her think Clay Matthews would do any better dancing to old music?

Caitlin met Jordan's careful scrutiny when he returned with her brown Betty teapot. He poured out two cups, set one down on the coffee table and motioned her to sit. The other he carried with him to his chair.

''Who left you those messages?''

''My, er, projects. They, um, want my help.''

''Projects? As in more than one?'' he queried, one eyebrow tilted upward ''I thought it was just Matthews.''

''It is. Or it was. Now Garrett Winthrop wants to see me, and Beth needs to talk. They used to be an item once.''

She took a sip of the tea he'd poured, grimaced, then quickly returned the cup to its saucer.

''Is something wrong? I thought you liked sweet tea?''

Though she searched his eyes, there wasn't a hint of malice there. That meant this disgusting concoction had to be an accident.

''Yes, I, er, I do.'' She left the cup where it was,

barely able to swallow after the syrupy mouthful she'd just imbibed. "Now about Clay. I was wondering if you'd help me out."

He gave her an odd look. "Help you with Clayton Matthews?"

"Well, sort of. I want to have a party, a kind of housewarming. And I thought it would be fun to invite a group of people."

"Such as?"

"Well, Maryann and Beth will already be here, after all, they live here now. And Amy, and Beth's sister Ronnie. It can be their housewarming, too. And I want to invite Clay because he's my friend." She opened her eyes wide and refused to look guilty. "He is!"

"Uh-huh."

"And Garrett and Beth always used to get along."

"How about Peter…"

"No!" she wailed and then realized how strange that sounded. "Uh, maybe next time, Jordan. I don't want too many people around. Especially with me in this condition, I mean." Her cheeks heated when he met her gaze and held it.

"And these other 'friends' aren't going to wear you out? But Peter will." He raised one eyebrow. "Clear as mud, Lyn."

"It's just a little open house. People do that, you know." She ignored the knowing look in his eyes.

"Hmm. Isn't it odd that you've got them all paired off?" When she wouldn't meet his gaze, he sighed loudly. "All right. What do you want me to do?"

"Play host."

"I don't know Garrett or Clayton that well, Lyn. And your roommates I see only occasionally." He tilted his head to one side, his glasses drooping to the end of his nose and he peered over them. "I get it. You're matchmaking, right?"

"Not really." She shrugged when one arrogant eyebrow arched even higher. "I'm not! I just want them to get together and talk. Then maybe they can see how much the other has changed, that this isn't high school. Maybe they can forget the mistakes of the past."

"Let bygones be bygones, start afresh." He groaned, putting his cup on the table with a thud. "I know I'm going to regret this."

"No, you're not. It's just a social evening, Jordan. Nothing to get all excited about." She averted her head from his too perceptive stare. "I'll put on some music, we'll talk, it'll be great."

"Caitlin, these people have histories. I don't think they can just take up where they left off and develop a lifelong love, or they would have done it already." He rose, walked around the table and sank down onto his haunches in front of her, one hand clasping hers.

"We've changed, all of us. You and I included. Time and distance does that to people. Affections change, too."

She stared down at him, wondering at the stain of red on his cheekbones. Did that mean he didn't care for her at all? Of course, he never had, had he? It had been her schoolgirl crush, all those years ago. Jordan had escaped as quickly as he could by dumping her on Michael.

Caitlin came back to the present with a jerk when Jordan, now flushed and discomfited, got up rather quickly and flopped back into his chair.

"What I'm trying to say is that the love they once felt, or that you think they felt, might be gone forever."

"It hasn't." She refused to believe that, not after talking to Beth and Maryann. There was something there, some spark that just needed a little nurturing. They deserved to find happiness.

"Okay. Nobody can say I didn't try." He raked a hand through his hair, mussing it worse than usual. "But you're not to go to a bunch of fuss. I'll get Mom to make some punch and I'll buy some chips and stuff."

"No." Caitlin swallowed down her dismay, trying not to let him see that she didn't want Eliza involved in such delicate matters of the heart. "I'll buy some of those frozen hors d'oeuvres or something so there's not a lot of work. I want to make my housewarming an occasion to remember."

"I'm pretty sure it will be that." His forehead pleated. "But fair warning. You may not want to remember it when those four see each other here." He shook his head. "You may wish you'd left them alone to get on with their lives."

"I won't."

Jordan knew she was up to something. Caitlin could see it in his face. Too bad. She was going to do this, with or without him. It would just be a little simpler

if she had him there. It would be nice to have him
there to lean on.

"Thank you, Jordan," she murmured. "I appreciate
your help. With everything."

"Don't be silly." His voice was brusque with gruff
courtesy. "I haven't done anything. Yet. And you may
regret asking me to help out, you know." He held up
a hand before she could get the words out. "I know.
Don't tell my mother." He sighed heavily. "Fine."

"Thank you, Jordan. You're a peach!" She grinned
at him, thrilled that he didn't even attempt to argue.

"A peach? First my own family tells me I'm fat,
and now you call me a peach." He shook his head in
disgust. "Wonderful. Just wonderful."

Caitlin giggled. "No, really. I mean it. I appreciate
this."

His eyes narrowed. "Good grief, Lyn, I'm not going
to have to dance with him. Am I?"

She giggled, the very idea conjuring up a myriad of
hilarious scenes in her head. "I don't think so. I wasn't
planning on including dancing."

"Good. Those big boots of his could be mighty uncomfortable on my delicate toes."

She felt his questioning glance study her more
closely, searching for an answer to a question he didn't
ask.

"Take it easy tomorrow. I'll come round after
church and see if you need anything." He paused, his
face tight with tension, as if something was bothering
him.

"Really, Jordan," Caitlin protested, hoping her

words would deter him from asking yet again. "That isn't necessary. I'll be fine. I just need a good night's sleep."

"I don't suppose you'd consider coming with me? Sing some hymns, hear the message, that sort of thing?" His voice was softly pleading.

She saw the glint of gold flash in those dark eyes as he studied her. Then he bent his head, one curling lock of hair falling over his brow.

"Right," was all he said, but Caitlin knew he got the point. She wasn't going to church tomorrow or anytime soon. She knew that Jordan would insist on coming over after, though.

"I'll see you in the morning then." He got up from the sofa and snatched his coat from the chair where he'd thrown it. "Try to get some rest, okay?"

She nodded. "I will. Thanks."

"Stop thanking me," he grumbled, preceding her to the door. "I'll start to wonder if there's something else wrong with me."

"There is." She giggled. "But we'll save that for some other time, when you're feeling tougher."

He shook his head, rolling his eyes to the ceiling. Then, before she realized what was happening, Jordan leaned down and brushed her cheek with his lips.

"Good night, Lyn."

"Good night, Jordan." She watched him drive away before she closed the door and wandered back inside her cozy apartment.

In a way she was relieved he kept dropping in. It was so nice to have Jordan around, taking care of her, managing some of the things she was just plain too tired to deal with. Besides, his company was restful and interesting at the same time.

Although it would never do to admit to it.

Neither would it do to question too closely her pleasure in having him around. Certain things were best not probed too deeply.

Especially the rush of pleasure she'd felt when he'd kissed her, innocent though the embrace was. Strangely enough, she wished he'd held her.

Why, when she was demanding to stand on her own, did she feel bereft whenever Jordan Andrews left her home?

Chapter Seven

❧

"Pregnancy and housecleaning do not go together." Caitlin surveyed the newly acquired gleam of her bathroom with a grimace. "But Junior, you've got to admit, this place is spotless."

Her first week of maternity leave and she was cleaning the bathroom. It hadn't been easy. The bathtub looked fairly routine, but at this stage in the maternal journey nothing was simple anymore. The sheer width of her body made cleaning in the crevices an arduous task at best, but she finished anyway. For some reason, a clean bathroom seemed important today.

As she rinsed off her rubber gloves and stored them in the caddy under the sink, one hand slipped round her hips to rub a tender spot. It wasn't a new ache. It had been paining her for days. Deliberately Caitlin turned away from her reflection in the full-length mirror, refusing to acknowledge it or her sore back.

"I'm fine, this is normal. I'm perfectly healthy and

nothing is going to go wrong. Right, Junior?'' She patted her stomach with a smile and got a swift kick of reassurance. ''Right.''

She wandered down the hall to glance once more at the baby's room. It stood waiting in the late-afternoon shadows, ready to welcome its new inhabitant. In the corner, the dresser was stuffed with tiny clothes Jordan's mother had either made or purchased over the past week. Eliza sent the various items with Jordan on his daily visit to boss her around.

She bent down to check the mural, then straightened in relief. No, there wasn't a snake there. Yet. She wondered how long it would be before he tried to sneak in that, or the boat Jordan continually insisted on discussing.

While Caitlin had her doubts about the durability of tiny crocheted sleepers or paper-thin booties, she couldn't bring herself to say anything that would dampen the joy Eliza obviously found in getting these things for her grandchild. And Caitlin appreciated the gestures of love Michael's mother had made toward her.

Her eyes roved appreciatively across the mural once more. Jordan had done a very good job. It was a lovely room to welcome a new baby, even without the extras he wanted to add.

The doorbell rang and Caitlin walked to the top of the stairs. ''Come in,'' she called, refusing to traverse the length of those steps again today.

''Caitlin, honey, it's me,'' Eliza Andrews called. After a moment she caught sight of her daughter-in-law. "I brought something for the baby's room. I hope you're feeling okay." Her voice dropped in concern. "I'm not bothering you?"

Caitlin felt a hint of frustration. Everyone treated her with kid gloves these days. As if she'd break.

"Come on up," she called. "I'm on strike. I refuse to navigate those stairs again just now."

Eliza joined her, thrusting a flat square box into her hands. "This is for you and the baby, Caitlin."

"Thank you, Eliza. You're going to have to quit this, you know." Eliza's wistful smile aroused Caitlin's curiosity.

"This is one thing I had to bring."

"Come and see the nursery," Caitlin invited, moving down the hall. Although she had contributed a number of items to the baby's room, Eliza hadn't yet been in it and suddenly Caitlin had an urge to show off her and Jordan's handiwork.

She left Eliza to look around while she sank into the rocking chair and unwrapped the box. Eliza's gift was the finishing touch to an already perfect nursery. Nestled inside the foil package was a delicately embroidered ivory shawl. Caitlin shook it out carefully, then spread it across the rungs of the crib, ready to welcome its new owner.

"It's beautiful," she whispered, trailing one finger over the intricate design.

"It was Michael's," Eliza told her, smiling softly in remembrance. "His grandmother made it for him and when he was through with it, I tucked it away. I thought he might use it himself some day. For his own child.''

"It's perfect. Thank you, Eliza. The baby will love it.'' Caitlin patted her soft hand.

"It's not that I'm trying to keep Michael alive or anything, Caitlin,'' the older woman apologized, her eyes solemn. "I know he's in heaven and happy. That's the one thing that makes his death bearable. But I thought someday the baby might want some history of his father's, some link with the past. If you don't think it's a good idea, I'll understand. I know you have to get on with your life.''

"I am getting on with life. And this is a wonderful idea! Thank you for thinking of it. To me, Michael will always be alive in here.'' Caitlin patted her heart. Her voice was full of tears and before long they were weeping all over each other. They didn't even hear Jordan arrive.

"What's all the bawling for?'' he demanded, relief in his eyes at the sight of his mother cradling Caitlin's dark head. "I thought having a baby is supposed to be a happy occasion. You two look like you're in serious pain.''

Eliza met Caitlin's raised eyebrows with a grin. "Son,'' she told Jordan affectionately, patting his broad shoulder, "women do not *bawl*. And these were tears of joy. I sincerely hope you're around when Caitlin goes into labor. Then perhaps you'll understand that children bring both joy and pain.''

Her blue eyes twinkled merrily, winking at Caitlin

before they returned to her big, boisterous son. "In fact, some children bring more of one than the other."

Caitlin giggled at the frown that crossed Jordan's usually smiling face.

"Mother, I hope you aren't insinuating that I have ever been anything but the wonderful, loving, caring, obedient son you have always told me I am."

"Obedient, he says. As if he would ever listen to his parents?" Eliza's snort was an audible guffaw in the quiet house. Her tears vanished as she looked to Caitlin for support.

Jordan raised his eyebrows in shock. "As if I would ever go against your wishes. Mother, please!"

"Enough, you two." Caitlin held up a hand. "You'll set a bad example for my baby. He's going to be the sweetest, most amenable child there ever was. Just like his mother."

Jordan coughed. "And if that isn't a bit of make-believe, I don't know what is." He offered a hand up to Caitlin. "Come on, little mama. We're going out for your walk. Then supper."

Caitlin groaned, her green eyes beseeching Eliza to support her. "It's too icy outside, Jordan. And too cold. I just want to stay home tonight. Take your mother out, for a change. She'd enjoy it."

But Eliza shook her head in an emphatic "no." "Thanks anyway, Caitlin. I'll go home to Stan." She picked up her coat and slipped it on then led the way to the outside door, stopping only long enough to slip on her snow boots.

Caitlin held open the door. "Thank you for the

shawl, Eliza. I will treasure it. Be careful on the roads,'' she added, noticing the icy slickness of the driveway. She closed the door quickly behind her mother-in-law, shivering at the blast of cold air.

''I am not going out in that, Jordan. And I don't care what you say,'' she informed him, swishing around him and into the kitchen.

The cupboards weren't quite bare, but it was close. Caitlin stared at the lonely can of tomato soup and shrugged. It would do. At least it was better than chancing her footing on all that ice.

''We can have soup and toast,'' she told him firmly as he entered the kitchen. ''That's nutritious and filling.''

''It's not tomato soup is it?'' he asked warily, glancing around her shoulder to peer at the label. ''I knew it.'' His voice was full of defeat.

''What's wrong with tomato soup?'' she demanded, whirling around to study him.

''Nothing,'' he muttered.

''It's just that I ate it almost every day for a solid year when I was going to college,'' he told her. ''I had to save my money to take this girl out, so I lived on soup. I got a great deal on a case of tomato.''

He ignored her snicker.

''I made a vow that when I graduated and started work, I would never eat the stuff again unless there was nothing else.'' He yanked open a cupboard door and stared at the empty shelf.

''Well, it looks like that time has arrived!'' Caitlin

grinned. "But that's okay. I love tomato soup. You can have toast."

"Caitlin!" Jordan let out an exasperated sigh. "How can you not have any groceries in the house? You're supposed to be eating healthfully and there's nothing in this fridge but a dried-up bit of lettuce."

"If you recall," she said matter-of-factly, stirring the thickening soup steadily, "these past weeks you have taken me out almost every single night for dinner. I hardly need groceries."

"Ridiculous," he replied, slamming the door closed and snatching up his heavy leather jacket from its usual position on her easy chair.

"Where are you going?" She pointed to the toaster. "Your supper is almost ready."

"That isn't a meal," he told her. "That's a bedtime snack. I'm going shopping and if you're nice, I'll bring some goodies back." His eyes glinted behind his glasses. "If there was a snowstorm, you'd starve to death here. Honestly woman, how can you be so careless of yourself?"

His chastising tone hurt. Caitlin felt a wave of misery close over her and seconds later heard herself burst into tears which made her even more disconsolate.

"I am not careless," she said. "I simply hate lugging those heavy bags back from the store and since I can't drive, I have to use the bus."

"I'm sorry, Lyn," he said at last, using his handkerchief to wipe the tears off her cheeks. His voice was soft and full of concern. "I never even thought of that or I would have taken you there myself. Just stop crying now, okay?''

''I am *not* c-c-crying,'' she blubbered, his gentleness affecting her more than his anger had. ''I never cry!''

Jordan tugged her into his arms and held her as she sobbed miserably on his shoulder.

''Of course you're not,'' he murmured, a wry grin tipping his lips. ''Any fool can see that. You merely have a leak in your eyes that allows moisture to fall out in huge droplets that roll down your cheeks and soak my shirt. Obviously not crying! How stupid of me.''

She pushed out of his arms, embarrassed by the whole thing. Turning her back to him, Caitlin filled the kettle and put it on to heat, striving for a tiny measure of control when her nerves screamed frustration.

''Caitlin?'' He turned her around and slid one finger under her chin, tipping her tearstained face up toward his. ''Just make a list and I'll pick up whatever you need, okay?''

''I don't need someone to look after me,'' she bristled angrily. ''I'm not a child that needs a keeper.''

She heard the sigh. Anyone would have. It was loud and forbearing as if there were thousands of things he *could* have said, and yet nothing he was willing to verbalize.

Guilt, frustration and tiredness welled up inside, each one vying for supremacy. She was fed up with figuring out which one was worse. All she wanted to do was give in to this need to cry.

Why couldn't everyone just leave her alone? She'd get through this. Somehow. In her own way.

"Just for right now, just tonight, let me be my brother's keeper, okay?" His gentle fingers turned her to face him, his golden eyes beseeching her. "Actually, that should be my sister-in-law's keeper.

"I promise, it will just be tonight." That tender note in his voice was her undoing.

Caitlin couldn't ignore him. "This one time you can help me out," she agreed finally. "Is it a deal?"

"Scout's honor." He held up one hand with two fingers pointing upward. "I promise I will never help you again. Not even if you beg me on bended knee. Now will you give me that list?"

"I could go myself," she told him, frowning. "I'm kind of picky about what fruit and vegetables I eat."

"Do you really want to go parading around a supermarket, pushing past people, standing in line and lugging everything across an icy parking lot to the car? I'm not going to take over your life, Caitlin. I'm just trying to help out."

"You have already *helped* me," she told him seriously. "It's not that I'm ungrateful Jordan. It's just that I have to learn to depend on myself. I have to manage on my own. I can't expect people to come running every time the Widow Andrews needs something." She peered up at him, trying to make him understand.

"I'm a grown woman, Jordan. I have to be able to

handle things as they come up. I have to be sure that I can manage it all." She smiled tiredly. "I know you think I'm obsessing about Michael, but I'm not. I understand that we're all human, that death is a part of life. That simply means you have to be strong enough to take it. Right now there is only me for my baby. He's depending on me and I have to learn to be self-reliant."

She waited, watching his eyes darken and narrow as he absorbed what she'd said. When he spoke his voice seemed leashed, held back.

"Yes, Lyn, people die. But can't you understand that while they're here, a lot of them just want to do what they can to make your life a little easier? Can't you see that it hurts us to see you struggling on your own when it's so easy for us to lend a hand?"

His face was serious, carved in lines of concern as he stared down at her. "We're not asking for anything from you, Caitlin. My parents don't expect anything from you. They just want to be there because you're their daughter-in-law and they love you. My sisters just want their friend back in their lives."

Caitlin squinted up at him through the mist of tears that seemed to constantly block her vision these days. She remembered how many times in the past week she'd put Robyn and her sisters off, pretending she was too busy to see them, have lunch, talk.

"Can't you accept just a little bit of that love, Lyn?"

It was a persuasive argument and she felt so alone. Caitlin stared at the table in front of her and admitted to herself that she did want to be part of their group again. She wanted to rejoin the human race, but on her own conditions.

"It's just that I have nothing to give them back," she whispered at last, sinking into a nearby chair.

"I'm empty, Jordan." She met his softened gaze. "Sometimes I think the last part of me that is capable of love only lives because of this baby."

He squatted in front of her, placing his hands on either side of her as his velvety soft gaze stared straight into hers. "Then just relax and let us fill the empty space. We'll do the work." He smiled softly. "All you have to do is accept it. That's all we ask."

One hand reached up to smooth her hair away from her tired face. "It's sort of like that with God, too. When we think we can't go another step, He's there to lean on and support us until we can catch our breath, gather our resources and continue with the journey." Jordan stood abruptly and zipped his jacket closed. His hand reached out and swiped the list from her fridge.

"For once in your life, Lyn, let someone else be in control. Just sit back and enjoy the ride." He grinned down at her. "I'll be back in a while. With real food."

Ten minutes later, as she sat sipping the tomato soup and munching on a square of toast, Caitlin thought about his words. Just like God, he'd said. Well, she didn't know much about God.

Oh, she had gone to church all her life and she was familiar with the hymns and choruses one sang in church. But she had never really thought of God as someone who was there to lean on. He'd always seemed an authority figure, somewhere way out there, sort of awesome and fear inducing. But the way Jordan spoke, God was like a person.

Caitlin leaned back in her chair and considered that. To be able to relax and let someone else shoulder the worry, that would be something. Not to feel guilty if she just gave in and believed that someone else would figure things out, to just go with what felt right to do today and not constantly worry about the future.

Of course, it wouldn't work for her. She had to plan each facet of her life. She had to make sure there were no surprises, she had to be prepared for anything life threw at her. Because if she wasn't, she would be hurt and abandoned just as she had been in the past. And she couldn't take that. Not again.

Caitlin cleaned up the kitchen and carried her tea into the living room, in front of the fire. A feeling of dread fell upon her as each moment ticked past on the old grandfather clock in the corner. What was taking Jordan so long?

He'd been gone for over an hour now. And the most recent check out the window had shown signs of a prairie storm blowing in. Everything was white, swirling snow. Caitlin could barely see to the end of the drive and as she peered out, her mind noted that the few cars that were out had to pass through the white drifts covering the road.

The phone peeled its urgent summons, causing her to jump.

"Yes," she murmured nervously, a trill of anticipation rolling down her spine. But the caller had a wrong number.

Please God, if you're there, don't let anything happen to Jordan.

She spent a long time saying that over and over, her television program long since forgotten. Caitlin was just adding another log on the fire when Jordan burst through the door carrying bags and bags of groceries. Arms loaded, he shoved the door closed with his foot.

"What in the world did you buy?" she demanded, aghast at the amount of the bill she found in the first sack. "I live alone, Jordan."

He grinned down at her. "But you're eating for two, right?" He hung his damp coat on the doorknob and picked up several sacks, lugging them through to the kitchen. "Come on, woman. You need to get this stuff put away."

But Caitlin was already sorting through the first bag. "Triple-chocolate-almond-pistachio ice cream?" she asked, one eyebrow raised enquiringly.

"It's my favorite," he told her grinning. "I knew you'd want to have something special to serve me when I come to visit."

Caitlin stared at him. "And the dill pickles?" she asked solemnly.

"Oh, those are for you. You know, pickles and ice cream. It's apparently all the rage with pregnant women." When she made a face he pulled out a package of freshly ground coffee and held it up. "Also for you, milady."

Caitlin sniffed as the fragrant aroma wafted across

the room. She closed her eyes at the wondrous essence of her favorite blend. He was at her side in a moment.

"Lyn, are you all right?"

"Perfectly," she whispered reverently. "I'm just enjoying the full-bodied zest of something other than herbal tea. Junior may stop me from drinking the stuff but even he can't object to my merely smelling it." She opened her eyes to find him grinning down at her. "It is not funny." She raised her eyebrows.

"It's hilarious," he returned solemnly, his velvet eyes caressing her. "How the mighty coffee drinkers have fallen. And by a tiny little baby!"

"That's not very nice," she mumbled, slicing a teeny piece off the gigantic slab of cheddar cheese he'd purchased. "I've never made fun of you for your little quirks. And you do have a lot of them, don't you?"

He only ignored her teasing verbal jabs and continued to lug in bags and packages from the entry.

"Grade A extra-large eggs, fresh whole milk, cream for my coffee, grapefruit, oranges, Granny Smith apples. Although why you want to eat anything so sour I can't imagine. They do nothing for your disposition." He held up a hand when she would have protested.

"Cantaloupe, lettuce, tomatoes, celery, a turkey..."

"A turkey?" Caitlin stared at him. "Are you crazy? I can't eat a whole turkey, it will go to waste. Jordan, really, this is too much."

He ignored her, stuffing groceries into her cupboards and fridge like a grocery store shelf-stocker intent on completing his job in record time.

"Jordan, will you listen to me?" Caitlin tugged on his sleeve, forcing him to abandon the jumbo box of rice cereal he was trying to juggle into a cupboard that was just too small.

"Jordan!"

"Yes, dear." He sounded like some wife-weary husband who added the appropriate comments but heard nothing that was said.

"Would you please stop that and listen to me?" He turned a blithe, unconcerned face toward her. "I cannot possibly eat a whole entire turkey myself. You'll have to take it back."

"In this snow?" He shook his dark head. "I don't think so. You can invite somebody over or something, couldn't you? Like me?" There was a twinkle in his eyes that should have alerted her.

"Not even you with your gigantic appetite could eat this thing," she muttered, poking the frozen bird with one finger. "It doesn't seem in very good condition, either." Caitlin pointed to the torn packaging in the inner covering.

"Oh, I had it sawed into four pieces," he told her smugly. "That way you can have four smaller meals instead of one big one and it will still be fresh. I'll roast some for you if you like."

Caitlin held the freezer door open for him and shoved the ice cream out of the way as she groaned. "Oh, no. Not in my kitchen. No way. I've seen you cook Jordan. It is *not* a pretty sight."

He chucked her chin with his forefinger as his dark head shook sadly. "Oh, ye of little faith. I'm a wonderful cook. I can cook the socks off my mother, if you want to know. You're going to be sorry."

"Oh, no I'm not," she retorted smartly. "I've seen the kitchen when you've finished one of your so-called specials." Caitlin raised her eyebrows scornfully. "I can't afford to hire cleaners for the next month. The last time you cooked, your mother said it took three weeks to get the spaghetti sauce off the ceiling. And I saw the pot you forgot to turn off." She shook her head. "Uh-uh. No way."

He smacked the bags together smartly and stuffed them into a drawer with resignation. "Fine, if that's the way you want to be."

"It is," she assured him, grinning as she bit into another piece of cheese. "I like the simple things— clean cupboards, shiny floor, laundry done. You know, the normal stuff."

"Anybody can be normal," he muttered. "It takes talent to make something really spectacular. Hey!" His face brightened. "You've never had my black forest cake, have you?"

"Down, Jordan. It's too late to start baking now. Did you have something to eat already or would you like a sandwich? For some odd reason there's a package of corned beef here. I hate corned beef. Too fatty."

He smiled from ear to ear. "That's just your professional nutritionist side talking. I had some at the store, samples you know. It really is very good. Especially with sauerkraut." He watched her shudder. "Some people have no taste," he complained sadly.

"That's for sure." Caitlin handed him a check, stuffing it in his shirt pocket when he didn't immediately take it.

"Thank you very much, Jordan. I really appreciate all of it. Are you sure you don't want to take some home with you?" she asked, holding the deli bag with his corned beef daintily between two fingers.

"Naw," he grinned smugly. "Keep it for the next time I visit. Instead of tomato soup. I didn't buy any of *that*."

"I noticed." Caitlin longingly eyed the succulent golden-brown butter tarts he'd purchased. They were large and oozing with calorie-laden sweetness.

"Let's see," she murmured, mentally adding up the calories. "If I just had one slice of toast..."

"I'm leaving," he interrupted her. "I think I'd better get going before I have to shovel my way home." His eyes narrowed as he watched her pick the tarts up and then put them down. "Why don't you just eat one if you want it?" he muttered curiously, when she finally slid the package into the cupboard and closed the door firmly.

"I've already overindulged with the cheese," she told him. "I can't have one of those, too. Besides, too much fat. I have enough already."

"You're not fat. You're pregnant." Jordan laughed at her as he studied her rounded figure. "Besides, you'll lose it all when the baby comes."

"I wish." Caitlin turned her mouth up. "A twenty-five-pound baby would be just a little big, don't you think? No, as it is I'm going to have a tough row to hoe to get back into my clothes after Junior shows up." She turned her back resolutely on the tempting bits of pastry sheltered behind the oak door. "I can't afford that."

"Can I have one for the road, then?" he asked grinning. "I need to keep up my energy." When she waved at the cupboard, Jordan helped himself to two of the confections. "It's really, really cold out," he told her wide-eyed stare.

Caitlin giggled and wrapped two more of the tarts in a napkin, then followed him through the living room.

"Thanks again," she said as he shrugged into his jacket. "I appreciate it."

The snow had blown up against the house when she tugged open the door. A little pile fell inside.

"See you tomorrow," he murmured, brushing a hand across her hair.

"Don't bother," she told him firmly. "It might be too slippery. I'll stay indoors and have a lazy day. I'll be fine. Good night, Jordan," she said when it seemed he would argue.

"Good night, little mama. Sleep well." Then he was gone.

"Sleep," she muttered to herself as she wandered back into the kitchen. But it was no use. She couldn't ignore the tarts.

Ten minutes later Caitlin sank into the big armchair

in her living room with a pot of tea and a tart nearby, the television turned on low.

"As if I could sleep with those things calling my name. I don't know why he wanted a list. He replaced tofu with turkey, low-fat cottage cheese with cheddar, and turnips with tarts."

Caitlin closed her eyes and sank her teeth into the creamy smooth sweetness, letting it fill her mouth with that delectable taste.

"Do lots of push-ups, Junior," she ordered. "You and I are off turnips for the next few days and we need all the calorie burn we can get."

Caitlin tugged her notepad closer, ignored the pastry crumbs dotting her shirt and set about planning her housewarming party. It would be a quiet evening. A little conversation, a little food, maybe even some romance for her friends.

What could go wrong?

Chapter Eight

"It's just an evening with some friends, Clayton. Nothing to worry about. Come on! We're waiting for you." Exasperated, Caitlin hung up the phone before the man could ask her the one question she'd avoided at all costs during the past week.

"He's not too thrilled about coming, is he?" Jordan's lip sloped up when she turned her head away. "Wants to know if Maryann is here, I'll wager." He laughed when Caitlin turned her back. "I thought so."

"What are you doing out here anyway?" she demanded, bending to check the tiny puff pastries in the oven. "You're supposed to be in there, keeping the conversation going!"

"Hah! What conversation? Gar, as I've been told to call him, sits there like a bump on a log, staring straight ahead. Beth is on the other end of the sofa, glaring at the fireplace. They won't even look at each other, let alone speak."

"And Maryann?"

"Maryann went upstairs, ostensibly to check on her daughter."

"What? You're not supposed to let her go up there!" Caitlin whirled around, hands on her hips. "Some host you turned out to be." With a flick of her wrist, she opened the oven, emptied the pan of shrimp hors d'oeuvres onto a plate and shoved them at him. "Here."

Obligingly, Jordan reached out and took one.

"They're good," he murmured in obvious surprise.

Caitlin sighed. Nothing was going right tonight.

"Of course they're good." She chuckled, whooshing a puff of air over her heated forehead. "And they're supposed to be for *our guests,* the ones *you* are supposed to be serving."

"Oh." He took the platter and moved toward the other room. "How long do I have to stay in there this time?" He looked like a little boy who had just been sent to his room.

"Until I come in and tell you otherwise. Now get them talking. You can do it, Jordan. You can talk about anything."

A man forced to walk to his own execution couldn't have looked more pathetic. Caitlin grabbed the tray of glasses from the counter and headed in after him.

The scene before her was pathetic. The other two inhabitants refused to look at each other, deliberately focusing their sights on some faraway spot. Maryann eventually returned to the room and took her seat, glancing worriedly from one to the other of her friends. Jordan shoved the platter in front of each of them in turn and then almost dropped it when the doorbell rang.

"I'll get it," he called, rushing toward the entry in jubilant relief.

Caitlin frowned at his retreating back, drew a deep breath and plunged in.

"Beth, how's your sister enjoying school in Oakburn? Does she get into as much trouble as we did?"

"She loves it." Beth's voice warmed. "She a real clown and the drama teacher wants her to audition for the spring play."

"That's great! Remember how you and Gar played Romeo and Juliet...?" Maryann's voice died away, her face flushing painfully as she realized that she'd just linked the two of them when it was obvious neither wanted to remember the past.

Thankfully, Clay chose that moment to come through the door.

"Clayton! How lovely to see you." *At last,* Caitlin added under her breath. "Would you like some punch?"

"I'll get it," Jordan offered.

"I'll help him." Gar got up and sauntered away, his icy gaze almost freezing Beth out.

"I, uh, that is, I think I should go with them," Clayton blurted.

Caitlin could have groaned. This was exactly what she hadn't wanted! Boys on one side, girls on the other. It was just like a junior high school dance. How could this matchmaking idea have gone so wrong?

When the doorbell rang again, Caitlin couldn't help rushing to answer it. The tension in her living room was thick enough to slice with a knife and she was at her wit's end.

"Please let it be someone who can help," she whispered and then realized that she'd just prayed to a God she wasn't speaking to. Who was she trying to fool anyway? She needed God in her life more than ever.

"Hi, sweetheart," Eliza said as she came inside. "Stan and I thought we'd drop over and see what you were doing. I saw Jordy's car here and figured you might like help." She peeked around the corner into the living room. "A party? Oh, honey, should we stay?"

Well, why not? Maybe Eliza and Stan could infuse a little warmth into the room. Caitlin certainly wasn't having much success.

"Of course! Come on in." She took their coats and hung them up, then ushered them into her living room. "What's that?" Caitlin motioned to the boxes under Stan's arm.

"Oh, he bought *more* games!" Eliza sighed heavily, but her eyes twinkled with love. "They're for four or more players so, naturally, we thought of you and Jordy."

Introductions were performed all around. Caitlin didn't know when or how it happened, but suddenly the room was filled with laughter. True, neither of the couples really looked at the other, and they sure weren't seated together. But it was a start, and it was far more fun than it had been.

The games Stan had picked up enlivened the evening immensely, especially the murder mystery. Two hours later they sat around sipping coffee and discussing it.

"I might have known I wouldn't guess." Beth giggled. " I never do and I love to read mysteries. But no matter how many I finish, the ending always comes as a complete surprise."

"Hey, Caitlin, you certainly picked the perpetrator out quickly. You and Jordan seem to have the same criminal mind-set." Stan cocked an inquisitive eyebrow. "Anything you want to tell us about?"

Six sets of eyes focused on them, a question mark in each one. Caitlin felt herself flush.

"You don't need to look at me as if I've robbed a bank of something! It was a perfectly logical assumption. The old man would have had longer to learn about toxins, wouldn't he?"

"Uh-huh." Maryann sipped her coffee slowly, eyes pensive. "And I suppose you know all about semi-automatic weapons and poisons, too. Right, Jordan?" She snickered. "Folks, we've got us a regular Bonnie and Clyde here!" She winked at the others.

"They know now, Lyn," Jordan boomed, dropping a casual arm around her shoulders. "That means we can start spending the loot we lifted from that last heist. What do you want to spend it on first?" His pinch on her waist told her to play along.

Well, she'd prove to him that Caitlin Andrews wasn't the dowdy old stick-in-the-mud he remembered from school.

"Oh, I don't know," she sighed, tapping a forefinger against her chin, fully aware of his hip pressed against hers on the crowded sofa. "It's all so difficult. Perhaps the tiara. Of course, they're very passé these days!"

His warmth and closeness were doing funny things to her blood pressure and she eased away from him on the pretense of checking the food. A few moments later she balanced on the arm of Stan's chair. Jordan noticed and frowned at her.

"Oh, a tiara is so boring." Maryann pooh-poohed the idea. "What else?"

"Then, of course, there is the villa. Spain's so lovely this time of year. You probably don't notice the cold as much as I do, Jordan, since you've just come back from the tropics."

And truthfully, it did feel cooler without his protective arm around her. But the atmosphere in this room, in her home was warm and friendly, exactly the way she'd always dreamed.

Caitlin let the others' conversations whirl around her while she thought about those dreams. She'd always wanted a real home, a refuge where she could feel safe and comfortable. Loved. Perhaps she'd finally found it? She glanced at the smiling faces, stopping on Jordan's longer than anyone else. What she saw in those golden eyes warmed her heart.

"Uh-oh! Caity's deep in a new intrigue!" Stan's voice finally penetrated her cloud of reminiscence, making her blush furiously.

"I was just telling them about the Lear." Jordan's

voice took the focus off her. "Once I get the computer system revamped to my specialized form, we'll be ready to take off. And no one will be able to follow us."

He said it to the others, but his warm brown eyes were on her, a question in their depths.

"Why, sir!" she drawled, fluttering her fingers at him and adopting her best Southern accent. "I'm about to become a mother! I simply couldn't fly away just now. Tell me, are there mint juleps in Spain?"

Everyone burst into delighted laugher at her perfect imitation of Scarlett. There was even a small round of applause. Then Clay's low voice broke in.

"I have to go, Caitlin. I've got some sick animals at home and I need to watch them pretty carefully." He got to his feet. "I'll see you Monday night, right?"

Why did he have to make it sound like some sort of a date? Caitlin asked herself as she nodded, found his coat and escorted him to the door.

"Do you think she noticed the 'Monday night' part?" he whispered, pulling on his Stetson.

"Maryann?"

He nodded.

"I'm quite sure she couldn't have missed it," she told him wryly. She sighed. This matchmaking thing was taking far more out of her than she had anticipated. By comparison, having a baby was child's play.

"Good. I don't want her to think I'm not attractive to other women." He stood staring down at her, his eyes roiling with emotion.

"I keep telling you that you're not unattractive,"

Caitlin grumbled. "You're just rusty. You need some practice. Why don't you ask Vivian Michaels out? She's a nice friendly girl."

"A little too friendly for my taste! I asked her out once a couple of years ago and she showed up at my house the next day with a cake."

"What's wrong with that? She was only trying to be friendly."

"Friendly? Hah!" His eyes glinted with anger. "She offered to cook my Christmas turkey." His face tightened into a mask of scandalized outrage. "I knew she was up to no good as soon as the words left her lips."

Caitlin choked down the laughter that burbled up inside with a gigantic effort. "Clay, Viv was probably just offering to help you fix Christmas dinner. She's alone a lot now, with her mother gone. She probably wanted someone to share some Christmas cheer with."

"She wanted to share a lot more than that," he insisted grumpily, shoving his arms into the sleeves. He zipped the coat closed with one motion. "Well, I'd better go." He stared at her for a moment, then his eyes opened wide.

Caitlin half turned to see who had come into the hall, but she found her chin grasped. Her head jerked up just in time to receive a kiss that landed to the left of her mouth, close to her jaw. It was anything but loverlike.

"Oh, excuse me!" Maryann's breathless voice told Caitlin everything she needed to know. Her heart sank as she heard the sound of footsteps rushing up the stairs to the second floor.

"Why did you do that, Clayton Matthews?" Caitlin demanded hands on her hips, glaring at him. "Why in the world did you do that?"

"Exactly what I'd like to know."

Sometime in the disaster of the past few moments, Jordan had joined them in the foyer. He stood tall and menacing, his eyes chilly as he glanced from her to Clay.

"I can kiss a woman," Clay blurted, obviously completely disconcerted by the other man's presence.

"I'm not debating that. I just want to know why it's Caitlin you're kissing."

"She's my friend. I like Caitlin."

"And she likes you. That's why she's trying to help you with Maryann. You remember Maryann, don't you, the woman you're supposed to like? The one who just watched you kiss someone else?"

His scornful voice stung Caitlin. She could only imagine how poor Clay felt. He'd tried the only thing he could think of to make Maryann jealous. Unfortunately, it had backfired.

"I do like Maryann." But as Clay glanced uncertainly from Jordan's twitching jaw to the staircase, Caitlin knew he was second-guessing his hasty decision.

Repairs between the two men were up to her and Caitlin searched for the right words. "Clay, Maryann is already a little skittish where men are concerned. I don't think making her jealous is the right way to attract her attention. She was married to a man who abused her trust. She won't risk her heart again, especially not if she sees you kissing me. You'll have to find a way to apologize, you know.''

"Yeah, I suppose you're right. Romance her, you said?" He sighed, chest heaving, face drooping at the thought. "You're sure it's the only way?" His look told her he was exceedingly skeptical.

"I think it's the *best* way."

Caitlin knew he wasn't too sure about that. But he didn't argue. Instead he shoved his feet into his number fourteen cowboy boots, hunched his shoulders and yanked the door open.

"Okay. Romance it is. I'll apologize tonight if she answers the phone. Sorry, Jordan. See you Monday, Caitlin.''

"Yes, I'll see you then. And Clay?"

"Yeah?" He raised one eyebrow.

"Don't worry about it so much," she murmured, going on tiptoe to brush a friendly caress against his cheek. "Everything will work out just fine."

"That's what I'm praying for." He stood a moment, bemused by her touch, one hand rubbing the spot. "Course, I prayed for it ten years ago, too."

"Just keep at it, Clay. It will happen." Jordan closed the door on the man, then turned to Caitlin. His forehead was pleated in a frown.

"Why'd you kiss him?"

She hooked her arm through his and led him back into the living room, shivering as a tickle of warmth crawled up her spine. Jordan was jealous? Of Clay?

The very idea was, well, exhilarating. She'd never had anyone be jealous of her before. It meant Jordan cared. Didn't it?

Beth walked over to them and smiled. "Thanks for a fun evening, Caitlin. But I've got to run. Night everyone."

"Good night, Beth," Caitlin said with a sigh as Beth walked out of Caitlin's apartment and across the hall.

"I've got to go, too," Garrett Winthrop's voice reminded Caitlin that neither of her schemes had worked out properly. "I'd like to talk to you sometime, Caitlin. Whenever you have a spare minute." There was a hint of authority there that told her he expected it to be soon.

Caitlin sighed. "I've started my maternity leave you know. I'm sure there will be lots of time before the baby arrives. Is next week okay?"

"It's fine. Nothing pressing. Just some things I need to know. For the bank." Gar bid the Andrewses goodnight, then followed Jordan out of the room.

Caitlin sagged against her chair, flopping into it with relief.

"Sweetheart, you're dead on your feet!" Eliza's caring hands gently massaged her shoulders. "Thank goodness you're off now. You were taking on too much."

"I'm fine. Really. And I did have a good time tonight."

"It was fun, wasn't it?" Eliza looked around the room. "I remember this house from when the Cardmore sisters lived here. They loved to have tea parties, you know. We'd get all gussied up and come over for cucumber sandwiches and iced tea in the summer. They had the coolest house in town.''

Caitlin nodded, trying to stifle a yawn as Eliza continued her story.

''That was before air-conditioning. How those two used to giggle and twitter.''

Stan shook his head in remembrance and tugged at his wife's arm. ''Come on, honey. Caity's falling asleep.''

''Of course she is! The poor girl's been on her feet all day, I imagine. I'll just load those few dishes into the dishwasher and then we'll be off. You can help.''

Caitlin chuckled at Stan's groan of agreement and watched as the older couple left the room. But she made no effort to hoist herself out of her chair. Instead she shifted her feet onto a footstool.

''Finally seeing the light?'' Jordan strode across the room and sat down in a chair across from her.

''Pardon?'' She knew exactly what was coming, but Caitlin pretended ignorance. He didn't have to rub her face in her capitulation.

''You know what I'm talking about, Lyn.'' His dark eyes mocked her. ''But I'm perfectly willing to play dumb if it means that you'll allow my family to help out once in a while.''

She closed her eyes. ''Don't bug me, Jordan. I'm too tired to argue with you tonight.''

''You look beautiful.'' The softly spoken words jarred her from her dream. ''Am I allowed to say that at least? I like that misty-green color on you. It makes your eyes stand out."

She snorted, glancing down at her stomach. "I look more like a pile of beached seaweed than anything wispy and you know it."

Caitlin fiddled with her skirt, unwilling to look at him. His words, his touch, even his presence made her nervous when he stopped acting like Michael's brother. She liked it, but it still made her nervous.

He sighed, exasperation evident in his body language. "I wish you could see what I see when you look in the mirror."

"I'm glad I can't," she said with a self-conscious laugh.

"You'd see a gorgeous woman who glows with life." He ignored her interruption. "Your skin has this luminous quality that the makeup companies would kill to emulate."

"That's because it's stretched so thin." She chuckled.

"Stop it! Stop decrying yourself. You're a beautiful woman, Lyn. Pregnancy has only added to that beauty." He stood up as his parents came back into the room, his voice changing as he asked them, "All done?"

"Clean as a whistle. There's nothing left for this little mama to do but to climb into bed and get some sleep." Stan leaned down and patted Caitlin's cheek as if she were one of his daughters. "Good night, Caity. Thanks for the party."

"You're the one who made it a party." Caitlin

smiled, accepting Jordan's helping hand as she hoisted herself from the sofa. "Before your arrival, we were dying fast."

"Why?" Eliza's eyes glowed brightly with curiosity.

"Let's jut say she's not as good at matchmaking as she thought." Jordan, tongue in cheek, ushered his parents to the front door. He found their coats, helped them on and wished them both good-night.

"Matchmaking?" Eliza's brow furrowed, then cleared. "Of course! I'd forgotten all about that. I've been so busy with you two...well, anyway I forgot."

"Good! I wish Caitlin would, too. You can't force these people to like one another simply because you think they should. They've got a history to get past."

"Rather like you and Caitlin." Stan's quiet voice drew their attention. "You two dated for a while, then broke up and Caity married Mike. Now here you are hosting parties together."

"Jordan's just helping out till the baby comes. That's all." Caitlin felt the heat burn her cheeks as Stan's glance met hers.

"I know." He smiled and squeezed her hand. "And I'm really glad he is. It just goes to show that God can work in any situation, if we leave it up to Him."

Caitlin wanted to stop him, to straighten out his obvious misconceptions, to get rid of that smug glint in his eye. But there was no time. Whatever Eliza and Jordan had been whispering about, they had not come to any agreement. Eliza's lips were stubbornly pursed together and Jordan, well Jordan seethed with something, though he cloaked it well.

"We'd like you to come to dinner tomorrow, Caitlin. After church. Jordan can pick you up for the early service. We'll all sit together."

"Mother, I told you…"

"I'm not sure I'm going," Caitlin prevaricated, glancing from one to the other as she handed out the gloves they'd left on the hall table. To Stan she passed the games.

"Good! Nine-thirty." Eliza thrust her arm through Stan's and hurried him out the door even though he was still juggling the games. "Thanks again. See you in the morning."

Caitlin tried to say something. But before the protest could form, Eliza snapped the outside door shut, leaving her and Jordan alone.

"I don't think…"

"You don't have to…"

Jordan shook his head and smiled. "Sorry. You go first."

"I was just going to say that you don't have to pick me up. I can get to church myself." She took off her shoes and padded back into the living room, toes scrunching into the thick pile. "What were you going to say?"

"Nothing." He followed her in, shutting the door behind him.

"Yes, you were. What were you and your mother arguing over?" She peered up at him curiously. "Was it about me?"

''In a way.'' His eyes avoided hers as he rearranged the cushions on the sofa. ''But don't worry, I set her right.''

''About what? What was she saying?'' Caitlin shifted from one foot to the other impatiently. ''Jordan?''

When at last he straightened, Jordan seemed to have recovered the calm good humor that was his trademark.

''She's got some silly ideas, that's all.''

Caitlin frowned, and shook her head. ''What are you talking about?''

Had she missed something? Maybe Michael's family were getting tired of having to care for ''little Caity.'' Maybe they wanted her to go to church so they could foist her off on some other poor souls.

''Jordan, please. What is going on?'' she pleaded, hating the knot of fear that twisted in her stomach.

He wouldn't leave now, would he? Not when she'd begun to rely on his strength and capability? Not now, when she'd only started to realize how much she needed him in her life, not so much as a link with the past, but as a connection to the future?

''I can see the fear in your eyes, Caitlin. And you can just stop it. I'm not going anywhere. I'll be here for as long as you and the baby need me.'' His crooked smile tilted down at her as his big warm hands closed around her arms, holding her in that strong but protective way.

Relief swamped her, blessed, light-headed relief that she wouldn't be alone to face this highest of all trials.

Jordan, dear, sweet, dependable Jordan would be there to lean on.

Caitlin ignored the little gremlins that giggled inside her head and told her that having him around was exactly what she *didn't* want. She'd be strong later, after the baby was born, when things were back to normal. That was the time to face life and the future alone, not now.

"Caitlin?"

She focused on the present and realized the same question still existed. "I'm okay. So what did your mother say?"

He sighed. A long, resigned whoosh of air that told her he didn't like saying the words, but that he wasn't willing to lie, either. That was Jordan. Truthful, no matter what.

"She thinks we make a good couple."

Caitlin didn't get it. She frowned lightly, tightening her fingers on his muscular arms. "I suppose we do. After all, we were trying to host this silly party together. Unfortunately, no one but us seemed able to talk to each other."

She stopped, searching his face as the silence stretched between them. There was something there, something that told her she'd misunderstood his meaning.

"Jordan?" The word came out quietly, half fearful at the glow of quiet purpose in his eyes.

"She meant couple as in a pair. Together. You and I. More than friends." He held her gaze with his.

"Oh."

Caitlin didn't get it, didn't understand what he was hinting at. Jordan *was* her friend. They laughed together, did things, had fun. That was all there was to it. Wasn't it?

"But I'm Michael's wife," she blurted out, trying to reconcile his words in her mind.

"You were. Michael's gone."

"I know that." Caitlin stepped back, dropping her hand from his arms. No, she wouldn't go there now. "It's late. I know you want to get going. I'll find your coat."

She scurried out into the hallway, half afraid of the glow that glimmered deep within those golden eyes.

"Here it is. Good night, Jordan." She waited as he shrugged into the warm jacket, smiling warmly as she stepped forward to the door.

"Lyn?" Jordan stopped her, his hand curving around her shoulder to stop her progress.

She turned back to him, wondering at the strange look on his face. The rugged planes softened as his hands drew her closer. Before she could do anything, his head came down and Jordan Andrews kissed her as if he'd been waiting forever.

It was over in seconds, but Caitlin didn't pull away. She couldn't. She merely stood there, locked in the circle of his arms, and stared blankly at his beloved face.

His hand came up to brush away the soft curls that fell around her cheeks. One finger traced a line from her forehead down her nose, past her lips to her upraised chin.

"Clayton Matthews has no business kissing you." The words were barely audible.

Then Jordan tilted his head and kissed her again, a warm friendly kind of kiss that Caitlin wanted to go on and on.

She didn't know how it happened but moments later she was free and Jordan was standing in the open door.

"Good night, Lyn," he murmured, stepping backward onto the step. "Sweet dreams."

"Good night, Jordan," she whispered to the closed door.

Chapter Nine

"Are you sure you should be doing this?" Clay Matthews shuffled awkwardly across the floor and took Caitlin's hand. "I mean, Jordan didn't seem too thrilled that you were helping me out. When I mentioned Monday, his face got all tight."

"Well, too bad. Jordan Andrews doesn't control my life. Now concentrate, Clay. You're not dragging around a sack of oats, you're dancing with Maryann."

"Maryann's not as big around as you," he muttered, pushing her forward.

"Gee, thanks." Caitlin rolled her eyes. "Can't you pretend, just this once?"

"If I pretend too much, I'd be too nervous to do anything."

Sighing heavily, Caitlin let him go and found the nearest chair, thankful she'd worn her sneakers for this. Her back ached like fire.

"Maybe we'd better delve into that area a little

deeper, Clay. Why does Maryann make you so nervous?'' And how come I never make anyone nervous? Concerned maybe, protective yes, but nervous? Nah.

While Clay rambled, Caitlin fell to thinking about Jordan's strange kiss and subsequent actions. He'd acted as if nothing had changed when he arrived the next morning to take her to church. And the dinner at his parents had gone off without a hitch, or another one of those knee-melting kisses.

They were pals, best buds, friends. So why did she feel so aware when Jordan scooped her hair out from her coat collar? And what about the way he'd so solicitously seen to her every need? He'd done nothing unusual, nothing to get upset about, and yet, every time his knuckles brushed hers, Caitlin felt herself tensing.

She'd told him she didn't need him, that she could manage. And when he'd dropped her off, she'd insisted that she wanted to spend last evening alone, in front of the fire. So why had she expected him to come in and play checkers?

It was crazy, that's what it was. And she was silly for even thinking about him like that. They were just friends and that was the way she wanted it. Right?

''Caitlin?'' Clay's somber eyes peered down at her. ''Did you hear anything I told you about Maryann?''

A ruckus in the front hall saved her from admitting that she hadn't heard a single word he'd said. ''I'll just see who that is,'' she murmured, scurrying across the room as Jordan's boisterous laugh rang out.

He was in the front hall, teasing Beth about her new boots.

"I doubt if you'll even be able to cross the street after a good blizzard, if you wear those things," he scoffed, trailing one finger down the new shiny leather. "The heels are way too high."

"That's good." Maryann giggled. "That way she can dig them into the ice. Traction." She and Jordan exchanged a look that had him slapping a hand over his grinning mouth.

"Well, I think they're gorgeous," Beth sniffed. "Caitlin, tell me what you think of my new winter boots."

As Jordan and Maryann turned toward her, Caitlin bent to examine the pliable leather and avoid his scrutiny. It was stupid that she felt as if he might see through her, peer into her brain. He might figure out that she'd skipped dinner.

"They're lovely," she offered. "So stylish. They'll look elegant no matter what you wear. I just wish I could manage to look as gorgeous as you do."

"You could never fit into those boots," Clay remarked from behind. "Your feet are way too big."

Maryann groaned, her eyes rolling with disgust. "Nice, Clay. That will really make her feel good about herself."

"It's the truth!" Clay's face turned a deep, dark scarlet.

"Don't you know you're supposed to tell a woman how lovely she is? Especially a pregnant woman. Believe me, we already know all our faults." Maryann glared at him, but a spark of teasing twinkled at the back of her eyes.

"I didn't say she had faults." Clay tilted his head to one side in confusion. "Did I? I don't think so. I just said—"

"We know!" Maryann turned her back on him and smiled at Beth. "I really do like them, Beth. Especially those heels."

"And I'll take care of telling Lyn how good she looks." Jordan's voice rumbled in Caitlin's ear, barely loud enough for the others to hear.

"High heels wouldn't look good on you, Maryann. You're already tall—" Belatedly, Clay held his tongue, his eyes just catching the glimmer of hurt in Maryann's face.

Caitlin could have groaned when she noticed the other woman had on heels.

"Gee, thanks," Maryann muttered, her face tinged a dark pink. "I think I'll go before you offer any more of your sweet-talking compliments on my appearance."

She hurried up the stairs, stumbling as she turned too quickly and her heel caught in the carpet.

"See, that's what I mean." Clay jerked his thumb toward the departing woman. "She always dresses up way too much for this place. Why doesn't she just wear normal clothes instead of those expensive dresses and fancy things?"

A resounding slam echoed back downstairs. Caitlin sighed, wishing she'd never come out here. Clay had singlehandedly done more to set back his own cause with Maryann than she could ever manage to correct, even if she paid for professional dance lessons for him.

She saw Beth jerk her head at Jordan and his almost imperceptible nod. Moments later he had his arm around Clay's shoulders.

"Clay, you and I need to have a chat, a man-to-man discussion." He shepherded the other man into Caitlin's apartment and firmly grasped the door handle to close the door.

"Well, maybe some other time. Caitlin was teaching me to dance!"

Clay's plaintive voice made Caitlin smile. She watched him stick his foot in the space.

"I haven't got a lot of time to waste talking, you know, Jordan." He sounded frustrated.

Jordan nodded. "Believe me, pal, I know just how little time you have! And we won't waste a minute of it. Besides, Caitlin's supposed to be getting a manicure from Beth right about now. Isn't that right?" he said over his left shoulder to the woman who stood holding her much maligned boots.

"Yes. Right." Beth scooped up the box and moved toward her apartment door. "Come on, Caitlin. Let's get at it."

Caitlin frowned at her hands and the fingernails she'd trimmed, filed and polished only that afternoon. That bit of pampering had filled in one of the long, lonely hours of her second Monday off work, but she didn't want to go through it all over again tonight.

"But I just…" She felt her arm yanked and scurried behind Beth into the apartment. "I've already done my nails today,'' she complained when the door had closed behind them.

''Fine. Then we'll do them again. Or we'll have tea. Or play Scrabble. Whatever. Let's just give those two a few moments alone together.''

''You mean Jordan and Clay? But why?'' Caitlin stared at her old school friend in puzzlement.

''Because Jordan can tell that guy a few home truths that you, even with all your careful wording, would never be able to explain to Clay Matthews.'' She ushered Caitlin through her bright red-and-white living room to the kitchen she'd decorated in the same vibrant colors.

''I shouldn't have said that,'' she admitted. ''It's not his fault. It's just too bad he grew up with six brothers and a mother too tired from running a farm and raising those boys to have any time left over to teach the social niceties,'' she grumbled.

''This looks really nice.'' Caitlin admired the other woman's panache in decorating. ''My place is dull and boring beiges and greens. Nothing like this.''

''Your place is perfectly beautiful,'' Beth staunchly defended. ''I didn't have much money to work with after setting up the shop, so I made my statement another way. The paint wasn't much and the stencils really add something.''

''I like it. Veronica's out?''

''My sister is making her millions baby-sitting for the entire town.'' Beth rolled her eyes. ''She desperately wants some new *cool* clothes, and since I need her help in the shop in the afternoons, she's decided to baby-sit in the evenings. She's been great about everything, moving here, changing schools, making new friends.''

''That's good.'' Caitlin wished she had a sister to room with. It must be nice to have someone to talk to when you needed an ally, someone who would sympathize unconditionally.

''I noticed you in church yesterday.''

''Yes.'' Caitlin sighed. ''Jordan and his mother wouldn't take no for an answer. In the end, I guess he was right. It felt nice to be back in the old place. I notice the organ hasn't changed.''

Beth giggled as she put on the kettle. ''Isn't it awful? That squeak has been there for years and nobody seems inclined to get rid of it. Sort of makes it feel more like home though, doesn't it?''

''I guess.'' Caitlin shifted from the bar stool to a kitchen chair. ''I don't know. The truth is, I feel a little strange sitting in that church. Sort of guilty.''

''Guilty?'' Beth sat down opposite her and frowned. ''For heaven's sake, what have you got to feel guilty for?''

Caitlin liked the way Beth sat there, waiting for her to explain. No pressure, no pushiness. Just the honest interest of a friend.

''It's, well, kind of hard to explain.'' Caitlin fought down the urge to pretend there was nothing wrong.

Beth sat where she was, her eyes softly sympathetic.

''I've blamed God, you see,'' Caitlin murmured, embarrassed at having to admit such a thing. ''I couldn't understand why Michael had to die, not when

He knew we were going to have a baby. It seems so callous, not something a caring God would do.''

"Yes, I suppose it does." Beth twiddled her fingers, grinning when Caitlin's surprised eyes met hers. "Hey, I never said I was perfect. I've often wondered why I had to grow up in the home I did. I didn't cause my dad's problems, so why should Veronica and I have to pay for them?"

Other people questioned God? The very idea of it was so new to Caitlin that she simply stared at her friend in disbelief.

"I was really angry at Him for dumping me in such a situation and then abandoning me. I used to envy you, Caitlin."

"Me?" Caitlin gaped, thinking of her scared, lonely teens. "Why would anyone envy me?"

"Because you lived with your aunt in a calm, fight-free house. You had it all together. Nobody yelled at you or called you an idiot. You were smart. You didn't have to look out for anyone."

"I couldn't have," Caitlin admitted quietly. "It was hard enough watching out for myself. And I had nothing together. I still don't."

"Besides, your aunt was no smiling violet," Beth added. "You don't have to tell me. I learned that later. That's partly how I found the nerve to face up to the ruins of my life and move on."

She walked to the stove, poured the boiling water into a brown earthenware pot and added two tea bags. "It's also how I found out God is bigger than anything I can lay before Him. I asked Him to show me what to do next when my marriage broke down and He led me up north. Even though we fought, I learned how much my husband loved me and I began to understand that God cared for me more than I could imagine."

She set two big mugs on the table, poured the tea, retrieved the cream and sugar for Caitlin and then sat down.

"Just because I made a whole bunch of mistakes with my life, just because everything wasn't a bed of roses, didn't mean God had dumped on me. Even though all my circumstances changed, my duty remained the same."

"Your duty?" Caitlin accepted the mug of tea and sipped carefully, trying to sort through what she was hearing. "What duty?"

"I should have explained better." Beth scrunched up her eyes and thought before starting again.

"You see, Caitlin, if I wanted God to show me His way, I had to make Him the king of my life. Once I did that I had to accept His authority. Nobody gets to question a king. He makes the decisions He does and His subjects deal with them." She passed a bag of chocolate cookies across the table.

"I needed to accept that my life was the way it was. Period. I couldn't change the past, I couldn't change the people. I could only move on, follow God's leading. That was the biggest relief. It was all up to Him." She grinned.

"And so here you are."

"Here I am, back where I started, thanks to you. Trying to do what God tells me, to follow His lead, even though I don't understand it. I just have to believe that His way is best. That's my duty."

"Duty. Hmm." Caitlin thought that one over, before glancing up into her friend's bright gaze. "What do you think my duty is, Beth?"

"Sweetie, I can't answer that. No one can. That's between you and God."

"I was afraid you'd say that. It just makes things worse." Caitlin heaved a sigh and closed her eyes. "God doesn't talk to me."

"How do you know that? Maybe you're just not listening. I do know that you'll never find out if you don't spend time talking to Him. Believe me, I know it's hard! But we only go on making more mistakes without some heavenly direction."

Beth's small delicate fingers, punctured by the thorns and rough stems of the flowers she handled, closed around Caitlin's.

"You have to let go of the anger and the worry and the frustration, Cait. I know it's hard to fathom, but God would never do anything to deliberately hurt us. We usually bring that on ourselves. We just have to learn from it and move on."

"That's almost exactly what Jordan said," Caitlin murmured.

"And he's right. Jordan wants to help. He wants to be there for you, to do whatever you want him to. He cares for you, Caitlin."

"That's the hardest part of all," Caitlin whispered, relieved to have finally said it out loud. "I can't care for Jordan. Not like I did for Michael, not the way I think he wants. I…it hurts too much.'' And even that wasn't the truth. Not all of it, at least.

''And you think he'll take off the same way everyone else did.'' Beth's voice was flat. ''I can't tell you he won't, Cait. Nobody can do that except God and He doesn't usually tell us His plans for the future.''

''So what do I do?''

''You let him be your friend. You let him share in the joy of the baby, let him be an uncle. And you leave the rest up to God. If He wants you to do something, He'll show you.''

''That's all?''

Beth grinned. ''Isn't that enough? Just take it one day, one step at a time. Jordan cares for you. Anyone can tell that by looking at his face, by watching him when he's watching you. But he's not Michael, honey. He's not going to rush you into anything. For now, I think it's enough for him to be there, helping you however he can. And you don't exactly repel him, you know.''

She didn't answer. She couldn't. She *wanted* Jordan nearby, wanted him to be there, wanted to count on him. She just didn't think she could risk loving him.

Caitlin shifted uncomfortably in her chair. She'd deal with apologizing to Maryann in the morning. Somehow. ''Do you think they're finished their man-to-man talk now?''

''I don't know. But they can take it elsewhere. You need your rest.'' Beth marched to the door, opened it and led Caitlin across the hall. ''Pregnant women need less stress in their lives, not more,'' she said loudly.

"All anyone seems to want me to do is rest," Caitlin mourned. "It's very tiring."

"I know you're tired. Hang on a sec." Her friend planted her knuckles against the wood and rapped.

Beth heard only what she wanted to hear, Caitlin mused. Maybe she was like that, too. She ignored the harsher parts of life, tried to gloss them over, so she wouldn't have to face them.

"Sorry, Lyn. Clay and I can take this somewhere else." Jordan smiled easily, his golden eyes glowing behind the glasses. "You get some rest."

Clay ambled to the door behind him. They both looked like they were hiding something.

"I wish everyone would stop saying that. I don't want to rest, I want to help Clay learn to dance so he can ask Maryann out." She slapped her hands on her hips and glared at the three of them. "If that's all right with you?"

Beth shrugged, murmured good-night and retreated to her apartment. Clay shuffled from one foot to the other uncomfortably but didn't offer a word of protest when she urged him inside her place. Jordan followed, closing the door behind him as Caitlin started the music once more.

"We do not require an audience," she told him firmly.

"I know. I'll just watch, see if I can help old Clay out with his footwork." Jordan flopped down on the sofa, his smile wide and endearing. "I won't be in the way, I promise."

No matter how much she glared at him, Jordan

didn't move. Caitlin felt uncomfortably self-conscious as she urged Clay to take the lead. He wasn't even trying.

"I'm not that old, you know," he blurted as he stood in the middle of the room. "I just can't seem to dance."

"Here, let me show you." Jordan slid his arm around Caitlin's waist, and wrapped his fingers around her hand. "You don't push her back and forth like a sack of potatoes, Clay. You glide to the music. You choose the path and she'll follow. See?"

Caitlin allowed herself to sway to the music, effortlessly following Jordan's lead. He was as sure-footed in dancing as he was in everything else and for once she appreciate his confidence. It was much nicer to dance with a man who knew where he was going.

The music was soft and dreamy. Caitlin closed her eyes and drifted as a plaintive saxophone drew the last few notes out, pretending she was young again, instead of the age she felt right now.

"You're a wonderful dancer," Jordan murmured, his mouth next to her ear. "You really get into the music."

Another tune started and he kept going, sweeping her out of her dowdy surroundings and into a magical place where everything was perfect. She could hear a waterfall and a bird twittered in the background. In her mind's eye she could see lush green grass and wildflowers swaying in the breeze.

"It's easy to dance when you have a good partner." Caitlin opened her eyes and transported herself back to reality. "But I'm supposed to be helping Clay." She glanced around, spying the other man who stood staring out the window.

"I know." Jordan let her go without another word, watching silently. "Ready to try again, Clay?"

"It's nice of you to try to help me, Caitlin," Clay muttered as he took her hand and started to move the way she'd instructed. "But I don't think there's much point. Even if I could master these steps and feel comfortable doing them, I wouldn't know what to say to her."

"Talk about anything," Caitlin encouraged. "There's no set subject you have to discuss."

Jordan smiled to himself. Lyn was getting a little frustrated with this particular pupil. He could see it in the crease at the corner of her mouth when she reminded the erstwhile lover that Maryann was a mortal woman who was perfectly capable of conversing on a number of subjects.

"Do you think she's beautiful?" he heard her say.

Clay snorted. "Of course she's beautiful. Anyone with eyes can see that."

"Then why don't you tell her so? You can compliment her on her eyes or her lovely hair or on what she's wearing."

Jordan winced along with Caitlin when Clay's big foot covered hers for the umpteenth time. She should have worn steel-toed boots!

"Her hair always reminds me of Naida's," Clay was saying.

Jordan frowned, hoping Caitlin would pick up on that.

"That's nice. But I don't think you should necessarily compare her to another woman." Her foot avoided his just in time.

"Naida's a sheep," Jordan murmured and watched as her eyes, now focused on Clay's, widened in a stare of shock. She forgot the music completely, staring at him as if he had just sprouted horns.

"You can't compare Maryann's hair to sheep's wool!" Shock rendered her incapable of dancing and Caitlin stood where she was, her mouth an O of astonishment.

"But I like sheep's wool," Clay insisted. "It's so soft. And the oil on it is really good for chapped skin."

Jordan held his breath, choking down the laugh that burbled inside as he caught sight of Caitlin's stricken face. Her mouth opened and closed several times as she sought for the right words, but evidently there were none. She flopped into her chair with an air of utter futility, her eyes begging him for help.

Jordan got to his feet, wondering how he'd landed himself in this fix. The only person he'd even consider playing Cupid for was Caitlin. He just couldn't bring himself to ignore the mute desperation in her eyes.

He'd help her. After all, that was his role now, wasn't it? Big brother, uncle? He'd told her he was there for her whenever she needed him. Well, Caitlin Andrews needed him now.

"Clay," he sighed, motioning the other man to the remaining chair. "It's not a good idea to compare

women, especially one you care about, to animals. Not
in that way. If you want to talk about your animals,
that's fine. But if you like her hair, just tell her that.
You don't have to pretend to be something you're
not.''

Ha, his conscience jabbed him. Wasn't that exactly
what he was doing right now, with his brother's wife?
He was pretending to be her good friend, the brother-
in-law who only wanted to help.

Well, he wanted a whole lot more than that! And if
he told the truth, he always had. Shock reverberated
through his system as the knowledge he'd deliberately
hidden burst forth into the light.

Vaguely Jordan realized with some part of his mind,
that Lyn and Clay were talking about goatskins. But
he couldn't deal with that now. The truth that erupted
inside his mind took his complete and total concentration.

He loved her! He always had. Even when he'd been
so busy playing chivalrous big brother, he'd been in
love with Caitlin. So why had he stood aside for Michael?

The answer was hard to accept.

Michael was young. He'd lived life to the max and
he didn't worry too much about the future. Caitlin, in
her shy, protected world, had gravitated to that like a
bee to honey. He'd seen it himself the first time he'd
introduced them. She'd been enthralled by Michael's
shining light, riveted by his boyish joie de vivre.

By contrast, Jordan felt old and boring. And he was!
He was older than both of them. He didn't want to

speed around in fast cars or go to exciting parties. He didn't have to search for a vocation. He'd always known he'd be in computers. The same way he'd always known Caitlin would come back to him.

Of course, he hadn't expected Michael to marry her! That had come as a total shock. And a revelation. Jordan came home after the wedding, of course. He had to, had to see it to believe it. He'd even been coerced into playing a part in the celebrations his parents had thrown. But as soon as he could, he'd left, using business as his excuse.

Because even though Caitlin was married to Michael, Jordan still loved her. It was despicable! It was wrong. It was a sin. He stayed away, praying desperately that God would take away this longing for the forbidden. And when Michael had died, driving *his* car, Jordan knew it was his fault because he'd hidden that love inside and nurtured it. He had no choice but to disappear from her life. He couldn't hang around Oakburn, knowing that he was in love with his brother's wife. That would have been traitorous.

But what about now?

He still loved her. Jordan had no doubts about that. It was a different kind of love, though. A more mature love. He was prepared to bide his time, let her get used to having him around again. Then he'd test the waters. Maybe in time, please God, she'd see him as something more than the bossy older brother.

"Jordan? Don't you agree?" Caitlin's earnest face frowned up at him. "About waiting," she prompted.

"There's nothing wrong with waiting," Clay insisted. "God will let me know when it's the right time."

"I think He already has." Caitlin's voice was firm. "After ten years Maryann is back, she's single and she has a little girl who needs a father. What more do you need? A lightning bolt?"

Jordan grinned at her vehemence. Caitlin never prevaricated. If there was a decision to be made, she considered both sides, weighed the arguments and chose. If it was a wrong choice, so be it. She dealt with the flak. But she didn't spend time dithering about which route to take. Maybe it was time to take a leaf out of her book.

"She's right, Clay. A man needs to be strong. Forceful. To go after what he wants. If your motives are pure, God will direct you."

Ha! Were his own motives pure? Jordan ignored that nasty little voice and weighed his options.

I love Caitlin he said to himself. *I want to marry her, to help her raise the baby. I want to be able to tell the world that I love her. I don't want to feel ashamed or embarrassed about my feelings any more.*

Yes. That was the truth. So now it was time to lay it all on the line.

Jordan glanced at the other man. Unlike Clay, he was certain he would know the right place and time to tell her. And he'd just have to keep praying that she would get past her fears of abandonment and realize that he wasn't going anywhere without her.

"Jordan? I've just told Clay we'll help him think

of some compliments when he comes tomorrow night. Is that okay with you?''

Jordan nodded yes while inside his mind screamed no! If Clay was going to hang around all the time, how would he ever get an opportunity to talk to Caitlin privately?

The following weekend Caitlin allowed herself to sink a little deeper into the softness of her chair as the conversation around her raged on. It was girls' afternoon at Wintergreen, as the Andrews women had officially dubbed it, and it was turning out to be fun.

''Women are more mature. They know what they want and they go after it. Why can't men understand that?'' Robyn sighed.

''Because men are romantics.'' Eliza sipped her tea calmly. ''They want us to be helpless, to need them. And we do. But we can also function perfectly well on our own in some matters. That's irritating to someone who sees you as the little woman.''

''That's what Jordan's like,'' Caitlin offered. She flushed a little when Robyn's eyes focused on her. ''Well, he is! He thinks I can't vacuum the floor just because I'm pregnant. He insists on bringing in a cleaning service which is silly because I always clean up before they come so they won't think I live in filth.''

A burst of sympathetic laughter agreed.

''It's not funny,'' she grumbled. ''Yesterday I wanted to clean out that hall cupboard. He insisted on bringing this chair out into the hallway and I had to sit there while *he* sorted through the junk left over from the move.'' She shifted uncomfortably. ''I'm pregnant, not paralyzed.''

''Jordan always was pushy. He's the type who walks little old ladies across the street, even when they don't want to go.'' Natasha's voice rang with the certainty of a younger sister from her position on the floor where she reclined against some cushions.

''He's good-hearted though, Nat. You have to give him that. He wouldn't willingly hurt a flea.'' Olivia snatched another brownie and bit into it with a sigh. ''He also eats like a whale and never gains an ounce. Why didn't you pass that gene on to me, Mother?''

''It belonged to your father. And he kept it for the boys. Michael always ate well, too.''

Silence, stark and bare greeted her words. Eliza stared for a moment, then rushed into speech. ''Oh, Caitlin, my dear. I'm so sorry! I didn't mean to upset you.'' She patted her daughter-in-law's hand worriedly. ''Sometimes I forget and, well…'' She stopped.

''It's all right, Eliza. Really. I know Michael's gone. And I'm sad about it. But I can still talk about him, remember him, without breaking down. I think.''

''Of course you can.'' Natasha's bracing tones were exactly what they all needed. ''Michael might have died, but you didn't. You're alive and it's only natural that you should go on with your life, find someone else to love.'' She studied Caitlin with a frown.

''Is this Clay guy the one you've chosen?''

''Natasha!'' Robyn, Olivia and Eliza all burst out at the same time.

"That's none of your business, Nat. Caitlin doesn't have to explain to you." Robyn's rueful glance met Caitlin's. "Just ignore her."

"No, of course I won't ignore her." Caitlin rubbed a hand over her forehead, wondering where to start.

"Good. So spill it all, Caitlin. I want to know what Clay means to you." Natasha's generous mouth curved down. "I somehow never thought of him as your kind of guy. But what do I know?"

"Exactly what I'd like to know." Robyn's eyebrows raised meaningfully, but whatever else she was going to say was drowned by her daughter's cries. "Come on, sweetie," she comforted Eudora. "Mommy'll kiss it better."

"Clayton Matthews is just a friend. Someone I'm trying to help out. He's not interested in me at all." Would that do it? Caitlin certainly hoped so.

Olivia assumed the lotus position, grinned and popped anther chip into her mouth. "The only time I ever saw him notice a woman was last week at church. He couldn't take his eyes off Maryann MacGregor."

"Exactly. He wants to ask her out, but he's a little bit shy." Caitlin shifted, knowing that to mention the subject was to elicit unasked-for advice.

"If I remember correctly, his mother had rather a rough time raising all those boys after their father left," Eliza murmured, staring out the window at the waning sun. "It's too bad someone didn't take him in hand long ago."

"So, you're not interested in Clay." Natasha took

another sip of her soda, lips pursed, eyes narrowed as she shifted fractionally on the sofa. "Who then?"

"Natasha!"

With one accord, the other Andrews women raised their eyebrows and rolled their eyes upward in exasperation. It was a trait they seemed to share with tacit agreement and to Caitlin those eye movements were more expressive than any words they could have uttered.

"Uh, you see, well," Caitlin swallowed, searching for the right words. "I'm not really looking for a, um, a man. It's not part of the plan. Not now I mean. That is, I haven't had time to think about it. Not with the baby and everything."

"You're so young, you don't want to spend your life alone, honey," Eliza said. "You need someone to share your life with, someone to laugh with, have fun with, grow old with. Someone you can give your heart to."

"I don't know anyone like that."

It was a lie and they knew it as well as she. If she'd learned anything these past weeks it was that Jordan was all of those things. He didn't mind when she was grumpy or angry, or when she lashed out at him. He took it all in stride and, in fact, encouraged her to express herself more often.

Jordan was comfortable, fun, and yet oddly exciting. She got the same rush out of seeing him come through the door that she'd gotten all those years ago when he'd dropped in at Aunt Lucy's to pick her up for youth group.

Was the reason she didn't want to talk about love because thinking about Jordan in that light made her feel guilty? Had she buried her feelings for the older brother when Michael came along, hoping that Michael could make her feel more secure, more in control? Or had she been so hurt by Jordan's obvious insensitivity to her schoolgirl crush, that she'd turned to Michael to pay Jordan back?

Maybe she hadn't been the best wife for Michael. Maybe she'd let herself fall in love with being married instead of being the kind of wife Michael had needed. Had Michael guessed that she'd only gone out with him that first time because she wanted to see Jordan?

Oh, where did all these questions come from? And why now, when it was too late to ask Michael if she'd disappointed him, if he'd known she'd once been in love with his brother? If he'd thought she was using him to get to Jordan?

"Are you planning on going to the fellowship supper next week at church?" Natasha asked.

"Jordan's taking me. He said I needed to get out of the house."

"That's nice." Eliza took Eudora from Robyn and put the little girl on her knee. "You know, Caitlin, I was looking at some old photos last night. Your wedding picture, actually. I know it wasn't that long ago, but you looked so young. You've grown up a lot since then, haven't you?"

"I like to think so." Caitlin closed her eyes to stop the tears that came as she remembered that silly, scared little girl. Had she really changed at all?

"I think you've changed a lot." Olivia looked up from her cross-stitch. "Michael used to say that you were his stabilizer, that you anchored him."

"Not well enough, otherwise he'd never have been driving so wildly." Caitlin felt she had to say it, they were all thinking it anyway.

"Caitlin. That didn't have anything to do with you! You couldn't have stopped him and you know it. Anyway, Michael was God's child. You couldn't have changed God's time no matter what you did." Eliza moved to wrap one arm around Caitlin. "Michael loved you, my dear girl. He thought the sun, moon and stars rolled around your head."

"He would be glad to know you're getting on with your life," Robyn agreed. "Michael loved life too much to want anyone not to live it."

"But I was so stupid. I was so scared that he'd leave me that I hung on too tightly. I'm sure he got tired of that." A lump rose in her throat that she couldn't swallow down. "Maybe I'm bad luck or something, I don't know. But everyone I love seems to leave."

"Caitlin Andrews you stop that right now!" Eliza stood up, tall and strong, her voice loving but firm. "Our God does not deal in luck!

"Yes, you've had a tragic life. But honey, don't let yourself become some kind of a tragic hero. You and Michael loved each other. And God blessed your marriage with Junior here." Eliza patted Caitlin's stomach.

"Open your eyes and look around you. God has given you people who care about you. We do."

The girls' heads nodded in exuberant agreement.

"So does Jordan, and your friends here at Wintergreen. We're your family and we're not going anywhere. So let's get on with life and move into the promised land. Okay?" Eliza brushed one hand in a tender caress across Caitlin's cheek.

"Okay. I'll try not to dwell in the desert anymore, Eliza." Caitlin smiled, grateful that these woman cared enough to stay with her, challenge her.

"And you promise you'll keep your eyes peeled for the wonderful things God is going to do in your life, the wonderful people He sends? You won't shut them out?"

"I promise."

"Promise what? What's going on here? Good grief! You all look as though you've been peeling onions." Jordan, tall, bossy and impossibly dear, stood in the doorway, frowning at all of them.

"Well? Are we going out for dinner or not?"

Caitlin glanced at Robyn, who raised her eyebrows at her sisters, but it was Eliza who finally burst into laughter. They all rose, searching for gloves and coats and purses.

"Yes, son, you're going out for dinner. And Caitlin's going with you. But Robyn and I have to get home. And Olivia's got a date with her hubby. Natasha, now..." Her voice trailed away. "I have to think about Natasha," they heard her murmur as she tugged on her boots, buttoned her coat and hurried out the door without even saying goodbye. "There must be someone for her."

Natasha grimaced, her face sour as she pretended to slug Jordan on the shoulder. "Thanks a lot, Jordy," she grumbled, her face fiery red. "Now she'll start in on me and heaven knows who she'll drag home! Last month she set up a blind date. A blind date!" She shook her head dismally. "He was as mortified as I was."

"This is my fault?" Jordan looked completely stumped.

"Yes! You're my big brother. You're supposed to protect me." Natasha's forehead suddenly cleared. "By the way, Caitlin wants to go to Chez Lee. She's simply dying to try their lobster. I told her you wouldn't mind taking her. After all, it is Saturday and you're allowed to stay out late."

Natasha scurried past to the door, her scarf trailing behind. "Bye, Caitlin. Don't let him bully you. And make him pay. Big time!"

"What did I do to her?"

"Years of bossiness, Brother dear. Now it's pay-back time." Robyn patted his arm, her eyes glowing with mischief. "But Caitlin really does want lobster. And onion rings. I don't know why. Ask her." She kissed Caitlin, grabbed her bundled-up daughter and headed out the door.

"I've got to go, too," Olivia murmured, tugging on her gloves. She hugged Caitlin close and then fixed her with a stern look. "No desert. Okay?"

Caitlin nodded, smiling as the last sister left.

"No desert? Doesn't she mean dessert? And why

not?'' Jordan's eyes worked open and closed as he tried to reason out the strange tableau.

"I've got to give you credit, Andrews," Caitlin giggled as she picked up the cups. "You sure know how to clear a room."

"And I wasn't even trying to get them to leave," he marveled. "I wish I knew what I did so I could do it again next time."

Caitlin burst out laughing, happier than she could remember being in months.

He followed her through to the kitchen, his hands full of used napkins and empty chip containers. "So where shall we go for dinner? We haven't got a reservation for Chez Lee's so that's out. But otherwise, take your pick."

He lifted the crystal bowl out of her hand and set in on the shelf she'd been stretching to reach. As his hands came down, one brushed the length of her hair, lightly fingering the russet curls, while the other rested on her shoulder.

For a moment, just one small unit of time, Caitlin relaxed against his massaging fingers as they manipulated the taut cord across her shoulder.

"You okay?" His gold eyes searched hers as he eased her into a chair. "No backache?"

"A little." She sat there, her head resting against his side, allowing the tiny thrill of joy to trickle from his fingertips to her heart.

"You're tired. I knew you shouldn't have asked Clay over again last night. It's bizarre, this coaching him in endearments.'' But his voice was soft and indulgent.

''No, it's not. He really cares for her, Jordan. I can't turn my back on that.'' She sighed when his fingers moved onto her scalp, easing the bands of pressure that clung there.

''Do you want me to make something? I know you're too tired to go out. I promise I'll sterilize everything when I'm finished. You'll never know I've been here.''

Jordan loved cooking almost as much as he hated cleaning up. And yet he was willing to do that for her, too. The small sacrifice brought a smile to her lips.

''I don't think so. But thanks anyway. I'm just not in the mood for anything that's here, in spite of your efforts to bring the entire store home. And we can have lobster another time.''

''I'm almost afraid to ask.'' He sat down in the chair opposite her, his hands gently caressing hers as he spoke. ''What are you in the mood for, Caitlin?''

He was so dear, sitting here like this, holding her. Would it be so wrong to love him? To let a tiny piece of her heart thaw enough to pour it out on Michael's brother.

''Caitlin?''

''Hmm?''

''What'll it be?''

''Chicken, I think. Strips. Golden crisp and steaming, with hot mustard sauce to dip them in, and some coleslaw on the side. And lemonade.'' She closed her eyes, dreaming of it all, and opened them again when she heard his snort of laughter.

"You're kidding, right? Coleslaw? Hot mustard sauce? Lemonade?" His eyes sparkled with laughter, his mouth creased in that teasing grin. "With your stomach? You'll need antacids all night long!"

Caitlin pretended to bristle. "Just because you don't like chicken is no reason I shouldn't enjoy it. I'll call the delivery people." She yanked her hands away from his and stood too quickly, causing the blood to rush to her feet. Caitlin wavered for a moment, then grabbed at the table.

"Are you all right?" His arm came around her shoulders and he helped her walk from the kitchen to the living room, easing her onto the sofa. "There. Put your feet up and watch the television for a while. I'll be back shortly." His eyes glinted with laughter. "But I'm warning you, the time will come when you won't be able to con me anymore."

Caitlin thrust her nose in the air and sniffed derisively. "As if I'd bother. I'm not helpless, you know," she sputtered, struggling to free herself from the soft cushy comfort of furniture that seemed intent on swallowing her up.

"Close enough." He grinned as she subsided with a sigh, then pressed a kiss to the top of her head and just managed to dodge the pillow she chucked at him. "And don't move or I'll give the chicken to someone else. See you in a bit."

"When I sell this sofa and get something I can get in and out of, you're going to be sorry." She shifted again, then sighed in resignation. "Threats," she called as he walked out of the apartment. "That's what you always use."

"That's because they work," he called back.

As usual Jordan got the last word in.

He was so easy, so much fun, so comfortable to be around. It couldn't be wrong to love a man like that?

Could it?

Chapter Ten

"I take it that waiting a week to get here was worthwhile?" Jordan escorted her out of the posh restaurant, a smile tugging at his mouth. "Chez Lee lived up to your expectations?"

Caitlin smiled as she grasped his helping hand and eased herself into his car. "It was excellent. I don't know when I've enjoyed myself more. Thank you, Jordan."

He didn't answer her until he was inside the car beside her and had eased the vehicle into traffic.

"You're welcome. I'm glad you enjoyed it. I was a little worried about you there for a minute," he joked, his eyes sparkling. "The waiter couldn't do enough. I'm sure he personally inspected every mouthful you ate. But when the maitre d' started hovering, with the dessert tray in his hands, I wondered if we shouldn't ask for some carryout."

Caitlin pursed her lips, considering the idea. "Hey,

you should have suggested it.'' Then she shook her head. ''No, better not. But I find I get that a lot lately. I call it the kid-glove treatment. There's a real advantage to being pregnant, you know.''

Jordan nodded his agreement. His mouth opened, then closed, as if he thought better of his reply. Instead, he turned on the CD player and tapped one forefinger against the wheel in tune to a concerto.

It only took a few minutes, then they were pulling up in front of Wintergreen. Caitlin waited for Jordan's assistance. Once out of the car, she wrapped her arm in his as they walked up the driveway.

''You look very pleased with yourself.'' He opened the door, waited for her to go in, then closed it, watching her curiously.

Caitlin grinned as she unlocked her apartment. She pushed open the door. ''I feel wonderful,'' she enthused. ''Spoiled and pampered and utterly coddled.''

He grinned. ''Wonderful is one of your favorite words tonight, it seems.'' His golden eyes sparkled with fun.''Well, it was a wonderful evening!''

''Don't hold back Jordan. Forget modesty and humility. Tell me how you really feel,'' Caitlin teased in return, brushing her knuckles across his lean cheek.

It was meant to be funny, but the tension in the room suddenly increased tenfold when he caught her fingers and pressed them to his mouth.

''All right, I will.'' The words were soft. In the glow of the single lamp she could see only shadows as they moved across his face. His eyes were dark-gold, molten, burning her in their intensity. He set her boots aside but stayed kneeling there.

"I'm in love with you, Lyn. I have been for a long time. I want to marry you." He lifted his hand up into the light, snapping open the lid of a black velvet box.

Caitlin gasped at the glittering magnificence that sparkled out at her. It was an exquisite diamond, pear-shaped and perched atop a wide gold band. Slowly she tore her eyes from it to the man who knelt in front of her.

"M-marry you?"

"Yes. I want to be able to come home to you every night, to stay here with you, instead of lying at home, alone, wondering if you're all right, if you need me. I want to be here for you and the baby. I want us to live and love and laugh together until the end. I love you, Lyn."

It sounded great, wonderful, inviting. It was the kind of fairy-tale life she had always wanted and never found.

It was too good to be true.

"Jordan, I don't know what to say."

"Yes would be nice." He smiled that silly, crooked smile that tugged at her heartstrings. "Maybe would be almost acceptable." He stopped when the tears began. "Don't Caitlin. Don't cry. Please?"

"I'm sorry. I can't help it. You've been marvelous, Jordan. So good to me when I was so cranky. And I've appreciated it more than you know. I don't know how I would have managed without you and your family here."

"But?" He leaned back on his haunches, hands falling to his side, the ring lying in her lap. "There is a but, isn't there?"

"I can't marry you, Jordan." Dear Lord it hurt to say that, to see the flash of anguish cross his eyes.

"Why?"

She heard the anger in that single word and hated herself for causing him pain.

"It wouldn't be right."

"Are you nuts?" He grinned, throwing his arms wide. "It would be fantastic. I love you. I want to marry you. I want us to live together as husband and wife."

"I'm Michael's wife." The words came out cold and harsh, bursting his exuberant bubble.

His eyes narrowed, lips stretched tight and thin.

"Were! You *were* Michael's wife. He's gone, Lyn. But I'm here, alive. And I'm still in love with you."

"Still?" What was he saying? Caitlin didn't know where to look or what to say. She hated to cause the hurt in his eyes and yet she simply couldn't marry him. Not with fear clinging to her like yesterday's news.

"I've loved you for years." His hands closed around her face, his palms firm against her cheeks as he forced her to look at him. "I loved you in high school, Caitlin."

"But you…" She avoided the yearning she saw hidden behind the playful banter and teasing familiarity. She couldn't let herself feel that.

"Look at me, Caitlin." His hands tenderly forced

her chin up, coaxing her to see what she wanted to have and didn't dare take.

"I loved you. But I was boring, wrapped up in my computers. I wasn't the kind of boyfriend you needed. Michael was young and vibrant. You needed someone like him, someone who wasn't dull and staid and too old for you. Someone who would help you to branch out, live a little."

"That's why you dumped me? To give Michael a chance?"

He nodded. "Yes. But also to give you a chance. I was older than you, Lyn. Sure you were brainy and two years ahead of your peers, but you needed that two years to mature. I wanted you to have that time, to sample life, go out with kids who'd have your interests." He grimaced. "Computer nerds aren't much fun."

She heard it all. Every word sank into her brain. But she couldn't believe she hadn't figured it out. Caitlin picked up the ring case and turned it round and round, then set it on the coffee table.

"And you didn't think you owed it to me to tell me?" Indignation reared its head. "You didn't think I had enough brains and common sense to tell you whom I preferred?"

"It was pretty obvious, wasn't it?" Jordan's damning words cut her protests short. "You started going out with him two days after I told you I couldn't see you anymore."

"Do you know why?" Caitlin resisted the temptation to touch him.

"I went out with Michael so I could see you. That's why. I thought seeing you like that was better than nothing. So yes, I went out with him, I went to the football games with him, I came over for dinner as often as I could. I let myself be included in your family because I couldn't pull away."

For once in his life Jordan Andrews appeared to have nothing to say.

"Eventually you went away to college and Michael and I were chumming around more and more. When we graduated, we chose the same college, took some of the same classes. We even rode home together at vacation."

"And eventually you fell in love. Right?" Hurt shimmered in Jordan's golden gaze. His hands clenched in his lap, belying the smile on his face. "I knew it would happen."

"It didn't happen right away. It sort of grew on us. Michael was all the things I wasn't and, I admit, I liked that. He wasn't afraid of anything. Life was like a big game to him and he was determined not to miss a thing."

She fell into a reverie, thinking about the many heated disagreements they'd had over his carefree attitude. How many times had she chided him for skipping an afternoon of work in order to fly a kite in the park or drive to the beach for a swim? How many times had he coaxed her away from her post-grad studies to go to a party or plan tennis or anything else that took his fancy?

"Caitlin, Michael is gone."

"Do you think I don't know that?" Caitlin slowly got up, stepped past him and walked to the window, staring out at the cold, black night. "It was my fault he died. Mine."

"It wasn't! He drove too fast under conditions that were not suitable. He took my car and even I know it was an accident." He stood behind her, not touching her.

As she stood there, Caitlin could feel the heat from his body, the sizzle that flickered between their minds every time Jordan came into the room. It had been the same back then.

"The night before he died we had an argument. Michael was angry at me, very angry. He said I was trying to hide from life."

She drew in a deep breath and turned to face Jordan.

"Michael asked me if I'd married him so I could live vicariously through him. He asked me if I didn't think I'd have been better off with you. Safer."

She could hear him suck in his breath and winced at the suffering she'd caused. But she couldn't stop now. She wouldn't.

"I told him I loved him. I told him I only wanted to be married to him. To be his wife. I promised I'd never be a drag on him again. I was so scared he'd leave, I would have promised him anything. Anyway, he said he forgave me. The next day he borrowed your car. The police say he was driving too fast for conditions."

"And you think that he took some extra risks just to prove that he could handle things?" Jordan shook his head. "It isn't true, Lyn. Michael had been driving that way for years. Dad used to lecture him on it, but Michael always laughed it off—said he knew what he was doing."

Caitlin shivered as the icy cold draft from the window washed over her. She'd have to get new storm windows, she decided absently.

"That doesn't matter. The point is, if he hadn't felt he had to prove that he could take risks and survive, I don't think he would have gone. My husband may have gone to his death believing I never loved him. That's what nags at me." She swallowed down her tears and turned to face him. "There could never be anything between us, Jordan. It would be like betraying Michael's trust in me. I told him I loved him."

She wondered about that now, wondered if she'd really loved him the way she should have.

"Lyn, you were always faithful to Michael. You loved him the best you knew. You were his wife. You didn't betray him by urging caution."

"How can you be so sure?" Caitlin jerked her head up to glare at him. "How can you know that? I don't."

"But—"

"Every day I ask myself if I supported him the way he needed. Did I tell him that I loved him when I should have? Did he *believe* that I only wanted him, that there wasn't anybody else for me by then? Was I telling the truth?" She shook her head.

"I can't be sure, Jordan. I can't be sure. And I can't help wondering if that's why God took him, because I didn't measure up."

There, it was said. The whole terrible awful truth. Let Jordan see how ugly her soul really was.

She wasn't surprised when Jordan didn't say anything.

"I thank you for your kindness and your friendship, Jordan. And I appreciate your help more than I can say. But friendship is all I can ever share with you."

"Like friendship is all you share with Clay and Garrett and all the others?"

She heard the frustration in his voice and felt bad for it. But there was nothing she could do about it. There was no way he could ever make her believe that Michael's death hadn't been a punishment for her failures as a wife.

"Clay and Gar are friends. And, thanks to you, I'm learning that I need friends in my life. But the past, the things that have happened to me, have made me who I am. I can't ignore them, Jordan."

She knew he wanted to say something, that he was about to tell her off. But his pager beeped and would not be ignored. Minutes later, as if through a fog, Caitlin heard him agree to fly to Minneapolis."

"Caitlin?"

She faced him.

"I have to go. A very important client has just lost his entire system to a virus. I've got to see what I can do to help."

"Of course." She forced a smile. "Go. Save the hard drive or whatever it is."

"I will." He nodded. "But first I need to say something. Will you come and sit down?"

She allowed him to press her into a chair and stayed there when he squatted in front of her. She even met his gaze when his hands closed around hers and little jolts of electricity shot up her arm.

"Listen to me, Lyn. I haven't got much time."

"I'm listening."

"I loved my brother. So did you. You were his wife and you did everything right. I know it, and I think deep down, you do too. Michael knew you loved him. I don't believe he ever doubted it. Nor should you. You were the best possible wife a man could ask for."

She smiled blankly. They were just words. He had to say them. What else could he say?

"But that was the past. I'm here now, Caitlin. Me. Jordan. And I love you here and now. There is nothing you could tell me, nothing you could say, that would change that love. And whether you believe in it or not doesn't change the fact that I love you. I always will."

He grinned that irrepressible grin. One hand pushed a swath of hair back off her forehead. With his forefinger he traced the lines of her eyebrows, her nose, the curve of her mouth and the stubborn tilt of her chin.

"You see, sweetheart, it's kind of like God's love for us. Whether we see Him or not, believe in Him or not, trust in Him or not, His love stays. Permanently. And there is nothing we can do to change that."

He stood then, sighed and moved away. One hand snagged his jacket and he flung it on. "It doesn't matter how long it takes you to trust in me. It doesn't matter when you call or what you ask of me, I'll always be there for you. Always. After all this time, my love isn't going to go away. It's going to grow and grow and grow. And whenever you're ready, I'll be waiting. Okay?''

When he didn't move or look away she finally nodded.

''There's just one more thing, Lyn. Though I'd like to, I can't be here all the time. So if you need help or assurance or just someone to calm the fear, you pray and ask God for help. He'll be there. And He'll answer. You just have to ask.''

''Goodbye, Jordan.'' Tears formed at the ends of her lashes, big, fat tears that she couldn't control. ''Thank you for everything you've done. Be safe.''

''It's not goodbye. I'll be back, Lyn. You'll see. But meanwhile, I'm leaving you in God's hands. You couldn't be safer.''

Then he pulled her into his arms and pressed his lips on hers, kissing her with the purpose and intensity of a man who knows exactly what he wants and has no doubt he'll attain it.

''Goodbye, little mama. I love you.''

''I love you, too, Jordan.'' But there was no one to hear the whispered words. No one but the wind as it whistled in through the open door.

Chapter Eleven

"The weather office is warning everyone to stay off the roads this Tuesday afternoon as sleet and rain combine with snow and high winds to create a huge outdoor skating rink. The storm is expected to continue until well into tomorrow."

Great, Caitlin thought, as she shut off the television. She was stuck at home without a single soul for company.

"It's the perfect time for a little one-on-one with the kitchen," she decided and pulled on a pair of rubber gloves. Two minutes later she was tugging one off to answer the phone.

"I'm fine, Eliza. No, I haven't been out. Beth is at the store and she intends to stay there overnight just in case the flower coolers go out. Maryann and her daughter are visiting out of town."

She paused and listened.

"Really it's fine. I've lots of food, plenty of wood

for the fire, and several really good books. I'll be snuggled in for the duration.''

By the time she rang off, Eliza seemed satisfied that Caitlin was only a phone call away.

''At least now she won't get in her car and drive over here,'' Caitlin muttered, rubbing a sore spot in the center of her back. Two minutes later she heaved herself up from scrubbing the baseboards to answer the phone again.

''Yes, Robyn, your mother just called. Everything's fine. No, I'm not doing anything too strenuous,'' she lied. ''Yes, I'll be fine.''

''Well, whatever you do, just sit tight and relax,'' her sister-in-law ordered before she rang off.

''I'd love to relax,'' Caitlin muttered wryly. ''But the phone keeps ringing.''

With a determined nudge, the worry of being alone receded to the back of her mind. Once the kitchen was clean, she concentrated on removing the mildew from the grout in the bathroom.

By six o'clock there was a glassy sheet of crystal-clear ice in front of the house and down the street as far as she could see. Freezing cold rain dashed down to the ground, sticking to whatever substance it met. Caitlin cringed when she spied the power lines, sagging with their ice-encrusted load.

''It can't be that bad,'' she told herself sternly. ''Mr. Wilson just drove into his yard.''

Unfortunately Mr. Wilson couldn't stop and Caitlin winced as his car plowed into the perfect splendor of his beautiful new oak-paneled garage door.

"That's going to cost some money," she murmured, watching as the elderly man carefully worked his way past the car and up the walk, slipping and sliding from side to side. "But at least he wasn't hurt."

She heaved a sigh of relief when he finally made it inside.

The telephone interrupted her musings and Caitlin absently rubbed her stomach as she answered. These Braxton-Hicks were getting really fierce.

"It's me, honey. Stan says this is our last chance to make it over. Are you sure you don't want us to come?"

"Of course not, Eliza. It's awful outside. Besides, I'm perfectly fine and I can do whatever needs doing around here without you guys risking your lives on those roads."

"You're sure? No baby yet?"

"Of course I'm sure and that question is getting old very quick." She paused, stuffing down frustration. "I'm just going to have some dinner, watch a little television and then head for bed. What could be simpler?"

"And you're not having any contractions? Your water hasn't broken?" Eliza's worried voice carried clearly over the line. "You're past your date, Caitlin, so you have to monitor these things very carefully now."

"I know. And I have been. But there's nothing unusual here, Eliza. Junior is just pushing a little. He thinks his momma is a football, I guess.'' She drew circles on her stomach, hoping to quiet the agile baby.

"Huh! Sounds like Jordan! He was determined not to leave without doing some damage. That boy can't be swayed once he makes up his mind.''

"No, I guess not. Any word from him?'' She hated asking it, but Jordan hadn't phoned her once in the past three days. She missed him, the sound of his booming voice, his capable hands, his tender glances.

"Not a word, though he often doesn't call when he's away on a job. He just shows up once the work is done. I hope he's not flying tonight!''

Something else to worry about, Caitlin thought after hanging up the phone. Imagining Jordan in an airplane in this ice storm made her physically sick and as the bile rose she rushed into the bathroom.

"Why is it that nothing with this pregnancy is going according to the books?'' she asked herself later, having recovered enough strength to down a few more tablespoons of the lukewarm broth. "Evening sickness in the ninth month is not nice!''

She gasped and grabbed her stomach as a fierce cramp seized her belly.

"Now you don't like tomato soup?'' she gasped, breathing more deeply as the sensation eased, then passed. "What a fussy kid.''

Caitlin stood carefully, rubbing her back as she inched forward toward the sofa. If she could just make it there and lie down, everything would be fine.

"Leaving the kitchen,'' she announced and then gasped as warm wet fluid gushed down her legs. "Oh,

no! My water broke!'' She hobbled through to the
laundry room, found some clean clothes and changed
as quickly as she could. She was just easing on her
slippers when the lights flickered.

''No,'' she cried out, gripping the closet door.
''Please not that!''

The lights stayed on until she arrived in the living
room. Then, suddenly, everything was dark. A crack
outside coincided with a flesh-searing contraction that
threatened to tear her insides out.

''Oh, God!'' she breathed with heartfelt appeal.
''The baby's coming and I'm all alone.''

The Lamaze lessons that seemed so simple mere
weeks ago fled her mind and it was all Caitlin could
do to sink into her chair and puff her way through one
contraction after another, wondering at the strength
and intensity of them.

Outside something shattered, then thundered to the
ground, reminding her of the past. It had been exactly
like this the night her parents had died. Her father had
been outside fixing a shutter when the call came about
her grandmother.

They'd scrambled into the car and started out for
the hospital, careening from left to right over the slick
surface, missing cars, posts and red lights by inches.
Only they hadn't missed the last one. A semi-truck,
unable to stop on the glare ice, plowed into them with
a sickening crunch Caitlin could still hear today.

How long had she lain there in the car, waiting for
whatever took her parents to kill her, too? How may
times had she begged God to send someone to help

her mother, to stop that awful wheezing sound she made with every breath?

She came back to reality with a thud. How long had she been lying here, panting her way through one pain after the other?

Oh, God, please send me some help. Why didn't I let Eliza come over? Why was I too proud to ask for help?

The questions boiled through her mind in lucid moments when she wasn't concentrating on her abdomen. During a particularly long lull Caitlin managed to light the big eucalyptus candle that sat on her coffee table, but the light was faint and flickering in the huge room. No streetlights shone outside.

Please God, send me someone. I'm sorry I haven't trusted You. I know I was wrong. I just couldn't shake off the past. But I never really stopped believing in You. Not really. Please forgive me?

The next contraction was the most painful yet and she whimpered in agony, wondering how she would get out of this fix. The telephone! She reached for it, dialed 911 and found the line dead.

Caitlin wanted to light the fire to ward off some of the chill that was seeping through her thin blouse, but she couldn't seem to make it to the fireplace before yet another contraction hit. She breathed it through, reminding herself of the two techniques she could recall. Breathe deeply and relax.

The minutes dragged past, counted off by the mantel clock. Caitlin lost track of everything but the fact that she and the baby were in trouble.

Call upon Me and I will hear you in the day of trouble.

The old Sunday school verse her father had recited so often popped into her mind.

"Okay, God. I'm calling. Please help me in this awful time of trouble. I'm afraid for the baby. Please don't take him. Please God."

She huffed and puffed her way through another pain and then froze as a noise at the front door caught her attention.

Burglars! Looting homes and shops while there was no one to catch them. What would happen when they saw the place wasn't empty?

Caitlin prayed harder, breathed deeper, and counted longer as the contractions dragged out. She strained to hear what was going on at the front door, but her attention strayed, her mind revisiting the terrifying looting scenes she'd seen on television just last week.

I'm here. I've always been here. Call on Me.

"Please, God," she whispered, shrinking as far back into the chair as she could. "Please help me. Send me someone. Please."

The front door creaked open and a shadow inched its way froward. Caitlin could see it all from her chair. Belatedly she wished she'd closed her apartment door. But she'd wanted to waylay anyone who could help her.

The person headed into her living room, carefully edging around the furniture with tentative groping hands. He was big, far too big for her to overpower. As he came closer, Caitlin prayed harder and refused to give in to the agony that racked her body. She bit her lip, closed her eyes and counted to twenty.

"Ouch!" A thud, a crash, and then a voice that was loud and unmistakable. "Good grief!"

"Jordan?" Caitlin could have wept with relief when his face, finally lit by that one flickering candle, swam into her tear-filled view.

He lit the three candles clenched in his hand and stood them on the table, eyes narrowing as he studied her. "Are you all right? I've been phoning for ages, but the line isn't working. Mom said she'd talked to you earlier, but I thought I'd check anyway."

Caitlin couldn't answer, she couldn't move. The best she could manage were short shallow puffs that kept the oxygen moving through her body.

"Caitlin? What's wrong?" He was there, beside her, holding her hands as she let the crest of it roll over her.

"I have to go to the hospital, Jordan. Now. Ooh, here comes another one!" She held on to his hand like a lifeline, refusing to let go until sanity returned.

"You chose tonight to go into labor? Honestly, Caitlin!" A ghost of a grin spread across his pale face. "You are the most stubborn woman I have ever known. I suppose you thought you'd do this alone, too!"

He stopped, winced, flexed his fingers and then held them out again. "Come on, kiddo. Hang on to me. Just keep breathing."

Caitlin renewed her grip on him and prepared for the next wave of unwavering pain. "As if I could stop breathing. I'm beginning to wonder if Robyn was right about you.'' She closed her eyes, concentrated on the searing agony going on inside her body and puffed her way through the contraction.

"Don't you start with me,'' she heard him mutter in a warning that belied his tender touch as he lifted her up and carried her slowly but surely to the front door.

"It's the lousiest night of the year to be driving, you know.'' Jordan's voice was quiet, conversational, with just a hint of steel running through it. "There are lines down everywhere because of the ice. For a woman who doesn't like to live dangerously you sure chose a funny time to have this baby.''

"He chose it. Not me. Ow!''

"But we'll make it, Lyn. We'll make it just fine. You keep hanging on to me.''

"As if,'' she puffed, tightening her hand on his shoulder, "I could do…*puff, puff*…anything else.''

He set her carefully inside his car, did up the seat belt and raced around to climb in the other side. She saw him fumble in his jacket for a moment before his cell phone appeared.

Another contraction hit and Caitlin heard little except Jordan's fierce order to have a doctor standing by.

"Jordan?''

"Yes, sweetheart?'' He revved the engine and slowly backed out of her drive. "What is it?''

"I'm scared, Jordan. Really scared. The contractions came awfully fast after my water broke.'' She swallowed and looked him straight in the eye. "Do you think my baby is all right?"

"I think your baby is just fine, darlin'. A little pushy, maybe, but hey, I'm in favor of pushiness." He grinned, his eyes glittering. "Still, we've got to get you to the hospital now. Couldn't hurt to get a second opinion. Will you trust me to do that?"

Trust him? Of course she trusted him. Jordan was a man of his word. But what if the streets were too icy? What if they had an accident? What if they couldn't get through? The worries swirled around her, sucking her in like an eddy of current.

"Lyn? Sweetheart, if you were thinking about letting God back inside, now would be a really good time. If you trust in Him, ask Him to help us, I know He won't let us down. Can you do that?"

Caitlin stiffened, preparing herself for whatever lay ahead. And then something tweaked at her brain.

"I did pray," she mumbled. "I prayed that God would send someone and He sent you." The very thought of it held her speechless for long tense moments. It was amazing! It was wonderful. It was... God. Talking to her!

He'd answered. She'd called and He'd answered her prayer.

"Just keep praying, honey. Your track record can only get better." Jordan patted her hand, shifted gears and started slowly down the glassy street, steering first left, then right to avoid the downed power lines that littered the area. "Trust God, Lyn. He won't disappoint you."

But Caitlin heard him only vaguely. For some reason the contractions had slowed. Her eyes took in the ravaged streets, the cars that slipped and slid across the road into other cars, smashing metal and grinding bumper to bumper. As Jordan fishtailed his car out of a skid, she was back to the night her parents had died.

"Ice storms are killers," she whispered, mesmerized by the flicker of sparks that shot out from a live wire just fifty feet ahead.

Jordan spared her one quick glance before he jerked the wheel to the right to turn down a different street. "You let God worry about the storm. You just keep praying."

"Watch out," she said as a car in front of them spun on a slick spot.

"It's all right, Caitlin. We're fine. God will take care of us."

"He didn't take care of me. Not at all." She peered out through the windshield, nodding as streetlight after streetlight flickered, then died.

"When my mother was in the car, dying, she told me, 'Be a good girl, Caitlin. Be strong.'" She nodded. "I'll be strong. I will be. I have to be."

Jordan fought to grasp the thread of what she was saying. She'd been in the car with her parents when they'd died? Why hadn't anyone ever told him? Caitlin had heard her mother take her last breath. She'd listened to the last bit of advice her mother had to give.

Be strong.

It was an awful lot to ask of a ten-year-old child. And yet Caitlin had been strong, far stronger than anyone should have to be. Bit by bit understanding flowed into his brain.

This was why she was so determined to go through life alone. It was what she'd always done when life threw a curveball. Be strong. He smiled grimly. Caitlin Andrews was the strongest woman he'd ever met. But it was time for her to learn to lean on someone else.

"Caitlin? Listen sweetheart, we're almost there. The hospital's right ahead. Can you hear me, darling?"

"Hurts," she whispered. "Hurts bad."

"I know, darlin'." He swallowed, carefully edging past the cars and trucks that lined the hospital entrance. He'd have to go around.

"If we trust God, He will always come through for us. Your mom and dad trusted God to take care of you and here you are, getting ready to be a mommy. Just trust a little bit more now. Just a little more. God will take care of you."

"Hard to trust, Jordan. So hard. Hurts to love." She sounded weak, her breathing short, gasping.

Jordan's heart thundered in his chest, but he refused to give up. His brain kept up a steady petition to heaven as he negotiated around the various vehicles that littered the area.

He parked in front of the emergency door. "Here we are, Lyn."

"Don't leave me," she whimpered as he stepped outside of the car.

Jordan hurried around to the other side, opened the

door and lifted her into his arms. "I'm not going anywhere, Lyn. I'll be right here beside you all the way."

"Ooh! Here we go again," she groaned, her fingers twisting in his hair as she wrapped one arm around his neck.

Jordan wanted to groan himself. He wondered if he'd be bald at the end of all this. When her other fist twisted up a handful of his shirt, Jordan lengthened his stride. He had to get her inside, and fast. Thank goodness for the portico that sheltered the driveway from the ice.

He set her down in a wheelchair and gave the doctors the pertinent information, watching as they wheeled her off into a labor room.

"I'll be right there, Lyn," he called to her. "As soon as you get into that bed properly. Just keep trusting."

She blinked, peering up at him as the door closed shut between them. Jordan winced at the sad hurt look in her eyes. She needed her faith now more than ever.

"Please help her," he whispered as he waited for her to reappear. "Please renew her faith and trust and help her to believe. She needs You now more than ever."

He opened his eyes when someone's hand pressed his arm. A nurse, stern but with kindly eyes stood peering up at him.

"She's in hard labor, son. And she's going to need someone to keep her spirits up. It won't be easy, so if you can't do it, you'd better say so right now."

"I can do it," he told her. "I can do whatever needs

to be done. There's no way you're getting rid of me now.'' He visually dared her to try.

To his surprise she smiled.

''Good,'' she nodded. ''Then hang on for the ride.''

Chapter Twelve

"If you even think of uttering one more chicken joke, I'm going to rearrange that handsome face. Ooh!" Caitlin's meager grin twisted into a grimace as she braced herself, hands closing around Jordan's arm.

"Breathe," he told her. "In and out, just let it go. That's good, darlin'. Very good." He kept murmuring compliments until she finally relaxed, her face drained and white.

"I am breathing, you know," Caitlin complained, her fingers unwrapping from his forearm. "It's not as if I can just stop!"

Jordan wondered if he'd have any skin left there when this baby finally arrived.

"Okay, sweetheart. Okay. You're doing fine. Everything's fine." He repeated the phrase as much to reassure himself as her.

"Stop telling me the same thing over and over."

She didn't look like she was joking. "I know what's fine and this isn't it!"

"All right." He kept his voice amiable. "What would you like me to say instead?"

"Caitlin Andrews is the smartest woman I know," she gasped, and returned her fingers to the permanent indentations in his arm. "Here we go again!"

"Caitlin Andrews is the smartest, most beautiful, least stubborn, most caring, forgiving and absolutely amazing woman I know," he whispered, brushing her hair back and dabbing at her forehead with a washcloth. He pressed a kiss there for good measure.

"That's more like it," she grunted.

Jordan could see her tiring little by little with each contraction. It had been hours and nothing seemed to be happening.

"Okay, darlin'. I'm here. Hang on. Here we go again." He brushed his hand over her tummy in circles, just the way the nurse had told him to. "Okay, Lyn. That's right. You're doing great! Junior's coming right along."

"He's sure taking his time." She puffed, face taut with tiredness. "Can I have an ice chip?"

"You've already had…"

"Andrews, give me that ice!"

She definitely wasn't joking now. Jordan slipped the chip between her teeth and watched as she sucked at it greedily.

"I'm just going to check you again, Caitlin. Try not to tense up." Dr. Warren smiled, her eyes sparkling above her mask. "You've certainly got a good helper in this guy. He doesn't complain at all."

"He's not allowed to," Caitlin muttered, her eyes dull. "He insisted on being here, and I'm not letting him go home early."

"That's for sure." Jordan grinned to show he didn't hold any grudges. "She likes to drag things out."

He kept his focus on Caitlin, but didn't miss the doctor's narrowed eyes, or quick flash of concern. When she raised her eyebrows, he nodded.

"Caitlin, Jordan's just about worn-out. I want him to go sit down and get a cup of coffee. Is that okay?"

Caitlin frowned, glancing from one to the other.

"You're leaving?"

"No way. Just getting a drink. You're not very good about sharing your ice." Jordan grinned, patted her hand and leaned down to brush her cheek with his lips. "I'll be right back, I promise. Meanwhile, the nurse will stay with you."

He gave her a thumbs up and headed for the door. "What's wrong?" he asked the doctor the moment they cleared the doorway. "What's the matter?"

Dr. Warren sighed. "She's not progressing at all and I'm getting concerned. Dilation hasn't changed. According to the monitor, the baby's heart isn't recovering as fast as we'd like after the contractions, either. It's probably tiring. So is Caitlin. I don't like it."

"What's the answer?"

"C-section. Get the baby out and give the mom a

break.'' Dr. Warren's eyes met his. ''You don't think she'll go for it.''

''I doubt it. Caitlin likes to be in control. She can't believe that things will be okay if she trusts someone else. I can't imagine she'll agree to an operation. Can we wait a bit?''

Dr. Warren shook her head, her forehead pleated in a frown.

''Not much longer. I think we should start preparing her for it. I don't see any other way.''

''I'll try to talk her into it, but you might just have to go ahead and operate.''

Jordan turned to go back in, his mind busy. Before he entered the room, he pulled out his cell phone and dialed his parents' home number to update them on Caitlin's condition. And once more he pleaded with them not to risk driving to the hospital.

''You're getting tired, Lyn. Try to relax.'' He said as he entered the room, though he knew it was a stupid thing to say as soon as the words came out. Evidently she agreed.

''Gee thanks, Jordan. Okay, I'll just close my eyes and pretend it's not happening. Ow!'' Her fingers dug into his arm extra deep. ''Sorry. Your method doesn't work very well. Oh, I want to go home.''

He stared at the fetal monitor, willing it to speed up. A moment later her eyes opened and her gaze followed his.

''It's taking longer for it to go up, isn't it?'' she whispered, her face growing even paler. ''I thought it was my imagination.''

"The doctors are getting a bit concerned," he told her plainly. "They're thinking about a cesarean."

"No way!" She puffed her way through the next pain, pinching his arm and glaring at him all the while. "I'm not letting myself be put under so I'll be helpless to fight for this child. No way! Besides, an operation would be hard on him, too."

"Lyn, remember what I said about trusting. God will take care of things if we trust in Him."

"It's so hard. Ooh." Finally she got through the crest of it and then watched the monitor as closely as everyone else.

"I'm afraid there's not a lot of choice, Caitlin. That baby needs to come out. Now. We're going to take every precaution." Dr. Warren looked stern. "We can't afford much more time."

Her face blanched, her big green eyes full of fear. "I'm scared, Jordan. It'll be like in the car, black and lonely, all by myself. I can't do that again. What if they make a mistake?"

"No one's going to make a mistake tonight, Caitlin. Dr. Warren is the smartest baby doctor I know."

Also the only one, but Jordan wasn't going into that now.

"And besides, God's in control. Isn't He, Lyn?" Maybe if he got her to admit it, she'd relax.

"I don't know." She hesitated, staring up at him, never looking away as the contraction tore through her body, her voice a faint whimper of agony.

Jordan stared at her intently, allowing some of her

fear to penetrate his brain. It was time to deal with this cleanly. Here and now.

"I want everyone to leave. Just for a moment." Dr. Warren tipped her head to one side and he nodded. "Just for a minute."

When they were gone, Jordan bent over Caitlin. He brushed his hand over her forehead tenderly, willing her to feel his love.

"Caitlin, I know you've had it rough. It's been a long hard path and it's taken a lot out of you. But you have to let the doctor help you. Help the baby. You have to face the fear, let someone else take control now. You can't do it all alone anymore."

"But what if something goes wrong?"

"There's always that possibility, sweetheart. But life is full of chances. You have to trust that God will do what's right for both of you. You have to get rid of the fear now. This is no place for being frightened. This is the place to put your trust in One who knows and cares about you."

"But to go under that anesthetic, to miss out on everything? Besides, anesthetics can slow down the baby's heart rate."

"I care, Lyn. And I'm not going anywhere. I love you and I love the baby. I'll be here. I'll be Michael's proxy, just for a while. I'll be here to welcome this baby into the world. I'll make sure everything's okay."

"And if something happens to me, you'll take over? You'll look after my baby?" Her lips trembled as she uttered the unthinkable.

Jordan placed his fingers across them, stopping the words. "Nothing is going to happen while God is in control. And He is, isn't He, Lyn?"

She nodded slowly, finally admitting it. Jordan heaved a sigh of relief.

"That's right. And this baby is His special gift to you."

"That's why I don't want anything to happen." She looked lost and forlorn in the big, sterile room with its chrome machines glittering nearby.

"That's why you've got to rely on God, to trust in Him. He's bigger, more powerful than the doctors. He'll take care of you both, if you'll ask Him."

He prayed fervently as the silence stretched between them. He could see her wrestling with the issue, trying to resolve it as she strained through another contraction. Finally she nodded.

"All right. I'll ask Him." She closed her eyes and prayed, voice soundless but lips moving.

He waited, willing the fetal monitor to speed up and desperately praying when it didn't. Lyn watched too, chewing her lip until the heartbeat finally resumed, her breath whooshing out in a sigh of relief.

"Okay, I'll let them operate."

"God *is* going to get you through this, Lyn," he murmured. His hand held hers firmly as the nurse injected a solution into the drip bag.

She whispered just before she lost consciousness, "I trust Him."

Jordan couldn't help a wash of relief as he watched the nurses readying her for surgery.

"Okay, let's move. We've got a baby to deliver, people." Dr. Warren patted Jordan's hand, holding him back as the nurses rolled Caitlin out of the room and down the hall. "She'll be fine."

"I promised I'd be there for the baby." He met her frown head on. "I intend to keep that promise."

After a long pause, the doctor nodded. "Very well. I'll let you watch. Under one condition. You don't faint on me. I haven't got time for a fainter. I've got enough to deal with."

"I won't faint," he told her, following her down the hall to the OR. "There's too much at stake."

The nurse swathed him in baggy green clothes and then showed him where to stand.

He held Caitlin's hand as the surgical team moved in. "I'm not going anywhere, Lyn. I'm right here."

"She's ready?" Dr. Warren waited for the anesthetist's nod. "Okay, folks. Let's get that baby here. Now."

Jordan didn't hear anything else. He focused his prayers on heaven, pouring an unremitting barrage upward as he watched the face he loved more than life.

"Please help her now. Please. She needs this baby to affirm Your love. Keep them both in the shelter of Your arms."

He didn't know how long he prayed. He only became aware of the others in the room when the nurse touched his arm. He let go of Caitlin's hand and set it gently back on the bed, reassured by the steady rise and fall of her chest.

"Here she is," the nurse chirped, her countenance

glorious. "A gorgeous baby girl." She settled the tiny bundle in his arms, her hands at the ready in case he failed this first test.

Jordan gulped.

A girl, a tiny perfect little girl.

Michael's daughter.

She had a patch of reddish brown hair and clear pink skin that felt delicately thin and oh, so soft when he grazed a hand over her flailing arm.

"Hello, baby," he whispered, smiling as her tiny fingers closed around his thumb. "Welcome to our world."

Time stood still as the baby lay in his arms. His brother's child. Alive and healthy. Jordan whispered a thank-you to heaven at the blessed weight of her in his arms. She opened her eyes, huge blue eyes that reminded him of his brother, and blinked up at him. He thought he could see a question there.

"Your daddy couldn't be here and your mommy's sleeping," he whispered. "You gave her quite a time. Anyway, I'm here to make sure nothing bad happens. I'll always be here. Whenever you need me." He wasn't aware of the passage of time or the other voices in the room. All he could see was the blind trust in those precious eyes.

A flash of light obscured his vision for a moment. Then the nurse held out a picture.

"She'll want to know you were there to greet her baby." Her voice was soft and caring.

"Thank you," Jordan managed to whisper. When she held out her arms for the baby, he fought the urge to keep her nestled close to his heart. "Is she all right?"

"She's perfect. Wouldn't you say so, Dr. Warren?"

The doctor was stripping off her gloves. She stood for a moment, watching as Caitlin was wheeled into recovery. Then her glance came back to the baby, now curled up in an isolette.

"She's doing very well. Her color is good, her Apgar rating was high. I'm not anticipating any problems." She laid a hand on his arm. "Caitlin is fine, too. Everything went very smoothly."

"I'll go sit with her until she wakes up."

Dr. Warren followed him out. "She's going to be upset."

"I know." He didn't want to think about just how furiously angry Caitlin would be. "But you tell me, was there another choice?"

The doctor shook her head, her eyes serious. "Not in my opinion."

"Then I can live with whatever comes. They're both alive and that's what I prayed for."

She led him toward the recovery room, let him wait outside until Caitlin was ready. Then when the small russet-haired form was wheeled back to her room, Jordan sank down wearily on a stool beside the bed and took Caitlin's small, delicate hand once more, tracing the veins that pulsed with her life blood.

"I'm here, Lyn. Waiting for you to wake up. You have a lovely daughter, sweetheart. She's just as pretty as her mother. Come on, darlin'! It's time to open those peepers."

He was jolted out of his stupor by the clench of fingers on his.

"Michael? I really do love you, Michael."

The whisper-soft garble of words stabbed him as deeply as any spear.

"I'll still trust," he muttered, his heart aching. "No matter what, I'll trust in You. Even if the only woman I've ever loved is still in love with my brother."

Chapter Thirteen

Caitlin allowed Eliza to lift the sleeping ten-day-old baby out of her arms. She smiled at the soft looks that covered the dear faces that had gathered around to welcome them back to Wintergreen. Maryann with her daughter Amy, Beth and Veronica, Clay, Garrett, Eliza and Stan, the girls and Jordan.

But when her gaze came to the baby, her gaze stopped there, her heart pounding at the love that swelled within. She was so tiny, so delicate, such a miracle. And her own mother hadn't been awake to witness her arrival.

She clenched her teeth, holding the smile in place with difficulty.

"She's such a darling, Caitlin. I can't believe she's finally here!" Robyn brushed a finger over the soft bloom of the baby's cheek. "And so big! It's a good thing you didn't have to push her out, Caitlin."

Caitlin smiled. "Yes, isn't it just?" She refused to

look at Jordan where he stood, leaning against the doorjamb of the living room.

"Are you feeling all right?" Olivia fluttered around her, bringing a pillow and a cover to make her more comfortable. "Is the incision still bothering you?"

"Not as much. It's been a while now and I'm feeling much better. It's nice to be home." That was a lie. She felt worse than she had in months, but it would pass. Anyway, what did it matter now that Micah was here?

"That's good. Well, come on everyone. Let's leave the little mother to rest, now that the baby's asleep."

They filed out, one after the other, pressing a kiss to her cheek before they left.

"Thanks for coming. I appreciate everything you've done." Caitlin smiled until they left, then sagged into her chair, relieved that she didn't have to pretend anymore.

"You're in pain. Here." Jordan handed her a white tablet and glass of water. "You can keep on ignoring me all you like, Lyn, but I'm not going anywhere. I promised."

"For the tenth time, I'm releasing you from that promise. I should never have asked it of you."

"I didn't make the promise to you, I made it to Micah right after she was born. And I'm not taking it back. Not ever. You can be as angry as you want, Caitlin, but I'd do the same thing again tomorrow."

She watched as he set the tumbler and pill down on the table and ensconced himself in her armchair. The anger, all the frustration welled up inside and she couldn't control the bitter words that poured out.

"I know, Jordan. And believe me, I'm grateful. That's what makes it so awful. It's just…" She gulped down the tears that clogged her throat. "I wanted to deliver Micah myself."

He got up, crossed the room and squatted at her feet. "I'm sorry, sweetheart. I know you're unhappy that you weren't awake when she was born. It doesn't mean anything, though. God still gave you a healthy little girl. She came through with flying colors. And you're getting better by the day. Can't you be happy about that?"

His hands closed around hers, warm and comforting and Caitlin felt overwhelmed with guilt. Why did she continue to harangue him when she knew it had to be that way?

That question was closely followed by a harder one.

Why did it always have to be that way? Why couldn't anything go according to the way she planned?

"You trusted Him, just a little, and He came through for you. Micah is the richest blessing He could have given you."

"I know." She kept her head bent, trying to ignore the wash of feelings that flowed through her every time she saw Jordan hold her daughter. "And I love her. She's so beautiful. She's so fragile! I'm just a little emotional lately."

He was as tender as any father could be, quieting her cries, singing her songs, even changing her diaper.

His love for the baby shone through in everything he did, including the small kindnesses he showered on her mother.

"I haven't thanked you for the flowers yet," she murmured, with a glance at the gorgeous red roses that overflowed her crystal vase. "You didn't have to do that."

"Yes, I did." He grinned, seating himself carefully on the cushions beside her. "I love you. And I'm proud of you. God has blessed me with the two most beautiful women in the world and I just had to share the joy." He pressed a kiss against her forehead.

"Look at that little miracle and tell me you're glad you had that operation. Caitlin. Please? There wasn't anything else we could have done."

The doctor had said the same thing the day she'd left the hospital. And Micah was a delight. Maybe it was time to let go of her anger, to give him a chance. After all, he'd stuck with her through everything. She'd been so ungrateful and he'd done so much. Why did she have to hide her feelings?

"I don't like being railroaded, Jordan. If you're going to stay in our lives, you have to stop being so pushy. I told you I didn't want milk and yet you still keep pouring me a glass. Those kinds of things do not make you likable." She smiled to show she was teasing.

"I'm already likable," he quipped, pressing a quick kiss to her lips. "It's just taking you longer to see it."

She pinched his arm.

"All right!" He held up both hands. "If you don't

want milk, fine. No big deal. How do you feel about pudding?''

''Jordan!'' Caitlin glared at him, but was unable to stop the corner of her mouth from turning up at his obvious caring. But then, that was the problem.

Jordan cared for her. In fact, he loved her. He'd told her far too many times for her to ignore it anymore. And Caitlin didn't know what to do about it. Here she was, mother to his brother's child, and he was acting as if he were the father. The whole situation was so confusing.

What do I feel? she asked herself for the twentieth time. What do I really feel deep down inside?

The answer wasn't easy, of course. Frustration and excitement, anger and thanksgiving, tiredness and exhilaration, pain and pleasure, happy yet sad. Everything. And nothing.

It was all mixed-up, confused. But she had Micah. That made up for all of it.

Did that mean God had answered her prayers? Or was this some sort of test?

''You're very beautiful, did you know that?'' Jordan trailed a finger down the length of her nose. ''Your skin glows and you look positively radiant.''

''I look like I just gave birth to an eight-pound baby girl,'' Caitlin snorted. ''And you can't keep changing the subject. You have to stop hovering, Jordan. We're fine.''

''I know.'' He smiled tenderly. ''But I like hovering, as you call it. Especially when it's over my two favorite women. So, now that the baby's here, can we talk about getting married?''

Caitlin gulped.

"I know you're tired and there are a hundred things going through your mind. My sister explained ad nauseam about hormones.'' He made a face, his mouth tipping downward in disgust.

"She did? Robyn?'' Caitlin frowned at his nod. "What did she say?''

"Oh, a bunch of stuff about women who had C-sections feeling guilty because they didn't have a normal delivery. I told her she was crazy.'' He reached out and touched the baby's arm. "As if there's anything to feel guilty about. This little girl is a miracle.''

"Yes, I'm beginning to realize that.'' Caitlin stared at the child who had come from her body. The thought of it stunned her. The perfectly shaped lips, the elegantly long fingers, the deep blue eyes. Micah was a miracle. And Jordan had helped get her here. She peered at him through her lashes.

"The thing is, I don't want to waste that miracle. I love you, Lyn. I want to marry you and take care of you and Micah. Couldn't we at least plan a date?''

She forced her attention away from him to stare at her fingers.

"Jordan, I've told you. I don't think I can marry you. Not now.'' *Maybe not ever,* she added silently.

"Sure you can. Doesn't have to be a big wedding, though I'd like to show you off to everyone. We could have the ceremony right here, if you want.'' His eyes shone down on her expectantly. "What do you say?''

"Jordan, I, uh, that is…the truth is, I'm not sure. I mean, everything seems so unreal to me. Everything is moving so fast. I just became a mother and now you're asking me to marry you. It's impossible to deal with!"

"Why?" His eyes narrowed, their golden lights piercing. "Are you going to say you don't love me? Because you do, Lyn. I've seen it in your eyes." His voice was so fervent she half wondered if he wasn't trying to convince himself.

"You've been really wonderful to us, coming round day after day, helping with the baby, taking care of things. And I appreciate it, Jordan. But…" Her voice trailed away as she searched for the words to express her confused feelings.

"You love me. You can't deny it. It's been there for a long time now. It's time you admit it, Lyn."

"I do like you, Jordan."

"Love," he insisted, his mouth tightening.

"I like the way you care for us, the way you make me feel loved and protected. But to get married? I don't think so, Jordan. Not yet, anyway."

"When then?"

"I don't know. Don't you see?" She was losing her focus and that was dangerous with those tiger eyes watching. "I feel like I'm only just getting back control of my life. Coming out of the anesthetic was like being back in that car, clawing my way to safety." She shuddered at the memory. "I felt like I was at the mercy of everybody while I recovered and I hated it."

His eyes demanded total honesty, and Caitlin acknowledged that she owed him that.

"If I let myself get involved with you, I lose that control again. I don't think I'm ready to do that just yet." She flinched as his jaw tightened.

"We are already *involved*," he said, lurching to his feet. "That's what love is all about." He glared into the fireplace as if he wanted to tear it apart.

"And now we get to the heart of the issue. Control. But what you really mean is that you want to go it alone, prove to the world that you can stand out there and take whatever it is that life deals you."

He turned around, his eyes blazing. "Why, Caitlin? Why is it so important for you to be strong and independent, even at the risk of refusing help for your unborn baby?"

"I didn't," she gasped, furious that he would dare to mention that now.

"Yes, you did. And I don't think it has anything to do with fear, Lyn. It's really all about anger, isn't it? You're furious at all the people you love who go away when you need them most. So you back away from love, hide out, protect yourself. That way no one can ever hurt you again."

"I don't do that." But she couldn't look at him, his words cut too deep. Was she really like that? Selfish and self-centered?

"Yes, you do, Lyn. And it hurts. I think you're trying to prove you don't need us." He sighed, raking a hand through his hair.

"Michael didn't *want* to die, Caitlin. Neither did

your parents or your aunt. They didn't *want* to abandon you. It wasn't their fault that God called them home.'' He stopped, watching her face.

Caitlin shook her head, all the while his words raced through it. Was it true? Was she angry with all of them? Was she trying to get even in some strange way?

''You're just jealous because I chose Michael,'' she lashed out, and then wished she hadn't. Jordan was moving closer, so close she feared he wouldn't let her hide any more.

He smiled tenderly, his hands gentle as they closed around her arms.

''I know you loved my brother, Caitlin. I've accepted that. You've just had his baby. That's wonderful. Nobody could be happier than me.'' He brushed a thumb over her blouse-covered arm, fingering the warm flannel.

''But he's gone now, honey. And you love me. There's nothing wrong with that. Love isn't meant to be hoarded, it's meant to be shared. It can grow and grow.''

He wrapped his arms around her and hugged her close, his voice soothing.

''For a long time I fought against the idea of loving you, even though I knew it was true. I thought it was disloyal to Michael. You were his wife, you chose him over me. I realized almost immediately that I'd been wrong to let you go back then, you know. I had to get away from here.'' He brushed his chin against her cheek.

"When I came home, after you were married, I realized that I loved you more than ever. But you weren't mine. Still, you were very happy. I could see that. I decided that I would go away again and that I would wait. I knew the love I had for you wouldn't die. I thought I'd see what God intended for me to do with it." His hands brushed down her back.

"But sweetheart, that love didn't go away and Michael did die. He didn't want to, but he's gone. And it isn't your fault. You can't make yourself pay for his death, or your parents'. That was part of your life. A hard part, sure. But you got through it." He leaned back, his generous mouth tipped down in a frown.

"You need to accept the past and move on, Lyn. You can't make anything better by hanging on to your anger. Let it go."

Jordan's eyes glowed with an inner light that made his words all the more tenable.

"You're not a child anymore, you know that God directs our paths. You've grown up. You don't have to hide away anymore, like a scared little girl who needs protecting. You don't have to prove you can handle life. You've done that. Now you can get on with your life, because you know that He'll be there, watching out for you."

His words hit a nerve. Caitlin felt the frustration rise inside her brain, red-hot and boiling. What did he really understand? The long lonely nights when the house creaked and moaned, the reminders that she had no one of her own, the longing she felt to let go of it all and be someone completely different? Someone not quite so pathetic?

Jordan Andrews thought that he knew everything about her, that he could direct her to do his bidding no matter what she wanted. Whatever he said was law! What did he know about her worries, her fears?

"You know nothing!"

"I know more than you want me to. I know you're letting the past control the future. Our future. But I won't let you ignore our relationship. I won't."

She shoved him away, walked over to the door and yanked it open.

"You think you've got me pegged, don't you, Jordan? You think it's so easy to just toss it all away, to forget about my parents dying so horribly while I lived and watched it, to see Aunt Lucy every day and know I didn't matter to her, to pretend Michael's death didn't affect me?"

She dashed the tears away, drawing on the facade that had seen her through years of going it alone.

"I'm strong because I learned that everything comes with a price. It just depends on how much you're willing to pay."

"I know all of that affected you, Lyn. It colored the past and altered your perceptions. But now it's getting in the way of your life today."

"Thank you, Dr. Freud! Why would you even think that I could love somebody who's so hard? Michael was your brother!"

"I know that." He stood before her, his shoulders straight, his eyes shadowed. "And I loved him. But I can't live in the past, Lyn. Neither can you. I love you. I want to move on with our lives. I want all of the things God promised us.''

He slipped his hand over the shining fall of curls that tumbled down her back. His touch was so delicate, so tender, Caitlin almost leaned into it.

But fear, her constant companion for years, held her back, restrained by her whispering *what ifs* inside her brain.

''I'm waiting for you, Caitlin. My family is waiting for you. We want you to join the living. They don't care that you locked them out of your life for so long. They're ready to welcome you back with open arms.'' Jordan swallowed. His hands dropped to his sides and his head tilted back.

Caitlin shivered, knowing something monumental would come out of those soft lips. She steeled herself.

''If your life isn't full and happy today, Caitlin, the only person you can blame is yourself. We're here, all of us. We want to love you. But you have to let us in. You can't keep withdrawing. You have to choose what you want, sweetheart. Fear, anger or love?''

Caitlin swallowed. There were tears at the corners of his eyes. His voice was sad, filled with regret.

''I can't come back, Lyn. Not until you're ready to face life and deal with its possibility of hurt. None of us controls life, that's up to God. But if we don't accept the pain, we miss the pleasure.'' He wrapped his arms around her and held her close to his heart, his lips against her ear.

''I love you and Micah so much. I want us to be a

family, to grow together. I want to share your pain,
your fears, your joys. I want to laugh with you and
grieve with you. But you have to want it, too. It's time
to grow up, Lyn. It's time to choose. What will it be?
Love? Or safety by yourself in your shell of self-
pity?''

Jordan kissed her so tenderly Caitlin thought she'd
melt. She could have stayed there forever, but mere
seconds later his arms fell away.

His lips touched hers one last time, his voice aching
in its intensity. When he looked at her, she could feel
the love in his eyes reaching out, desperately trying to
touch her frozen heart.

''Choose love, Caitlin. Please, choose me.''

And then he was gone.

Chapter Fourteen

"Choose me."

Caitlin shook herself out of the fog Jordan had left her in.

She closed the door, entered her apartment and started up the stairs, determined to get on with her life. She was a single mother, alone, with a baby. She had responsibilities. She had to be strong.

The sound of brakes applied too heavily rang through the house. Caitlin stopped, her eyes wide with fear. Jordan! Was he hurt?

"Not again! Please God, not again! I can't lose Jordan, too. I love him so much."

The knowledge coursed through her like a lightning bolt, awakening her to the folly of letting him go.

She'd let him walk out the door without telling him how much she loved him. Not the same as she'd loved Michael, it was true. This love was different. But it was a deep and lasting love that would be a foundation for the future.

Caitlin raced for the front door, ripped it open and stood on tiptoes, staring to the west as her heart beat double time. What was the pain of the past compared to the grief she now felt, knowing she'd turned him away, knowing she loved him more than life.

Relief swamped her as she spied his car, patiently waiting at the end of the block for a young boy to cross the intersection.

Jordan, dear Jordan. He was fine. He was alive!

Caitlin sank down onto the thickly braided rug inside the front door of Wintergreen, her mind whirling with the wonder of it.

She loved Jordan Andrews. Loved him. With all her heart and soul and mind. Of course, she had loved Michael, too; but that was a different kind of love. She'd been young and needy. She'd expected Michael to care for her, to protect her, to cherish her. She'd never even considered what her young husband might need from her, and never found out how their marriage would have worked, what she would have contributed to their union.

But she had to consider it now. Jordan was here, alive and well, and in love with her. He didn't want a little girl for a wife, he wanted a woman who was prepared to stand by his side and face the world head-on, good or bad.

"He needs me to be there for him," she murmured,

trying to sort it all out. "He wants me to share his life."

But to share meant giving herself, freely, without holding back. Could she do that? Anything less would be cheating, a childish pretense that would hurt him. And she and Micah would suffer as much as Jordan. They needed him in their lives, needed his comfort, his compassion, his strength.

But most of all they needed his love, backing them, supporting them as they supported him. There would be problems, certainly. But, oh, the joy she'd share. How wonderful it would be to just let go and love him.

Jordan was gone.

He wouldn't come back. Not now. Not when she'd turned him away, mocked him for pointing out how childish she had been. He'd given her the chance, asked her to trust him, and she'd turned him away, let him walk out of her life and Micah's.

Bleakly she watched the taillights of his car disappear.

Caitlin pushed the door closed, then burst into tears at the enormity of what she'd done. Jordan had left believing that she didn't want him, didn't need his arms around her, his lips close to hers. How could she have denied herself the one thing she most wanted?

"Caitlin? Caitlin, what in the world is wrong?" Maryann stood inside, staring. After a moment she hunched down beside her, tugging at her shoulder. "Is it the baby?"

"Why doesn't she answer? What's wrong with her?" Beth's concerned voice only encouraged her tears and Caitlin sobbed all the harder.

"I forgot to tell you... What in the world is going on here?" Eliza's worried voice broke through the others' conversation. She listened to the others for a moment, then tugged on Caitlin's arm.

"Tell me what's wrong?" she encouraged, a tiny smile twitching at the corner of her lips.

"She keeps asking for Jordan."

"Ah! I thought so. Come on, dear. Inside before you catch your death." They urged her to the sofa. "Spill it all," Eliza ordered.

"I've ruined everything," Caitlin sobbed after the whole story had poured out. "He'll think I only want him here for Micah if I tell him I love him now. He'll think I can't stand on my own two feet!"

"Good gracious. I've never seen you so out of control. Mop up, my girl. We've got work to do. I haven't coaxed and coached things this far to let everything fall apart now."

Eliza motioned to Beth and Maryann and Caitlin watched as they formed a circle in the middle of the room.

"What are you talking about?" she asked uncertainly. There was something in Eliza's glance that sent a squiggle of reservation up her spine.

"We're talking about your future, my dear. A wonderful happy future that you deserve and that I intend to see that you have." She smiled. "You don't think

I'm going to throw all my hard work away, do you? No sir!''

Caitlin thought she looked like a cat that had lunched on a canary and now just finished a very big bowl of thick cream.

"Now go with Maryann, my dear. She'll help you change. Beth and I have things to do. First of all we need flowers. Lots of flowers.''

"What things? Why do I need to change?'' Caitlin dashed the tears from her eyes, frowning at them all. "What are you doing?''

"Playing Fairy Godmother,'' Eliza giggled as she brushed a stack of baby clothes into Maryann's arms and waved her arm toward the stairs. "It's my best role.''

Caitlin flinched, stunned by the glow of anticipation in those eyes that were so like her baby's.

"Come on, Caitlin. Let's get you pretty.''

Caitlin trailed Maryann up the stairs, her forehead creased. "What are they doing?''

"Planning a nice romantic dinner for you and Jordan. And it's about time!''

Two hours after he'd left Lyn's, Jordan was headed back. He kept his foot pressed to the floor, ignoring the yellow lights and honking horns. Caitlin needed him his mother said. There was no time to dillydally. This was important.

He made the corner to her cul-de-sac on two wheels, barely missing a station wagon that was illegally parked by a hydrant.

"Calm down," he ordered his racing heart. "Everything's fine. The baby's not sick, Lyn's okay. Mom would have said if it was serious. Take a deep breath. You're not a kid going out on his first date!"

It didn't help much. He still lurched to a stop in front of the old Victorian house with a squeal that would have done a teenager proud.

"Probably burst a pipe in this mausoleum," he consoled himself as he loped up the walkway and took the stairs three at a time. "Or the furnace went out. Yeah, that's probably it. The furnace."

He punched her doorbell four times in rapid succession before he could physically force his hand down. The door was oak and really solid, but he figured if she didn't answer in about twenty seconds, he would kick it in.

The door opened.

"Hi." Lyn, his Lyn, stood there smiling, her hair gleaming as it flowed over her shoulders in a river of curls. She wore a dress in some green velvet stuff that showed she hadn't kept so much as an ounce of Micah's baby fat. If she had, it was well placed. "Come on in."

Jordan stepped through the door, puzzled by her calm demeanor and elegant dress. Surely that oaf Matthews wasn't going to show up again?

"Uh, Mom said you needed me?" He let her take his coat, then followed meekly when she led the way into her apartment.

"Yes. Yes, Jordan I do."

Inside the door, he stopped short and stared. There were candles everywhere, flickering on the soft light of late afternoon. A fire glowed in the hearth, flowers bloomed on the mantel. To Jordan it looked like home.

"Come on in. Dinner's ready whenever we are." She smiled at him and he got lost in that look. Her eyes glowed with something warm and exciting. What was it?

Jordan swallowed when she turned around, and followed her, trailing behind, through to the dining room.

"Have a seat."

He stayed where he was, his eyes fixed on the gorgeous bouquet of red roses sitting in the middle of a table prepared for an intimate dinner for two. He looked at her again. She was smiling that smile again. His palms started to sweat. Something told him this wasn't a dress rehearsal for Clay.

"Uh, Caitlin?"

"Yes?" She stood there, waiting, her hands clasped together in front of her.

"What exactly is this about?"

She smiled. It started in her eyes, but the effect was transported across her entire face.

"I just thought you might like to enjoy a nice romantic dinner before I ask you to marry me."

Jordan gulped. He couldn't move, couldn't look away from her. His whole body was on full alert. Was she serious? It was too good to be true, wasn't it?

Then he saw her fingers knot together and knew that she was just as nervous as he. That unlocked the block of his chest. He walked over to where she stood and took her hands in his, warming their icy coldness with his warmth.

"*You're* going to ask *me* to marry *you?*"

She nodded. "Mmm-hmm."

"Why?"

"Because I love you. I have for a long time. I've tried to run from it, pretend it isn't there, blame it on Micah. I can't do it anymore. I'm too old to play games. I don't even want to."

"What do you want?" He didn't know how he got the words out of his mouth, his heart was beating so fast.

"I want to be your wife, to live with you, to share your dreams. I don't want to run away anymore, Jordan."

He pulled her into his arms, prepared to forgive anything as long as she loved him.

She tugged back. "Wait a minute, Jordan. I have to say this first."

"It doesn't matter, Lyn. None of it. I love you, you love me. That's what counts. And Micah, of course." He grinned, ecstatic that he wouldn't miss any time away from the little girl.

"It does matter, Jordan. Micah is Michael's daughter. I can't change that. I don't want to." She took a deep breath and continued.

Jordan watched the flicker of candlelight on her face and wondered uncertainly if they would ever get past Michael and find their own place.

"When I married Michael, I was a child. A girl who was so afraid of life that she grabbed on to the first anchor she found. I loved him without knowing what love meant and he was gone before I could find out." She searched his face, eyes dark with worry. "Do you understand?"

He nodded.

"When you came back, I realized that I didn't really know anything about love. Michael was the giver, I was the taker."

"He wanted it that way, Lyn. Michael loved you."

"I know." She sighed, unshed tears making her jade eyes glisten. "But I've grown up now, Jordan. I've learned that God is the only shield I need against trouble. He'll always be there, no matter what. I can face anything with you. Anything."

"I love you," he whispered. Then he kissed her as he'd longed to do so many years ago, just last week, early one morning when he'd visited her at the hospital and found she was coming home.

"I love you so much."

She relaxed against him, her fingers twining about his neck. He would have kissed her again, long and satisfyingly, except that she tilted her head back and raised one eyebrow.

"What?" He was half-afraid to ask.

"Well, I was just wondering if this means you'll marry me. Please? Forever. As long as we both shall live."

A sparkle in her eyes told him she already knew the answer, so he pretended to prevaricate.

"Hmm. I'll have to think about it. Does Micah come as part of the deal? She's already my daughter in here." He tapped his chest.

She frowned. "Of course!"

"And will you promise to love, honor and *obey* me?" He burst out laughing at the dour look on her face.

"You're pushing it, Jordan! I meant for this to be a happy evening. I mean, I have the ring and everything." She pulled the black box out of her pocket.

"Oh, you got me an engagement ring?" He flipped the lid open and lifted out the ring he'd chosen weeks ago, shaking his head as he turned the ring from side to side. Its facets shimmered and shone in the candlelight.

"I have to tell you, Lyn, this is a little gaudy for me."

She held out her left hand and slipped her finger inside the ring before he could move.

"I'll just look after it for you then, shall I?" Her eyes sparkled up at him.

"For how long?" he demanded, replacing his arm around her waist.

"Forever," she promised, sealing the deal with a kiss.

A long time later Jordan glanced at his ring on her finger.

"I have to tell you, I don't think this is such a good

deal,'' he complained, snuggling her head against his shoulder as they both watched the baby sleep.

"Why?" She stared at her hand, twisting her finger this way and that in the moonlight. "I think it's a great deal."

"What do I get as a reminder of your promise of love?" he demanded. "How do I know that you won't run away the first time I muddy the kitchen floor or forget to wash the porridge pot?"

"You never mentioned porridge." Caitlin frowned.

"I didn't?" He brushed a knuckle down her nose. "I love porridge. Especially if it's a day old or so."

She reached up to stroke one hand across his chin.

"I'll tell you what. The day we're married, I'll give you my promise embedded in gold and fixed on your finger for life. As long as you promise to wash the pot when you're finished."

He pretended to consider it.

"I guess that would be okay. When and where are we getting married?"

"At Wintergreen, of course!" She looked scandalized that he hadn't thought of it. "After all, it's only fitting that the Widow of Wintergreen renounce her status as an independent, self-reliant woman. And when else would we get married but at Thanksgiving."

He nodded, liking the idea more and more.

"The garden will be buried in snow, of course, but we could have everything in here. That way, we'll be well and truly married before Christmas."

"Why's that so important?" He blinked at the glitter of mischief in her eyes.

"Because I've got the perfect thing to go into your stocking. So what do you think?"

He must have liked the idea. Jordan was too busy kissing her to reply.

Epilogue

"I can't believe I let you talk Caitlin into this." Jordan glared at his mother with a look that wasn't totally pretend.

"All this falderal when all we wanted was to get married. Look at me! I look like a turkey."

"You can say that again." Robyn grinned as she straddled Eudora on her hip. "Smile!" She snapped yet another picture, giggling at his threatening look. "I love it."

"Mother!" Jordan clenched his fists to stop himself from strangling them both. "Can't you do something?"

"Of course I can. Go away now, Robyn, dear. I have to get your brother calm so he won't forget his vows. I want everything to be nice for Caitlin."

"We wanted Thanksgiving you know," he sputtered, shoving the huge poinsettia out of his way. "We were going to have a small ceremony. A *private* ceremony.''

''How ridiculous! I'm glad I was able to help her see the light. Now bend down, Jordan. Your bow tie is crooked.'' When he didn't obey immediately, she pinched his arm. ''I don't know why you men fuss so much. It's only a wedding, after all.''

Jordan rolled his eyes, but controlled the groan. She wouldn't thank him for pointing out the ruckus she'd created over the wedding cake, nor the fact that she'd ordered more flowers than three weddings required.

''Caitlin's home, *our* home,'' he corrected himself, ''looks like a garden.''

''Do you think so, dear? Oh, thank you.'' She hugged him tight and then bustled out of the room. ''Try not to get dirty, Jordan. And stay put. I have to go help Caitlin.''

Jordan grinned and then checked his watch for the umpteenth time that morning. Six more minutes. Then they could get on with this production and he'd be one step closer to being married. He fell into thought dreaming about that.

''Good grief, Jordan!'' Robyn shook her head in disbelief. ''The whole place is waiting for the groom to come out. Caitlin thinks you've changed your mind. What's the problem?''

''Robyn, you're a wonderful wife and I'm truly glad that you love me as much you do. And I thank God every day that you're not afraid to stand up for what you believe. But right now darling, and I mean this in the nicest possible way, go away.'' Her husband gently eased her out the door and smiled as she stomped away.

"I told you I can take care of my wife." He winked at Jordan. "Ready, big guy?"

"Yes," Jordan sighed happily. "More than ready."

He sucked in his breath when Caitlin moved slowly down the stairs. Her suit was the palest pink, the short trim jacket giving way to a long straight skirt with a scalloped hem. She held dark-pink roses and lilies. A fluffy little veil sat perched on her head.

To him she was the most beautiful sight in the world as his father led her down an aisle formed between rows of chairs and up to the area circled by dark pink poinsettias, where he stood with their minister.

"You're late," he whispered, taking her hand.

"So were you." She smiled and the tension left him. This was right, this was good, this was blessed.

"'Old things are gone. Behold, all things are as new.'" The minister's words rang around the room like the bells on Christmas morning.

"I now pronounce you husband and wife. You may kiss the bride."

From her grandmother's arms, Micah mewled a tiny cry, then shoved her fist in her mouth. Seconds later her lashes flopped closed and she slept, a furtive smile curving the corners of her bow-shaped mouth as her parents celebrated their love.

* * * * *

Dear Reader,

I hope you've enjoyed *Baby on the Way*. I've learned so much from writing Caitlin's story. Have you ever had one of those weeks when nothing seems to go right? Or maybe it's lasted months, or years! It's hard during those times to remember that God loves us more than we can ever know or understand. Isn't it amazing that in spite of our frustration and anger and worry, He can make something beautiful out of us, if we'll just allow Him to work?

My hope is that you will find the silver lining in every cloud that God sends your way. I wish you peace and joy, but above all, I wish you abundant, restoring love in every moment of your life.

Lois
Richer

WEDDING ON THE WAY

Be strong and take heart,
all you who hope in the Lord.
—*Psalms* 31:24

Chapter One

One year and three months after Beth Ainslow's return to Oakburn, betrayal still burned in Garrett Winthrop's craw. Though he'd done everything he could to ignore her, the petite strawberry-blonde just wouldn't leave his mind alone. Especially since they'd once been engaged, but she'd left him to marry someone else.

Gar had continued to date Cynthia Reardon for a while, but soon realized how foolish that had been. He couldn't go out with one woman when his mind was busy with thoughts of another.

He leaned back in the booth of the local café and heaved a sigh of disgust. How had the presence of one delicate five-foot bit of femininity managed to wreak such havoc on his always calm, always well-organized life?

"I can't believe you didn't tell me she was moving back to town." Gar stirred his coffee three extra times before finally laying down the spoon and facing his friend. "You owed me that, Clay."

Clayton Matthews pushed back his cap and surveyed his friend with a cheeky grin. "Believe me, if I'd known her return would get you this upset, I would have alerted you. But it's been over a year now—you should be used to her. Besides, I've been a little busy with my own love life, remember?" Clay grinned the happily smug smile of a man newly married.

That blissful glow irritated Gar immeasurably. He gulped a mouthful of the steaming brew and winced as it stung all the way down.

"Anyway, what's the problem?" Clay pretended to hide his mocking smile behind his mug. "Are you still carrying a torch?"

"No!" Gar slammed his cup onto the table, and then flushed as every eye in the place focused on him. "It's just that she waltzes back into town, and first thing you know, she's got her finger in every pie. Take that downtown restoration idea we've been working on."

"*You* take it. I'm a farmer, I don't know diddly about downtown restorations."

And Clay seemed totally opposed to learning more, Garrett decided privately.

He forged ahead anyway, intent on proving his point. "What right did she have to advise the Forsyths to sell their building instead of rent it? I've been working with them for months, I know their situation, and even I didn't say that."

"Maybe you should have. She has the right of a

woman with a perfectly good brain, Gar. And she's not afraid to use it. Maddie and Harold Forsyth are in their sixties. They want to travel, not get tied down to renters and renovations. Besides, according to coffee row, Beth aims to buy that building someday. The present location of her flower shop is a little small, I hear.''

Garrett jerked upright, his eyebrows rising. "What? How would she buy it? Did she suddenly inherit a fortune or something?''

Clay shrugged. "Beats me. All I know is what I hear.''

"Well, good old Denis Hernsley wasn't rich. I checked.'' As soon as he said it, Gar felt like an oaf for talking that way about Beth's deceased husband. He winced as Clay's eyebrows lifted. Money was not a measure of a man's stature. He knew as well as the next guy—and better than most—that a few dollars in your pocket meant nothing when it came to true happiness.

"Sorry, Clay. I just meant that she had to have money come from somewhere to start the flower thing.'' He frowned, trying to puzzle it out.

"Insurance money, I s'pose. And it's a good thing she got it, too.'' Clay shook his head in disgust. "Jordan Andrews told me that his wife Caitlin, as a friend, asked Beth to move into Wintergreen because she was homeless. She and her sister Ronnie were living in one of those company houses way up north in Alberta. When Denis died in an oil rig accident, the oil company absolved themselves of the necessity to provide housing, and Beth and Ronnie were out in the cold. So to speak.''

''Ronnie? Veronica was living with them all this time?'' Garrett hadn't heard that before. ''I thought she went to an aunt after her dad got sick a few years back. Why would she be living with Beth and not her father? The girl's underage. She's only fifteen!''

Clay scratched his forehead. ''I don't believe Ronnie's lived with Mervyn since Beth left town. And I can understand why. He was an awful old coot when he'd had a drink. Besides, he used to disappear for days. That's no life for a kid.''

Garrett didn't understand any of this. For the past fifteen months his younger brother Ty and Ronnie, who was now fourteen, had spent most of their time together, a good part of it at his parents' home, Fairwinds. So why hadn't he heard about this before?

Gar was sure someone—his dad maybe—had told him all those years ago that Veronica had gone to live with an aunt. Why would Beth have dragged her little sister along when she herself was only eighteen, a new bride, and hardly prepared for caring for someone else? He cast back in his mind as something twigged his memory...

''We'll have to take in Veronica.''

He could still see it so clearly. She'd called the dorm several times before Christmas that year, asking over and over when he'd be home. Involvement in the drama department and a production they were staging took every spare moment Gar could afford. He hadn't wanted to abandon it before the final performance, so he'd put her off, promising to return for a weekend, an afternoon, lunch together, and then changing his mind at the last minute.

How many times had he wished he'd changed his answer that last day? How often did he hear, over and over, the desperation in her, but he'd gone over it too many times. It was over, done with. Why couldn't he just leave it alone?

"Why're you asking me all this stuff? Why don't you ask her yourself? She's coming in now." Clay swallowed the last of his coffee and searched his pockets for his wallet. "I've got to go. Got a little project on the go and I need some hinges. Take it easy, Gar."

"Yeah. Right." Gar watched Clay pay his bill at the old-fashioned register and walk out the door. What he wouldn't give for such a simple life, and time to do the things he loved most. He'd devoted so much time to the bank—and for what? His father's approval? Approval that never seemed to come, no matter how hard he tried.

Gar stuffed down the traitorous thought. How foolish. He was perfectly happy working at his father's bank. It was Beth's fault he was questioning himself—

"Are you leaving?" Beth's tentative voice roused him from his daydream. "I don't mean that you should. It's just that the place is full, and I thought if you were going—" She stopped, took a deep breath and shook her head. "Never mind. I'll wait."

Gar reached out and grabbed her arm, halting her

progress away from him. It was time to forget the past, to move on.

"Have a seat," he offered quietly. "I wanted to talk to you anyway."

"Thanks. I think." She frowned, peering at him from beneath her lashes.

It could have been ten years ago, Gar decided. She looked barely a day older, except that now she wore her hair short, in a sort of pixie cut, instead of that bouncing blond-red ponytail. Her slight compact form still looked great in jeans and a shirt, and she still darted around like a sparrow.

It was only when he looked into her eyes that he saw a change. When she stared back at him, Gar saw something in those blue depths that made him wince. She'd been hurt. Because he'd avoided her?

"How are you?" She accepted the menu and a cup of coffee from the waitress and added a liberal amount of sugar and cream. "I haven't seen you for months. Been busy?"

"Not as busy as you." He couldn't stop the burst of words. "What right did you have to advise my clients to go against my advice?"

She blinked. "Your clients? Your advice?"

Gar clenched his jaw. "You know very well that the Forsyths have been meeting with me for months to discuss their property."

"Oh. Actually, I didn't." She placed her order and then leaned back against the seat. "I simply asked them if they were thinking of selling their building, and they told me they'd rather rent. That's when I found out they were planning on traveling, and I said I didn't think they'd want to be bothered with renters.''

"So you told them to take the money and run, whether it was a good price or not.'' He nodded, his voice pinched tight. "Yes, I'm aware of your sentiments on the matter.''

She laughed, a light tinkling sound that grated on his nerves. Her eyes were wide with innocence.

"I don't have any sentiments, Gar. I just wanted to know about the building.''

"You couldn't afford it even if they did want to sell.'' He immediately regretted saying it, but there was no way to recall the harsh words.

"Really?'' She looked at the sandwich set before her and immediately removed the pickles. "So what are you so cranky about then? Did I step on your toes by asking about it?''

"I'm not 'cranky'.'' He stopped, lowered his voice and searched desperately for some measure of control. "I am not cranky. I am merely asking you not to counter my advice to *my* clients.''

"Okay.'' She nodded once, then took a dainty bite of the sandwich and chewed appreciatively. "This is so good. I never roast a chicken anymore.''

"I didn't know you knew how. You never used to cook much.'' Gar clamped his lips shut. When would he learn to forget the past?

Beth shrugged. "You never used to be so crabby. Things change.'' She took another bite. "Do you go away in January? I remember your folks always used to leave Minnesota to go to Arizona when it got cold. It's certainly been cold enough since Christmas.''

''I'm not in my dotage yet,'' he muttered dryly. ''And I have no desire to play bingo, bridge or whist for hours on end.''

''Nobody said you had to go *there*.'' She grinned. ''Though I don't know how you could resist. All those seniors with their money just sitting gaining interest. Don't you salivate over the prospect of investing it for them?''

Gar glared at her. ''You used to worry about money a lot more than I did,'' he reminded her dourly. ''You were always fussing about how much things cost.''

''That was then.'' Beth took a sip of her coffee before she studied him with that thoughtful look he remembered so well. ''I've realized that money doesn't matter one iota when it comes to happiness. There are far more important things.'' She shrugged. '''The Lord giveth and the Lord taketh away.'''

Gar shifted uncomfortably, not liking the question he was going to ask, but needing the answer. ''How's business at the Enchanted Florist?''

''A little slow since Christmas, but actually, not bad. I projected my sales to be a little lower, just in case, so I'm doing fairly well. Why?''

She blinked those innocent green eyes at him, and Garrett felt like a creep. ''Just wondering. The Forsyths seemed to think you were looking to expand.''

She nodded. ''I am. The place I've rented is far too small. I didn't realize I'd need so much counter space to work.'' Beth rolled her eyes. ''My assistants and I nearly killed each other before Christmas. There were so many arrangements to be done, we had to take shifts.''

She nibbled the last bit of sandwich away from the crust and daintily covered the leftover edges with her napkin, exactly as she would have done ten years ago.

Garrett couldn't help smiling. So much had changed, and yet so little.

''Why are you asking?'' Her eyes drew his attention.

''I just wondered how—I mean, well—'' he felt his cheeks burn, and looked away from her inquisitive expression ''—I was just wondering.''

''You want to know how I can afford it.'' She plunked her mug on the table and glared at him. ''Where did I get the money? That's it, isn't it?''

He nodded finally, feeling like a firsthand louse.

''Well, don't worry about it, Gar. I didn't walk away from my marriage to Denis with a bag full of money, though he was a good provider. In fact, it's a lot more expensive to run the shop than I'd originally planned on. Especially when I have to freight everything in.''

He felt like a heel for questioning her. Vainly Gar tried to backtrack. ''It doesn't matter.''

Beth held up one hand. ''No, you asked, therefore, you want to know. I don't know how I'd afford to buy it. I'm just trusting God day by day. Where He leads, I'll follow.''

Gar could hardly believe he was hearing this from the woman who once couldn't go an hour without planning exactly when she had to be home. This lais-sez-faire approach bothered him.

"I suppose I'd have to ask for a loan." She got up from the table and dug in her purse. "I'll know better when the time comes. Right now, I have to concern myself with supporting Ronnie until she's finished college."

"I wanted to ask you about that." Gar lurched to his feet, dug in his pocket and tossed a bill on the table, ignoring her frown of protest. "Clay said you had Ronnie with you after you were married. What's with that?"

He held her arm to escort her through the crowd and out the door, but Beth jerked free and whirled to face him, her eyes glittering with some suppressed emotion.

"Does it really matter, Garrett? I left Oakburn, got married, and Ronnie lived with us. Okay? That's in the past. Why don't you just let it go?"

Gar saw Beth's cheeks flush bright red as she became aware of the stares of the other patrons. She strode quickly across the room and out the door, trying to ignore them all.

This time his height and long legs gave him an edge, and Garrett used it to good advantage. He followed her out of the café and caught up with her as she jaywalked across the street.

"I can't let it go because I feel like you're hiding something. I thought it then, too, but I brushed it off. Now I need to know what happened all those years ago.'' He peered straight into her eyes. ''Please level with me, Beth. I think you owe me that much.''

He could see the fire lick into her eyes. He could feel the defensiveness as she straightened to her full five-foot-two-inch height. Most of all, he could hear the anger as she spoke, carefully enunciating every word.

''I owe you?'' Her emerald eyes dared him to repeat it. ''I owe you nothing, Garrett Winthrop. We were going to be married, but the timing wasn't right. You needed to finish school, and I needed to do other things. God led us down different paths. You and I made our decisions ten years ago.''

''But that's just it,'' he protested, his frustration growing. ''I didn't make any decision.'' He frowned. ''I'm just trying to understand, Beth.''

''I think it's better if you focus on accepting the past, and move on. I'm going to.''

With that she turned and shoved the door to her shop open, pausing for one tiny moment to cast a look over her shoulder. As he searched her eyes, Gar thought he saw something there that looked remarkably like pain. But that couldn't be, could it?

Beth had dumped *him,* not the other way around.

''The nerve of that man!''

Beth flounced around her apartment later that night in a fit of pique, straightening things that didn't require straightening as she vented to her two friends. ''I owe him? Hardly!''

''What on earth did the poor man say that triggered

this?'' Maryann Matthews asked, cutting through Beth's stormy thoughts.

"It was more what he hinted. As if I owe it to him to explain my life history just because we once dated!"

"Beth, you have to admit you did a little more than date." Caitlin offered her admonishment quietly. "You were going to marry the man, remember?"

"Yes, but he didn't want that. He found someone else. I know that for a fact. Never mind how." She held up a hand, forestalling the questions written all over their faces. "It was over. And it still is, so don't get any ideas."

Beth glared at Maryann and Caitlin, daring them to mention any matrimonial plans they might have for her. When they simply blinked at her, she flopped onto her rickety used sofa with a sigh.

"The whole town has informed me that Garrett Winthrop and Cynthia Reardon are the perfect couple. She's the perfect kind of woman for him—so pleasant, so smart, so finished. As if I can't see that for myself." Beth glared down at her ragged sweats and made a face. "But sometimes I wonder what I'm even doing here. What does God want from me?"

"I guess we'd all like to know that upfront." Maryann sipped her coffee, her face thoughtful. "Unfortunately, that's not usually the way it works."

"I wanted to have a new beginning here—a fresh start. I wanted Ronnie to have a place that was good to grow up in, a place she could get to know Dad without all the awful history. I wanted to give her good memories." Beth sighed. "Everything seemed so simple when we were up north."

"It always does." Caitlin's eyes were shaded. "Maryann thought it would be easy to come back, I thought it would be easy to put the past behind me. I guess it's a group thing with us." She chuckled. "The Widows of Wintergreen. It's as if the old house is some kind of refuge for wayward widows who need to get over their past hang-ups!"

"In a way, maybe it is." Beth chewed on the edge of the blackened cookie her sister had gleefully presented earlier. "It's the one place we can get reacclimatized to life in this Minnesota town. Get beyond the past."

"I'm not sure it's that easy, Beth." Maryann got up to saunter over to the window. "Before I married Clay, I'd been trying to put the past behind me. The thing is, it just won't stay there. It affects the present and the future, even though we wish it didn't."

Beth shifted uncomfortably. She knew Maryann had suffered in her first marriage, although the other woman had never said much. But life back in high school couldn't have been as hard for Maryann and Caitlin as it had been for her.

"Maybe we've gone about things the wrong way. Maybe we should have just laid it all on the table and tried to go on from there, instead of hiding the hurt. I don't know." Maryann returned to her seat.

"I don't want to talk about the past," Beth insisted. "I want to talk about the future, as I see it."

"And that future doesn't include Gar?" Caitlin's eyebrows lifted.

"How can it? He's not in my league, he's got his own life now. And it includes someone else." Beth faced her friends' curious looks. "Not that that's important. I didn't expect him still to be single. I thought he'd have married one of those debutantes he saw at college. I thought he'd have kids by now."

Maryann made a face. "Garrett was head over heels in love with you, Bethy. He didn't even know the rest of the female population was alive. I don't suppose he could turn that off the day you left. It must have been very difficult for him. Even Cait and I didn't understand why you had to go so quickly." Her blue eyes darkened. "I do know you weren't in love with Denis. Not at first."

"No, I wasn't. I think I stopped believing in that kind of love the day Garrett refused to marry me." She cast her mind back to the first days of her marriage and smiled. "Denis helped me get past that. He was a wonderful man, you know."

"You're avoiding the truth, Beth." Caitlin shook her head vehemently. "You can't just toss out something like love by merely declaring that you won't feel it anymore. Tell us what you really believe, honey. Are you still carrying a torch for Gar?"

They wouldn't give up. She knew that much about her high school friends. They'd keep probing until they got an answer. But how could she admit that after all this time, after being virtually ignored by Garrett for more than a year, she had realized he still held a piece of her heart? How could she deal with that without opening herself up to the same questions she'd asked ten years ago?

Sure, she had her own business now, was self-sufficient, had learned that she was worth caring about. But she still wasn't the kind of person who lived in the Winthrop mansion, wore silk and cashmere, and held afternoon teas and glittering soirees.

"I can never go back, Caitlin. Maybe you and Maryann are different, I don't know. But for me, I've learned what my deficiencies are, and I'm still not the kind of wife that Gar needs." She tossed the burned cookie back onto the plate and picked up her hot chocolate.

She'd have to tell a bit of it, Beth decided. They wouldn't give in until she did.

"I'm from the wrong side of the tracks, girls. My father is a drunk who never got over my mom's death. When he went on a bender, it wasn't a lot of fun."

The two pretty faces across the room were distorted by frowns of disbelief.

"Beth, honey." Caitlin's voice brimmed with compassion. "I always knew there was something wrong, but we never guessed this. I'm so sorry."

"I know. So was I." She refused to cry.

"Me, too." Maryann got up to offer a quick hug. "I suppose we should have asked more questions, probed a little more."

"It wouldn't have mattered." Beth sighed wearily. "I wouldn't have told you anyway. It was my shame to bear."

"Why your shame?" Caitlin was frowning. "Your father drank, not you. Besides, everybody gets hurt in life. It's part of living in this world."

"Part of living a certain way, maybe. I'll guarantee Gar never had to be embarrassed about his father's actions. The Winthrops are the perfect picture of civic responsibility, the perfect married couple, the perfect parents. They have the same hopes and dreams, they share a common history. No one looks at his father and shakes his head in disgust."

Beth swallowed down the welling of self-pity that rose inside, and carefully set her cup on the table. She choked over her next words, the pain building inside as she pretended fact was fiction. There were some things she just couldn't tell even her best friends. "Imagine, just for a moment, if Dad staggered into one of those fancy dress balls the Winthrops hold every Valentine's! Gar would have been humiliated by me even before Dad opened his mouth and started his ugly diatribe."

The stunned looks on the other women's faces told her how well she'd kept his secret. They thought this was a hypothetical situation. Of course, they would. They'd been long gone from town when that had happened.

"Beth! I didn't realize it was that bad. Did he *hurt* you?" Caitlin's voice was barely audible.

"No. He wasn't that kind of a drunk. He'd rant and rave, then disappear for days. We never knew when he'd come back, or even *if* he'd come back." Her voice dropped in embarrassment. "Sometimes he was gone so long, we'd run out of things. The scariest part was the not knowing." Beth shivered, remembering those long dark nights.

"I couldn't stay and live that way with Ronnie seeing so much ugliness. So one day, before he passed out, I got him to sign her care over to me." She shrugged, pretending the entire matter was of absolutely no consequence. "Then I went looking for a job to support us both."

"Why didn't you tell someone?" Maryann stood and paced the length of the room. "There were people who could have helped."

Beth shook her head, her face tight with the effort of retaining control. "Uh-uh, Mare. I couldn't face the embarrassment. The whole town was already gossiping about the white trash Gar was engaged to. I couldn't make it any worse for them. Besides, his dad..." She stopped, glancing from one to the other. "It doesn't matter anymore now. It's finished." What was the point in delving back into it all over again, trying to figure out if she'd been wrong to take the opportunity Denis had offered when Gar was away at school and run with it, to listen to Mr. Winthrop's advice and get out of Gar's life before she ruined it.

Maryann shifted uncomfortably on her chair, her forehead pleated in a frown. "The youth group could have prayed for you—helped you."

"Do you think I didn't pray?" Beth let the hoarse laugh escape. "I prayed almost hourly for some way of escape. Sometimes I was so afraid to leave Ronnie alone, I took her with me on some of our dates. Gar didn't seem to mind back then.'' She shrugged. "But God didn't answer my prayers.''

"How do you know?''

Beth smiled sadly as she shook her head at Caitlin. "I was there, remember? I lived through it.''

"But, Bethy, maybe that's the answer. Maybe God meant for you to meet and marry Denis. You had a good marriage, didn't you?''

"Yes, in a way. We cared for each other, and he was the kindest, most caring person I could have asked for Ronnie to grow up with. He understood me. I guess that could have been part of God's plan, for Denis to take care of us. Right?'' She fiddled with her hands, ignoring the satisfied looks Maryann and Caitlin exchanged as she tried to reason it out in her mind.

"Did you ever tell Gar about your dad?'' The question came softly, surprising her.

"No!'' She stared at them. "Of course not. How could I? I didn't want him to know about all that ugliness. Anyway, I'm sure he heard it around town. Everyone knew Mervyn Ainslow tipped the bottle too often.'' Even now the stigma of being the daughter of the town's drunk stung.

"We didn't!'' Maryann's eyes were wide and unblinking. "But we're veering off the subject. We want to know how you feel about Gar now.''

"I don't know. I still find him attractive. I think he's done very well for himself. I want the best for him.'' Beth gathered up the rumpled napkins and used cups, loading them all on the tray she'd painted about this time last year. "I can't really tell you any more than that."

Tears filled her eyes as she carried the tray into the kitchen and disposed of the dishes in the sink full of soapy water. She could hear the other two moving about, and she searched desperately for a shred of composure.

"Bethy? I think God brought you back here to face the past and find out something about yourself." Caitlin's voice sounded behind her as warm caring arms hugged her close. "I'm sure if you told Gar why you needed to leave, that you had to find work—"

"No! You two are not to say a word of this to anyone. Promise?" She whirled around to glare at them both, urging them with her eyes to support her on this. "I don't want to resurrect the past. I'm trying to maintain my self-esteem in this town and show them that Beth Ainslow isn't worthless. I'm not smart, but I went to college and graduated, even if it was night school and by correspondence. I'm not some poor pitiable creature anymore. Let Garrett think what he likes about me, if he thinks about me at all. I don't care. Neither does he."

"But you do care, sweetie. That's why it still hurts." Maryann sighed when Beth shook her head. "And you're focusing on the wrong things. Self-worth doesn't come from your roots, or what people think about you, or even from the pain you've endured. It comes from knowing your value to God and what you make of what He gives you. Believe me, I know that better than most."

Beth started to protest, but Maryann held up a hand. "All right. If that's the way you want it, I promise I won't say a word. Not that I see Gar much anymore. Life on the farm doesn't allow for many chance encounters."

"You love it and you know you do," Caitlin giggled. "And your new husband just loves showing off his new furniture upstairs. It's a good thing your father-in-law decided to rent the place after you two got married, Maryann."

"Willard likes being on his own. And it's easier for us, too." Maryann's troubled gaze met Caitlin's, and some secret message Beth couldn't interpret passed between the two.

"Promise me, Caitlin. Not one word to Garrett or anyone else about the past. Promise." Beth refused to look away, and sighed with relief when Caitlin finally nodded.

"I think it's a mistake, Beth. But if that's what you want, I won't go against your wishes. I just wish—"

"If wishes were horses, I'd be a rancher." Beth smiled at them both to show that she wasn't suffering. "I'm too old to believe in fairy-tale endings anymore, girls. There's not going to be a prince to sweep me off my feet and carry me to his castle." She frowned. "I don't even want there to be. I just want to get on with the future." She followed them out of the kitchen.

"I know you're hurt." Caitlin handed Maryann her coat and pulled open the apartment door. "But most of the time, the future and the past are interwoven.

You're a product of the past, Beth, but with God's help, you can rise above any circumstance and build a future that shows the real you.'' She leaned down and pressed a kiss against Beth's cheek. ''Night, Bethy. Thanks for the cookies. I won't ask for the recipe.''

''Funny. Very funny. I'll tell Ronnie you loved them. That way she'll make you guys a batch of your own burned ones for her next home-economics project.'' Beth grinned at Caitlin's less-than-enthusiastic smile. ''Night, Mare. Drive carefully. Tell Clay hello.''

''I will. I love you, Beth. And I think you're a wonderful friend.'' Maryann also hugged her, then scurried out the front door, her shoes tapping on the steps. ''It's snowing again,'' she called before she tugged the door closed behind her.

''I hope Ronnie's okay. She was going out with some of the other kids. I hate it when it starts to snow and she's with a new driver. Anything could happen.''

''Give it to God,'' Caitlin murmured, pulling open her own apartment door. ''All of it.'' Her eyes twinkled with happiness. ''It's surprising what wonderful things He can make out of our mistakes. Two of those surprises are right in there, waiting for me. If He did it for me, He can do it for you. Night, Bethy.''

''Good night.'' Beth waited until Caitlin was inside before she walked back into her own apartment, her mind turning over all the things she'd shared tonight, things she'd kept bottled up for ten long years.

She tossed another log into the fireplace, poked it

halfheartedly and then curled up in front of it, her back against the sofa.

"As if Garrett could still love me now," she muttered in disgust. "What a ridiculous idea! As if his father would let him, even if he were interested. Which he is not!" She shook her head in annoyance. "There's no point in even thinking about it, silly, because it just isn't going to happen."

The past hurts came back with a vengeance, and she suddenly wished she could go back to the security of life with Denis. "He was so kind," she muttered, remembering those blessed years of safety and sanctuary when she'd been able to probe her own thoughts and fears and begin dealing with them. "I did everything I could to make it work."

And it had worked. She and Denis had grown close, Ronnie had found friends, life had become full and busy. Beth had even taken a job at the local florist and learned, under Helen Smith's apt tutelage, how to make the most of every flower that came into her hands. In her spare time she'd taken all the courses she could. She'd filled her brain with all the things she'd once longed to study but hadn't had the funds or opportunity to tackle. And she'd fed her hungry heart with books, hundreds of them.

In the process, with Denis as her mentor, her bitter heart had healed there among the flowers in a place where ice and snow prevailed for much of the year.

"I'm older, hopefully smarter, and I can earn a living. I'm not a drain on society like Dad is. I can give Ronnie a home and maybe even veterinary school," she told the empty room. "I'm not that stupid needy child from the past."

She freely admitted that she'd been gullible back then. And a little too eager to avoid facing down anyone who seemed to have more than she did.

"If I had it to do again, I don't know whether I would take Charles Winthrop's advice or not. But then, maybe the girls are right—maybe I did need Denis and life with him to find out who I am."

The fire crackled and spit, and a glow of red danced on the walls. What was the best way to channel her energies now, outside work, to keep her mind off Garrett and the past? She spied the phone pad on a table nearby and stared at the scrawled message regarding a new youth center. Could she help?

I can do this. I can't change the past, go back and explain everything to Gar. He wouldn't understand that scared little girl. But I can do this. I can make sure Ronnie and teenagers like her have a place to go where kids can mix and mingle freely without feeling out of place.

She dialed the number slowly, thoughtfully.

"Renata? This is Beth Ainslow. No, I went back to my maiden name. Yes, it's good to hear your voice, too. It's about the youth center. I'd like to help." She scribbled down dates and times and nodded. "Sure. That's fine. I'll be there."

After they exchanged the latest news, Beth hung up and went back to her meditation by the fire.

Denis was such a good man. Why hadn't she kept his name? But it's time to face up to it. Inside I am an Ainslow, and it's time to face up to that. Denis would agree with that.

Wintergreen's front door opened, and the old oak floor squeaked as someone tiptoed across it. Beth held her breath as the lock in her own door turned and her sister slipped inside.

"Hi," she murmured quietly. "I was wondering where you were."

"Oh, you're still up. Good. We went out for coffee after youth group. Then I went back to Tyler's farm. Bethy, those horses!" Ronnie flopped down beside her sister and closed her eyes, blissfully sighing. "Someday I want to have horses like that, Beth. They're so beautiful."

"You were at the Winthrops'. Again." It wasn't a question. Beth felt her heart sink to her boots.

"Uh-huh. Garrett was there. He showed me around. It's a fantastic stable." She shifted, her face turning toward Beth. "Bethy, why didn't you ever tell me that you loved Garrett? And why did you marry Denis if you were in love with someone else? Do you still love Gar?"

Beth wilted.

Here was the question she'd avoided for ten long years. How could she possibly answer Ronnie when she didn't know the answer herself?

Chapter Two

On Friday night Garrett punched the buzzer for Jordan and Caitlin's apartment and then stood back to admire Wintergreen. The old house loomed above him in the dark January evening like a specter from the past, even though there was nothing remotely ramshackle about it.

"Come on in, Garrett. You don't have to stand out here. You know that." Jordan thumped him on the back in a friendly manner, and held the door wide open. "Clay's here already. He's playing with my daughter because his isn't coming over for a while. Amy's at her figure skating lessons with some other children. Caitlin and Maryann are out, too."

Jordan motioned him in, then left the apartment door ajar. "Parts delivery," he explained. "I've got a monitor that keeps acting up."

Gar walked into the warm inviting apartment and admired the renovations. He'd only been here a couple of times lately, but the place intrigued him just the same.

"Have a seat."

"Clay." Gar nodded in greeting, accepted the mug of coffee from Jordan and took the big armchair. "You guys wanted to see me?" He didn't bother with social niceties. What was the point?

"Well, sort of. Though I've been meaning to ask you over for a while. Christmas and Clay's wedding sorta put the kibosh on my plans. We guys gotta stick together, you know." Jordan grinned but the glow didn't quite reach his eyes.

"We do?" Gar wondered at this sudden need for male bonding.

"We're thinking of forming a men's club." Clay handed the one-year-old Micah back to Jordan.

Gar hid his grin as he watched the farmer remove a glob of pureed peas from his shoulder. "A men's club? What for?"

"To give us something to do when it's ladies' night out!" Clay peered at him with a frown. "What do you do with all your spare evenings?"

"My parents are frequently away so I've been staying at their place, looking after Ty. That takes a lot of time."

"Looking after Ty?" Clay's bushy eyebrows rose. "He's almost eighteen, isn't he? How much looking after can he need?"

Gar grimaced. "You'd be surprised. He's been hanging out with that motorcycle gang that came to town last fall."

"Yeah, hanging out with them and Ronnie Ainslow!" Jordan didn't pretend that wasn't the point of the whole conversation. "She's nuts for those horses your parents keep."

"I know. Ty's taken her riding lots of times. She's a natural, though Dad doesn't seem to like her coming out so much lately. Says he's afraid she'll get hurt, and he'll get sued." Gar leaned back to give the illusion he was relaxed. Truth to tell, he felt as if he were sitting on a crate of red-hot nails. These two wanted something from him. He just had to find out what.

"It's good, in a way. I mean, with her wanting to be a vet and everything." Jordan glanced up from his play with Micah. His golden eyes peered through the hank of hair that had fallen forward. "Sure gonna be expensive to put her through that."

Gar set his cup down and leaned forward, elbows resting on his knees, pretending a nonchalance he didn't feel. "Okay, fellas. Why don't you just say what you want from me and we'll take it from there?" he said quietly.

"Suits me." Clay glanced at Jordan, who nodded slightly. "Money."

"I beg your pardon?" Gar frowned.

"I said, we're after money. Every year your family gives a big donation to the school to use for awards to the most promising student. It would be really nice if there were a scholarship this year for the student most likely to go into veterinary training." Clay shrugged. "Or something like that. I'm not sure how they word it. Ty would probably know. I guess you'd have to put a bug in the principal's ear.''

''And I would do this because…?'' Gar opened his eyes innocently wide.

''Because Ronnie Ainslow needs you to. There's no way Beth can afford a school like that—not with that little life insurance policy she got after Denis died. She most likely needs that to run her store.''

''How do you know about her finances?'' Gar glanced from one to the other, seeing the flicker of guilt on their transparent faces. ''Who've you been talking to?''

''It's just that we were talking to Ty the other day,'' Clay sputtered finally, ''when he came over to study with Ronnie. I was here delivering some of my furniture.'' He gulped. ''Anyhow, he mentioned that Ronnie was real worried about asking Beth to help her choose a school. Apparently you have to start early.

''Anyway, Ty told us the fees are awful high. The girl's afraid her sister can't afford the school she wants, and she's thinking about changing her plans. We don't want to see that happen.''

So Ronnie and Ty had been discussing their future? Gar frowned as he wondered just how friendly the two actually were.

''And Ronnie's a natural with animals. She brought me in that dog that was hit last week, and it's perking right up.'' Clay cleared his throat. ''You're the guy who knows all about compound interest and the value of investing early, aren't you? I'm sure if you run a spreadsheet analysis or something, you could see how valuable such a scholarship could be when she finishes school."

Gar almost laughed. These two were suddenly worried about financial evaluations? It was ludicrous. He studied each of them for several moments. There was something behind this. Jordan didn't even bother to look away. He faced Gar head-on.

"Do it, Gar." Jordan's voice held no pretense. "Do it because it's in your power and you'd do it for any other kid who showed so much promise. Because we asked you to."

"And because you think I owe it to Beth. Is that it?" The dawn of recognition hit Gar between the eyes. "Because I didn't marry her and she's had such a hard life. I'm right, aren't I?"

Clay's mouth dropped onto his chest. He gulped once and then emitted a high-pitched squeak. "Huh?"

Jordan wasn't nearly so delicate. "If you feel that guilty, Bud, I guess it wouldn't hurt to offer a consolation prize."

"I do not feel guilty." Gar strained to keep the even tone in his voice. "She's the one who left, the one who married someone else." He swallowed. "Anyway, it was ten years ago. Actually, eleven now. If I ever did feel any guilt, it's long gone."

They were pushing this too far, shoving their noses in his business, Gar fumed silently. His relationship with Beth was private. Not that he had one at this point. Or expected to. It was just...

"You guys are making me nuts," he finally exploded.

"Sure, blame us. I didn't *say* you should feel guilty—did I, Clay?"

Clay obediently shook his head.

"No, of course I didn't." Jordan blinked innocently as he cuddled a sleepy Micah. "I was just suggesting something you might like to do for the good of the kids in the community, to help someone you know is having a tough time. You used to sort of like doing stuff like that. Remember Mrs. Carver?"

"Who?" Gar wondered if this happened to every man who got married. Neither Jordan nor Clay seemed able to keep the same thought in their heads for more than three minutes—it was very frustrating. "I don't know any Mrs. Carver. And what's that got to do with anything?"

"Yes, you know. The old woman who had that monstrously huge lawn at the end of Clagmore Drive. Every year she'd try to find someone to clean up those leaves, and every year all the kids in town were suddenly busy." Clay grinned. "Except you. You'd go out there and slave away for a whole Saturday just to earn a few bucks."

"Money was important to me. We had to earn our own, you know. My dad didn't believe in just doling it out." Gar shook his head. "What does this have to do with anything?"

"The point is, you didn't do it for the money, and we all knew that, Gar. You had a soft spot for the old girl." Jordan smiled sheepishly. "You've always been a giver."

"And, uh, Beth's finding it a little tight right now,

or so I heard." Clay coughed delicately behind one hand. "January isn't the best month for the flower business. If her sister had a scholarship put away, say, even a small one to count on, that would take some of the pressure off. And then there's this summer camp. Ty showed me the brochure..." His voice trailed away as he caught a glimpse of Gar's face.

It was pointless to argue with them. They were like a couple of old busybodies, arranging things behind everyone's back. Apparently they'd even sucked Ty into it. Garrett mentally calculated the amount left in the bank's budget for donations, and nodded.

"Fine. I'll ask the principal to have her fill out an application and bring it in to the bank." He surged to his feet. "Is that all?"

"No." They said it in unison, glancing at each other in surprise.

Garrett exhaled, then sat back down, shifting uncomfortably under the intense scrutiny. "Well?"

"The thing is," Clay began, "we were kind of hoping this could be anonymous. You know, no strings attached."

"I don't think Beth would let Ronnie accept anything from the bank, especially if she found out we were behind it." Jordan looked a little unnerved by the prospect. "We, uh, sort of came by this information in a nonpublic way—if you know what I mean."

He knew. Garrett sighed, wishing he'd had a board meeting or something urgent to attend tonight.

"Yeah, I know exactly how you got this information, Jordan. You eavesdropped, or else you pried it out of Ty." He glared at their unrepentant faces.

"I also know Beth wouldn't accept a plugged nickel from me. She doesn't care where I go, what I do, who I see or don't see. She's free and single and she doesn't have to answer to anyone." Gar forced the frustration out of his voice. "Thanks, guys, but I got the point the last time I had coffee and she happened by."

"It sounds to me like you're just a little too worried about what Beth Ainslow thinks. And if you ask me, you completely missed the point," Jordan grumbled, just low enough for Gar to hear.

"Actually, I didn't ask you, Jordan. But what, exactly, is the point? Don't tell me you two geniuses are setting yourselves up as matchmakers?" Gar glanced suspiciously from one to the other.

"Matchmakers? Who?" Jordan blinked.

"Us?" Clay squeaked, eyes innocently rounded behind his glasses. "No way."

"Because if you are," Gar went on, ignoring their studiously blank faces, "let me tell you that there is no point. The Beth Ainslow that lives across the hall from you, Jordan, is nothing like the Beth we knew in high school. She's cold and hard and determined to be the consummate businesswoman. She's not into the past. Not at all."

"Actually, according to our wives, she's exactly the same as she was then." Jordan set Micah down on the floor with a set of toy keys. "Caitlin says she's still hiding something that she won't share with anyone."

"And Maryann says she's booking herself up with fund-raising for a community youth center so she won't have to stay home alone at nights." Clay winked at Jordan and then blinked in pretended surprise. "Hey, that's an idea! Why don't you get on the committee, too? Then you two could both work on the center. You are a member of the town council, Gar. It wouldn't be that hard to get yourself appointed."

Gar frowned. "The community center? I haven't heard anything about her being on that board. I'm pretty sure I'm not sitting on it anyway."

"You should pay more attention." Clay went to answer the door, and seconds later returned with his stepdaughter Amy. The little girl greeted everyone, then flopped down on the floor to play with the baby. "Our taxes pay you guys to keep your eyes peeled."

You couldn't win with these two, Gar consoled himself. Just when you thought you had them beaten, they veered off the track onto something else.

"I'm on enough committees, I don't need any more." He ignored their fallen expressions. "I sure don't need to add any more meetings to my schedule. And the youth center idea is just getting off the ground. It'll mean hours of meetings."

"You could do it for Ty's sake, couldn't you?" Jordan's smug grin made Gar nervous. "He'll benefit, too, you know."

"How?"

"Instead of hanging around with the wildest crowd in town, he could be drawn in to the community center. Provided it was a cool—or hot—place to be. You know how kids are." Jordan winked at Clay. "If you can remember that far back."

"Cute, Andrews." Gar thought about it for a moment. "It could be mighty uncomfortable, you know. She's made it more than clear that I've been completely wiped from the slate of her mind."

"Well, what do you want her to say?" Clay rolled his eyes. *"Welcome home, darling"?* He snorted. "That's only in the movies, Garrett. Even I know that."

Gar sighed. Why had he come here? They reveled in embarrassing him, making fun of him and taunting him with these reminders of the past.

"Admit it, Gar. You still carry a torch for Beth. Maybe it's only flickering right now, but with a little fanning—"

"I do not carry any torch for Beth Ainslow! That was over long ago—the day she married someone else. I don't care about her one way or the other. So don't expect me to go kissing up to her now, because I have no reason to do that. She's the one who broke the engagement. She should apologize to me."

The words barely left his lips when a gasp of surprise alerted him.

Beth stood in the doorway, all five foot two of her diminutive frame bristling with anger. Her lips pursed together in a tight line as she glared at him. Her pint-size feet brought her to stand immediately in front of him.

Garrett turned and groaned, his whole body slumping with defeat. Talk about bad timing! He got to his feet slowly, knowing he'd said too much.

"I have nothing, *nothing,* to apologize to you for, Garrett Winthrop. But if it will make you feel better, I'm sorry I dumped you ten years ago. I thought, hoped, you'd be over it by now. There, feel better?" She wheeled around and stalked to the door, her strawberry-blond hair glittering in the lamplight.

Gar swallowed, remembering the hurt look in her eyes. He'd done that, without even meaning to. *Help me, God.*

Gar hadn't wanted to hurt her. He'd simply lashed out. He followed her to the door and laid one hand on her arm to stop her.

"Beth, I didn't mean to say that. I was just—"

She turned around, jerked her arm away from his touch and fixed him with her jade-green eyes.

"Just what? Spouting off? Angry? Still? Grow up, Garrett. This is a new era. We're adults now. It's time to move on." She glanced past him to Jordan. "I stopped by to tell you that Caitlin and Maryann will be delayed. They're discussing a Sweetheart's Banquet for sometime in February. Good night." Beth glanced at Gar, then turned and marched out of the room.

"Uh, thanks. Good night," Jordan called.

Gar turned and watched the other man's face as the apartment door across the hall slammed shut. Jordan winced, his eyes squinting.

"Uh-oh." Clay, who'd risen moments ago, now flopped back down in his chair.

"Auntie Beth is mad," five-year-old Amy informed them all.

"No kidding! And it's all your fault." Gar scowled at the two men. "If you hadn't dragged me over here on some bogus excuse, I wouldn't now be the scum of the earth on Beth's shoes."

"It's not that bad." Jordan closed the door, apparently forgetting about his parts delivery as he returned to his seat. "She's just a little miffed."

"Yeah, right. And the Pacific is just a little pond." Gar stumbled over to an armchair and sank into it, thrusting his head into his hands. "Why do I get myself into these situations? I always end up the fall guy when I get near you two. When will I learn to shut up?"

"What you've got to do now is apologize." Clay grinned. "I've learned that much in my short marriage."

"How could I possibly apologize for saying she means nothing to me?" Gar stared dismally at the carpet.

"You weren't telling the truth, were you?" Jordan murmured, his eyes bright. "Because you actually care quite a bit for Beth Ainslow."

"He does?" Clay frowned. "But he said—" He stopped at the growling sound emanating from Jordan's throat. "Oh—" he nodded "—I get it."

"Gar?" Jordan was unrelenting.

"I don't know what I feel anymore." Gar raked a hand through his hair in frustration. "I loved her, you know. Really loved her. For years. I thought she felt the same, but then she just walked away. Without saying a word. It hurt.''

''And now she's back.'' Jordan handed Amy a coloring book and a crayon from a box hidden inside the coffee table. ''So?''

''What are you suggesting? That I try to pick up where we left off?'' Gar made a face. ''I'm not eighteen anymore.''

''Uh-uh. You can never go back. If anybody knows that, it's us. Right, Clay?'' Jordan didn't wait for a response. ''What you need to do now is find out what you really want. I think you still care for her. That's why it hurts so much.'' He picked up Micah and cuddled her in his arms. ''It's up to you, buddy. But I'll give you one piece of advice.''

''Just exactly what I need. More of your advice.'' Gar rolled his eyes. ''Okay, spout off. And then mind your own business.''

Fortunately Jordan didn't take offense. ''Forget the past. You can't change it, you can't make it go away. You can't alter her decision. She did what she did, and you don't know why. That's life. You might find out and you might not, but either way, it really doesn't affect the here and now. Deal with it and then decide what you want. If it's still Beth, go for it.'' He held Gar's gaze with his own for several moments, nodded and then walked over to the stairs with Micah.

''I've got to go change her. You guys are welcome to help yourselves to whatever you need.'' He climbed the stairs, murmuring sweet words of love to his daughter.

"Wow! He's been married—what? A little over a year? And he thinks he's an expert on everything." Gar sniffed as he lunged to his feet, showing Clay what he thought of Jordan's lately acquired perceptions. "I'm leaving." He buttoned up the coat he'd never removed and walked to the door. "See you, Clay."

"Gar?" Clay leaned down and whispered something to Amy, then walked toward him. "Can I say something?"

"Why not?" Resigned to hearing more than he'd ever wanted to on the subject of love, Gar stayed where he was.

"Jordan doesn't know everything, and sometimes his advice is a little off the wall. But in this case he's right." Clay jerked his head in the direction of Beth's apartment. "You need to let go of the past before it poisons the future. Maybe if you told her what was in your heart, you'd find out why she did what she did. Or maybe it wouldn't matter anymore."

Clay opened the door. "Either way, good luck, Gar."

"Luck? Ha!" Gar closed the door and stood in the hallway fuming. "If it weren't for bad luck, I wouldn't have any luck at all. Of all the lamebrain things to say."

Beth's door opened a crack and she peered out above the chain, eyes narrowed. "Are you talking to yourself?"

"Actually, I was hoping to talk to you." He moved to stand in front of her door. "Just for a moment."

"I think you've said *everything* there is to say."
She began to close the door. The emphasis on 'everything' couldn't be missed.

"Wait!" Gar thrust one loafer into the space and winced at the pressure against his toes. Given an opportunity, would Beth push even harder? "I really need to talk to you, Beth."

"No, you don't. You need to go home. And when you get there, send my sister home." She stood, waiting for him to remove his foot. "Well?"

Gar made up his mind. "You can let me in, and we'll talk in the privacy of your apartment, or I can stand out here and bellow for the whole world to hear. There are two very snoopy men across the hall who would relish relaying every word to their equally nosy wives. Your choice."

"Gar, be serious!"

But he'd made up his mind and he wasn't changing it. It was long past time they had this out. He, for one, needed a fresh start.

"I'm perfectly serious. Take your pick." He stayed exactly where he was, feeling the door press more tightly against his toes. "You have one minute to decide."

She glared at him for almost the entire time. But when he glanced at his watch and opened his mouth, she sighed, slid the chain off and opened the door. "Fine. Have it your way, say what you want. Then we can close this chapter for good."

Gar walked inside, slid his scarf and gloves off and laid them over the back of a dilapidated rocker. *You just have to be firm,* he told himself proudly. *Insist on what you want.*

But wasn't that the problem? He didn't know what he wanted.

Not when it came to Beth Ainslow.

I could use a hand here, God. Otherwise, I'm not going to be able to get both feet out of my mouth.

Chapter Three

"Well?" Beth stood in front of the closed door, hands planted on her hips, and waited, her mouth a thin tight line.

"Do you have to be like that?" Gar ambled over to the sofa and gingerly sat down, wondering if the rickety old thing would hold him up. "I just want to talk. I'm not into whipping and public stoning anymore." It was a poor attempt at humor, and her eyes told him so.

She flounced over the worn carpet and sat down across from him, her legs curled like a pretzel beneath her.

"So talk."

"You're not being very nice," he chided. "It's just a conversation, Beth. I'm not going to threaten you or demand you explain anything."

She frowned at him, her green eyes pensive. Finally she let out her breath, a big sigh of resignation, and nodded. "Fine. I'll be as gracious as I can be under the circumstances."

"And what are these 'circumstances'?" he asked mildly. "We were engaged once, but we never got married. That's all."

"That's all?" She peered at him suspiciously. "Are you sure? That isn't what you said before. And you just told those two men that I mean nothing to you. I don't understand why you're here. Shouldn't you be accompanying Cynthia to something or other."

"Cynthia is just a friend," he muttered, his cheeks burning. "A close one, but only a friend." He sucked in a deep breath and let it out on a whoosh of truth. "The only woman I ever loved was you."

Oh, God, please help me now! he prayed seconds later as tears, big and fat, welled in her beautiful eyes.

"Don't cry, Beth. Please, don't cry." He felt as helpless as the newborn kittens Ronnie had helped their cat deliver last weekend.

"I'll cry if I want to," she sniffed, dashing the tears from her eyes. "I don't have to ask your permission."

She was so frustrating. That much hadn't changed. "Okay then, cry. I can't stop you." He sat there, feeling powerless and painfully belligerent and wondering why he'd decided to come in here tonight. Why hadn't he gone straight home and reamed out Ty for blabbing to his friends?

"Anyway, I'm not crying. I had something in my eye." Beth's eyes still glimmered with the sheen of unshed tears. "Thank you for saying that."

"That I loved you?" He shrugged. "It's the truth.

I accepted that a long time ago. I thought it was mutual.'' He avoided her gaze, tapping his toe against the worn Persian rug she'd laid in the living room. ''I guess I had some growing up to do.''

Beth didn't say anything, didn't offer an explanation, didn't even meet his glance when he finally looked up. Instead, she seemed to be studying the flames in the fireplace, a frown marring her smooth forehead.

''The thing is, I'm not sure where we stand now.''

Her head jerked up at that. Gar barreled on. He needed to get this said. ''I mean, are you mad at me for something? Did I do something you couldn't forgive? Should I get permanently lost?'' He said everything but the one question that had plagued him for ten long years. *Did you really love me?*

He pretended not to study her as he peered over through his lashes. She straightened, drew a deep breath and stared directly at him. Gar held his breath, mentally preparing himself for what was to come.

''The problems I had in the past didn't really have to do with you, Gar. They had to do with me. With who I was and what I had to sort through. There have been many things I've had to deal with these past few years, but none of them were caused by anything you did.''

''Why don't you just tell me?'' he murmured, as the words trembled on the edge of her lips. ''I promise I'll listen.''

Beth studied him for several tense moments, took a deep breath and plunged in. Gar forced himself to listen carefully to every word while studying her expressive face.

"When I was eighteen, I had this idea that marrying you would solve all my problems. Of course, you couldn't do that for me. Nobody could. Actually, it was a good thing that God led me away from Oakburn, where I could confront the real issues in my life."

Gar frowned. "God led you away? How do you figure that?"

He didn't get any of this. There was something she was trying to tell him.

"There are some things I probably should have told you years ago," she murmured. "Things that would have explained some of how I acted. I think the time has come to tell you now. If you want to hear them."

"Yes, of course. But we knew each other pretty well, Beth. I don't think there's much you can say that I don't already know about you." He saw her grimace, and hastily backtracked. "I'll listen to anything you have to say."

"Do you remember that Easter sunrise service we had that year? The one where we dedicated our lives to serving God, to knowing Him as a real Father?" She waited for his nod. "I had the wrong idea of a father then, Gar. I didn't understand what God the Father meant, and when I thought about it, the only picture I ever got was my dad."

"And?" He waited for her to continue, watching as her fingers fiddled with the fringe on the scarf she wore.

"Did you ever meet my dad?"

He frowned. "Yeah, a couple of times, I guess. When we were dating, he was away a lot. I figured he was some kind of workaholic. After college, well, I was busy. I only saw him once in a while." He waited for some comment, but it never came. Instead, Beth seemed intent on her next words.

"My father was as far from the ideal father as you could get. After Mom died, he couldn't seem to dig himself out of his depression. I think Ronnie and I reminded him of what he'd lost, and that's why he drank so much."

Drank *so much?* "Your father always seemed fine to me. Sure, he drank a little, but he had it under control. Didn't he?"

She shook her head, her eyes clear.

"No, he didn't. Oh, he always had a good reason for anyone who cared to ask, but the truth was that he had a serious problem and it affected our home. Everything I did revolved around that problem and how it impacted on Ronnie and me. It wasn't a pleasant life."

"Were you in danger?" he asked, anger surging through his veins.

"No. He'd generally disappear until he was sober again. And if you let him ease back into the routine without comment, he was fine." She met his gaze. "I couldn't tell you, Gar. I was too embarrassed. I figured you'd realize how totally unsuitable I was to be going out with you. That's why I never asked you to come to my house. I know you must have wondered."

Gar figured that for someone the rest of the town

considered a relatively smart man, he was incredibly dense. "Actually, I never really noticed. Ronnie was with us, so I guess I just accepted that you had to care for her. Anyway, there was always lots of room at our place, and my dad liked to keep an eye on us."

How well he remembered those intensely scrutinizing eyes.

"Yes, I did have to watch Ronnie. I was more of a mother to her than a sister."

Gar noticed that she avoided mentioning her father. For some reason he'd never understood but intuitively known, the two of them had never really gotten along. Was his drinking the reason?

"And Ronnie was the reason you left here? Married Denis?" he prodded, watching the array of emotions fly across her face.

"Sort of." He saw her draw a lungful of air. "After you went away to college, I was alone a lot. I couldn't find a permanent job, Dad got laid off, and Ronnie and I had nothing in the house, sometimes for days, when Dad would disappear after a bender."

He wondered how dearly it had cost her to say that. Knowing Beth's pride, Gar figured it wasn't easy to reveal how desperately hard up they'd been.

"Surely there was someone who could have helped. The church or a social agency?" He saw her lips tighten and knew it was a stupid thing to say. Someone should have noticed without being told.

"I suppose if they'd known, they would have," she agreed dully. "But I didn't want anyone to know how awful it was." She smiled sadly. "Pride. Silly irresponsible pride that meant Ronnie went without when she didn't have to.'' Beth shook her head. ''I'll never forgive myself for that.''

''And you left because…?''

''I left because I had to get a job in a place where I could earn some money and provide for both of us. We were destitute. I couldn't live like that anymore, and I wouldn't let Ronnie stay home alone, with *him*. After a lot of heart-searching and debate, I became convinced that leaving was the only thing to do. By then I knew I wasn't going to marry you. You needed someone more your equal. I borrowed some money to start out, and left to try and start over.'' Her voice trailed away.

Gar glanced up and saw a flash of pain enter and leave her eyes. She was still hiding something—something she wasn't ready to tell him. Should he ask?

As he watched those delicate narrow shoulders bow under the strain of a memory that obviously still stung, Gar knew he wouldn't probe farther. He'd seen the shame on her face, and knew that she hated talking about those days. He wasn't too crazy about rehashing them, either. Wasn't it better to let it all go, and see what could happen from hereon?

''I'm glad you told me.'' He stayed where he was, watching as she drew herself erect, her dignity draped like a cloak around her. ''And that's why you wanted to see me that weekend? To tell me you were going away?''

She nodded. ''I owed you that. I didn't want to send a letter. I thought it was something I needed to do in person. I wanted to tell you to get on with your life, not to worry about us. Eventually, though, I had to write it. It was the hardest thing I've ever done.''

A letter? Gar frowned. He'd never gotten a letter from her. But then, maybe she hadn't mailed it. After all, it couldn't have been easy for an eighteen-year-old girl to uproot herself from everything familiar, and, with little sister in tow, take off for parts unknown. He'd ask about it later.

''I'm sorry, Beth. If I had known, I'd have done everything I could to get back here and help you out. You should have told me.'' He felt the old anger rise and shoved it down with resolution. Jordan was right. There was no profit in rehashing what could have been.

''I've been reminded many times lately that all of that is in the past. And this is the present. So where do we go from here?''

He held his breath, waiting for her answer. And as he did, he prayed that it wouldn't hurt too much when she told him she hated him.

''I don't know. There are so many things to think about.'' She smiled tremulously. ''I don't want to make any more decisions right now, Gar. It was hard enough to come back here when Ronnie decided she had to meet Dad. Now, I just want to relax and take one day at a time—see what God has in store for me. I want to focus on business and prove to the world that Beth Ainslow isn't a total write-off. Is that okay?''

''I'm sure nobody ever thought that you were a write-off, Beth,'' he offered, seeing the glint of tears return to those vivid green eyes. "What about me? Will it bother you that I'm around Wintergreen to pick up Ty? He seems to home in on this place after school."

"No," she said firmly, her clear gaze meeting his. "I'm glad Ronnie's found a friend, and I'm glad it's Ty. We can't go back to what we had, but maybe we can still be friends. Someday. If you can put the past behind you, I can, too. You're welcome here anytime, Garrett."

He pressed home his advantage. "And if I asked you out?"

Beth shook her head. "I don't think that's a good idea, Gar. Not with everyone already speculating about you and Cynthia, and probably me, too. Right now, what I really need is a friend."

"Then you've got one." He stood, once more buttoning the coat he'd never removed. Beth stood, too, peering up at him, her bare feet reducing her height considerably from the heels she usually wore.

"Thank you," she murmured, holding out her hand.

Gar took it, heart thumping as her smooth alabaster palm lay warmly against his. "If you need anything, anything," he repeated, "promise you'll let me know."

"Oh, you'll know." She grinned and self-consciously pulled her hand away. "Probably before the week's out. I'm going to apply for a loan."

He liked that impish gleam that sparkled deep in her eyes. It reminded him of happier times. "I just happen to know the boss,'' he quipped. ''I'll put in a good word for you.''

Her smile immediately fell away, but she hid it, walking in front of him to pull open the door.

''Thanks for talking to me, Gar. I was kind of dreading this confrontation, but you've made it much easier for me.''

''I'm glad.'' He didn't know what else to say, so he bid her good-night and left the old house, her earlier words still ringing in his ears.

Ronnie and I had nothing in the house, sometimes for days.

How did I miss it? Why didn't I see something, anything? he wondered as he drove to his parents' house.

''Well, Garrett, where have you been all this time? Your mother and I ate long ago. We were hoping you'd be here.'' His father stood in the marbled entry, his eyes probing. ''Some secret assignation? Cynthia called three times.''

Gar frowned. ''Why would you think I was meeting someone secretly?'' he asked as he hung up his coat.

A look of something—relief perhaps—flickered in his father's eyes. ''Just a joke. I'm having a second cup of coffee in the den if you want to join me. That Cynthia is a real nice girl. Well-mannered. Her family is from good stock. Is she someone special?''

Gar trailed along behind into the elegantly appointed oak-lined den his father had inhabited for years. But his mind whirled with what he'd just heard.

"We're just friends. Dad, what do you know about Mervyn Ainslow?"

His father's nimble fingers hesitated just a moment before they poured out two cups of coffee from the silver coffeepot. He added cream and sugar to his own before passing Gar a cup of black.

"Ainslow? Oh, you mean Ronnie's father." Charles Winthrop sank back into his tufted leather chair and sipped his coffee. "Not a lot. As I recall, the man had a drinking problem. At least, that's what I heard years ago."

"And the church deacons didn't offer to do anything for him, or for the girls? Especially with their mother gone?"

His father glanced up warily. "Why would you ask that? Is the man in trouble or something?"

"No. He's in a nursing home right now. I was just wondering how Ronnie and Beth had made it through back then. Nobody in this entire town seems to have lifted even their pinky to make sure the kids were okay." He stared at Charles, waiting for his denial. To his surprise, there was none.

"I'm afraid we're guilty there, son. Most of us just didn't want to see how bad Merv really was. He missed Loretta terribly, I suppose. Just as I would miss your mother."

"Sometimes they had no food." For some reason Gar felt inclined to push the issue. He wondered at the sudden whiteness of his father's face. "Are you all right?"

"Certainly. Just a little indigestion." His father buried his nose inside his cup, only to jerk it out moments later. "Why bring all this up now?" he demanded.

"I was talking to Beth tonight. She told me a little about why she left town ten years ago."

Charles surged to his feet and hurried over to replace his cup on the tray. With his back turned toward his son he asked, "Did she call you—ask you to go there?"

"No. I was at Wintergreen to meet with Jordan and Clay." He frowned, watching as his father fiddled with the cream pitcher. "Is everything really all right, Dad?"

"Certainly. Fine. Perfect. Think I'll go talk to your mother for a while." Charles stalked across the room and pulled open the door. "That young girl is here again," he muttered. "I'm not sure it's a good thing for Ty to be hanging around with her so much. He forgets his responsibilities."

Gar followed his father down the hallway and watched as he began to climb the stairs.

"Why shouldn't she come around if she wants to?" he demanded, frowning. "Ronnie's a perfectly fine girl, and she might even help Ty get his grades up. He should be looking for a college soon, you know."

His father quickened his pace. "She's not our kind, son. Childhood friends are one thing, but the boy needs to think about the future. So do you. See you later."

"Yeah, see you," Gar muttered, then added to himself, "What did I say wrong this time—?"

"He does that all the time. Talks to himself, I mean. I think it's a big brother thing. Or maybe senility."

Gar whirled around to see Ty and Ronnie standing behind him, huge grins spread across their faces. Apparently they hadn't heard his father's last remarks.

"Hi, you two. What are you doing?"

"Looking for something to eat. We missed dinner."

Ty didn't look worried in the least, and Gar couldn't help but smile. In the old days he'd gone out of his way to make sure he was on time for meals. Tardiness meant a long-winded lecture—and he'd hated those. Apparently Ty wasn't as concerned.

"I guessed you'd be here with the old folks." Scorn laced through Ty's squeaky voice. "You gotta get a life, Gar."

"For your information," Garrett enunciated, leading the way to the kitchen, "I was out. And I'm starved, too. I missed dinner."

"Boy, you're really living it up!" Ty shoved his way in front of Garrett and yanked open the fridge. "Cook left some sliced chicken, some kinda salad stuff and—wow!—lemon pie." He pulled everything out as he spoke and piled it on the counter. "Come on, Ronnie. Let's eat."

Gar whisked away a slice of the pie before his brother appropriated it all, helped himself to several slices of chicken and a healthy portion of the Caesar salad after Ronnie had chosen barely enough to feed a mouse.

"You eat even less than your sister used to," he remarked, smiling at her as he offered a can of soda.

"I think she got more carryout containers than anyone else in town back in those days." The reason for that suddenly hit him, and he gulped. How could he have been so stupid as not to have seen why?

"Beth's never eaten much," Ronnie murmured, shaking her head at Ty's offer of pickles. "But she's crazy for sweets. I gave her this huge chocolate Santa for Christmas, and it was gone before noon." She giggled. "We had a great time."

Gar remembered his Christmas at Aspen, and suddenly wished he'd stayed home. He'd been trying to avoid her after Maryann and Clayton's wedding, but she'd stayed in his mind so effectively that he might as well have planted himself at Wintergreen in the front hall and watched Beth come and go. Instead, he'd spent New Year's wondering who she was celebrating with.

"Just ignore him," he heard Ty mutter around a mouthful of food. "He's kinda spaced." He bounded up from his stool at the counter and snapped two fingers in front of Gar's face. "Yo, earth to Gar. Anybody home?"

Gar sighed. No respect, that was the problem. Everyone else seemed to think he was worthy of it— everyone except his own kid brother. "What is it, Ty?"

"I asked where you were that you had to miss dinner?" Ty rolled his eyes at Ronnie before returning to his seat. "I figured you'd be eating out with good ol' Cynth. She's kinda dull, like you."

"Cynthia Reardon?" Ronnie's eyes widened.

"She's gorgeous, Ty. So elegant and refined. I wish I was more like her. Instead I'm plain."

"No, you're not," Ty replied. "You're good-looking in a different kind of way. And you know how to have fun. Cynthia's as stiff as cardboard. 'Good evening, Mr. Winthrop,'" he mimicked in a falsetto. "'Thank you so much for inviting me over to your ball. I just adore those sculptures.' Yuk!" He shuddered.

"Ty, that's unkind and totally untrue. Cynthia is very bright, and a kind woman besides. She's certainly forgiven you for any number of faux pas." Gar placed his dishes in the dishwasher and turned to face his brother. "But, for your information, Cynthia and I are just friends."

"Does she know that?" Ty's eyes dared him to answer that. "She's looking for more than friendship."

"Well, that's all I'm offering." He ignored his brother's snort of derision and turned to Ronnie. "I'll drive you home, when you're ready."

"Thanks." She smiled, putting her own dishes away. "But I don't want to put you out. Beth said she'd come and get me."

"Your sister has been working all day. Why don't we give her a break. You call and tell her I'll drop you off, okay?" He waited for her nod and then glanced at Ty. "I'm going up to change, and then we can go. Try and get your homework finished, will you, Ty?"

"Nag, nag, nag." Ty's mouth turned down. "The parents already have one golden boy, why do they

need another one? I'm not cut out for bank stuff, Gar.
I want to do something else.''

"Like what?" Gar stopped where he was, frowning
as he undid his tie.

"I'm not saying. You'll just tell me how dumb it
is." Ty turned back to Ronnie, a dejected set to his
thin shoulders. "Come on, Ron. Let's go get your
stuff. It was fun riding through the woods, wasn't it?"

"It was wonderful! You're so lucky to live here."
Ronnie waved at the huge expanse of snow-covered
lawn that stretched out beyond the patio doors in the
dining room. "You can have all the pets you want
without bothering anyone."

Gar left them there, chattering, as he headed up to
his room. He caught the tail end of Ty's complaints.

"Yeah, but you've got the real freedom," his
brother murmured. "You don't have to fit a mold. You
can be anybody you want. That's way better."

Gar thought about that as he changed into jeans and
a sweatshirt. Was Ty really so unhappy with his life?
He himself had never minded school, had reveled in
the academic subjects and had made the team in three
sports. Tyler seemed to have none of those interests.
Gar wondered why that was. Was he missing something there, too, just as he'd missed Beth's problems.

He vowed to pay more attention. And he'd speak to
his father about having Ronnie out more often. Despite
his father's worries, Gar was certain that Veronica
Ainslow was a great influence on Ty. And driving her
home gave him another connection with Beth.

That was good.

Wasn't it?

Chapter Four

A week after her meeting with Gar, Beth forced her fingers to unclench. Then she pushed the glass paneled door of the bank open and resolutely stepped inside. The most expensive building in town bustled with activity, yet still managed to gleam with buffed elegance. The brass railings and glass partitions shone, totally free of grubby fingerprints and dust.

"I wonder if their cleaners do houses," she muttered to herself as she walked steadily past the tellers to the loans department. Yeah, right. Like Winthrop's cleaners would touch her dinky apartment.

"Hi, Beth. Chilly one today, isn't it?" Glynis Johnson smiled from behind her big oak desk. "Need those thermal things these days."

"Don't I know it." Beth pulled off her gloves, hoping she looked businesslike. "I had to refuse a shipment of long stems this morning. They were frozen solid."

"Oh, poor things! I don't know how you can stand to see those beauties ruined like that." Glynis pulled a sheaf of papers from the top basket of her desk. "Now, I suppose you'd like to get through this as quickly as possible. No businesswoman I know wants to be away from work when the door is open."

"Thanks, Glynis. I appreciate your help, and the way you've kept this quiet. I know this town is like a bubble where everyone knows everyone else's business, but I really don't want this to get around. Not just yet, anyway." She took the folder full of papers and opened it, gulping at the myriad rows and columns that confronted her.

"Don't pass out! It looks like a lot, but it's not really that bad. We just like to have a bit of history to base our decisions on. If you need help, I could take a few minutes and show you—"

"Thanks, Glynis, but it's all right. I filled out all those forms before I ever opened the Enchanted Florist. I can handle these." She glanced around. "Is there someplace I can sit?"

"Sure, use this office. It's empty at the moment." Glynis opened a door to her left and indicated the empty desk and chair. "If you need help, just yell. I've got a pretty light day."

"Thanks. You're very kind."

"Not at all. Things always slow down when Gar goes out of town. But he always brings back twenty times more work for me, so I don't feel bad about relaxing once in a while." She grinned and pulled the door almost closed behind her.

So Garrett wasn't in the bank today? Good. That made it easier to do this. She laid out the sheets, took a deep breath and concentrated on the first one. She could do this. She had to do this. Ronnie was counting on her.

Twenty minutes later, voices disturbed her.

"I'm sorry, Mr. Winthrop. I didn't know you had asked the Thomms to come in today. I'm sure the office will be free in a moment."

Beth jerked to attention, then quickly shoved the sheaf of documents inside the folder. "It's all right, Glynis. I'm finished anyway." She stood, eyes trained on the door. "Hello, Mr. Winthrop."

The elder Winthrop stared at her, his eyes chilly. Finally he responded. "Miss, er, Mrs.—" He stopped. "I'm sorry, I don't know how to address you."

She was fairly certain the remark was supposed to make her cower, but she refused to be put down. She had a perfectly good reason for being here. "Beth," she enunciated clearly. "Beth Ainslow. Surely you remember?"

"Beth has an appointment to talk to you in—" Glynis consulted her watch then smiled at them both "—in two minutes." She reached for the folder. "All finished with these?"

"I've done as much as I'm going to. I think the *pertinent* information is all there." She ignored the frowning look Glynis gave her. "Is Mr. Winthrop free now?"

"Uh, yes. That is, I believe so. If you'll come this way, I'll let the Thomms in here." She led Beth out of the office and to an etched-glass door with the name and title Charles Winthrop, President embossed on the frosted pane. "Have a seat, Beth. I'm sure he'll be with you shortly."

Beth sat because her legs wouldn't allow her to stand any longer. The room had been redecorated since the last time she'd been here, but the walls were still warm with the mahogany paneling. Under her feet, the carpet was the thickest broadloom she'd ever seen, it's brilliant jade color rich against the wood.

"I can't do this," she decided, and gulped nervously as she eyed the expensive brass fixtures lying neatly on the desk. Who used a brass letter opener these days?

Nothing had changed. She didn't fit in here any more now than she had then. What did she know about mortgages and profit-and-loss sheets? Who was she to be in here, bearding the lion in his den?

"Miss Ainslow, I have no idea why you need to see me privately. I don't believe we have anything to say to each other." Charles Winthrop strode across the room, seated himself behind his desk and folded his hands on top of the immaculate blotter. "Do we?"

"Uh, well, that is—" Beth heard herself stammering and felt a heat wash over her cheeks. Nothing had changed. Nothing! She was still intimidated by this man and his wealth. She had nothing, she was a nobody. And he was rich and well-known, needing nobody, nothing and no one.

"Yes, Miss Ainslow? Why did you ask to see me?"

Something in his tone, some underlying note of concern made her look up. She studied his face—leaner, lined with worry, drawn tight even though he'd apparently just returned from a skiing holiday. And something inside her clicked.

Charles Winthrop was a businessman. He earned his money by using other people's money. He would loan her money and charge her an exorbitant amount for that. It was a business arrangement. But that's all it was. There was no hidden hierarchy. No more than there was when a customer came in to her shop hoping to do some business.

She straightened in her seat, shoulders back, chin up. She was an equal here, a businesswoman prepared to offer him an opportunity, not some lowly eighteen-year-old filled with self-doubts.

"I'm here to enquire about a loan from your bank, Mr. Winthrop. I'd like to purchase a building that I've learned will be going up for sale. My present location is far too small to generate the kind of sales I am currently projecting and achieving." She took a deep breath and waited for his response.

"Well." Charles Winthrop folded and refolded his hands, chagrin contorting the patrician lines of his face. "I see." He recovered quickly. "We must have some information before we grant loans, Ms. Ainslow."

Beth smiled, noting that he'd settled for her maiden name, but attached the "Ms." lest anyone misconstrue her as single.

"I've given Beth the forms and I believe she's completed them, Mr. Winthrop." Glynis edged through the door, carrying a tray with two cups of steaming coffee. "I thought you might like your coffee while you discuss this."

She seemed totally unaware of the tense atmosphere that hung between the other two, but went quietly about handing out the cups and offering cream and sugar, then glided back out the door. Beth took a sip for fortification.

"I believe you'll find what you need in here," she murmured, handing across the file folder with its contents.

He took it, set it on his desk and then peered across at her. "Are you sure there isn't someone you'd like to consult first? Perhaps someone with a bit more, er, experience in such matters? A new business is generally on rather tenuous ground until it has proved itself for a period of time."

Beth nodded. "Yes, generally speaking I'd agree with you. Except when that business is suffering because it cannot grow any more under the present circumstances." She sat back and folded her hands in her lap.

"Thank you, but I don't need to speak to anyone, Mr. Winthrop. My degree has given me some knowledge in this matter, and I feel confident I can handle the purchase myself, with my lawyer's advice, of course." She took a deep breath of confidence. She wasn't that insecure little girl from ten years ago. She was a businesswoman, and she needed this loan if she hoped to expand and build up business enough to support Ronnie when she left for college.

"As you may be aware, I am now renting. I'm obligated only by the month. I can give notice at any time, and it seems to me that January would be a good opportunity to do that. Once we are a little closer to Valentine's Day, I'll be receiving larger shipments and I'll need the additional area for arranging displays."

He nodded. "Yes, I can see how the extra space could be valuable. But surely that space isn't income-generating. It's work space. Perhaps if you worked later at night, or came in earlier..." His voice trailed away. "I'm sorry, perhaps you are already doing that."

It sounded smug and overbearing. But maybe it wasn't a put-down, Beth considered. Maybe he was just trying to be sure she'd considered other options. Well, she had. And thoroughly. But no matter how much she shifted and reorganized and rearranged, there simply was not enough room. She knew that—now it was up to her to convince him of it.

"Yes, I have. We worked in triple shifts through the Christmas season to accommodate our customers as best we could, but I'm afraid there are still unexpected funerals and walk-in customers who don't want to pick something up tomorrow or the day after. We simply must have more room." She held her temper in check and calmly listed the reasons for her decision.

To his credit, Charles Winthrop listened to her plans for expansion into Belgian chocolates and the ever-popular stuffed animals. He nodded when she spoke about the market in items other than fresh flowers, and she couldn't help but feel a warm glow at his obvious surprise. She'd done her homework, and done it well.

"So, as you can see, this isn't some fly-by-night idea of mine. I intend to stay in Oakburn and make this business grow strong and healthy." She held his gaze, never wavering under the intense scrutiny.

"And your plans for the future?" His voice hinted at something.

"My sister would like to go to veterinary college when she's finished high school. That will be fairly costly, but if at all possible, I'd like to send her. That's why I want to get things going on the right foot at my store." If he was asking about Gar, Charles Winthrop was going to have to come right out and ask her.

"I see. You plan to stay at your current home, then? Continue to pay rent at that house— What's it called?"

"Wintergreen." She frowned. "Caitlin has been very kind. And yes, the apartment suits me quite well. Ronnie is near the school and there is always someone around."

"And your father?"

The softly voiced enquiry made her sit up straighter, sent her shoulders back.

"I'm sure you're aware my father is in the local nursing home where he is being taken care of. He has all he needs there. I am not responsible for him financially, if that's what you're asking." She swallowed the rest of the words. This wasn't the time to defend a man who had no defense, even if she wanted to. She needed this loan.

"Why did you come back?" The question seemed forced, as if he hadn't wanted to ask it but couldn't help himself.

Beth shifted uncomfortably. "Ronnie wanted to see Dad again. She doesn't have much memory of him, and she wanted to fill in the gaps before it was too late."

"Perhaps it's better that she doesn't. I understand from my son that he was absent quite frequently."

The well-polished scorn in those tones sent her hackles up, and for the first time in her life Beth defended the man she'd been sure she hated.

"My father loved my mother. When she died, he couldn't get past his grief. Yes, he drank. Too much. And yes, I suppose you even know that he left us alone for days on end. When he was home, he did the best he could. Perhaps that's the most anyone can do." She glared at him, daring him to say more.

Long minutes passed as he sat there, ensconced behind his elegant desk, studying her from behind his gold-rimmed glasses. She couldn't read his face. He'd had too much practice hiding his emotions. Nothing much had changed there.

Beth was fed up with the whole event. Certain that it was pointless to continue, and needing desperately to get away from this cloying atmosphere, Beth gathered up her purse and coat.

"Thank you for your time, Mr. Winthrop, but I have to get back to work. I'll leave those papers with you. I'm sure you'll need some time to decide." Actually, he'd probably already decided. And no doubt the answer would be a resounding "no." At least she'd tried.

She pulled open the door to his office, looking back over her shoulder as she did. "Please have Glynis phone me as soon as you've made your decision. I'd like to get moving immediately, if possible. As you already know, I always pay back my loans."

She nodded and then stepped through the door, careening into a solid mass almost twice her size.

"Beth?" Strong lean hands held her steady as she caught her breath. "What are you doing here?"

"Gar." She pulled herself away, mentally aware of the fresh lime tang of his cologne—he still used the same one. "Talking to the president of this bank. Excuse me, please."

Beth moved past him and down the glossy floor in a straight beeline for the door. She did not want to be there when Garrett discussed her loan application with his father. And he would. As a member of the board, a registered financial consultant and second in command, Gar's opinion would be sought.

Once outside, she breathed in the cold, crisp air and glanced up at the bright blue winter sky. Whatever happened, she'd done her best. It was in God's hands now.

Back at the shop her part-time helper was busy explaining the variety of cut flowers that could be assembled on such short notice. Beth checked the messages lying by the phone and frowned. The nursing home? What did they want?

She dialed the number. "This is Beth Ainslow. I understand someone called me."

She listened as the voice on the other end of the line explained that the home was having a potluck supper for the families. "I have your note here and just wanted to be sure you are aware of this opportunity to spend time with your loved one."

My note? Beth peered out the huge plate-glass window and groaned as enlightenment dawned. Ronnie! It had to be. She was so determined to get to know her father.

"And this is tonight?" Beth nodded, her voice quiet. "Thank you for phoning. Goodbye."

She had no doubt that Ronnie knew all about the supper. She'd been to the nursing home many times, and except for Christmas Day, all without Beth. There were notes plastered all over the fridge at home about upcoming events.

Beth knew she'd have to go. If she kept on avoiding her father, the whole town would begin speculating as to what had happened in the Ainslow household. Next would come a debate on why she'd *really* left town.

"He's old, he's half senile, he can't hurt us anymore." But even as she recited the words, Beth knew it wasn't the present she feared as much as the resurfacing of the past.

"She's applying for a loan? Why?" Gar listened as his father explained, running over the figures she'd neatly printed on the forms he held. "Expanding already, huh? Good for her. You'll approve it, of course.''

''Approve it?'' His father glared at him. ''Have you lost all your sense, Garrett? She has very little collateral, almost no assets, and her ideas are risky.''

''I think they're very sound and she's proven them by the looks of these statements. She's good at what she does, Dad. Why not give her a chance? That's how Grandpa started this place, remember?'' Gar watched the fine pink flush rise from his father's collar.

''That was a long time ago. People didn't default on their debts then like they do now.'' Charles straightened the immaculate piles of paper on his desk, then glanced up. ''I recommend we refuse.''

''Then I'll stand as guarantor myself.'' Gar met his father's startled glance. ''She deserves a chance, Dad. And she's not going to default. If that business fails, it won't be because Beth hasn't put every single ounce of effort she has into making it a go.''

''You don't feel obligated, or something, do you? I mean, it was just a silly, childish crush that the two of you shared in school. You were both too young to know better. You've moved past that with Cynthia.''

Gar shook his head. ''Cynthia and I are just friends. How many times have I told you that, Dad? And I'm not so sure my feelings for Beth are in the past. I didn't have a 'crush' on her, I was in love with her. And she loved me.''

Charles sprang to his feet, his eyes blazing. ''What do you mean, son? It was over years ago. She ran out on you.''

''She left Oakburn to get a job so she could support her sister and herself.'' Gar stared at his father's angry face. ''Why does all this bother you so much, Dad?''

''She's been married, Gar. *Married!*'' Charles flopped back down in his elegantly tufted chair. ''How could this girl have loved you if she married someone else?''

It was a question Gar had asked himself a hundred times. And he'd never found an answer. Wasn't it funny that now one came immediately to mind.

''She was alone, with a child to support. I'm sure Denis Hernsley was a nice man and his, uh, support would have been appreciated.'' He couldn't make himself say the word *love*.

''Exactly! If she loved you, why didn't she come to you? Why go to him? She must have loved him, don't you think?''

Gar shook his head vehemently. ''No, I don't think that at all, Dad. I think she was a mixed-up kid who couldn't handle her life here and tried to do the best she could somewhere else. And I think it's up to us to see to it that she gets a fair shake in this town. We owe her that much, don't you think?'' He frowned as his father's face blanched.

''W-what do you mean, Gar?''

''I mean that someone in this town should have seen what those two were going through ten years ago. Somebody should have reached out a hand of hope and helped them. And I'm one of those people. I was engaged to the woman, and I didn't see what was right in front of my face.''

"It wasn't your fault, Garrett. You were just a kid. It wasn't mine, either." Charles wiped his pristine white handkerchief across his forehead. "Mervyn Ainslow is a drunk. Nobody but him can change that."

"I'm not debating that, Dad." Why was the old man getting so hot under the collar? It was as if he knew something no one else knew. Gar shook his head. How ridiculous. "All I'm saying is that those two girls should have been able to count on the church, the community, someone. Oakburn goofed up back then, Dad. But we're not going to make that mistake again. Are we?"

He fixed his father with a stern look that dared him to deny Beth the opportunity to make good. If worse came to worst, he would invoke his grandmother's help, plead for her to insist on helping someone who deserved a chance.

"Well?"

Charles sighed and signed his name to the bottom of the application. "Very well, she can have the loan. But the bank will assume the risk. I won't have you tying yourself up with someone else's problems for the next ten years." He thrust the papers at Gar. "Besides, I thought you were advising the Forsyths to hang onto that property. Now, suddenly you want them to sell?"

Gar ignored the jibe, shuffling all the paperwork for Beth's loan into a neat pile.

"As someone recently pointed out to me, the Forsyths are retired and their biggest dream is to travel. Why should they have that building hanging around their necks the whole time? The cash from this sale will give them a lot more enjoyment than that pile of brick and mortar.''

Charles sniffed. ''Miss Ainslow's advice, no doubt?''

''As a matter of fact, it was. That's one thing you have to admit, Dad. Beth has her head on straight.'' He grinned at his father's dubious look. ''I'll go tell her.''

Charles mumbled something like ''straight to the money,'' but Gar ignored him and left the office. On his way out he hugged Glynis so close that her feet left the floor. The woman gave a shriek of dismay and then giggled with delight as he set her down.

''Mr. Garrett, you shouldn't be doing that to an old woman like me. I could have heart failure!'' She straightened her prim white blouse and long black skirt.

Gar burst out laughing, his knuckles brushing her talcum-scented cheeks. ''Never, Glynis. You're much too young and healthy.'' She preened before his eyes, and he strode across to his own office, grinning from ear to ear.

It took two seconds to dial the number he'd memorized months ago. ''Beth, it's me, Garrett. Your loan has been approved. We can go ahead with the paperwork right away, if you'd like.'' He listened to her shocked silence and then her burst of questions. ''Dad makes up his own mind. But we'd be fools if we didn't look to the future with an eye to keeping Oakburn growing, now wouldn't we?''

She agreed, her voice breathless with relief. He could almost see those blue eyes soften and lighten.

"How about coming out for dinner tonight? To celebrate?"

"I can't, Gar. But thanks for asking." Her voice immediately changed, grew harsh and cold.

"Oh." He swallowed down his disappointment. "I'm sorry, Beth. I didn't mean to take anything for granted."

"It's not that. Ronnie's arranged for us to attend a potluck at the nursing home. I-I think I'd better go."

He knew how hard it would be for her to go there and pretend that she was glad to visit her father. Somehow he felt sure that when Beth looked at her father, she remembered the past, and the bitterness of it welled up inside all over again. She'd talked of moving on, but she would have to deal with those feelings first.

"I'm sorry," she whispered, a catch in her voice. "Maybe another time."

"Nah, I think tonight is as good a time as any." He made some swift calculations. "I'll pick you and Ronnie up at Wintergreen. What time—six?" She muttered something about the residents eating early, and he scribbled a note to himself. Not that he was likely to forget.

"Okay, five-thirty it is. And don't worry about food. Nettie's got a whole fridge full of stuff that Dad and Mom will never eat. I just happen to know that today is her baking day."

"You don't have to do that, Gar. It's not necessary. I can grab something from the deli."

"Why bother? Now, get to work. You've got a lot of planning to do." He grinned, pleased that he'd been able to do this much for her.

"I do, don't I?" Her voice thrilled with wonder.

Gar hung up, filled with determination to be there when Beth encountered Mervyn. If the old man was in one of his foul moods, he'd hightail Beth out of there so fast her head would spin. Potluck or no potluck.

He picked up the phone and called home. "Hey, Nettie. This is your favorite person. No, not Ty." He grimaced, unwilling to accept that he'd been replaced in the cook's hierarchy of love. "Gar. Your *very* favorite. What can you give me to take to the potluck at the nursing home tonight?"

As he listened to the string of items that ensued, Gar finally answered the voice inside his head. No, he didn't feel guilty. And he wasn't trying to buy Beth— not that he could. He simply wanted to help an old friend get past this next hurdle. If it meant spending some time with her, so much the better. He'd take whatever time he could get.

There wasn't anything wrong with seizing opportunity, was there?

Chapter Five

"The whole town must be here." Ronnie almost danced up the sidewalk, her arms laden with the fresh rolls Nettie had donated for the potluck supper.

"And then some." Beth glanced around nervously, spying several vehicles she knew, and a lot of faces she recognized but couldn't put a name to. "I probably shouldn't have come. The Arnetts are having that big anniversary party on Saturday and I've got tons of work to do."

It was a stupid time for a reunion, she admitted privately. Why hadn't she come here one afternoon when Ronnie was in school and spoken to her father alone, without any witnesses?

Because you were afraid he'd rant and rave like the last time. And you know he's right. You could have brought Ronnie to see him umpteen times in the past ten years.

Yeah, I could have. But why would I?

*So she and Mervyn could get to know each other.
Ronnie's not like you. She doesn't hold grudges.*

"Are you okay, Beth?" Gar's hand beneath her arm
lent support that she was only too ready to accept.

"Yes, I'm fine. I just wish I hadn't come. There are
so many people." She walked slowly through the
doors and down the hall, barely following Ronnie's
eager form as she burst her way through the crowd in
a rush of energy.

"And they're all busy with their own families," Gar
murmured in her ear. "No one is paying any attention
to you."

It was a lie, but it was a nice lie.

"Yeah, they are," she muttered, nodding at the
groups of people they passed. "And why not? The last
time I was here, they had to sedate my father. Not
exactly a great reunion." She heard a chortle and
turned to look.

Gar's mouth was creased into a huge grin; his eyes
danced with mirth. "Sorry. I just got this mental picture and—"

"It set you off." She shook her head in reproof,
amazed that he hadn't lost his sense of the absurd.
"Still, Gar?"

He shrugged. "I can't help it if I have a good sense
of humor."

"More like a distorted one." She felt the tension
draining away as his eyes laughed down into hers. She
shrugged. "Okay, maybe it was kind of funny. In a
weird sort of way."

"There you go." He stopped inside the huge dining

room. "Is there someplace I can put this stuff, or am I doomed forever to carry three dozen butter tarts."

"Shh!" Beth placed a finger across his lips. "If you blab it to everyone, there will be none left." Suddenly she realized what she'd done and jerked her hand away.

Gar seemed unfazed. "There won't anyway," he prophesied, gloom distorting his handsome features. "Nettie's cooking never hangs around for very long." Then he grinned, and the blaze of it warmed her cold heart. "Fortunately, I have personal access to a private stash in the freezer. So, do you see him anywhere?"

"There. With Ronnie." Beth pointed to the small, shrunken man who sat huddled in an armchair, his eyes searching the room. When he saw her his eyes widened, but it was the sight of Gar that seemed to shake the old man.

Beth strode across the room, determined to get it over with. "Hi, Dad. How are you?"

The question was perfunctory, and everyone, including Mervyn, knew it.

"Cold," he barked, glaring at them. "Stupid place never cranks the heat up. Drafty old place." He jerked his chair forward, away from the windowledge he'd sat down beside, and in so doing almost upset Gar's load of tarts. "What's that stuff?"

"Food." Gar set the containers down on a nearby coffee table and then shrugged out of his coat.

Beth couldn't help but notice the quality of the blue cashmere sweater he wore, and contrast it with her own acrylic pullover. There was no comparison. It was like comparing diamonds to cubic zirconias. She swallowed as he tugged the sweater off, displaying his powerful chest concealed by a black turtleneck.

"Put this on, Mr. Ainslow," he offered, holding out the expensive sweater. "I'm roasting. If I wear that I'll pass out for sure."

The room wasn't overly warm, but neither was it cold. Beth knew he was just being kind. But she couldn't afford to pay for that sweater. Neither could her father.

"Isn't it lovely, Dad?" Ronnie slid a hand over the knitted garment. "It's so soft. Here, I'll help you." She carefully slipped the oversize garment over the white head and then tenderly smoothed each hair back in place as her father shifted the sweater into place. "You look very nice."

"Feels better. Thank you." Mervyn studied Gar for so long that Beth wanted to scream. "Do I know you?"

"Garrett Winthrop. Charles's son. How are you, Mr. Ainslow?"

"Didn't think I knew you, but I expect you know right well how I am." Mervyn glared at the outstretched hand, but finally shook it. "When are we going to eat, anyway? A body could die of starvation in this place."

"I'm hungry, too. Should we find a table or something?" Ronnie glanced around, apparently unabashed by the grumpy behavior.

Beth could have crawled into a hole. Her own father

looked right past her as if she weren't even there. Why had she even bothered to come?

"I expect you're pretty proud of your daughters, aren't you, Mr. Ainslow? My brother tells me that Ronnie's in the running for a scholarship for her high marks. And Beth's shop is doing very well."

"Flowers!" The old man snorted. "Who needs that drivel in a dinky little town like Oakburn? It'll never fly."

"Actually it's flying higher than anyone expected." Gar's voice was even as he seated himself across from the older man, his gray eyes intent. "Beth's moving into a new building pretty soon, you know. She needs the extra space."

The sting of her father's words faded just a little as Beth listened to the proud ring in Gar's voice. He was such a wonderful man, spending his valuable time here, trying to coax a grumpy old man to smile.

"Humph! How's she going to pay for it?" Mervyn glanced at her for a minute, and Beth could see the malice in his eyes. "Your dad going to fund this expedition, too?"

"The bank has given her a loan." Gar's tones were even, though he cast an odd, questioning look at Beth.

"You got it?" Ronnie flew across the small area and hugged Beth. "Oh, how lovely! Now we can really show off your stuff. Wait 'til good old Oakburn sees those Valentine's arrangements you've got planned! The ones you did last year were awesome, but *these!* We'll have to hire someone to handle the extra customers."

"It is exciting, isn't it?" Beth turned back to her father, holding out the bouquet of flowers she carried. "I brought these over for your room. I thought they might cheer you up."

"How're flowers supposed to cheer me up?" Mervyn grumped, but there was a glint of something in his eye. "I suppose you'd better put them in my room, then. Ronnie, go put those things in a jar of water, would you?"

"Sure thing, Dad." Ronnie took the flowers and danced off down the hall, barely containing her excitement.

"Girl's full of vim and vinegar," Mervyn murmured appreciatively. "She'll go far in life."

"I hope so." Beth sank down into the nearest vacant chair and smoothed her slacks nervously. "She wants to go to veterinary school, you know."

"Smart girl! She can make a bundle off them rich folks that have their animals doctored all the time." Mervyn peered up at Gar quizzically. "Wasn't it a Winthrop who used to dole out a king's ransom for someone to take care of horses. Waste of money."

"Dad loves his horses. He doesn't consider that a waste." Gar smiled pleasantly at the curmudgeon, and then turned to Beth. "I think he recognizes me," he whispered. "He's just faking it."

"Why bother?" she asked back, and then sat up as an aide came to speak to them. "Yes, we'll be glad to sit over there. We brought these." She handed over the food and then grasped her father's elbow. "Come on, Dad. I'll help you up."

"I don't need help getting out of a chair!" Mervyn slapped her outstretched hand away before slowly standing.

Once erect, he wavered back and forth. Beth held her breath, afraid he'd fall down. She breathed a sigh of relief when Gar finally took her father's arm and led him toward the tables. Ronnie caught up with them halfway there.

"We'd better get seated pretty quick or we won't get a seat at all," he said, steering Mervyn toward a table near the window on the farside of the room. "This looks like a good spot."

"The cat comes in and out that door. I hate cats. Sneaky, preying things." Mervyn frowned. "It's cold here."

"You'll soon be warm. Now, Beth and I will go get some food while you and Ronnie save our places. What would you like?" Gar stood patiently waiting, seemingly unperturbed by the other man's continuous complaints.

"I suppose it's all cold stuff. What does a man have to do to get a hot meal around here?"

"I'll ask." Before Beth could say anything, Gar was escorting her toward the buffet. "Come on. I'll choose his plate. There must be something here that he likes."

"He used to love fried chicken. Not mine, of course. It wasn't as good as Mom's. Not that that ever stopped him from eating it!" She took four plates and handed him two. "I really appreciate your helping out,

Gar. I'm just sorry he's so miserable today. It's not very pleasant for you, and you've been so kind.''

"Beth, don't worry about me. I'm fine. I just feel kind of sorry for your dad. He's stuck there all day, staring out the window, when you know he'd rather be snowshoeing across country. He used to love to hunt, didn't he?''

Beth was surprised. "I didn't know you'd remember that. It was a long time ago.'' She thought about her father's change of life-style. "I guess it is sort of constricting. But I can't look after him properly at Wintergreen. He needs oxygen most of the time, and medication for his heart. I'd have to stay home.'' She shook her head in frustration. "It's a no-win situation.''

Gar's hand covered hers. "You're doing the best you can, Beth. Nobody could ask for more than that. Besides, I'm not so sure your father would want to live with you. He seems to have made a few friends here.''

He tilted his head to one side, and Beth followed the motion, then gasped as her father's hearty laugh rang out, his face wreathed in a grin as he joked with an elderly woman who shuffled past in her walker.

"He's smiling,'' she breathed in astonishment. "Imagine!''

"Yeah, imagine.'' But Gar was staring at her, his face intent. "Don't start to feel guilty, Beth. You did the best you could. That's the most you could do.''

She put a scoop of potato salad on Ronnie's plate, then served herself with lettuce.

"He blames me, you know," she said finally, aware that though he kept moving through the line, Gar was waiting for her next response. "He said I should have at least brought Ronnie to see him, even if she didn't stay with him. He doesn't seem to understand that I wasn't just a few miles away. I couldn't simply pack her up and send her, and it would have cost so much for both of us to fly down."

Gar picked up a couple of rolls and butter, waited for Beth to add meat to her plates, and then stepped aside, out of the way of scurrying staff.

"Did you want to?" he asked softly.

Beth searched his face, but there was nothing there to hint at malice. He wasn't just chipping away at her. He really wanted to know. Slowly, she shook her head.

"No, I didn't. I never wanted to come back here, even if we could have afforded it. When I left this place back then, I thought I'd left for good."

He nodded. "You did the best you could. Let it go."

As she followed him back to the table and watched her father scrutinize the choices Gar had made for him, Beth couldn't help wondering how she was supposed to let the past go when her father wouldn't.

Two hours later they left the home, Ronnie running back to tell her father one last thing she'd forgotten to impart.

"Those two seem to really hit it off." Gar grinned. "Not that your sister has a problem talking to anyone, but she seems really close to your dad."

Beth nodded. "It's one of the reasons I came back,

even though he seems to hate me. Ronnie really needed this connection to her family. I just hope I won't live to regret it.''

''What do you mean?'' Gar stood, frowning, as he held the car door open. ''Why should you regret it?''

''You don't know what he's like when he takes a drink, Gar. If he ever gets hold of a bottle, he'll stomp all over her tender feelings. Alcohol doesn't bring out the best in him.''

Gar slammed the door shut and walked around to the other side. He climbed in and started the car, switching the heater on high before he spoke.

''There is no liquor allowed where he's staying, Beth. And anyway, I'm sure he's past that now. You yourself said it was partly because of your mother's death. That was a long time ago. He's had time to deal with it.''

Beth pulled her wallet out of her purse and opened it to display the photo she'd tucked inside so long ago. ''This was my mom, Gar,'' she murmured, holding it out so he could get a better look.

''You could be identical twins!'' Gar stared at her, then at the photo. ''It's amazing.''

''Maybe now you see why he finds it so hard to have me around, why he resents me. I must remind him of her constantly.''

''Yes, I suppose you must.'' Gar stared at the photo until Ronnie returned to the car, breathless and chatty.

''He's playing cribbage with some other old guy. They have quite a sparring match going, but I don't think Dad will better him.'' Ronnie perched on the edge of the back seat so she could pat Gar's shoulder. "Thanks for backing Beth up. He razzes her a lot, and I know it hurts her."

"Maybe you can drop me at the store," Beth broke in, her face warm with embarrassment. "I have a fair bit of work to do there. Will you be okay for a while, Ronnie?"

"Aw, come on, sis! You promised I could have Ty over tonight. We're working on that biology project together, and I was going to help him decide on the title page."

"He's doing the title page and—let me guess—" Gar pretended to consider for a moment "—you're doing all the work, right? That kid is a freeloader."

"No, he's not!" Ronnie protested indignantly, her eyes flashing. "Ty's been a really great friend. Besides, I'm just repaying him."

"Repaying him? For what?" Beth frowned, wondering how she was ever to keep up to the orders that had begun to flood in if she was constantly chaperoning teenagers.

"Just a little agreement the two of us had. Nothing bad, really. He's helping me with a little problem, and I'm helping him." Ronnie leaned back in her seat. "It's okay if you can't handle it tonight, sis. I know you've got to get those orders ready. I guess I'll have to phone Ty as soon as we get home. I hope he hasn't left yet." That plaintive note crept into her voice.

"I could stay." Gar's response was hesitant, almost apologetic. "I haven't got anything scheduled for tonight but paperwork, and even that isn't urgent. I don't mind watching the two of them at Wintergreen. Or they can come out to Fairwinds. Mom and Dad would like that.''

''That's very kind of you—'' Beth stared at her sister's vehemently shaking head.

''No, we can't do that. It has to be at Wintergreen. I've got all my research and stuff already set up there in the library we made. It'll take me eons to pack it all up and then unpack it. Besides—'' Ronnie checked her watch ''—Ty should be showing up right about now.''

Gar turned the corner, and, sure enough, there was Ty climbing out of his father's luxurious sedan, which then pulled away.

Ronnie burst out of Gar's car and sprinted over to where Ty stood. A hurriedly whispered conversation took place. Beth sighed and accepted the hand Gar offered as she levered herself out of the low-slung sports car. Whatever they were up to, it was apparently top secret. But she wouldn't pry. Let Ronnie have her secrets. At least something besides her father was occupying the girl's mind.

''Ty and I would really like to have Gar stay. If it's okay with you, Beth?'' Ronnie's wistful expression was the same one she used to wheedle extra candy out of her sister every Christmas.

Beth had never been able to resist Ronnie's soft doe-eyed look, so she turned to Gar. ''What do you think?''

''I think she should find somebody else to con,'' he

muttered for her ears alone. "I also think that you're too soft. If you don't want me here, just say so."

"Oh, no. It's not that. It's just that I was worried that you'd have something else to do. Something more important." Beth knew she was babbling. She clamped her lips together while she searched for her misplaced decorum. "If you don't mind hanging around here, it's fine with me. I just don't think it's a good idea for them to be alone here."

"I agree." He followed her up the stairs and into the house. "With those two in cahoots, Wintergreen would probably be reduced to hundred-year-old ashes in mere minutes." He patted a balustrade fondly. "Since I like what Caitlin's done with the old girl, I'll protect her."

"Oh, brother!" Beth rolled her eyes as she unlocked her door. "Here you are, then. Enjoy, soak up the ambience, or whatever it is. I'm going back to the shop."

"I could take you," Gar offered. "These two could manage for five minutes."

Beth shook her head, smiling as she thrust her keys back in her pocket. "No, thanks. Climbing out of that thing more than twice a day is dangerous to my health."

"You don't like my Vette all of a sudden?" His eyebrows rose. "Why?"

Beth pulled on her gloves, relishing her response even before she gave it. Gar was pleased with himself, a little too pleased that she'd been coerced into doing what Ronnie wanted. His shoulders were all puffed up with conceit and his eyes glittered the way they always had when he thought he'd snuck in the last word.

"Garrett Winthrop, you aren't sixteen years old anymore. That's a hot rod, a toy car. It's not the kind of vehicle a man who advises people on their finances should drive. It's too—" She searched for the right word. "Risky," she finally managed.

"Risky?" He looked affronted. "My car isn't risky! It's got a powerful motor that can overtake most anything on the roads around here."

Beth nodded, biting her lip to keep from smiling. "I know. And when people look at you sitting in that shiny black bat-car, what do you think they see?"

"I dunno." Confusion crossed his face. "What do you see?"

"A little boy who never grew up." She pulled open the door, then turned back and wiggled her fingers at him. "See you later."

"Beth, wait a minute! What do you mean? I'm not a kid—"

She shut the door on his protestations and burst out laughing. *That* would give him something to think about aside from her shabby furniture and cheap furnishings.

Now, if she could just keep her mind off him for the next couple of hours, she might actually get some work done.

Chapter Six

"Folks, if we can bring this meeting to order." Herbert Fitzwater pounded the hammer, which was acting as a gavel, on the block of spruce. "Come on, folks. We've got us some business to do here tonight."

Gar glanced around the table, searching for but not finding Beth's tiny figure. Where was she? He'd volunteered for this committee, and Beth was the only reason he was here. He had figured he could almost call it a date, and it was sure better than sitting for three hours in her living room, staring at blissful, smiling photos of her, Denis and Ronnie as he had during his last visit to Wintergreen.

So where was she?

"All right now. That's better." Herbert grinned his semi-toothless smile, and pawed through the sheaf of papers in front of him. "Now, what's next, Eustace?"

"You might call the roll, Herbert. How d'we know

if everybody's here? We can't just hope we got all our members.''

Gar knew Edgar Bonds wasn't in the least happy with being included on this board. What he did like was the stipend he was paid for attending. This was probably his one contribution of the night, but Gar could have kissed him for it. Surely now they wouldn't start without Beth.

''I counted seven around this table, Ed. That's the number we're s'posed to have. Now let's get down to business.''

Gar was about to protest, ask for a recount, do something—anything—to stop them, when the door to the council chambers flew open and Beth rushed inside. Her cheeks were red from the cold and her hair stood up in little golden-red spikes that the wind had created.

''I'm so sorry. I had a last-minute customer.'' She tugged her coat off as she spoke and placed it across one of the empty tables.

Since no one else moved, Gar got up and offered her his chair. Once she was seated, he retrieved another for himself and set it to the left of hers, raising one eyebrow at Gertrude McGillicuddy in the hope that she would move her chair just a tad south.

''Excuse me,'' he whispered as Herbert slammed the hammer down once more. Gertrude frowned ferociously, but did eventually shift her considerable bulk enough to let him find a place at the table. Beth pushed his writing tablet and folder over, and he took them with a smile.

"Put that hammer away before you hurt someone, Herbert!" Gertrude sniffed and leaned her shoulders back against the chair, her chin jutting out in anger. "Let's get on with it, shall we? And we're supposed to be eight, not seven, if you check the latest roster that clerk printed. You never could count."

Somewhat abashed by the crankiness of his former schoolteacher, Herbert laid down his hammer and began explaining exactly what their duties were to be. "Now, we've already got the building. Tom Pettigrew set that up for us by organizing the old town hall. What we have to do now is decide what's to go in the place and how it's to be run. Anybody got any suggestions?"

"I do." Beth's voice jerked Gar out of his in-depth study of her fingernails. "I think it's imperative that the center, once it's set up, not depend on the town for huge amounts of money. I've taken the liberty of drawing up a proposal for a budget, using the amount that the town has already allocated to furnish the center."

Gar accepted his copy in stunned disbelief. Surely this was his field. Shouldn't he have been approached to run the financial aspects of the whole thing? Not that it mattered. Beth probably hadn't considered the depreciation of the building or the need for a canteen or something like it. And there would have to be revenues to offset some of the expense. He glanced down and swallowed his smug feeling of superiority as he read over her proposal.

"Garrett, you're the head honcho when it comes to

new business in Oakburn. What do you think of this?"
Edgar, newly roused from his sleep by Gertrude's
wayward cane, waved his papers back and forth across
the table, creating a slight draft that sent the others
scattering to rescue their fluttering pages. "Does she
know what she's talking about?"

Yipes! Now they'd done it. Beth would be furious.
And he didn't blame her. Who wanted to be put down
by an oaf like Edgar? He stared at the sheets she'd
handed out, searching for an answer as he got to his
feet.

*What do I say, Lord? I don't want to hurt her feel-
ings.*

Tell the truth.

Ha! That was easier said than done. Gar kept his
head bent, kept his eyes on the paper.

"Garrett?" Herbert thunked the table again. "Has
the boy gone deaf? Poke him, Gertie."

Gertrude straightened, her face a tight mask. Garrett
knew they were about to witness an all-out war between two angry factions that had been feuding for as
long as he could remember. He had to do something.
When in doubt, stall.

"Just a minute, Herbert. I'm reading." Gar forced
his eyes back on the page and prayed desperately for
a way out of this debacle. He didn't want to be involved in another of these petty disputes that the senior
citizens waged just for the fun of keeping their wits
sharp.

Come on, Lord. What am I supposed to say now?

"Speak the truth in love."

"Well?" Edgar had awakened long enough to glare at them all balefully.

"I think," Gar began, feeling his way as he went, "that we should ask Beth, er, Miss Ainslow, to explain these to us. She's gone to a lot of work on this." He smiled at Beth, then sank down onto his chair with relief. Whew, that was close.

"He's right. I have spent a good deal of time researching the number of young people likely to use the center in the next five years because I want to make sure that it's a place where my sister, among others, can enjoy herself without getting into trouble."

Gar listened in amazement as Beth calmly and clearly delineated her study for everyone's benefit. He couldn't fault her on either presentation or accuracy. She'd researched her subject well, and had obviously come prepared to deal with any skepticism she found.

"Any questions?"

He felt so proud of her, standing there, her hair glowing in the bright fluorescent light.

"Very thorough. Always did think a woman was better at these things." Gertrude crossed her arms over her thin chest with smug satisfaction as she glowered up the table at Herbert. "I say, let's go ahead with it."

"Not so fast, Gertie. I want to know where she got all this information. And how are we going to pay for all this stuff she says these kids need?" Eustace tented his fingers and peered at them as if he'd never seen such beauty before. "In my day we made do with a sled and a hill. Or we talked and listened to the radio.

We didn't need Ping-Pong tables and CD players.'' He snorted in disgust.

Gar sat where he was, marveling that Eustace had managed to say so much at one time. He jerked to life when a sharp finger jabbed him in the ribs. Gertrude was scowling.

"Pay attention, boy!"

"I studied several different youth facilities in towns across the state. The successful ones had certain planned events, but a lot of the time the centers operate like an open house between set hours. Of course an adult or two is always in-house, just in case, but mostly the kids are responsible for the property themselves.''

"How do they manage that?'' Edgar sniffed derisively. "I can't even get my kids to look after their bikes.''

"Not firm enough.'' Gertrude nodded knowingly, her face pinched and tight. "That's the problem with parents today. They want to blame everything on their children, when they're simply too weak to make rules and abide by them.''

"My kids are no worse...'' As Edgar launched into a spiel about the youth of today, Gar got to his feet.

"Excuse me,'' he said loudly. "Point of order, Mr. Chairman.''

"What?'' Herbert jerked to attention, knocking the hammer to the floor; it narrowly missed his toes. "What is it?''

"If we are to make any progress tonight, I think we need to get on with business. Now, Miss Ainslow has given us plenty to think about. Economically, I'm sure you'll all agree that her plan is very workable. What we should focus on is finding some funding for this project.''

''I was kind of enjoying hearing about Ed's brats, but I suppose you're right.'' Herbert conceded the point with regret. ''What do you suggest, Miss Ainslow?''

''Please, I've been Beth for twenty-eight years now. I think you can still call me that.'' Beth grinned, then shrugged. ''Actually, I think the kids themselves should be invited to attend our meeting. There's no point in planning something they don't want. If they're in at the beginning, they can suggest fund-raising ideas that they'll be willing to help in.''

''Let the kids be part of it?'' Herbert considered this soberly.

Gertrude McGillicuddy wasn't quite so hesitant. She turned to Gar and frowned. ''The girl has a good solid brain,'' she murmured, just loud enough for the whole room to hear. ''Seems to me you messed up good when you let her go.''

Gar heard Beth gasp. He knew that she would insist on setting the record straight, but, for once, he didn't want that. ''Yes, I sure did, Miss McGillicuddy. I messed up very badly.''

Gertrude pinned him with the same look that had cowed every kid in her Sunday school class. ''Time to learn from your mistakes, isn't it?''

Gar nodded, glancing toward Beth. ''Way past time,'' he murmured.

"Maybe you're right, Gar. We should study this."
Never one to make a decision hastily, Herbert gathered
together his papers and nodded sagely. "Okay, so
we'll meet next week, same time, and let the kids have
their say. Meeting adjourned." The hammer retrieved,
Herbert slammed it against the board, which promptly
split in two.

"Well, that was quick." Gar got to his feet, a grin
itching at the corners of his mouth as he watched the
others speedily vacate the room. "You sure know how
to clear a room."

Beth made a face. "I'm not so sure I can take all
the credit." She chuckled. "They didn't look any too
pleased to be here when I came in. Besides, I'm pretty
sure there's an important hockey game at the rink tonight."

"Want to go for coffee and discuss the next step?
I'm sure you've got it planned out. You seem to have
done a lot of work on this project. I don't know how
you find the time." He placed her prospectus carefully
inside his folder and shoved the folder in his briefcase.
"There's a ton of information here. I didn't realize
you had so much experience at this. Glynis said your
loan application was more complete than any she's
seen in a long time."

"Thank you. But you don't have to say that."

He saw the blush color her cheeks a faint pink, and
guessed she'd had few compliments on her business
acumen.

"I never say anything I don't mean." He held out
her coat. "Coffee?"

She studied him with a wary look. "I guess. The kids are at my place studying again. At least, that's what they're supposed to be doing. Caitlin's going to check on them." She slid her arms into the sleeves, and murmured a thank-you when he set the heavy wool on her shoulders.

"They seem to be whispering a lot these days. Whenever I come into the room it stops, and Ty gets this sad, innocent look on his face. He used it when he stayed for supper tonight, too. What do you suppose they're up to?"

Gar slid on his own jacket and shrugged. "I have no clue. And, to tell you the truth, I don't want to know. It's too scary." He grinned to show he was joking. "Though I will tell you that lately I've begun to realize that shielding Ty from Dad's anger isn't always the best thing. It's better for him to face up to his responsibilities."

"What responsibilities?" Beth asked as she bundled her information back into the leather portfolio she carried. One last glance at the long polished table and she led the way to the door. "He's barely eighteen. Besides helping out with the horses, which he adores, what else is there for him to be responsible for around Fairwinds? Your parents have a huge staff to take care of things."

Gar nodded, holding the outside door of the municipal offices open for her.

"Yes, I know. But there are certain things Dad expects from his sons. Up to now, Ty has avoided hearing too much about that. Mostly because I've shielded him.''

"And now?" Beth hugged her case close. "What's changed?"

"For one thing, he's getting older. He won't be in school forever. Ty's going to have to decide on his future. Dad would like to have him in the bank, of course." He held out his arm. "You'd better take my arm. In those heels you'll land flat on your, er, back." He grinned at her frown, then grabbed her arm when she tripped on a ripple of ice. "See?"

"I don't know what it is about my shoes that makes people feel they have to comment on them. I like heels. They make me feel like someone somewhere might actually notice what I have to say. It's no fun being a shrimp, you know." Her fingers deliberately pinched a little tighter as she slipped and slid her way over to his car.

"I have nothing against your choice of footwear, Beth, so you needn't frown like that. I was merely offering an opinion about the likelihood of your remaining upright while prancing about on the ice in those." He raised one eyebrow as she swung her legs into the car. "Although, I suppose you could dig your heels in like spikes."

He burst out laughing at her indignant look, but managed to hide the fact as he slammed the door shut and walked around the car. By the time he was inside, next to her, he'd organized his face into a mask of control.

"Now, what were we talking about?" he asked innocently after shifting into gear.

"Ty," she returned immediately. Her forehead pleated in a frown as she peered up at him through the gloom. "What if he doesn't want to go into banking, Gar? What if he wants something completely different for himself?"

Gar stared at her, his brain working. Something his brother had said earlier pricked at his brain, but for the life of him he couldn't remember exactly what. He shoved the thought away. It didn't matter. What bugged him now was why she was asking.

"Not go into banking?" Gar laughed. "Why wouldn't he? Ty isn't the most industrious person in the world, and the bank is already set up. He can slide into place with a minimum of fuss. It's perfect for him."

"Is it?" Beth looked as if she wanted to say more but didn't dare.

Several minutes elapsed as he drove to the coffee house on the edge of town.

"Did you always want to work with your dad?" Beth pressed. "Didn't you ever dream of starting something yourself? Something that was totally yours, with *your* name on it?"

"The bank has my name on it. At least, it's where it counts—on the bottom line." Gar risked a glance at her face and found her peering out the window at the passing businesses. "I've always known I was being groomed to take Dad's place, just as he took his father's place. What's wrong with that?"

"Oh, there's nothing wrong with it. As long as that's what you want to do. I was just wondering what would happen if you had decided you wanted to study, say, geology. Maybe be an astronaut. Or maybe find a cure for cancer." She spared him a glance, then resumed her scrutiny of the empty town streets.

"A doctor? Me?" He laughed. "I don't think so. Numbers have always been my preference, Beth. You know that. Surely you can't have forgotten our math tutoring sessions?" He winked at her, hoping she'd remember how little time they'd actually spent on the problems cited in the texts.

But Beth only smiled vacantly, her big green eyes clouded with something he couldn't name.

"I remember," she murmured. "I remember everything."

Gar was so busy studying her, he almost missed the vehicle that careened through the intersection. The big shiny cab of a semi narrowly missed his bumper as it sped through a red light. He jammed on his brakes and yanked the steering wheel hard right, hoping to avoid any further damage from the truck's cargo, which followed obediently behind the cab.

In slow motion he saw the tractor-trailer slide past them, its big, unwieldly length ready to cut off their avenue of escape. He hit the brakes hard, praying for help as he tried to steer a separate path.

The icy patches negated any braking prowess he had, and Gar played with the wheel as they slid uncontrollably. Everything moved so fast that he could only hold his breath and pray Beth would escape. Seconds later, through some miracle of rubber on ice, they were heading toward the curb as the semi roared past, horn honking. The car came to a grinding halt mere inches from the yellow cement curb.

"Are you okay?" He turned his head and found Beth jammed against his side, her face white as a sheet as she hung on to his arm. Her seat belt held her in place, but it didn't stop the fear from crowding into her eyes. He took her arm. "Beth, are you okay?"

She nodded slowly, her fingers tightening on the fabric of his jacket. "I thought we were going to slide right under it," she gasped. "We could have been killed!"

"We're fine. It's okay." Gar gathered her shaking body into his arms and held her for several moments, willing the fear to recede. "Nothing happened. You're all right. I've got you."

When she finally stopped shivering, he leaned back to peer down into her face. What he saw there made his breath catch.

"Beth?"

She stared at him the way he remembered from so long ago, and to Gar, time retreated back to those glorious days when he'd been totally and completely in love. The longing he saw reflected in her eyes echoed that of his own heart, and he couldn't stop himself from brushing the red-gold strands off her forehead and tracing his lips across the thin, delicate alabaster skin.

"Oh, Beth. I've missed you so much." When she didn't answer, just clung a little tighter to his lapels,

Gar bent his head and took her lips, tasting their sweetness like a man denied sustenance.

And wonder of wonders, Beth returned his embrace. Her hands pulled him closer, her lips met his and answered their request with one of her own.

When she finally pulled away, Gar was lost in a world of make-believe, where he and Beth were walking down the aisle together.

"I'm sorry. I shouldn't have done that." She straightened back into her own seat, her face warm with the blush that made her freckles stand out on her pert nose.

Gar lifted a hand to trace them, and then remembered that this wasn't the past. This was the here and now.

"I don't want your apology," he mumbled, shifting in his own seat. He tilted his chin defiantly and dared her to look away from him. "I enjoyed kissing you. I always have. You probably forgot."

"I haven't forgotten anything."

He barely heard her response, so soft was her voice. Perhaps she hadn't meant for him to hear. But though he searched her face for an answer, she shut him out. The pixie face that could flash in a grin of amusement or freeze in a mask of disdain was now frustratingly empty, devoid of all response.

"Perhaps you'd better take me home," she murmured. "I don't really feel much like coffee anymore. Besides, the kids will wonder what happened."

"I doubt that," he muttered. But he did as she

asked, making an illegal U-turn in the middle of the now-deserted street. "Should *I* apologize?"

"No, of course not. Put it down to the moment," she scoffed. But she avoided his eyes.

"It wasn't the moment," he told her honestly, enjoying her frustrated glance. "I've been wanting to kiss you for ages." She was going to interrupt, so Gar switched tactics. "Beth, my grandmother has been asking me to bring you for a visit. I wondered if you'd come Sunday after church."

"Your grandmother?" She stopped, thought for a moment, then raised her eyebrows. "But doesn't she live in Paris or something?"

"She did, until my grandfather died five years ago. Then she only wanted to come home. Now she lives just outside of town on a small acreage in the hills, near my place. I usually stop in at least once a day."

"I didn't know you had a place, either." She grimaced. "I guess I'm still a little behind the times."

"I built it when I moved back here. When I still believed you were coming back." He watched for some flicker of surprise, but sometime in the past few years Beth had become more adept at hiding her emotions. Only a spark of interest flickered in her eyes.

"Why would your grandmother want to meet me? We have nothing in common."

She avoided his admission so easily. She was running scared, ignoring everything to do with the past. Gar smiled a half smile. It was a good start. At least she wasn't indifferent to him. He'd take what he could get and run with it.

"Well? Is Sunday suitable? Shall I tell her you'll come?" He pressed home his request, anxious to ensure that his two favorite women finally met.

"I think Ronnie wants to go to see Dad on Sunday."

"We'll drop her off on our way. After we've had lunch." He had it all planned out. Now, if he could just get her to cooperate.

"You don't have to buy us lunch. I always put something on to cook while we're at the service. Why don't you come to our place?"

It was on the tip of his tongue to refuse, to insist that she deserved a break, a trip to the nicest place in town. But something in her eyes stopped him.

"Okay, that'd be great. Can I bring something?"

She laughed, and it was a light tinkling sound that made the world seem a better place. Gar couldn't tamp down the hope that sprang up inside.

"What's so funny?"

"You are! Exactly what would you like to bring? What's your specialty, Gar? If I remember correctly, you set the kitchen at Fairwinds on fire once. Have things changed so much?" She giggled at his affronted look. "I didn't think so."

"I can cook. A few things." He pulled up in front of Wintergreen and parked the car before turning to face her. "I can. I make a good pot of tea. And I know how to make toast and those pizza things you put in the microwave."

"You *have* come a long way!" Beth's voice mocked his accomplishments. "For a guy who used to routinely incinerate everything he touched, I guess that's progress.'' She opened her door and climbed out, then leaned in to add, ''Don't bother bringing anything, Gar. Except maybe Ty, so Ronnie will have somebody to talk to.''

Gar climbed out of the car and walked around it, then took her arm before marching her up the shoveled walk to the house.

''Seems like we've always got those two around,'' he muttered, rolling his eyes as two heads peeked out from behind Beth's door. ''See what I mean?''

Beth stamped the snow off her boots and led the way inside. ''They're harmless,'' she chided. ''Take your coat off. I'll make some coffee. And you can sample Ronnie's cookies.''

She turned away quickly, so Gar did as she said, convinced by her manner that there was something she wasn't telling him. Or maybe it was just the after-effects of their near-accident?

''Hi, you two. Get any studying done?'' He frowned as Ty made some secret hand signal to Ronnie. ''I guess not.''

''We got a lot done, actually, Gar. Ronnie's really good at biology, even if I'm a dud.''

''You're not a dud. You just don't care about it like I do. Besides, you got a way higher mark in home economics than I did.'' Ronnie's eyes sparkled with teasing as she glanced from Gar to her sister and then back again.

''You're taking home economics?'' Gar wondered what else he'd missed. ''Why?''

"No choice. The school has this brilliant idea that the males of the species are not properly prepared to fend for themselves when they get out into the big, wide world. Guess they think we're all as incompetent as you, bro."

Beth stuck her head out of the tiny kitchen. "He's not incompetent, Ty. He just *really likes* all those forms of carbon."

When they all burst out laughing at him, Gar decided it was time to turn the tables. "It's not as if you take after your sister, Ronnie. She never did catch onto biology, either, even after Mrs. Beetle diagrammed the inside of a cow's stomach."

"Yech!" Ty pretended to gag. "More than I needed to know."

"I guess everybody has a talent. My home ec teacher says I shouldn't plan on owning a restaurant." She sighed. "I can't understand why Mrs. Arnold gets so worked up when I alter her recipes. It's not as if her heavy old bran muffins don't taste better with a few chocolate chips."

Ronnie disappeared into the kitchen and returned with a plate of charred, barely recognizable cookies, which she offered to Gar. "Try one of these. I substituted a few things, but they're not bad."

Gar reached out gingerly and lifted up the top one, which also happened to be the biggest. He bit into it experimentally, and then stopped as his teeth came into contact with something hard and unchewable.

"Aren't they good?" Behind Ronnie, Ty was making faces, holding his throat and openly mocking his brother.

"Different," Gar said. "I've never really tasted anything like this before." He stopped when Beth appeared with a tray of hot chocolate.

"And you probably won't again, right?" she muttered sotto voce. "Can't say I blame you. Don't eat it all, or you'll get awful heartburn."

"I substituted coconut for the peanut butter, and some cheese and stuff for the oil. I don't like greasy stuff." Ronnie seemed unperturbed by the color of the ghastly tasting concoction, never mind the charred edges and crisp chocolate chips. "But I didn't change the chocolate. You should never alter chocolate."

"Absolutely." Gar slipped the rest of his cookie into his pocket and gulped down a mouthful of the steaming hot chocolate. He glanced up in time to see Beth's wink. "Come on, Ty. You need to get home. Your curfew isn't far off, and from what I've heard, you've missed a couple lately."

"Aw, Gar!" Tyler unfolded himself from the rug in front of the fireplace with a moan meant to sway the hardest heart.

"Forget it. I'm not covering for you in this, buddy. You're late, you take the heat. Let's go. Thanks for the hot chocolate, Beth. And the cookie, Ronnie." He took his coat from Beth and slid it on, checking to be sure her natural color had returned. "By the way, Beth and I are going to Gran's on Sunday, Ty. Maybe you and Ronnie can think of something to do."

Gar frowned as he watched his brother make the

motions of a high-five behind Beth's back. "What are you two planning now?" he demanded.

"Us? Planning something?" Tyler gave a fake laugh that didn't quite come off. "Don't be silly, Garrett. What on earth would we be planning?"

"Yeah, like what? You make us sound like criminals. Come on, Tyler. I'll walk you out." Ronnie threaded her arm through Ty's.

"Walk me out? I can walk myself out. It's not like there's more than one door, Ron." Ty squawked once when the girl yanked on his arm. Then enlightenment seemed to dawn. "Oh, sure. Lead on, Macduff. Walk me out."

"They're acting very unusual, even for them. And they look guilty." Beth stood behind him, frowning at the retreating pair, who were whispering madly. They stopped once to glance back over their shoulders, then scurried out the door.

"I know it. I'm sure they're up to something. I just don't know what. Doesn't really matter, I suppose." He shrugged the feeling away and studied her once more. "You're okay? You won't have a bad dream or something?"

Beth grinned that spunky smirk that told him she probably would, but that she wouldn't admit anything of the sort to him. "I'm perfectly fine, Gar."

"That's good." He smiled, enjoying the curious look that came over her face when his arms slid around her waist.

"It is?" She stood peering up at him. "Why?"

"Because I'm going to kiss you good-night, and I

don't want you blaming the effect on our traffic incident earlier.''

''Oh.''

She didn't move away, so Gar took that as a good sign.

'''Oh.' That's all you're going to say?'' He frowned.

''What did you expect me to say?'' Her jade eyes glinted.

''I don't know. Scream 'yes' maybe. Throw your arms around me and kiss me back. Act surprised. Something.''

''Sorry.'' But she didn't move away, didn't lower the slim arms that had crept up to his shoulders.

Gar decided to quit wasting time. He held her face between his palms, bent his head and touched her mouth gently with his own, deepening the kiss when she responded.

''Gar, we have to— Oh, sorry.'' Ty left again in a hurried scramble, and then they were alone again.

''They're going to get the wrong idea,'' Beth whispered as she lowered her arms, her face touched with pink.

''What's the right idea?'' he murmured, enjoying her confusion.

''No more questions. Good night, Garrett.'' Her laughter bubbled out, a joyful sound in the silent room.

''Good night.'' Knowing a good exit line when he heard one, Garrett grabbed this one and ran with it. ''See you Sunday, if not before.''

''Uh-huh.''

He hastened out of the building and down to the end of the walk, turning just once to see her framed in a window, her arm flung across Ronnie's shoulders. Satisfied that she seemed back to normal, he climbed into the car and turned the volume knob of his CD player down to a dull roar.

"You two are getting pretty cozy. Especially when you're supposed to hate her guts." Tyler didn't bother pretending he hadn't seen anything. "I didn't notice Beth protesting, either."

Gar started the car and drove away from Wintergreen at a sedate fifteen miles an hour. "I don't hate her," he murmured. And the words rang true through his mind. "I never did."

"Sure sounded like hate to me the few times I heard you mention her name."

Not hate, Gar told himself with new awareness. I love her. More than I ever have. I love Beth Ainslow, and I couldn't care less if she had married six men. If she loves me, and I think she does, that's what I want more than anything.

"Did you hear me?" Ty asked, switching the stereo off. "I asked you a question. Should I repeat it?"

"No, Ty. And don't hold your breath waiting for an answer, because I'm not going to give you one."

"Why not?" Tyler's belligerent voice rang loudly through the car's small interior. "I want to know if you're going to date her again."

"That's none of your business, brother dear."

"Sure it is. I like her sister a lot. If you two are going to be fighting all the time, I'd like to know ahead of time. That way Ronnie and I can avoid both of you.''

"We're not going to be fighting," Gar informed him, a tiny smile twitching at the edge of his mouth.

Now why was he so positive of that?

Chapter Seven

"Are you willingly going to tell us about that meeting the night before last, or are we going to have to pry it out of you?" Caitlin looked determined enough to try, so Beth nodded.

"All right, I'll tell you both. But please don't read too much into it. Promise?"

"Oh, will you just spill it?" Maryann tossed her needlepoint onto a nearby chair, slipped her shoes off and crossed her feet beneath her. "And hurry up. You've kept us on tenterhooks for days."

"Hardly days. It was on Monday night."

"And this is Friday. Days." Maryann sniffed, nose in the air.

"Okay, days. I have been working this week, you know. Stop nagging me, Mare. Give me a break."

"I'm not nagging. It's perfectly reasonable to expect some details. You guys pried into my life—remember?"

"I've never pried!"

A shrill whistle barely stopped Maryann's exasperated protests. Beth whirled around to stare at Caitlin.

"You two are in my home, at my invitation, so I'll give the orders. Is that clear?" Caitlin stood, hands on her hips, as she regarded the other two with a glint in her eye.

"It's clear." Maryann sighed. "Sorry, Beth. I was nagging. Guess I'm just overly curious."

"So am I." Caitlin flopped down beside Beth and pointed a finger directly at her. "Now I'm ordering. You. Tell all. Now. Got it?"

"She's a tyrant. I wonder if Jordan knows." Beth held up both hands. "All right. I'm telling, I'm telling. We talked. That's all."

"And I'm the tooth fairy." Maryann nodded at Caitlin. "I heard they were seen parked on Main Street."

"You're kidding. Ooh." Caitlin fluttered her lashes and gave a coquettish laugh. "Just like the teenyboppers."

"We were parked there because we narrowly missed being killed." Beth nodded, smugly confident that she now had their full attention. "It's true. A semi went through on a red light, and we were in the intersection. It was scary."

"I'm sure it was, dear. But actually, I was enquiring about your meeting about the youth center. You remember the one. Garrett Winthrop also sits on that committee." Maryann smiled sweetly, her teeth bared in a threat.

"It was great. I could hardly believe it myself. Of course some of it was due to Gar." Beth fed them every detail she could remember, from presenting her proposal to Gar's asking the other committee members to give it a chance.

"So you see, Beth. You worried for nothing. Gar doesn't hate you. He obviously thinks you've got talent and brains if he got the others to read your paper." Caitlin nodded as if she'd known it all along.

"It felt so good to stand there and actually know what I was talking about. After the first few minutes, I felt like I could field any of their questions." Beth allowed herself to preen, just a bit. "I did the work, I organized it into a presentation, and last night we had a quick meeting with some of the youth. They're going to help out with a number of the decisions."

"Which is exactly what you wanted. Congratulations, girlfriend." Maryann thrust her hands into the air in a silent cheer. "I knew you could do it. You always were smart when you put your mind to it."

"No, Mare, I wasn't. That's the thing, you see. I've always felt so intimidated by people in power. I felt dumb and out of it." She shrugged, her lips lifting in a smile of remembrance. "But when I saw Miss McGillicuddy sniping at the others, I realized that they're just ordinary people like anyone else. And when it came to the center, I had more information than they did because I'd studied up on it. Gar even complimented me on my work."

"I don't know why not. You're smart as a whip,

Beth. We've always known that. It's just taken *you* a while to figure it out.'' Caitlin smiled benignly.

Beth felt as if a sudden calm had collapsed her sails. ''But don't you see? I'm finally on a par with the rest of the town. I can hold my own when it comes to a discussion. Gar and I were throwing around projected costs last night, and when he started doing a spread-sheet on his laptop, I knew exactly what he was talking about. It was great.''

''Of course you knew that stuff, Bethy. You've got a degree in business, haven't you?'' Maryann pre-tended to stifle the yawn that stretched her mouth wide.

''Well, yes. But still, it was quite something to feel as if I mattered.''

''You're worrying me now, Beth Ainslow. You al-ways mattered. And it doesn't mean a heap of nails to me that Gar or anybody else noticed it. God made you—and He doesn't make any junk.'' Caitlin's voice was firm. ''When will you stop looking to people for approval? Their opinions don't matter a whit. It's God's opinion of you that really counts.''

''I know you're right, Caity. And I do believe that, really. It's just that I guess I hadn't realized how much I'd changed since I left here ten years ago. I really do feel like I've earned my place here now.''

''No, no, no! That's not it at all.'' Maryann shook her head, startling them with the loudness of her voice. ''Sorry, I didn't mean to yell. But you haven't *earned* anything, Beth. You always belonged here. If you feel more comfortable now, that's great, but you didn't have to leave and struggle for ten years, or get a degree, to be part of this town. You were always a part of it.''

''It didn't feel like I was.'' Beth hid the sting that those words caused. ''I felt like an outsider who was unworthy. I had nothing to offer.''

Caitlin shook her head vehemently. ''Wrong. Honey, you're still holding on to this picture of yourself scraping and climbing to get out of the past, to reach your destiny. It simply isn't true.''

''Isn't it? I was the local drunk's daughter. I had nothing to call my own. We starved half the time, and the rest of it we wondered where our next meal was coming from. How could Gar have married me then? I'd have ruined him.'' She closed her eyes and sighed, willing the ugly memories to recede. ''And if I didn't spoil things, my father would have.''

''And *that's* why you left.'' Caitlin nudged Maryann, whose eyes were also wide open in amazement. ''You did it to save Gar from any indignity you thought he might suffer because of you or your father. I'm right, aren't I?''

Both women sat staring at her, demanding that she answer the question. When she could stand it no more, Beth finally nodded.

''Oh, you silly fool,'' Maryann scolded as she wrapped her arms around Beth. ''I think you've caused yourself far more problems than your father ever could have.''

''How can you say that? He was always showing up drunk.'' The embarrassment of it still shamed her, reddened her cheeks and made her want to run and hide.

"Listen to me, Beth. Drinking was your father's problem. If there's any shame to be borne, it is not yours. Nor are you any better because you got away from it. Your self-worth doesn't come from your father's binges any more than mine came from my parent's devotion to God." Maryann took her by the shoulders and forced her to look up and accept the truth shining in her eyes.

"She's right, Beth." Caitlin poured out more tea. "You've got to face this thing you have about your past and deal with it. It happened. You can't gloss over it or run away from it, or pretend you've risen above it. It will always be there. And maybe it did help shape who you are."

"But none of that has anything to do with your heart," Maryann continued, nodding at Caitlin in approval. "Your worth is built on God. You're His child and that makes you valuable, no matter whether you're as rich as Croesus or a ditchdigger. We don't think you're more worthy to be our friend because you've opened a business or earned a degree." Maryann squeezed her hand.

"Nor did we think any less of you when you told us the whole story about your past. We already knew the real Beth Ainslow, you see. She's a woman who cared enough about her sister to get her away from danger, to ensure her sister's safety at the expense of her own happiness." Tears formed at the end of Maryann's long lashes.

"She's also the woman who loved a man enough to get out of his life rather than damage his chances for happiness. That's what you're worth, Beth. And it has absolutely nothing to do with how much you earn. We love you because you're you. Trust me, we wouldn't bother with just any old insecure pal.'' Caitlin laughed as she wrapped them both in her arms and hugged for all she was worth.

Beth indulged them in their group hug, but the questions still whirled around in her brain.

"It's been a long, hard road, but we're glad you're back here with us. Now, what about Gar?'' Maryann was unrelenting.

"What about him? Nothing's really changed. We're still on totally separate courses. And we have nothing in common.''

"You knock some sense into her, Caitlin. I give up! Anyone with two eyes could see that the two of them were meant to be together.'' Maryann stuck her nose in the air.

Caitlin shook her head slowly, her eyes pensive as they met Maryann's. "I don't think I can do that, Mare. This is something Beth needs to work out for herself. You and I will just have to pray that her eyes are opened.''

"My eyes are wide open, Cait. And I can see exactly what would happen if Gar decided to pursue that political goal his father keeps dangling. In an electoral race, my past would come up, or I'd embarrass him somehow and he'd have to cover for me. I can't let that happen.''

"Then why are you going to see his grandmother on Sunday?" Maryann demanded.

"Good question. Will you burst out laughing if I tell you I don't know why?" Beth murmured the words quietly, the admission weighing heavily on her mind. *Why am I spending more and more time with a man I'd vowed would have no part in my life?*

"There's hope for you yet, girlfriend." Something about the way Caitlin smiled as she leaned back in her armchair made Beth take a second look.

What did Caitlin know that she didn't?

"Gran, this is Beth Ainslow. Beth, I'd like you to meet my grandmother."

Beth took the porcelain hand carefully in hers. Mrs. Winthrop's skin looked like parchment that threatened to crack and fall to pieces if treated too roughly, but her grip was firm and sure. The tiny frail-looking woman fit in perfectly with the gingerbreadlike cottage in which she lived, but Beth suspected she was anything but delicate.

"My dear, how wonderful to meet you at last! I've heard so much about you. Do come in. I'm about to have some tea. You'll join me, of course."

"Oh. Thank you." Beth followed the tiny figure through to a cozy room filled with antiques covered in petit point. She chose the sturdiest looking chair and sat down on the edge, mindful of its delicate molded legs. "What, exactly, have you heard?"

"Wonderful things, dear. Just wonderful. My grandson can't say enough good things about you." She picked up the bone china teapot and poured three cups.

Beth's eyes opened wide as she digested this information. Gar talked about her to this woman? She studied him, hoping to see the topic of their discussions written across his lean face.

"Oh, not Garrett, dear. No, he's much too reserved for the kind of chitchat an old woman likes to hear. Tyler is the one who's been filling my head with your accomplishments. There you are."

Beth accepted the tea and sipped it carefully, fully aware that the china with its Limoges pattern was an heirloom and probably irreplaceable if she broke it.

"The boy seems quite infatuated with your sister."

"They get along very well. It's nice for Ronnie to have a friend."

They chatted desultorily back and forth for several minutes before Mrs. Winthrop spoke directly to Gar.

"I want to talk to this young lady alone, without you monitoring every word, Garrett. Why don't you take a walk?"

It was not a question, it was an order. Gar obeyed, though his eyes silently protested her decree. Minutes later he left the room, though he didn't bother to close the door.

"There, that's much better. Now tell me, my dear, will you be marrying Garrett soon?"

Beth stared at the twinkling blue eyes and swallowed hard. "We're not, uh, that is, Garrett and I aren't getting married." Strangely, it hurt to say those words out loud, and Beth didn't quite understand why. She was resigned to her new life, wasn't she?

"Really?" Mrs. Winthrop patted her silver-gray curls, her elegantly arched eyebrows rising. "Why not? You're in love, aren't you?"

"We were. Once. It was a long time ago."

"Yes, I know about that. You went away and married someone else. My grandson found that very hard to accept. He was so sure you loved him." The steel in those blue eyes wouldn't allow Beth to look away. "You did love him, didn't you?"

"Yes, I did. Very much."

"And something happened to change that. What was it, dear?"

The voice was compelling, daring her to lay it all out in the open. Beth resisted only a moment before deciding to pour out her heart. She related the past as quickly as possible.

"So you see, I didn't have any other choice. I had to go."

"Yes, I do see, Beth. I see quite clearly. But all that's in the past, and yet you still continue to see my grandson. Why is that, if not because of love?"

"I care for him very much, of course. But nothing much has changed. Gar is still an important person who feels called to do certain things. His world is far different from the world I'm in." Just saying it hurt immensely.

"All that claptrap is merely a shield to hide true feelings. Answer me, girl. Do you or do you not love my grandson?"

Beth couldn't look away from the determined face, couldn't think of a way to avoid the probing questions. After several tense moments she nodded.

"Yes, I do. I think I love him more now than I did before."

Oh, the relief of saying that! The admission made her heart soar.

"It isn't his money you're attracted to?"

"Of course not! The money has nothing to do with it."

The periwinkle eyes darkened. "It did once, though, didn't it? I thought so." She nodded her head sagely, lips pursed. "Money and power, both used wrongly."

How did she know? Had her son told her? But no, Charles Winthrop had promised never to reveal that secret. Beth swallowed hard.

"I-I'm not sure what you mean." Beth hesitated, searching desperately for a way to avoid this discussion.

"Come now! You were eighteen, you had no money to pay rent or buy food. How could you have managed to get away from Oakburn unless someone helped you? If Garrett weren't head over heels in love with you, he'd have asked these questions long ago." Dinah Winthrop frowned. "It was my son, wasn't it? He bribed you to go."

"Not bribed, no." Beth let out a breath. "He simply explained the realities to me. Gar was in his first year. He had at least three more to go. And even when he was finished with college, money would be tight for us."

"And that's what decided it for you? The money?" A frown of dismay marred the delicate face.

"No. It wasn't the money." Beth allowed the shame of it to wash over her again. Even ten years later she felt totally humiliated by that awful scene. "Your son and his wife invited me to their home one night. It was a wonderful evening. I had a new dress, and I felt like people were finally beginning to accept me for who I was, to accept that I was going to marry Gar."

"Go on." The sweet gentle voice barely penetrated her musings.

"There were a lot of celebrities there, people your son knew and did business with. They came in limousines. The women wore jewels and expensive perfume. To me it was like a movie set."

"Yes, Charles likes that sort of thing. I suppose it helps solidify his contacts in the business world, though you'd think he'd be beyond that ego-soothing by now."

"The mayors from three nearby cities had come also. I'd never seen anything like it. I was beginning to think the evening couldn't get any better, when Mr. Winthrop asked me to dance." She stopped, swallowing painfully. "Then the dream cracked and broke into a thousand tiny pieces."

The old woman merely waited, her bent fingers folded calmly in her lap. Her eyes glittered with some suppressed emotion, but she said nothing.

"My father somehow managed to elude the security people that night. He'd had more than his share of the drinks that were being served, and I guess that's what made him so bold. He accused Mr. Winthrop of causing my mother's death.''

"Was it true?"

"I don't know. I don't think so." Beth shook her head. "I don't remember much of what he said. All I remember is everyone staring at me, pitying me. He ranted and raved around the room, calling names and demanding that someone arrest your son. Then he turned on me.''

"Don't go over it again, dear. It must be very painful for you to remember." There were round spots of bright red color on the woman's cheeks.

"He turned on me, said I was degrading myself by hobnobbing with my mother's murderer." The words slipped out on their own accord, accompanied by a single teardrop. Beth stared at her hands, mortified.

"He said I was a nothing, a nobody who was trying to burrow her way into a place where I was out of my depth. That was when I realized that I didn't fit in and I never would. I wasn't the right kind of person. I didn't have the training or the social graces to brush that scene off and go on pretending that my father's diatribe meant nothing to me, or to anyone there.''

She swallowed hard. "It was true, you see. I was a nobody. And I had nothing to offer Gar. Nothing. I couldn't support him in his business because I didn't know anything about how that world worked. I came from the opposite side of the tracks, and nothing had prepared me for life in a place like Fairwinds.''

"And?"

"I was worried about my past harming the man I loved. What if Dad had said those things in front of Gar—condemned him the same way he condemned me?"

The cuckoo clock in the corner called out four o'clock as a log hissed sparks in the fireplace. But other than that, the room was broodingly silent.

"I couldn't put him through it. I couldn't ask him to put up with all that hate, all that blame. I couldn't rake over the past, especially when your son told me that he'd been the one to turn down my mother's plea for help the day she died." The tears flowed unchecked now.

"It was just a business decision. It wasn't personal. I understood that. But my dad had made it into some kind of vendetta, and he wouldn't stop his accusations, no matter how many times Mr. Winthrop offered to give him a new loan." She gulped. "The whole place was buzzing with the gossip."

The old lady's lips were tight with reproof now. Her fingers grasped the arms of her chair tightly, clearly outlining the blue veins on her hands.

"My mother had been gone for some time. I didn't care about the past, but I knew there was something I could do about the future. When my father's drunken absences got longer, and conditions at home grew much worse, I decided to go away—to leave before Ronnie got caught in the awful mess."

"That was a very smart, brave thing to do. It can't have been easy."

"Actually, it was." Beth smiled, dashing away her

tears. "Mr. Winthrop came to see me. He explained that he felt it would be best if I went away for a while, got some training. I could come back, later on, when he'd smoothed things over. Gar was going to be tied up with college anyway, so why not prepare myself for when he came back. I let your son believe that I would be back someday when I told him I was taking Ronnie and leaving Oakburn to look for a job."

"And Charles gave you money, didn't he."

Beth nodded. "A loan, yes. He said he'd wished hundreds of times that he'd given it to my mother, lent a hand when it would have done some good. Since he couldn't help her, he'd help me."

"You took it." It wasn't a question. The old lady's eyes were fixed on the blue chintz love seat across the room.

"I took it and promised to pay him back. I gave him a letter for Gar, and I left town before the gossip got even more unbearable. A few months later I met a wonderful man, a man who fell in love with me— the real me. He wanted to marry me, to take care of Ronnie." Beth smiled, remembering that strange proposal.

"What was he like?"

"Denis was a lot like me, I guess. He'd grown up poor, worked his way up through the ranks until he built himself a reputation on the oil rigs. He was good and solid and dependable, and I knew he would never let me down. I didn't have to pretend around Denis. I could relax and be myself."

"You loved him?" The voice broke through her reverie.

"He was my friend, my advisor, my comforter, my partner in raising Ronnie. After a while I think I did grow to love him, but in a different way than I loved Gar. There wasn't any excitement or razzle-dazzle, not the way there is when I'm near Gar." She squinted, wondering if she'd offended this regal old woman. "Do you know what I mean?"

Mrs. Winthrop smiled, nodding. "I certainly do, my dear. And razzle-dazzle is a perfect description. It's the way my dear husband made me feel, too. Anything else is second best."

"I suppose. But I didn't feel like that about Denis. He was just—" Beth frowned, thinking it over "—Comfortable is the right word, I guess."

"What will you do now?"

"Go on building my business and seeing Ronnie through school." Why did that sound so bleak and unfulfilling?

"I understand she's a very bright girl. You've done well."

"Yes, Ronnie's far smarter than I ever was. And I mean for her to make something of herself. I don't want her to ever feel as inferior as I did. I want her to be strong and secure."

Not that anyone could possibly believe Ronnie would ever be unsure of herself. The girl was comfortable wherever she went. *At least I've done that for her.*

"That's commendable, my dear. And I'm sure your

sister will be fine. But aren't you putting an awful burden on her as well?''

Beth frowned. ''I don't know what you mean.''

Dinah Winthrop smiled as she picked up the poker and stabbed the glowing logs to new life. Her actions sent up a sheet of sparks that spooked the cat lying on the mantel.

''You're projecting your own wishes on her in exactly the same manner that my son projects his will on his children. Haven't you noticed?''

Beth shook her head. ''No, not at all. Mr. Winthrop wanted Garrett to go into banking, of course. But that was what Gar wanted, too.''

''Yes, Garrett was more malleable than Tyler, I'm afraid. He let himself be made into a carbon copy of his father—''

''I don't think that's quite accurate, Grandmother.'' Gar strolled into the room, his words echoing off the plaster ceiling. Both women started in surprise. ''I am *nothing* like my father, and what I've heard just proves it. I would never turn away a woman desperately searching for help for her family.'' His tones were measured. But his eyes blazed with anger as they lighted on Beth. ''Why didn't you tell me?''

''H-how much did you hear?''

''All of it, I hope. I'm not all that obedient when it comes to being shooed out of the room like a naughty little boy. When I came back from speaking with Cook, you were talking about leaving town. I always wondered why you'd left, Beth. I don't know why I didn't guess that you'd had help." He shifted from one foot to the other, hands clenched at his sides.

"I never wanted you to know about it." A tide of red burned Beth's cheeks as she realized how much she'd given away. Had he heard her profess her love?

"Just to set the record straight, I never got any letter."

"But you must have!" Beth stared at him, trying to assimilate this new information. "I specifically asked your father to give it to you the next time you came home."

"I didn't come home for quite a long time, Beth. I learned about your departure a week before Christmas break. A friend wondered why I hadn't gone home to say goodbye." He smiled grimly. "I called and called but you weren't there. Father or no father, I made up my mind right then to find you. I was out of school for six months, searching for some information, some thread that would have led me to you. I couldn't find a thing. You hid yourself well, Beth."

"You looked for me?" She couldn't believe what he was saying.

"Of course. You didn't think I'd just let you go, did you?" His face tightened, lines of fury radiating from his eyes.

"Yes, I did." Beth nodded, then swallowed when his face grew darker. "I hoped you'd understand from the letter that I wasn't right for you, that I couldn't change myself into that kind of person."

"I didn't want you to change! I liked you the way you were. Are. Whatever. And may I repeat that I *did not* get any letter.'' He bellowed the words, and then instantly offered his grandmother an apology. ''I'm sorry, Gran. You don't need to hear all this.''

''On the contrary, dear boy, I'd like to hear even more. The situation has bothered me for some time.'' She refolded her hands in her lap and smiled. ''Go on.''

''I don't really think we should air our problems in front of your grandmother,'' Beth protested. ''I'm sure she'd like some peace and quiet.''

''No, she wouldn't.'' Gar's voice was firm. ''Dinah thrives on people. And even though she's supposed to live quietly nowadays, she never does what the doctors say. So stop using her as an excuse.''

Beth straightened her shoulders, affronted. ''I do not require an excuse. We weren't even properly engaged, if you recall, Garrett Winthrop. You said we'd do it up right when you graduated.''

His eyes opened wide. ''I proposed, you accepted. I even gave you a promise ring. In my books that's called being engaged. The time line doesn't have a thing to do with it.'' He stood in front of her, arms folded across his chest in a belligerent attitude that spoke volumes.

''Oh, you make me so angry sometimes! Don't bother acting so hoity-toity with me, Gar. I know very well that you were dating other girls in college. And you found one especially attractive, didn't you? I believe her name was Carrie. And now there's Cynthia.'' Beth flopped back onto her chair with a huff, her face hot.

"I am *not* dating Cynthia Reardon. If one more person tells me I am, I'll…"

"You'll what?" Beth demanded. "Did you ever stop to think that everyone is saying it because they believe it's the truth?"

"Just like they believed you ran away because you were pregnant? I suppose I'm to blame for that erroneous conclusion, too?" As soon as he said it, Gar groaned and slapped a hand to his head. "I'm sorry, Beth. You're the only person I know who can make me say things I shouldn't."

Beth stared at him. "They thought I was pregnant?" She couldn't take it in, couldn't absorb what he was saying. "They thought that you and I…that we had…oh no!" She closed her eyes and wept. "The talk that must have gone around. And you were here through it all."

"I'm tough, I managed." He smiled softly. "And anyway, who cares about the talk, Beth? It doesn't matter. Don't you see that yet?" Gar knelt in front of her, his big warm hands covering hers. "What we need to get at is the truth. All of it, no matter how much it hurts. Okay?"

She nodded.

"And I'm going to go first." He got up, hooked a chair over and sat down in front of her, his face inches from hers.

"I wasn't going out with anyone, Beth. Sure, groups of us went out for coffee sometimes, but there was never anyone special. You had my heart. Carrie was just a friend."

"That's why you invited her to your graduation? My dad told me that when I telephoned one night," she added at his raised brow. "It was *our* dream, Gar. Ours. And you shared it with her."

"Because you weren't there to share it with, and I was lonely. Don't you see? I waited, I even looked for you that day. But you never came."

"I was there," she whispered. "You didn't see me, but I was there. In my heart. I even wished you congratulations."

He sat silently, staring into her eyes for a long time. Then slowly, gradually, a smile started in his eyes and worked its way down to his mouth.

"Congratulations to you, too. I guess you noticed I wasn't at yours, either."

She allowed herself time just to stare at him, to absorb the wonder of a love that—no matter how hard she tried to believe otherwise—had never really died. A love that couldn't be killed no matter how much she told herself she didn't care anymore.

"So what now?" It was Dinah's voice, brimming with laughter as she sat perched in her chair. "Where do we go from here?"

"I don't know." Gar turned from scrutinizing his grandmother to Beth, his eyes asking a question she was afraid to answer.

"I don't know, either. I have to rethink it all, reevaluate what I've learned. Nothing is as it seemed." Beth shook her head, hoping to clear it. But nothing could dislodge what she thought she saw burning deep in Gar's eyes.

Did he still love her? She didn't know. But until she did, she wasn't making any life-altering decisions. Not again.

"Nothing is the same, you're right. Things are better. We've cleared the air between us. But I think we deserve to hear the whole story. And there are two men who can explain it to us." Gar surged to his feet, planted a hearty kiss on his grandmother's cheek and grabbed Beth's hand.

"Thanks for tea, Gran. But we have to go now. There's someone—actually two someones—we need to talk to."

A shiver of fear trickled down her spine as Beth rose to follow him.

The truth was about to come out. Why was she so afraid?

Chapter Eight

"Beth and I would like to talk to you about the past, Dad. Alone." A hardness tinged the melodic timbre of Gar's low voice.

Ty and Ronnie glanced up from the puzzle they were assembling. Beth could see the questions on both their faces. She wanted to tell them not to worry, to get on with their own lives. She longed to do that herself. But she couldn't. She and Gar couldn't move ahead until the past was straightened out.

"I'm sure the children won't mind if we talk here." Charles's voice was amiable enough, but there were frown lines on his forehead and his now-whitened cheeks.

"I don't think you want that, do you, Dad?" Gar stared hard at his father and only slightly relaxed when Mr. Winthrop finally got to his feet. "Let's go to the study."

Two minutes later Beth was ushered to a wine-colored chair that sat in front of a huge desk. Nervously, she folded her hands in her lap, then unfolded them and laid her fingers out straight. She knew Gar was furious. He hadn't said a word all the way here, other than to ask her politely if she was all right or needed the heat turned up.

In truth, Beth felt icy cold when she saw the way his gray eyes glittered. She glanced at him now, noting the way he sat in his own chair, his back straight, his shoulders rigid. The truth had to come out, but at what cost? Would it drive a wedge between the two who had always been so close?

"I want to know everything. And I'm not going to stop asking until I get the truth. No games, Dad. That's gone on for years now. I think that's quite long enough."

"You can't fault me for doing what I thought best." Charles sat behind the desk, leaning back in his chair as if he were afraid Gar would lunge at him.

Beth found it interesting that he didn't even pretend not to know what they were talking about.

"Best for whom? Me? Beth? Best for Mervyn? Just who were you helping by paying Beth to leave town?"

"I didn't pay her." Charles sputtered indignantly at such a description. "I merely made her a loan."

A nasty smile tightened Gar's mouth. "I'm sure you did. And probably collected interest. Am I right?" He glanced over at Beth, inclining his head a bit when she nodded.

"Of course I'm right! That's the whole reason for

this family, isn't it, Dad? We've got to make more and more money. Doesn't matter at whose expense.''

"Now just a minute, son. She had to leave. Mervyn was getting worse. He disappeared for days sometimes. That's no environment for a child!''

Beth glanced at Gar. He was so hurt. He'd never suspected his father of doing anything this underhanded. How difficult it must be to find out the truth this way.

"No way at all for young girls to live." The younger Winthrop agreed, a hint of a smile touching his angry lips. "And, of course, you did everything in your power to help Beth and Veronica, didn't you? I mean, you saw to it that someone took over some groceries, made sure the pastor looked out for them, even sent a friend after Mervyn to make sure he didn't hurt himself. Well, didn't you?''

Charles looked at the floor, his hand clenched by his side.

"No, I didn't think so. You looked the other way instead. It's so hard to see children starving, isn't it, Dad? Kind of eats away at you.'' Gar surged to his feet and strode around the room, his hands thrust into his pockets.

Though Beth ached for him, she couldn't think of a thing to say that would make any of this easier to swallow. So she sat where she was and whispered a prayer that this relationship between father and son wouldn't be totally ruined by the past.

"Son, I don't think they were starving. They always seemed healthy enough to me.''

"Don't you dare call me 'son'! Right now I'm so ashamed of you, I'm almost sick to my stomach. How would you know how the girls managed? You never bothered to find out. Is that what happened when Beth's mother came to you for a loan? You turned away and focused on other things?"

What little color was left in the old man's face now drained completely away, leaving him gray and shriveled.

"How did you—"

"'Be sure your sin will find you out.' Isn't that what you've always preached to me, Dad? I guess yours have come home to roost, haven't they?" He smiled grimly. "What did you say to Mrs. Ainslow that made her so despondent she didn't check the intersection for oncoming cars?"

Beth frowned. How had he known how her mother died? Gar hadn't been any older than she.

"I couldn't grant that loan, Garrett! She had nothing, *nothing* to back it. We had a lot of shareholders back then, folks who depended on the bank for their income. I was responsible to them and to my own family to be sure the bank was covered."

"The bank? The bank is made up of people. Human beings whose lives are more important than earning another few dollars!" Gar glared at his father, his face tight with strain. Only his eyes burned. "You know Grandfather's edict as well as I. 'Whenever possible, help.' How could you let her just walk away?"

Charles Winthrop bowed his head, his hands fidgeting in his lap. When he finally looked up, there were tears in his eyes—eyes that begged for understanding.

"I've gone over it a thousand times in my mind. And I've wished ten thousand times that I could change the past. But I can't. I couldn't then and I can't now." The thin shoulders slumped as the old man admitted his mistake. "I knew Mervyn was right. I killed Loretta Ainslow as surely as if I'd pushed her into that street." He looked up at Beth, his face drawn and haggard now. "I'm sorry, Beth. So sorry."

A well of forgiveness opened inside her at the sight of that pitiable man. He'd made a wrong choice and it had cost him years of pain. Why continue adding to it now? What difference would it make to anyone?

"It doesn't matter now," she whispered softly, leaning forward to cradle his cold, blue-veined hand in her own. "It's in the past."

"How can you say it doesn't matter?" Gar blasted his barely concealed indignation at her words, his voice seething with hurt as he raged at the injustice.

His words hit Beth with a fierceness that shocked her, yet drew her nearer. She felt a tender sympathy for both men—Charles because he had to live with his consequences, and Gar because it hurt to see how imperfect a parent could be. His pain was at least partly on her account, and she felt cherished. She sat silently as he continued.

"All right, he made a mistake with your mother. But he didn't learn a thing, no matter how guilty that mistake made him feel." He turned back to his father and demanded, "How could you do it all over again with the woman I loved?"

The anguish in those bitter challenges ate at Beth like acid, as Gar audibly agonized over his father's perfidy. She wanted to go to him, hold him close and promise that she would soothe away the hurt. But Gar was not a child, and the anger festering inside needed to be let out. She could only watch and listen. And pray for him.

For them both.

"You knew how much I loved Beth. You watched me hunt for her. I begged you a hundred times to hire a private investigator but you refused. And all the time *you* were the one who had sent her away, convinced her that the money mattered more than the love. How could you do that, *Dad*?" The sarcasm in the last word was unmistakable.

"I was doing what I thought was best." Charles gave Beth an apologetic glance. "I mean no disrespect, my dear, but you were not our kind. That was evident at the party. You had no knowledge of the industry, and even less as hostess. You were afraid of your own shadow, and there were those who would have been happy to decry both you and my son."

"Our kind? What is 'our kind,' Dad?" Gar's scathing voice made a mockery of the apology. "Because if 'our kind' means lying and cheating and even stealing, then I'm proud to say I'm not 'our kind' either."

"Stealing?" Charles huffed up, indignant at the accusation. "I've never stolen anything."

"You stole a letter that was addressed to me from

Beth. You promised her that you'd give it to me and then you lied to me, the son you profess to love. You cheated us out of ten years when we could have been together, happy. Explain that, *Dad.*"

Charles hung his head. "I destroyed that letter as soon as she left town. I couldn't allow you to stop your education."

"You couldn't 'allow' it? What right did you have? Certainly not the right of a loving father."

Beth had always wondered at the term "broken man." But that was exactly what Charles Winthrop was now. Broken and bent as Gar heaped accusation after accusation on his head. Ill and elderly, the arrogant man seemed a mere shadow.

"That's enough, Garrett." Beth stood and walked over to the tea cart. She poured out a tumbler of water and held it to the old man's lips while he took a sip. "You've asked your questions, gotten your answers, laid down your judgments. Now leave it alone. You're not helping anyone with all this anger." She smiled at the old man, patted his shoulder, then returned the cup to the tray.

Gar grabbed her arm, his face a contorted mask of questions that demanded answers.

"What? How can you say that? He spoiled our lives!"

She shook her head, studying this man in a whole new light. "No, he didn't. Oh, maybe he helped make things more difficult, just as my father did." She thought about that time as a wry smile lifted her lips.

"But the truth is that you and I spoiled our own lives."

"*I* didn't spoil anything." Gar flopped down on the sofa, obviously disgruntled by her lack of support.

"Yes, you did. If you'd come home when I begged you to, if you'd listened to what I had to say, we could have talked things through. But you didn't. You were too busy playing Romeo." She laughed, in hindsight, at the silliness of it all. "And I was a fool to leave without forcing you to listen to my explanation. I let all my doubts and fears take over. I didn't trust you enough. I didn't trust God enough, so I made my own solution."

"Yeah, some solution. Marrying Denis."

The sour look on Gar's face sank in as Beth realized exactly why he had always decried her husband. He was jealous. She walked over to stand in front of him.

"Funny you should think Denis was the wrong solution. That's the one part of this whole debacle that I'm almost positive must have come directly from God. I needed someone strong, someone who could teach me to rely on God and myself. Denis was that man." She smiled, her hand gentle as it brushed through Gar's spiky hair.

"Marrying Denis didn't mean that I loved you any less, Garrett. I've always loved you. Maybe more now than ever before. You're a part of me. That could never die."

He stood and wrapped his arms around her waist, tugging her closer to his heart. His eyes glowed with a fierceness that sent a thrill of wonder through her.

"Do you mean it? Really, Beth? You still love me?"

She nodded, her eyes welling with tears of joy. "I really mean it."

"I love you, Beth. And I *am* going to marry you. Maybe it's ten years late, but there is a wedding on the way." He leaned around her to glare at his father. "And there's nothing you can do to stop it."

Charles Winthrop got up slowly, his body stooped. He walked around the desk slowly, holding the edge for support. But when he looked at his son, there was a warmth, love and deep compassion in his eyes that Beth understood.

"On the contrary, Garrett. I'm going to do everything in my power to speed it through. As soon as possible. I wish you both the very best."

Beth slipped out of Gar's arms and stepped over to the old man. "Thank you," she whispered as she kissed his paper-thin cheek. "For understanding."

His eyes met hers, questioning. Beth smiled and patted the thin hand.

"He'll come around. I'll make sure of it. Just takes a little time."

"Thank *you*, my dear. I don't deserve it, but I'm grateful for your forgiveness."

There wasn't anything she could say to that in front of Gar, so Beth merely smiled.

"I'll go tell the children the good news. I have a hunch it won't come as a surprise. They've been planning something like this for a while." Charles pulled open the door and then stopped. "Besides, I've a little something to discuss with Tyler. The boy's grades are dropping every semester.''

"Now that we've had our showdown, I guess my little brother's going to have to face the music.'' Gar stood behind Beth, his arms closing around her waist. "It's about time, too. He's been dragging his heels long enough.''

Beth turned and placed a finger on his lips. "Forget about Tyler,'' she murmured, her eyes taking in every detail of his handsome face. "Did you just propose to me, Garrett Winthrop?''

"Yes. And no matter what you try, this time it's going to happen. I suggest Valentine's Day. Does that give you enough time?'' His lips nuzzled her cheek in a tender caress.

"I don't need much time, just enough to talk to my dad.''

Gar frowned. "Are you sure you want to? I mean, it might end up hurting you if he can't get past his bitterness.''

Beth hugged him close, her head against his heart. "Then that's a choice he'll have to make. I can't make it for him. I finally realized that I do care for him, but it's time he faced up to his part in our awful past.''

"But it is the past, isn't it? It's not going to interfere with our future?'' The anxious note in his voice and the frown on his face ushered out the last doubt that had lingered in her mind.

Gar loved her. She loved him. What else did they need?

* * *

Gar followed Beth into the nursing home with doubts plaguing every step. He wasn't positive this was a good idea. Mervyn had carried his grudge for a long time. It wouldn't be easy to let it go.

"Stop mincing along! He's not going to bite you." Beth shook her head in disgust, then wrapped an arm through Gar's. "I'll defend you if he does. Or dress your wound. How's that?"

"Not very comforting," Gar muttered, and pushed open the door to Mervyn's room.

"Hi, Dad. How are you today?" The forced cheeriness in Beth's voice was evident.

"Same as yesterday. Probably the same as tomorrow. Not that you care."

"Of course I care. I always have, in spite of the way I acted. That's why I'm here to see you today." Beth sank into a chair near her father's and explained what they'd learned this afternoon. "I guess the end result is that Gar and I still love one another and we intend to be married. On Valentine's Day."

"What? You're allying yourself with the son of the man who killed your mother?" Mervyn snorted in disgust as an angry red flush suffused his face. "How can you do that?"

"I can marry Gar because I love him. Just as I loved him ten years ago. Only more so now." She winked at Gar, her fingers reaching for his.

Gar squeezed her hand but stayed where he was, leaning against the wall. He wanted to be prepared for whatever Mervyn tried to pull. Something told him this wouldn't be a pretty scene.

"You have no idea of the pain that family has put us through." Beth's father glared at them both.

"Yes, Dad. I do. But it's a pain you also contributed to."

"Me?" Mervyn coughed in amazement, his eyes wide. "I did nothing."

"Exactly." Beth sat back in her chair as if she were lounging, but Gar could tell she was strengthening herself for what was to come. "Why did Mother go to the bank that day, Dad? You'd had an argument the night before, I remember. Did her trip have anything to do with your disagreement or the fact that you were off on a bender when she was killed?"

Flustered and indignant, Mervyn's mouth opened and closed several times like that of a fish gulping water. If it hadn't been so sad, it would have been comical. Gar watched the man fidget in his seat, and swallowed down his anger. There were elements of a tragedy in his past, but he had moments, good moments, to remind him of the way things could be with his dad.

The real tragedy was that a relationship had never been allowed to develop between this father and his daughters.

"You're acting just like the Winthrops now, girl. That figures!" The words were sharp, but it was just a show, a shallow pretense.

"Did Mom go to ask the bank for some money so she could buy some food, Dad? Or maybe she needed that money you spent on your drinking buddies to pay for those pills she had to take." Anger glittered in

Beth's green eyes as she thrust her head back. Her hair blazed reddish-gold. "Did you drink away my mother's life that afternoon?"

"You're just like her, Bethy. Her gold hair got full of those red-colored sparks when she was mad, too. Boy, did she have a temper." Mervyn's eyes glazed over with memories. "She stood up for what she believed and she never took 'no' for an answer. She was determined to take that job over in Moss Creek, and if it meant we had to get a car, she was going to get it. Nothing could have stopped her."

"But she had a job. She cleaned at the bank." Beth glanced at Gar, but he shrugged.

He had no idea what had happened all those years ago, except that Mrs. Ainslow had been hit by a vehicle while crossing the intersection. But he intended to find out the truth now. And then, please God, they could finally put it all behind them.

"She wanted something better than I could provide. She was determined that you girls wouldn't suffer because of us and the problems we had. So she went to *his* father to ask for four hundred lousy dollars to buy that car. A pittance!" Mervyn glared at Gar, malevolence on his face.

"But that wasn't good enough for his old man. No, he had to humiliate her further by reminding her that we were behind on the loans we already had."

"I'm guessing that she had no idea how deeply you were in debt. Right, Dad?" Beth didn't wait for a nod. The look on Mervyn's face said it all. "How can you blame this on someone else? How can you act as if

it's not just as much your fault? You pushed her into
that humiliation by drinking away every dime she hid
in that old tin coffee can.''

Mervyn stared. ''How did you—''

''Oh, don't worry, Dad. She covered for you. But I
wasn't stupid. I knew what was going on. When she
thought we were asleep she'd start crying. Did you
know that, Dad? She'd pray a little prayer over and
over. 'Please, God, take care of my babies.' Then
she'd start that awful coughing.'' Beth chewed on her
bottom lip as she fought for control.

''I'm sorry, Bethy. I'm so sorry.'' That broken
voice tugged at Gar's heartstrings.

But Beth wasn't in a forgiving mood. ''You weren't
one bit sorry. Don't you see? If you had been sorry,
you would have thrown away that bottle and knuckled
down to taking care of us after she died. We could
have consoled each other. Instead, you got your consolation in an alcohol-induced haze that lasted just
long enough for me to have to stay up all night, worrying if you were ever coming home.'' She burst into
tears then, great racking sobs that tore at her thin body.

Gar would have gone to her then, taken her in his
arms and consoled her. Even physically removed her
from the room. But the look in her eyes held him back,
so he stayed where he was, chafing at the inner voice
that told him to keep still while she bared her soul.

''Do you know what my memories are of the time
after Mom died? What would we eat? How could I
make sure Ronnie would be okay? Were you going to
go away and leave us again? Every day. All day. All

night." She stood and dashed the tears from her face, her eyes raging.

"You're not sorry in the least, Dad. You're still doing the same thing to me today, using me or the Winthrops or anybody else who's handy to justify a situation you created. Even now you play Ronnie off against me, blame me for taking her away, and fill her head with stories that have no relationship to our ugly reality."

"You took her away from me. My own little girl." His voice cracked. "I wanted to protect my wife, make things right for her. Just like I want to make sure you and Ronnie are okay."

Mervyn stretched out a hand, which Beth ignored. Gar watched as the old man pulled open a desk drawer and took out a small flask. Gar knew exactly what was inside, and he saw by the look in her eyes that Beth did, too.

"Yes, I can see how badly you want that," she scoffed. "You'll blank me out, make all the bad stuff disappear. For a little while, anyway. And Ronnie and I will be left to deal with the pieces, the scandal and the dubious distinction of being known as the town drunk's daughters. Thanks a lot, Dad."

As Gar watched, Beth stormed out of the room, tears pouring down her white cheeks. He wanted to follow her, but some little voice inside told him to stay.

Mervyn sat where he was, stunned by the words that she had thrown at him.

"I failed her, didn't I?" The old man stared at his hands.

"We all did, Mervyn. Me, Dad, you. We should have been there for her, but we weren't. And in spite of everything, she managed to take care of herself and raise Ronnie." He smiled gently, holding out his handkerchief for the old man to use. "That's quite a daughter you have."

"She looks exactly like her mother. It used to make me crazy when I'd come home from work and she'd be standing there with those great big eyes in that heart-shaped face. I missed Loretta so much, but everywhere I turned, there was another reminder of her in Beth." He lifted the flask to his lips as if to take another sip.

Gar reached out and stopped him, knowing this was the last chance Mervyn would get to alter a pattern that had developed years ago between himself and his children.

"Do you love your kids, Mr. Ainslow?"

Mervyn frowned, but at least he lowered the flask from his lips. "Of course I love them. They're all I have left."

"You're going to lose them." Gar paused, letting his words sink in. "Beth gave up everything to come back here because Ronnie wanted to get to know you again. Your eldest daughter kept her sister away as long as she could, carried the stigma of your failures on her shoulders and kept your misdeeds to herself so her little sister could grow up free and happy."

He picked the flask out of the wrinkled hand and

set it on the table. Then he put the girls' pictures on the table beside it. "You start drinking again and you're going to lose them both. For good."

The tired eyes flashed with anger, but Gar ignored that. He was fighting for his future happiness. And Beth's. He wouldn't give up easily.

"Beth and I are getting married, and there is nothing you or anyone else can do to prevent that. But I'm only too well aware of how much your behavior has shamed her, how she's covered up for you, lied when you disappeared on one of your binges, taken over your role as father when she needed a father herself."

"Hah!" Mervyn's hand reached out to grab the flask, but Gar stopped him. "What do you know?"

"I know this. If you begin drinking again, I will take Beth away from here, and Ronnie will come with us—after she's been told the truth. You will never see either one of your daughters again. This is your last chance to be a father, Mervyn. Your children or your bottle. Choose."

"You don't understand!" The pathetically sad face made Gar squirm. "I have these dreams. I'm sure Loretta is here. I reach out and I almost touch her and *whoosh*—it's gone. Then I remember. And it hurts." His voice was tortured, proof that he still yearned for what he couldn't have.

But Gar remained undeterred. There were two lovely young women who desperately needed to know that their father cared about them. He was fighting for that.

"I know all about your dream, Mervyn. I've had

the same one for the last ten years.'' He swallowed hard, forcing himself to continue. ''It's my wedding day. I'm at the church, at the front, waiting for Beth to walk down that aisle. The music starts, the congregation stands, and I know it's finally going to happen. Then I wake up and I'm alone. Still.'' He smiled grimly. ''Believe me, I know about that kind of longing.''

Gar moved to the window and stared out at the glistening white snow that shone in the moon's bright glow. He thought about the agonizing that always followed those awful dreams.

''The thing is, God's given us both a second chance, if we want to take it. I intend to make my dream a reality. I am going to marry Beth.'' He turned to face his future father-in-law.

Mervyn sat there, morose and frowning, but his attention was on Gar.

''What about you? Are you finally going to build a family, or are you going to throw it all away for a lousy drink that will only dull the truth for a little while? Is this bottle what you want for a family? Last chance, Mervyn. Decide.''

The clock ticked away the minutes, one by one, as Gar forced himself to keep his eyes focused on the man in front of him. There would be time for Beth and him later, he was confident of that. But there might never be another time to reach Mervyn Ainslow, to give Beth back the father she longed for but was afraid to trust. He waited, silently praying.

With slow, hesitant movements, Mervyn got to his

feet. He picked up the flask and clutched it tightly in his hand. Gar felt his heart sink to his feet.

Oh, God, why? Why can't You heal this hurting family?

He closed his eyes and prayed harder than he ever remembered praying.

"You might be marrying her, but she's still my daughter." Mervyn stood at the sink, allowing the amber liquid to dribble from the glass bottle into the sink and down the drain. "And that will never change."

Thank you, God!

"Gar?" Beth stepped inside the room, rubbing her hands up and down her arms. She refused to look at her father. "I'm freezing. If you're going to stay here a while, I'll walk home."

"Bethy?" Mervyn stood where he was, still holding his flask over the sink. When she turned to glare at him, he let the bottle drop and faced her, his eyes moist.

Gar saw a flicker of hope in her eyes as she glanced from her father's hand to the sink and back again.

"I'm sorry, Bethy. I've failed you and Ronnie so badly. It would serve me right if you never came here again." Mervyn swallowed hard, then took a step forward. His face was sallow.

"I've been a lousy husband and father. I know that. But if you'll let me, I promise I'll try to change."

"You've said that before," she muttered, averting her eyes to stare at the floor.

"And then I went on another bender. I know. I embarrassed you at that party and I felt so bad, I just wanted to disappear.'' Mervyn gulped. ''When I looked at you, I saw her. And that hurt something fierce. I wanted her back.''

''But instead I was there, demanding you be a father to Ronnie and me,'' Beth whispered. Her eyes were dark, glistening with unshed tears.

''I had to lash out, I was so angry. And then I had to get away. I couldn't stay there and see you and not be reminded of how much I loved Loretta, and of how badly I failed her. And you. It hurt too much.'' The poignant words trailed away.

A long silence hung between father and daughter as they stared into each other's eyes. As Gar watched the wordless communication, he prayed.

''You can't run away anymore, Dad. We don't have that much time to waste. If you want to be our father, it's got to start now. Ronnie needs you.''

Mervyn nodded, but his eyes were intently studying the young girl who'd grown into a woman. Gar had a feeling that the old man was finally seeing the beautiful woman who stood before him as herself, his own dear daughter—not some dream-like replica of her long-dead mother.

''And you?'' Mervyn's voice was stronger now. ''What about you, Beth? What do you want?''

''The past is finished, done.'' The corners of her wide mouth tipped up in a wry grin. ''And to tell you the truth, after today I don't care if I never hear about it again. I want the future. With Gar. And you. I want Ronnie to be proud of you, to know you as I remember you—before the drinking.'' There were tears now, but they were hopeful tears.

''And?'' Mervyn stood where he was, waiting.

Beth gulped down a sob. ''I want you to walk me down the aisle when I marry Gar. I want my family to be there for me.''

''I'll be there.'' Mervyn's voice sounded rusty; it squeaked in places. ''I promise you, Beth. I'll be there, stone-cold sober.''

At last Beth flew into her father's embrace, her sobs joyful at this reunion with the man whose memory had haunted her for years.

As he watched them hold each other, Gar heaved a sigh of relief. *Thank you, God.*

Now, if they could just get on with the wedding!

Chapter Nine

The ride home was slower than it needed to be because Gar took a detour. Beth didn't mind. She basked in her father's words and reveled in the thrill of having Gar's arm around her shoulders, snuggling her as close as they could get with the stick shift between them.

"Where are we going?" she asked, glancing around and seeing nothing familiar.

"I'm abducting you. And it's a secret hideout, so close your eyes."

Beth complied, content to let the pictures waft through her mind. *A wedding.* Two days ago she wouldn't have dreamed this was possible, and now suddenly she was positive it would happen, perhaps sooner than anyone imagined.

"Keep your eyes closed now."

"They're closed already! What is this all about, anyway?"

"You'll see."

She was aware that the car had stopped, felt Gar move, and then shivered as a gust of cold air rushed in when her own door was opened. Moments later she felt herself being lifted out of the car. She giggled at the strange feeling of being carried who knew where. She clasped both arms around his neck, relaxed and enjoyed it.

"What are you doing with me?" she demanded.

"I'm ensuring that for once in this relationship, we have some privacy," he told her. "You can open your eyes now."

Beth did so, and glanced around, startled by the beauty of the room she'd just entered. She slid to her feet, taking in the lustrously polished cedar walls, the stone fireplace and the soaring ceilings. A glance out the window showed they were somewhere out of town, but she couldn't see much except for the snow-covered hills that gleamed under a full moon.

"Where is this?"

"This is our home. Or at least, I hope it will be. I built it a few years ago in the hope that when you finally came back, you'd live here with me. I haven't stayed here much, though." He looked sheepish. "I never told you this, but I've been waiting for you to come home. I've had this dream of you here."

Come home? Had she really? Beth touched a hand to his cheek and stared into his eyes. She smiled and nodded, finally willing to accept that anywhere with Gar would be home. Things didn't matter.

After several solemn moments, Gar moved toward the fireplace and lit the little pile of paper and kindling that lay waiting. When the fire grew stronger he added more and more sticks until it was a well-established blaze. Then he rose, dusted off his knees and walked back toward her, stopping once beside a big chest. Beth heard him open a drawer, but was too busy looking around the beautiful room to pay any attention.

"Come on, Beth. Sit down." He ushered her to the big golden sofa, and, when she'd sunk into its softness, he knelt in front of her. "I have something I want to say."

"Okay." She loved him, she wanted to marry him, to live here with him. So why did this all feel so strange?

"I've been in love with you for years, Beth Ainslow. There have been times, lots of them, when I've wondered if you would ever come to this place. And I promised myself that if you did, I'd do this properly." He stared into her eyes, his own glowing dark with suppressed emotions.

"I love you. I always will. I finally realized that I don't care about the past anymore. My focus is on the future." One hand picked up hers, squeezing it gently. "Will you please marry me, Beth?"

She couldn't hold back—a "yes" burst out of her, heartfelt and confident. She saw his smile of satisfaction, then noticed the ring he was holding out.

"This was my grandmother's, given to her by her husband when my dad was born. The stone was a very rare find by a man they'd loaned money to when they didn't have much to loan. Grandfather asked him to keep the stone until he could afford to buy it, and his friend agreed. It took him almost ten years, but he finally bought it on the day my dad was born. He said they'd waited so long to have children, he wanted to commemorate God's goodness.''

"What a lovely history!"

"Dinah gave it to me several years ago and told me I should only give it to the one woman I wanted to share the rest of my life with. Will you wear it until we can get a proper engagement ring?''

The unusual garnet glowed with a rich yellow-green against the heavy gold setting. As she stared at the strange colors, tears came to her eyes.

"Garnet is January's birthstone," she whispered. "And your birthday is next week. I'd love to wear it *as* an engagement ring, Gar," she whispered, sliding her finger into the ring. "It's perfect because it will remind me constantly of you."

Gar leaned forward and kissed her, his lips warm with promise. "It's not the usual thing," he warned. "We could get you a diamond if you like, or some emeralds to go with your beautiful eyes. I just wanted you to have this ring tonight because today is a huge step forward for us." One finger caressed her cheek lovingly.

But Beth shook her head, holding her hand out to the firelight. "This ring is absolutely perfect," she whispered, tipping her head back to stare at him. "It's exactly like you, unusual. And I love the history behind it. A diamond engagement ring is common, but this one reminds me that though we had to wait, God is always faithful. Thank you." She kissed him back.

"You're welcome." He grinned, watching her twist her hand to catch the light. "They almost named me for that stone, you know. Thankfully, my mother thought Garnet was too effeminate a name for her son." Gar made a face and then patted the floor, shifting so there was room for her to sit beside him on the rug in front of the fire.

"Can you possibly be ready by Valentine's Day?" he asked quietly. "I know it's only a little over two weeks, but I don't want to wait anymore, and since it's so close, the day for lovers seems the perfect time to get married."

"A Valentine's wedding would be nice," Beth agreed hesitantly. "But I'd rather pick a different weekend."

"Why?" He seemed startled. "Valentine's Day is supposed to be all about love."

"I know. But it seems...well, trite. And besides, that's my busiest day. I'd rather not be racing around doing both things at once. What about the week after?"

Gar frowned, and Beth steeled herself for what she knew was coming. His disappointed look said it all. But she had to make her feelings clear.

"Beth, you don't have to worry about the store now. I make more than enough money for both of us. We can afford to let business slide for one weekend." His eyes begged her to reconsider.

But Beth frowned, then shook her head. "The Enchanted Florist isn't just some hobby I want to play at, Gar. This is what I do, it's part of who I am. And

I'm not going to stop doing it after we're married." She prayed he knew that much about her. "I love working with flowers. It fulfills a part of me that needs expression. I put together the idea for the Enchanted Florist at the lowest point in my life. I believed in myself and worked hard to make that dream come to fruition. I intend to see it through."

She saw an angry look pass over his face, though Gar did his best to hide it. He fiddled with his hands for a moment, then wrapped one around hers, enclosing the ring and her hand inside his fist. To Beth it was akin to losing herself in him. She felt embarrassed by that, irritated that she could even think that about the man she loved.

She thrust the traitorous idea away and concentrated on what he was saying.

"I wasn't suggesting that you forget about the store, Beth. I just thought we could take a little time for us, to celebrate our marriage. If you want, I guess we could get a justice of the peace and fit the ceremony in between orders."

"Gar!" Beth felt the tears well in her eyes. "I don't want that at all." She dashed the tears away with her hand. She wasn't a child anymore. Surely she could articulate her feelings. If she could ever figure them out.

"I never really thought about this before, but—" she gulped nervously, searching for some control "—maybe what we both need is some time to reacquaint ourselves. Ten years is a long time to be apart. People change."

"I haven't changed." His lip took a stubborn downward tilt. "I'm still in love with you. And it's been eleven years, not ten. That's a long engagement, even for us!"

"I love you, Gar. More than I even thought I did before." Beth curled her fingers into his, and nudged her shoulder against his. "But you have changed. And so have I. I've changed from that person you knew back then. I grew up, learned some things. And I don't want to go back to being that scared little girl who depended completely on you for her happiness."

"I liked that girl." He said it grudgingly, his eyes downcast, avoiding hers.

"I didn't. You don't want a child for a wife, Gar. You want a woman who isn't afraid to move into the future. You have your business—you're good at it, too. Why is it wrong for me to love working with flowers?"

"It's not wrong," he huffed, kicking the fire grate. "It just interferes with things."

"With what, exactly?"

"With what I'd planned, what I thought you wanted. I hoped we'd be able to get married, have a honeymoon, start our life together soon. We've waited a long time already." His disconsolate-looking face made her smile. "You don't have to prove anything to me, Beth. I already know you're more than capable of doing anything you set your mind to."

"Thank you." Beth reached up and cupped his cheek in her hand, turning his head so he faced her. She chose her words with care. "Darling, we're going to be married. I'm not letting you go. But when we're married, I want to be fully awake and aware. I intend to enjoy every moment. I don't want to be half dead from the rush of Valentine's Day when I focus all my attention on you, Mr. Winthrop.''

He pulled her into his arms and kissed her breathless. ''Do you realize we've completely reversed roles? I used to be the rational one, the guy who thought through every move. Now, for the first time in my life, I'd like to be impetuous, and you're the voice of reason.''

''Eerie, isn't it?'' She giggled. ''I'd better go home,'' she murmured ten minutes later. ''I want to talk to Ronnie, tell her about us and Dad.'' She got to her feet and looked around the dimly lit room for her coat. When Gar didn't rise, she glanced down and saw the frown on his face. ''What?''

''You *are* going to marry me, aren't you? You're not just saying that, putting me off?'' Uncertainty formed a tiny furrow in his forehead, and his dark eyes swirled with unspoken emotion.

Touched by the worry in his voice, Beth pulled open her purse and snatched out her calendar. ''I'm not letting you off that easily, buster,'' she teased, trying to lighten the atmosphere. ''Valentine's Day is on a Sunday this year. I'll marry you two weeks later. That's still in the 'love' month.'' She raised her eyebrows and rolled her eyes as she drawled ''love''. ''How does that suit you, Garrett Winthrop?''

''It's a little too long, actually,'' he murmured as

he rose and kissed her once more. "More than a month away. How will I survive?"

"You'll manage," she assured him smugly. "Come on, Gar. We've got a lot of things to discuss on the way home."

"Like what?" He pressed the screen in front of the fire a little more securely, pulled on his jacket and switched out lights as she walked outside. "All I have to do is get my tux cleaned."

"Uh-uh. I don't think so!" Beth shook her head, climbed into his car and did up her seat belt, her mind racing. "Who's going to stand up with you? And what time should we have the service? What colors do you like? And how many guests should we invite?"

Gar stared at her quizzically for several moments, then came back to reality as he slammed her door shut, rounded the hood and climbed into his own seat. He pressed the key into the ignition and backed out of the drive. "Did I mention that I like the idea of eloping?"

"Don't even think about it," she warned. Then her face brightened. "I've got to find a dress. A real wedding dress." She mused on that for a good part of the way back before noticing his silence. "Is something wrong?"

"You never said if you liked the house. Not that you have to. We can sell it if you don't. Build something else maybe?"

Beth smiled.

"It's a lovely house," she murmured quietly. "And I love all that cedar. You did a wonderful job."

"But?"

"Why do you say that?" She blinked innocently.

"I can tell there's something you aren't saying," he told her with a smart-aleck grin. "You haven't changed that much, no matter what you say, Beth Ainslow. Spill it."

"It's just that I'm not sure if I can live this far out of town. Right now the store is just a few minutes from Wintergreen, and I can run back to it after dinner if I have to do the books or finish something. But this drive seems more like twenty minutes."

"Thirty, if you don't speed." He stared straight ahead. "I was hoping we'd have some time to ourselves."

"We will," she assured him. "Lots of it, I promise. But I'll still be in charge of Ronnie, and I have to think about the future. Don't forget about her."

"I have not forgotten about anything," he mumbled, face gloomy as he focused on the road. "I just hope you don't."

Beth pretended she hadn't heard the cranky note in his voice. They would both have to make adjustments. But they could do that. Couldn't they?

"Why so glum, chum?" Jordan Andrews slapped Gar on the back before flopping down beside him on Beth's old sofa. "This is your engagement party. You're supposed to be ecstatic, aren't you? Or did I get that part wrong?"

"I am ecstatic," Gar muttered as he stared into the ruby gleam of his punch. "Completely and totally ecstatic. Deliriously enraptured."

"Could have fooled me. You look like your dog just died." Jordan took the glass away and set it on the table. "What's the matter?"

"To answer your questions in order, I don't have a dog, everything, and nothing."

"Well, that's about as clear as this sludgy hot chocolate. Care to elaborate?"

Gar knew Jordan. He knew the other man would no more leave this subject alone than a hungry dog would leave a big, juicy bone. Jordan might be a computer nerd of the highest order, but he always tried to make everyone as happy as himself. It was an annoying trait that merely emphasized the differences between them.

"I don't really want to tell all, thanks. It just has been a little hectic lately. I feel like I never get five seconds with Beth, and when I do, somebody decides we need a party with half the town invited." He saw the red flush on Jordan's cheekbones and sighed, wishing he'd taped his beak closed. "Sorry, pal. I know you and Caitlin meant well. You did invite everyone, didn't you?"

Jordan nodded. "Yup! Everyone we could think of. We thought you and Beth deserved a party to celebrate. It's been quite a week, hasn't it? You guys finally get engaged, the youth center gets under way, Beth moves to her new store, and your dad announces his plans. Sorry if we ruined your evening."

"Nah, forget it. I'm just tired, I guess." Gar glanced around the room at the hoards of busily chattering people, and decided he was too tired to hang around here much longer.

"I'm not surprised. That new merger your dad's working on will be a doozy for the bank, won't it?"

"Yeah, I guess." Gar decided to 'fess up. Maybe it would help. "The truth is, Jordan, I don't care much about that merger. First Federal has had some problems in the past. And they're totally averse to taking on clients they term at-risk."

"And you don't like that." Jordan nodded. "That's easy to understand. Your grandfather didn't operate on the same principles. But it's a whole new world, Garrett. What went on then, what was perfectly acceptable to Gramps in his day, simply isn't feasible today."

"And that's good?" Gar glared at him, disgruntled to think that someone else was against his ideas for self-funded economic growth in Oakburn.

"I didn't say that. You are in a bad mood!" Jordan's head lifted as Beth's joyful laugh rang around the room. "At least someone is enjoying herself. Now, back to the point. Which is? What's at the root of your unease, Gar?"

"Tyler." It wasn't easy to admit, and Garrett wasn't ready to spill everything. But lately Ty's actions had been bothering him. "I don't know what's up with that kid lately. I've been covering for him for months. His grades are down, he's dropped all athletics, he isn't on the debate club anymore, and I almost have to carry him physically into the bank."

"So, the boy's going through a phase. Leave him alone and he'll grow out of it." Jordan took several sweets off the platter his wife passed before him and popped one into his mouth. "He's a kid, he's supposed to explore things."

"He can't afford to fool around too long, though. If he doesn't do something about those math marks, he's going to be attending summer school. And I assure you that my father will come down hard on him then." Gar shook his head at Caitlin's offer, smiled at her, then leaned back. "Lately all he wants to do is hang around with Ronnie."

"So? What's wrong with that?" Jordan sniffed. "Nobody's more college-oriented than that girl. She'll steer him right."

"I'm not so sure of that. I don't like to talk about this with Beth, but I think the two of them are spending too much time together. They're always out riding. Or else they disappear for hours, and when you ask, they say they were talking." He snorted in disbelief. "What in the world do they have to talk about? They're with each other almost every moment of the day as it is now. There's no time for anything new to have happened!"

"Ah, young love." Jordan wiggled his eyebrows and made calf eyes. "What's the matter? Don't you remember what being a teenager is like?"

Gar frowned, reliving the scene he'd inadvertently glimpsed yesterday. "That's just what has me worried. I don't think they're the least bit in love. More like best buds, pals."

Jordan shook his head, his eyes glinting with laughter. "You need to have a frank talk with someone, Gar. Refresh your memory."

"No, I'm serious." He hesitated, then relaxed. "Today I went looking for them when Dad was about ready to throw a hissy fit. Ty's supposed to work at the bank Friday afternoons, but he never showed. I went out to Fairwinds, and sure enough, he was there, with Ronnie, sitting on a fence on the river property by the Sullivans. They were talking a mile a minute."

"About…?" Jordan prodded.

"I didn't catch all of it. She told him he had to go with what he thought was right, that he couldn't allow me or Dad or anyone else to sway him. When they spotted me, they both hushed up. I felt like a fifth wheel."

"As you were supposed to. Nobody likes to be spied on." Jordan held up a hand as Gar began to protest. "I know, you weren't spying, but it may have looked like that to them. What did Beth say about it all?"

"Like I had time to discuss it with her!" Gar heaved himself to his feet. "The only thing I know is that we're getting married on the last day of February. The rest of our wedding is a mystery. We had more communication when she lived up north." At Jordan's raised eyebrows, Gar flushed and shook his head.

"Sorry. But part of that is true. Beth is run off her feet with this Sweetheart Banquet thing. And Valentine's Day. And maybe even the wedding, for all I know. There's no time to just relax with each other, to talk."

"So help her out."

"Huh?" Gar wondered if he was losing his hearing.

Surely he was a little young for that. Or maybe it was his mind. How early did the little gray cells start keeling over?

He glanced at Jordan, but his friend certainly didn't look bothered in the least by his age. In fact, he was even now ogling a tray of chocolate-covered almonds.

"Tell her you'll take over the wedding. All she has to do is get herself a dress. You look after the rest. You tell her the details, of course. If she objects, you change them. If she doesn't, she lives with it." Jordan shrugged, intimating that the outrageous idea made perfect sense to him.

"You might also bribe Ronnie into helping out at the store more and riding less. Try clothes. Girls always like more clothes. My sisters taught me that early." He shoved his glasses farther up his nose. "It's just an idea, of course."

"And a good one." Gar rubbed his hands together in glee, his brain busy. "I know two grumpy old men who would just love to help out with this wedding. And getting Dad out of the office would give me some freedom in these negotiations." He struggled up from the sofa, freeing himself only after an intense battle with the overwhelming cushions.

"Don't leave me here."

Gar grinned and held out a hand to Jordan. "I'll get you out on one condition, pal."

Jordan stayed where he was, his golden eyes suspicious. "What's the condition?"

"You help me out with the wedding without any interference from your wife. Is it a deal?"

"Is what a deal? What are you two up to now?" Clay Matthews's voice seemed loud to Gar.

"Keep it down, will you? And if you make the same promise, I'll let you in on our little secret."

Clay nodded, his face full of curiosity. "Okay, but can we get Jordan out of that thing? I think he's going to hyperventilate if he folds up like that for much longer."

Gar heaved the big man out of the sofa and waited a moment while he caught his breath.

"You two are to meet me tomorrow morning at 9: 00 a.m. at the bank. We have a lot to talk about."

"But it's Saturday," Clay protested. "I like to sleep in on Saturday. Besides, the bank's closed."

"Exactly." Gar grinned at both of them. "Be there." He put his glass down on the table, slapped a hand on each man's shoulder and smiled. "As much as I thank you for this party, Jordan, I'm going to collect Beth. There's something we need to discuss."

Then he turned and prepared to thread his way through the mob of well-wishers that surrounded the tiny blonde he loved more than life. As he went, Gar heard Clay's confused question.

"What's so important the guy has to leave in the middle of his own party?"

Jordan's answer was low-voiced, almost secretive. "Be at the café at eight-thirty and I'll tell you. But for Pete's sake, don't tell Maryann where you're going. No women."

Gar smiled as he pressed past the mayor, two members of the youth center committee and a woman who'd been dealing for eons with his family's bank.

"Excuse me, folks," he said loudly. "I need to steal this beautiful woman away from you for a while."

Amid the catcalls and silly, mocking remarks, he bundled Beth into her jacket, shoved her gloves into her hand and propelled her out the door, stopping just long enough to grab his own coat.

"Garrett Winthrop! What in the world are you up to?"

He ignored the plaintive sound of her voice and ushered her outside, his hand firmly planted on her back.

"What are you doing? Our guests—"

"Can wait. I need to discuss something with you."

"Really?" Her green eyes glowed in the streetlight. "What's so important that it couldn't wait until after the party?"

"Our wedding."

She groaned. "Gar, you know how busy I've been. I just haven't had time to do anything yet."

"I know." He smiled to show he wasn't upset, linked her arm in his and set off at a brisk pace toward the park. "Beth, my love, I'd like to propose something."

"Again?" She grinned up at him, her eyes sparkling. "I thought we did that already."

"Be quiet, woman. I'm serious." And in the dark snowy night, with the lights and laughter of Wintergreen behind them, Garrett explained his idea, adding new twists as he went.

"Well? What do you think?" He waited breathlessly for her response, praying she wouldn't turn him down.

"I say, I'm marrying the smartest man east of the Pacific Ocean. As well as the brashest, the nerviest, the sweetest, most thoughtful fellow God could have given me. And I'm taking you up on it, all of it. Just remember two weeks from now, when you're buried under To-Do lists, that you *offered.*"

"Oh, I'll remember. Just make sure *you* do when I pick the wrong color."

"Colors don't matter to me." She laughed at the very idea. Seconds later a frown replaced that smile. "Unless it's black. I don't want a black wedding."

"Trust me," he encouraged as Beth's arms wrapped around his waist and she hugged him close. Garrett smiled to himself.

All right, Lord, he prayed silently. *One problem down, one to go. Why don't I feel Ty will be as easy to handle?*

Gar fancied he heard a light burble of laughter drop down from heaven along with the fluffy snowflake that landed on his nose. But it must have been his imagination for when he looked up, cold, wet snow got caught in his lashes and he couldn't see a thing, let alone hear any voices.

I can do it, he told himself confidently. No problem.

There was that laughter again. Must be someone else in the park.

Chapter Ten

"They did what?"

A week later Beth sighed, rubbed her fist against her temple and counted to ten, fifteen, no, twenty. She glared at the speaker phone malevolently as she pulled her finger free of a rose thorn.

"They went to Minneapolis, Gar. To see an exhibit. They went with the youth group."

"Oh, yeah." A long pause. "I thought that was for a rock concert. That 'cool' singer, what's his name?" His voice echoed back, full of confusion.

"Denise D'Angelo is *her* name. And yes, they went for that. But when she phoned, Ronnie said they saw the ad while they were there and decided to go to an exhibit." She stared at the layers of greenery that waited to be formed into table edging, and felt tiredness swamp her.

"My brother went to an *art* exhibit? Willingly?" The disbelief was obvious.

"Gar, I'm up to my neck in plans for this over-done banquet that my dear, sweet friends came up with. Believe me, I would not choose this moment to play a joke on you." She swallowed a mouthful of cold, stale coffee, and made a face. "Anyway, what's so bad about Ty going to an exhibit? We can all do with exposure to the finer things in life."

"But an art exhibit?—" he huffed "—Unreal."

Beth frowned. "Ronnie didn't actually say 'art.' I don't think," she mused. "I guess I just assumed that part. What other kind of exhibit is there?"

"You're asking me? I haven't a clue. And when it comes to Ty, I would have said it would be either food or horses. What was wrong with coming home with the rest of the group?"

"I don't know." Beth puffed, blowing cool air onto her forehead. "I don't know any more than I've told you."

"Kids! If they'd only think first."

"You're wasting time, Gar. Of course, I would have preferred that they got on the bus with the rest of the group, but it's too late to say that now. They missed it, and someone has to go get them."

A long, drawn-out silence greeted her words. Then a sigh.

"You're not asking me to go, are you? Because I can't. Not now. I'm in the middle of sorting through Dad's latest brain wave."

Garrett's tone was less than cordial. In fact, he sounded harassed, as if he'd been hit with one too many things in the past hour.

Beth knew exactly how he felt. Three funerals of prominent citizens, an impromptu wedding and then this banquet with all of Caitlin's changes and Mary-ann's add-ons. Not that she resented the business or the income. No, she was thrilled with both. But how would she ever get everything ready?

"Then when? I don't suppose it would hurt them to stay overnight, though according to Ronnie, neither one of them has enough for a hotel room." She tried to think of another idea, but lately all she saw was more and more work.

"Can't you go?" The request hinted that it was her turn. "After all, I've been doing all this planning and stuff for the wedding."

"Along with our fathers." She nodded. "I heard. And for your information, I've been working, too, you know. You act as though I have nothing to do but wait for your phone calls!" Beth heard the words as if they came from someone else's mouth, and shame filled her. "I'm sorry, Gar," she apologized. "I'm just very tired. Okay, if you can't, you can't. I'll have to drop what I'm doing and go."

She stared at the mess that lay around the work-room, remnants of a Saturday that should have been finished two hours ago. Everyone else had left at six, but she'd stayed on, determined to make a dent in the Valentine preparations that were now only a week away. Boxes of expensive Belgian chocolates sat in the cooler, waiting for her to get the showcase ready. If it didn't happen soon, she would lose a lot of money.

"I can leave in about fifteen minutes if I hustle."

Silence. Then a rustle of paper came through the phone.

"I'll go with you," Gar announced. "I need a break, and I need to see you. That's more important than work. We can go over wedding things on the drive. How's that sound?"

Beth's heart lifted. "Actually, it sounds wonderful. I've barely seen you this week. And I don't think we've had more than a three-minute conversation since that party last week."

"It's that crazy youth center. They keep changing their minds. I knew it was a mistake to let Jordan talk me into sitting on that board. Carpet, no carpet, pop machine or food booth, CDs or cassettes. The list goes on and on."

Beth straightened. "Jordan talked you into that? I thought you were asked as part of your council duties…" She let the words trail away, shook her head and refocused. "Never mind. I don't care how you got on it. All I want to do is see the thing opened. Why did they have to choose February for that?"

Gar laughed and the sound was music to her ears. She'd missed him.

"Guess they figured it would be a quiet month. Shows what they know." He cleared his throat. "We're wasting time, Beth. I'll pick you up in ten minutes. Okay?"

Fifteen minutes later, accompanied by chips and sodas, she leaned back against the car's leather upholstery and breathed a sigh of relief.

"It feels good to sit down for a while," she mumbled, resting her head on the back of her seat. "My legs are so tired!"

"I feel like I've been sitting for days." Gar shifted uncomfortably.

"The negotiations?" When he nodded, she smiled sympathetically. "How's it going?"

"It's not. We're at an impasse. Dad's not too happy with me right now, but I'm not going to go along with something I don't feel is good for Oakburn."

"What do they want to do?" she asked curiously. She flicked open a can and placed it in the cup holder.

"Call in a few loans for starters. From people who can't afford to pay them right now. Thanks." He took a drink and replaced the can.

"It's a good thing you borrowed your dad's car. We'd never squeeze the kids into yours." Beth opened her own drink and then offered him a package of chips. "Is the bank overextended or something?"

He shook his head. "Not at all. We're well covered. Sure, we've got a few bad debts that we will probably never recover—who hasn't? Still, all in all, I think we're in pretty good shape. It's just that these guys want to make it as much of a sure thing as possible."

"I guess we'd all like to know that we weren't taking any risks. But if we don't, nothing much gets accomplished in life. Ronnie and I were talking about this the other day. She thinks she should find a college nearer Oakburn, just in case I need her." She smiled, remembering her sister's generous offer.

"What about me? Don't forget, we'll be married."

He looked offended by the very idea, and Beth forced down a smile.

"I'm not forgetting, neither is she. I think she feels that I'll need her moral support."

"For what?" Gar's disgruntled voice was barely held in check. "I'm not an ogre."

"Close," Beth teased, her head tilted to one side as she studied his profile. "You do furrow your brow something fierce when anyone dares question you." She laughed out loud at his frown. "But really, I think she's more worried about me standing up against your father. Ronnie thinks I'm a wimp."

"She doesn't know you very well, then. Even I know better than that." Free of the town, Gar set the cruise control and leaned back to relax. "You've always gone after exactly what you wanted."

"Not always. And never with your family. I let all the gloss and hype that surrounds your dad overwhelm me. Don't worry," she hastened to add, "I'm not going to do it again. But I do have to guard against taking the easy way out."

"That's what I've been doing with Ty. I know how overbearing Dad can get, and I always try to shield him. But he's got to learn to face responsibility. Tonight is just another example of his immaturity. It's time he grew up."

"He's a teenager, Garrett. They're supposed to be irresponsible once in a while." Beth rushed to the kids' defense, unable to understand Gar's anger.

"That's a good excuse, isn't it? 'Poor little kid, let's let him ride on someone else's coattails for a while.'

No way! I took my duties seriously when I was his age.''

''Maybe a little too seriously.'' The words slipped out. Obviously, tiredness loosened her tongue.

''What does that mean?'' His dark eyes veered from the road just long enough to glare at her. ''Are we going back to blaming each other?''

''No, of course not! It's just...'' How could she explain what she meant?

''Just what?'' His tone told her it would be better if she stopped now.

But she couldn't. The questions lay there, waiting to surface. Wasn't it better to deal with her doubts now, before things got blown out of proportion?

''I've often wondered this, Gar. Tonight I'm going to ask it.'' Beth took a deep breath and plunged in. ''What would you have done if you hadn't known you were expected to follow in your father's footsteps?''

The silence that stretched between them told its own story. Taut with strain, full of things unsaid, it hung there.

''I've always known I would be at the bank,'' he muttered at last. ''It's a part of who I am, of what I was brought up with. And if you think I resent that, you're wrong. I like banking. I like the challenge of finding ways to make people's dreams come true.''

Beth nodded. ''I know you like the numbers part of it. But the dream part, that's what you do in your own time, in your own business. It's not something that you really do much of at the bank, is it?''

Gar took another swallow of his drink, his eyes

fixed on the dark ribbon of highway ahead. Occasionally he'd glance at her, but she couldn't discern his true feelings. So why did she doubt him? Why did she feel he kept hiding something about himself—some part that he never let anyone see?

"The flower shop was your dream. We filled that request." The words had a harsh edge to them.

"But I wasn't a good risk, and I doubt whether your father would have granted my loan without some pressure from you. Am I right?" She waited, knowing deep inside that it was the truth.

"It doesn't matter how the dream gets filled. The fact that it does should be enough."

"Maybe." She chewed on another chip, considering his words.

"But we're straying from the topic."

"Which was?" He sounded irritated.

"Duty. I think you would have done something completely different if your father hadn't groomed you for the bank since the day you were born." She held up the chip bag and waited while he found several with his free hand.

"Maybe. But I had a duty, and I did it. It didn't kill me, I make good money at it and there are times when it is very fulfilling. That's what I want for Ty."

"And if he doesn't want to spend his life in the bank?" She held her breath and waited as he absorbed such a rebellious thought.

"He will. He knows that's his place." Gar drove steadily on for a few minutes, then leaned over to pat her hand. "Why don't I catch you up on our wedding? It's going to be at least another hour 'til we get there."

And that's the end of it, Beth mused to herself, only half listening to his description of the guest list. He doesn't even want to consider that there could be an alternative life choice for Ty.

If we have kids, are they going to have to be involved in the bank, too? she mused to herself. Or will they have the freedom to find their own niche? She tilted her seat back more comfortably, murmured her consent to matching wedding bands, then closed her eyes. Just for a moment.

She dreamed of four towheaded boys dressed in three-piece suits, marching to the beat of an unseen drummer. Somehow she knew these were her children—hers and Gar's. But they didn't want to go to the bank. They wanted to go play in the park.

"Beth? Come on, wake up. We're almost there." Gar's hand lifted from her shoulder as he manipulated the car in and out of traffic. "What street did you say this place is on?"

"Just a minute. I wrote it down somewhere. Oh yeah, here it is." She blinked groggily.

"The corner of Fifth and Fifteenth." She straightened as the city lights flashed past. Eventually they reached the right corner. "There, that's Ronnie in her pink jacket."

Gar eased the car to the curb and pressed the automatic door locks so the two teens could tumble into the back seat.

"You guys are lifesavers," Ronnie gushed. "I just

couldn't think what else to do. The bus had gone by the time we got back to the hall. Sorry, sis. I know you were up to your eyeballs in work.''

"It's my fault, not hers. I had to see that display when I saw it advertised in the paper. I just didn't think it would take so long to get back." Ty fastened his seat belt and then looked at his brother's rigid back. "Thanks for coming, bro."

"'Didn't think' is right. Do you realize I was in the middle of some important negotiations? And Beth has piles of work to do, too. We can't just dump everything and run off to rescue you because you 'didn't think.'" Gar stared straight ahead, but his voice was tight with anger.

"It's okay, Gar. I'll catch up. Ronnie'll help me." Beth tried to smooth things over.

"Well, that's just lovely. Good for Ronnie. But who is going to give me a helping hand? It won't be Tyler. He hasn't got the foggiest notion of what's going on nowadays, because he hasn't been in to do his *job* in weeks."

Beth's temper started a slow simmer. "Garrett, do we have to go over this again now? They know they made a mistake. They won't do it again. Can't we just relax?"

"Relax?" He stared at her as if she had suggested he rob a bank. "You don't learn anything by relaxing and letting your standards drop."

Beth was glad the light was temporarily red, because his attention was certainly not on his driving. She closed her eyes and prayed for control of her tongue. Behind them a horn honked, and she grabbed the seat as he lurched forward, his foot heavy on the gas.

"Garrett. Slow down. I don't want to get killed on the way home." To her relief, he did lift his foot until they were through the city. "Are you two hungry?" she asked, turning to glance at the repentant pair.

"Starved," Ronnie admitted.

"Do you think we could pull in over there and pick up some burgers and fries?" Beth pointed to the drive-thru, considered the car they were in and changed her mind. "Or maybe we should go inside. We don't want to mess up your father's car."

"No, we wouldn't want to do that." The stinging mockery came from tightly clenched lips.

Beth ignored him. Once parked, she climbed out and motioned to the others. "Come on. I'm buying." Gar stayed in the car. "Aren't you coming inside?" she demanded as the others slipped and slid across the icy parking lot.

"I'll stay here, thanks."

Beth sighed. She'd disagreed with him and now he was pouting. Surely this wasn't a good omen.

"Get out of the car, Garrett Winthrop, or I'll make the biggest scene you ever hope to see." She kept the teasing out of her voice, her eyes solemn and her mouth in a straight line. "Now!"

"Sometimes, you're a royal pain," he muttered finally, easing himself out from behind the wheel.

"The feeling is mutual. They're kids, for Pete's sake. Will you cut them some slack?" Sure that he was following her, Beth walked inside the fast-food place and ordered for them all, not even bothering to consult Garrett who'd gone to find a table.

While Ronnie and Ty chatted about the concert, readily answering Beth's questions, Gar sat silently, his face gloomy. They were slurping up the last bit of their milk shakes when he finally spoke.

"So what was so great about this art exhibit that you had to go across town to see?" His long lean fingers picked up a French fry, inspected it and then placed it in his mouth as his eyes pinned them down.

"Oh, it wasn't an art exhibit." Ronnie grinned, her eyes dancing. "It was an exhibit by a group of international chefs. You should have seen the stuff they made. Ty's eyes were this big." She made a circular motion with her fingers. "He's going to try a couple of the recipes out next week."

"Chefs?" Beth repeated.

"You went to look at food?" Gar sounded shocked. "Why in the world would you do that?"

"'Cause Ty's gonna be a world-famous chef someday. You should taste his caramel banana torte!" She rolled her eyes, head lolling back. "It's to die for. Ow! Why'd you kick me, Ty?"

"Cooking is a good hobby to have," Beth offered, smiling at the red-faced boy who now shifted uneasily in his seat. "You can come and practise on us anytime. Especially if you're making cookies. Ronnie's are disgusting!"

"Oh, it's not a hobby," Ronnie burst in, her eyes

glittering with excitement. "Ty wants to train as a chef. He's even found the best school."

"What?" Gar's voice roared above the crowded room, causing patrons to turn and frown at him. "You want to be a cook? A *cook!*"

He made the vocation sound as if it were a fate worse than death, Beth fumed silently. She saw Ty focus his eyes on his lap, his hands twisting beneath the edge of the table. His cheeks burned a bright, embarrassed red. When he finally glanced up, she saw the defiance in the depths of those usually laughing eyes.

"Yes, a cook. A chef. That's what I want."

"Well, you can forget it right now. I suppose it's okay as a hobby, but it's not something you do for the rest of your life. Get a mitt and get in the game, kid. We're talking about a career."

"There are some very good careers for chefs." Tyler's voice was soft but steady. Clearly, though he hadn't expected to discuss it tonight, like this, he'd done some preparation. "And they work in fascinating places. Someday I'm going to open my own restaurant. I'm going to train in Europe."

Beth silently applauded the smooth controlled tone, though she knew the boy was hurt by his brother's scoffing.

"Don't be a fool. What do you know about cooking?" Gar's voice raked out scathingly. "Nothing. You've never done it. And I'm sure it doesn't begin to pay well. It takes years for these men to make it to the top."

"I've been working in the kitchen for months, Gar. Those things you took to Ronnie's dad at the potluck, I made those. And I don't care about the money," Ty added.

"Of course you don't. You've never really had to earn any, have you?" Gar shook his head, completely disregarding Ty's answers. "I don't understand any of this."

"I don't think we need to discuss it right now. Are you two finished?" Beth gathered up the soiled papers and cardboard containers as she waited. "Want some dessert?"

"No, thanks."

They both looked glum, deflated, as if they'd lost their oomph. It hurt her to see Ty's disillusionment with the brother he'd trailed after since he'd learned to walk. She'd have to talk to Garrett, make him understand. Somehow.

"Okay, let's get on the road, then. You two can snooze for a while. Gar, do you want me to drive?" She stood, holding the tray as she stared into his eyes.

"Believe me, I'm wide awake now." The scathing response made her bristle.

"Fine. Let's go." She slipped the car keys out of Gar's hand and tossed them at Ty. "You two go ahead. We'll be there in a minute."

"Don't start with me, Beth. I'm furious. This is why the kid's been avoiding work. He's been playing at cooking."

"What's wrong with that? Other than the fact that

it isn't *your* choice?'' She stood directly in front of him, daring him to answer.

"Ty's future is with the bank. There's security, a good income. Everything's all set up."

"And he doesn't want it. So now what?''

Gar stood, easing her out of the way as he flexed his shoulders tiredly. "I don't know. He'll have to give up this silly notion, of course. Dad will have a heart attack."

"Well, then he'll have a heart attack. Hopefully he'll get over it." Beth smiled to soften her words. "Gar, Tyler can't live his life the way you or your father want. It's his life. He only gets one chance at it and he has to make the best of that. Let him do it his own way."

"Don't be foolish."

She smiled sadly. "Foolish? I don't think so. I know exactly how Ty feels. I had a dream once. I wanted it so badly, I could almost taste it. I put my heart and mind and soul into learning everything I could to make that dream come true. And eventually, when I opened the Enchanted Florist, it did."

She peered at him quizzically. "Haven't you ever wanted something so badly that you were willing to do whatever it took to make it reality, Garrett?"

He sat there, silent but brooding, filled with anger, his mouth taut.

"Yes," he enunciated finally. "I have. But I didn't get it. And I managed to survive."

"I see." She tapped her finger on the table. "You get so much joy and pleasure out of your father's bank that you now want Ty to ignore whatever hopes and dreams he has because you're positive he'll find his true calling there, too. Am I right?''

''He's too young to know—'' Gar began.

''But that's exactly the same mistake your father made about us!'' She couldn't believe they were doing this again. Hadn't they learned anything? ''He thought you were too young, I wasn't good enough, we needed to grow up. And he was *wrong*.''

Garrett stared at her in astonishment, his mouth open.

''Don't you see, Gar? This is always at the root of our disagreements. Now it's a barrier between you and your brother. You want both Tyler and me to give up what we've chosen for ourselves, what we really enjoy.''

She swallowed, searching for the right words. ''It's not right to do that to anyone, Gar. I wouldn't ask you to give up the bank. Not ever. I know how much pleasing your father and helping the people in Oakburn means to you. You wouldn't be the same person, the man that I love, if you didn't put every effort into helping people get what they want out of life.''

He gave a wry smile. ''That's my job, ma'am. I'm a financial advisor. I help people achieve their dreams.''

She nodded. ''I know that. And I think it's wonderful work. But what else do you want from life?''

''I don't know what you mean. The bank takes up all my time now.'' He looked mystified.

''Exactly! And that isn't good.''

"It's not?" He adjusted the ketchup bottle, moving it first to the left, then to the right. "Why?"

Beth took a deep breath and plunged in. "What would you do if everyone in Oakburn was on the road to achieving what they wanted from life—their dream? What would you do next?"

"Do?" He frowned. "Look for new clients."

"There aren't any more clients, the bank is doing fine, your father is happy, your life is on a roll. Now, what do you want?"

His eyes clouded in puzzlement. "I don't know."

"But don't you have a whole list of things you'd like to try someday, if you have the chance?"

"What kind of things?" He looked nonplussed. "You mean hobbies?" He gave the word a distinctly horrible sound.

"Not necessarily. Just things you want to do." Seeing that she was getting nowhere, Beth decided to help him out. "For instance, I've always wanted to ride in a hot air balloon. Or go to Hawaii."

"I've already been there, but we could go again." He looked pleased by the thought.

Beth sighed tiredly, wondering if she'd been wrong to even bring up this subject. But it worried her. Was he so driven by his father's idea of success that he had no ambitions that were totally his own?

"Isn't there anything that really thrills you?" she finally demanded. "Anything that you'd like to try, just once, to see if it's all it's cracked up to be?"

A faraway look came into those rich gray eyes, and Beth could almost see the wheels in his mind turning.

"Okay, you've thought of something. I can see it as plainly as the nose on your face. What is it?" She waited, breath suspended.

"You'll think it's silly," he stalled, pretending to fiddle with his collar.

Beth reached out and placed a hand on his arm. When he looked up, she met his embarrassed gaze and smiled steadily. "I won't think it's silly," she promised. "Tell me."

His eyes assessed her seriousness. Eventually he nodded, apparently satisfied that she could be told.

"I'd like to go sky diving," he muttered at last.

"Sky diving?" She gulped.

Garrett, the man who never took a risk without thinking everything out logically and carefully, wanted to throw himself out of an airplane at six-thousand feet with nothing but a dinky piece of silk to depend on?

"I knew you'd think it was juvenile." He picked up his gloves, pulled them on, and then, finger by finger, removed them. "I do, too. My father would never allow it."

Indignation surged to the fore. "Never allow it?" She gathered her belongings, squashed the empty containers into a garbage can and pulled her purse over one shoulder. Then she turned her attention back to him. "You're twenty-nine years old, Garrett. Don't you think it's time you decided whose life you're living? As for me, I've got to get some sleep. Valentine's Day is only one week away. Let's go."

The ride home was not restful. Silence, filled with foreboding, stretched among them. Several times Beth heard Ronnie and Ty whispering. But she ignored them.

Instead, Beth focused on what needed to be done for the banquet that had gotten out of control. By the time Gar pulled up in front of Wintergreen, she was more than ready for sleep. She leaned over to kiss his cheek.

"Think about what I said, Gar. Everybody has to make their own mistakes. Even Ty. Good night to you both. Ronnie?"

In a calm, dignified manner, she made her escape, while he sat puzzling over her words. She shooed Ty back into the car, kept Ronnie behind her and closed the door firmly on both of the Winthrops.

"Let him chew on that for a while," she muttered as she climbed the stairs to bed, more exhausted than she'd been in months.

Chapter Eleven

"I hate this Sweetheart's Ball. How did it get to be a ball anyway? This started out as a banquet." Beth grumbled and complained as she rearranged the red and white carnations in their vases for the fifth time that afternoon. "And if you move these one more time, Caitlin Andrews, I'll pinch your fingers!"

Caitlin chuckled, her eyes dancing. "A little moody, aren't we?" she teased. "For a girl who just got engaged, who's getting married in two weeks to the most handsome Garrett Winthrop, you're just the teensiest bit cranky, my dear."

"Nerves I guess. I want everything to go smoothly so I can get working on my wedding plans." Beth sighed. "I haven't even chosen a dress yet: Why can't the men be here helping? It's Saturday, all three of them are free and yet here we are, decorating for this ill-conceived banquet tonight!"

"It was not ill-conceived." Maryann sniffed. "I

think it's a wonderful way to spend a Saturday night, and especially here at Fairwinds. It's so romantic!''

Beth groaned as her friend's eyes grew hazy and her hands forgot that they were supposed to be twisting a streamer. ''Romantic? We'll be lucky to stagger in here after doing all this work.'' She began spreading rose petals down the center of each table as Maryann had requested. ''They could have been hanging those things, instead of asking you to go up a ladder.''

''Not this morning they couldn't.'' Maryann giggled. ''This is the only morning they could get a plane. I never thought Clay could look so green.''

A premonition, dark and suffocating, rose in Beth's stomach.

''A plane? What do they need a plane for?'' she asked, carefully dropping one petal at a time as her heart sank to her toes.

Caitlin frowned at Maryann. Obviously her friend had spilled the beans. ''They wouldn't say,'' Caitlin admitted. ''But I think they're going to get something for tonight. Jordan said you'd be thrilled.''

''Oh, no! Oh, please, no.'' She dropped the basket of petals on the floor, grabbed her coat and headed for the stairs. ''You guys finish up. I'll be back later.''

''Beth, where are you going?'' Caitlin's voice followed her up the steps.

''To stop something before someone gets himself killed.'' Beth muttered the words to herself as she slammed her delivery van into reverse and took off for the municipal airport.

By the time she had arrived at the air field, parked

the van and rushed to the fence that enclosed the landing strips, she'd gone over every word she could remember of Gar's—the predominant one being sky*diving*.

"He wouldn't do it," she told herself firmly, scanning the sky, which looked wintry dark and ominous. "He'd never do something so foolhardy. I'm wasting my time out here."

The low drone of an airplane engine carried on the wind, and Beth searched anxiously, expecting to see a human form come hurtling through the air toward her. Something did fall, and for a moment her heart stopped. But then she realized that it was a flurry of small papers, and they were being tossed and turned in the wind.

It wasn't Gar.

Relieved and feeling somewhat foolish, Beth returned to the van to collect her scattered thoughts. This silly panicking was doing no one any good. And she had far too much to do.

Lips tightly pursed, she drove back to the shop to help Ronnie and her assistant, Melinda, deal with the influx of customers.

"Yes, we do have delivery tomorrow. I know it's Sunday but my sister wanted to be sure people had the option if they wanted it. Sure, where do you live?" Ronnie shoved the phone between her neck and her shoulder and busily scribbled down an address.

"We'll have it there. Thanks for calling."

"Looks like you two have been running." Beth took off her coat and hung it up, eyes widening at the number of orders hanging on the To-Do peg. "Really busy?"

"Yep, you could say that." Ronnie blew her bangs off her forehead and stepped from behind the counter. "I have to help Mr. Peterson decide on something for his wife. He's been here about an hour. Can you do the phone?"

Beth nodded and picked up the receiver. "Enchanted Florist."

Between phone calls, special orders and time spent on arrangements, Beth was kept busy for the rest of the morning. She wasn't worried about returning to Fairwinds until late afternoon, when she would put the finishing touches on everything. For now, it was important to concentrate on every customer that she could.

"Hi." Garrett stood grinning in front of her worktable, his cheeks red from the cold. "Pretty busy, I see."

"Drowning." She smiled back and reached for another vase. "But I love it." She arranged the tiny pink rosebuds with fern, added some baby's breath and a ribbon, and admired her work.

"Have you got time for lunch? There is something I need to discuss about the wedding."

"Now?" She shook her head, paper-clipped the form onto the card and pushed the pick into the vase. In one fluid motion she set it in the cooler, while her other hand automatically reached for the next order.

"It's kind of important," he murmured, watching

her hands fly. "I, uh, probably should have told you before this."

"Can't we discuss it here? It is my busiest day, Gar. I don't want to go for lunch. I'll get behind. Further behind."

He frowned, tipping back on his heels as he thought about it. "I suppose. You see, the thing is, I wanted—"

"Can I help, Dave?" Beth couldn't help interrupting. A young man stood waiting for her attention, and she had to acknowledge him. The other girls were busy elsewhere.

"I want to get some flowers. Something special."

Muttering a quick "Excuse me," Beth hurried toward the man. "Okay. What kind were you thinking of?"

Helping Dave didn't take long but there was a constant stream after him and it was some time before she remembered Garrett. She wasn't surprised to find he'd left. There was plenty to do at Fairwinds to get ready for the big event tonight.

"What did Gar want?" Ronnie asked later that afternoon, when a lull in customers allowed them to sip a cup of hot chocolate together.

"I don't know," Beth admitted. "I had to wait on a customer."

"Congratulations, Beth." Old Mrs. Arbuthnot smiled toothily, patting her purse. "You can mark me down. I'll be there for the wedding."

"Oh. Uh, that's really nice, Mrs. Arbuthnot. We'll look forward to having you there." Beth waited 'til the older woman had left, then turned to Ronnie. "Gar invited her to our wedding? But she wasn't on the list. We barely know her!"

"Maybe she's a friend of his." Ronnie turned away, dumping out the rest of her drink.

"But how would she know the time and stuff? She sounded like she had a personal invitation."

"Beats me." Ronnie wiped her hands down her green apron, fingered the logo that was printed on the pocket and scuffed her toe on the floor. She completely avoided Beth's glance.

As the door chime pealed its summons, she jerked forward. "I'll get it. You finish that. You've got a long night ahead."

That was odd. Ronnie never hurried to wait on a customer. She was always espousing the belief that people bought more if they could browse first.

Beth shook her head. No point in puzzling over it. There was too much to be done. She got up and wearily checked her stock. So far, so good. Her second year in business was proving she hadn't been wrong about the Enchanted Florist. She could do this, pull this off. She just had to focus.

"I'll take these to Fairwinds and set them up. You go home and change. Have a bubble bath. You're dog tired." Ronnie picked up the arrangement baskets and carried them to the back one by one. "I asked Ty to be here to drive me, just in case we got behind. I figured today would be a little rushed."

"Thank you, sweetie. You're a doll." Beth glanced

around the empty shop with a satisfied smile. "We've done really well. But I'm going to have to pull an all-nighter after the banquet."

"No way! We were talking it over and we've all decided to put in an extra couple of hours tonight. That way, everything should be ready for tomorrow. We haven't got any sweethearts anyhow, so we don't much care about the banquet." Ronnie grinned at the other two women whom Beth had hired.

"This once I'm going to take you up on that." Beth tugged on her coat and grabbed her purse. "Thanks very much." She glanced at her watch. "Yikes! Is it six-thirty already? I'll have to hustle."

"Good thing I laid out your dress this morning, isn't it?" Ronnie preened, obviously pleased with herself. "Now get going. Gar is going to pick you up in twenty-five minutes."

Beth got.

At home she showered, blow-dried her hair and applied her makeup faster than she'd done in years. By the time Gar rang the doorbell, however, she was also satisfied that she *looked* better than she had in years. Evidently, Garrett agreed.

"Wow!" He walked around her twice, admiring the ruby gown with its side slit and pearl-encrusted bodice. "You look fantastic." He leaned over and kissed her. "I'll be the most envied man there."

"You look pretty spiffy yourself." She touched the glistening white shirt with one finger, admiring its silken sheen. "I don't think I ever saw you in a bow tie before."

"And after our wedding, you won't again," he muttered, tugging at his neck. "I hate 'em."

"Thank you, darling." She stood on tiptoe and pressed a kiss against his cheek. "I know you did it for me."

"I did something else for you, too," he muttered soberly. "I tried to tell you earlier, but you were too busy."

"Shouldn't we be going? You could tell me on the way." Beth reached for her faux fur coat and slipped her arms in while he held it up. "Ready?"

He nodded, holding the door so she could precede him. Once in the car, Gar seemed to find it hard to begin.

"You'd better tell me now, if you're so anxious to discuss something. We'll be there shortly."

"I hired a plane today," he blurted out.

"I know." She smiled, remembering her panic.

"Oh. You know and you aren't mad?"

"Why should I be mad? You didn't jump, did you?" She frowned at the thought.

"Jump?" It took a few moments for her meaning to sink in. "No! Of course not. Heights give me a headache. I hired the pilot to drop wedding invitations on the town."

Beth blinked, certain she'd misunderstood. "Pardon?"

"I did. I got sick and tired of your dad, my dad, my grandmother, my mother and every other Tom, Dick and Harry telling me not to forget someone. So

I had an invitation made up, and I distributed them all over the town. From the plane.''

She blinked.

''Oh. How many invitations?'' she managed to ask.

''I'm not sure. A lot.''

''Oh.'' She swallowed. ''Uh, what else is happening with the wedding plans, Gar?''

''Why? Worried?'' The grin on his face didn't ease her anxiety.

''If you want the truth, then yes.'' She made a face at his mocking laughter. ''Are there turtledoves being released in the town square at noon? Who's catering? And where are we going for our honeymoon?'' She frowned. ''Or are we even having one? I should know so I can cover the store,'' she mumbled, avoiding his smugly superior look.

''I'm not telling you where, but I will tell you we're taking two weeks. Just you and me, without your sister or my grandmother or anyone else.''

''I like your grandmother. She's been a real encouragement to me.''

''Well, she's discouraging me. Every time you and I get five minutes together, she calls. And talks for hours. It's hard to compete.''

He turned the corner into Fairwinds, then tossed her a glowering look. ''And don't think you're going to sit in the study and chatter with Dinah tonight, either. I'm counting on us spending some time together, even if we do have to compete with a hundred or so other people.''

"Dinah's going to be here?" Beth stared at him. "How come?"

"She's being escorted by your father. Apparently, according to her, he needs to get out more often."

"Oh, Gar, do you think that's a good idea? I mean, she's so sophisticated. Dad's, well, recovering." She felt her cheeks heat at the frown he cast her way.

"My grandmother likes Mervyn because of who he is," he said sternly. "She couldn't care less about his faults or problems. She just wants to be his friend. She says he makes her laugh."

Suitably reprimanded, Beth said no more. But as he escorted her inside his parents' sprawling home, and she took in the elegance of the rooms, she couldn't help wondering how her father would feel entering his enemy's home. She didn't want him to be embarrassed or feel out of place, but the truth was, he didn't have much in common with any of these people, young or old.

Neither, for that matter, did she. Except that she was going to be Gar's wife.

"Come on, let's get some punch. Dinner's in twenty minutes."

Beth soon forgot about her father amid the happy chatter and laughter of the merry group. Once they'd sat down at the elegantly appointed tables, the oldest sweethearts were announced and received a pair of tickets to a stage production in a nearby town.

Jordan Andrews was at his best as host, and he made everyone howl with laughter at his silly jokes. "We'll be having these contests all through the eve-

ning, so don't be surprised if you win something.
You're all fair game.''

He proposed a toast, and everyone clinked glasses
as the waiters carried out their meals and began serving.

''I don't see your parents,'' Beth murmured, leaning
to one side as the waiter placed her plate in front of
her. She caught a hint of Gar's aftershave, and smiled.

This felt right, good. She was a part of this; she
belonged here because she belonged to Gar. The delicate china, crystal glasses and silver serving dishes
didn't impress her nearly as much as they had the last
time she'd been here. They were just objects.

''Today is the day my parents were married, thirty-
five years ago. They flew to Paris this morning to celebrate.''

''Isn't that romantic?'' Their tablemates smiled and
began chatting about true love.

But Beth didn't hear most of it. She caught a
glimpse of her father seated beside Dinah Winthrop,
and her breath stopped in her throat. He looked nervous, ill at ease in the poorly fitted black suit that had
definitely seen better days. His plate sat before him,
but he made no effort to eat anything; he fiddled with
first one fork and then another.

To her credit, Dinah was smiling and obviously doing her best to make him feel comfortable. From time
to time she'd lean forward, touch his arm, ask a question. Beth could see the movement of her father's lips,
his answering smile—but there was still confusion in
his eyes.

''Excuse me,'' she murmured, easing away from the table. ''No, go ahead and eat, Gar. I just want a word with Dad. I'll be right back.''

Garrett frowned, but he sat back down, his eyes intense. She could feel them burning into her back as she threaded her way to Dinah's table.

''Hello, Dinah, Dad. You two look stunning.'' She carefully placed her hand on Mervyn's shoulder, hoping to infuse a little confidence as she smiled at them both.

''So do you, dear. Absolutely lovely. You have a beautiful daughter, Mervyn.'' Dinah's expressive eyes thanked Beth for her help. ''I persuaded your father that this was one event he couldn't miss, even if he had to escort an old woman like me. And then they gave us this table for two. Wasn't that lovely?''

Mervyn seemed to relax, just a little, as he covered Dinah's hand with his own. ''I'm glad she asked me,'' he told Beth. ''I didn't realize you'd fit in here so well. You look as if you were born to this kind of thing.''

Beth couldn't stop the laugh that burbled up inside. ''Looks can be deceiving, Dad. I'm still just plain old Beth, but I dress up okay.'' She glanced around, saw Jordan heading for the microphone and murmured, ''See you later.'' Then she hurried back to her place.

Gar held her chair. ''Your food is cold.''

Because she was concentrating on his words, Beth missed whatever it was Jordan had said that made the room erupt in clapping. She turned to see her father stumble to his feet, his face beet red as he took Dinah's hand and half bowed to the assembled group.

Once the old woman was seated, Mervyn ducked into his own chair, keeping his eyes down.

"Now it's time to vote for the cuddliest sweethearts," Jordan boomed. "I've already had one nomination for Maryann and Clay Matthews." The crowd burst in whistles and catcalls. "Yes, I suppose you can't expect these newlyweds to remember they're in public and not hold hands under the table, can you?"

Beth met Caitlin's grin with her own, and they both smiled as a red-faced Maryann jerked her hand out of Clay's.

"You haven't been doing too badly in that department yourself, Jordan!" someone called out. Everyone agreed, and Herman Nethers took over the microphone just long enough to demand that both pairs stand and accept the prize of chocolate kisses.

"You'll have to share, but I'm sure you two don't mind. They're not nearly as good as the real ones, anyhow." Herman laughed at his own joke long and hard, until his wife nudged him and he sat down.

"We're going to have the waiters clear the tables now. While you're doing that, prepare for a very sweet dessert."

The waiters worked fast, removing dishes and re-filling wineglasses as they went. Beth frowned when she noticed that someone had given her father a glass of wine, but she relaxed a little after noticing that it hadn't been touched.

"He's fine, Beth. Dinah will look after him. Just relax and enjoy the evening." Gar's hand closed over hers.

Beth grinned. "I don't think you should do that anymore," she told him quietly. "Everyone seems to be watching us already, and we don't want to be the focus of one of Jordan's contests."

"Why not?" Gar demanded arrogantly. "I'd win hands down."

"How do you figure that?" one of their tablemates demanded.

"I've got the most beautiful girl in the world."

Beth's face flamed with embarrassment, but she squeezed his hand back anyway. "Thanks," she whispered, for his ears alone.

"I have a lot more to say, if you'll just pay attention." His eyes glowed, and Beth allowed herself just a moment to wonder what he'd planned.

The desserts were decadent slices of chocolate-covered cheesecake with a delicately swirled raspberry coulis.

"They did a wonderful job with the meal," Nelda Parker murmured to Beth. "It always tastes better when you don't have to cook it, doesn't it?"

"You've never cooked this before," her husband complained.

Nelda sent him a mock frown.

"Folks, if you don't mind, we'll move out of this area and allow our waiters to clear the tables. The Winthrops have kindly opened the library, the solarium and the salon for our use."

As everyone got up, Gar took the opportunity to introduce Beth to people she didn't know—his friends, acquaintances and business associates.

"Beth and I are getting married in two weeks," he told them proudly.

"Yes, we saw the invitation." Myles North grinned at Beth and slapped Gar on the shoulder. "I must say, I never thought of your idea for distribution before, though it certainly gets the message across. You can count on Celia and me."

"Thanks, Myles. And don't knock it. If she backs out now, I've got a lot of witnesses to my intentions."

Beth wanted to sink into the floor at the reminder that she'd run out on him once before and left Gar to face a lot of embarrassing questions, but he apparently wasn't aware of her thoughts. After several more introductions, he took her hand and steered her back into the dining area, to a quiet corner where candles still burned among the potted plants she'd arranged earlier.

"I needed a minute alone with my fiancée," he murmured as one hand slid into his jacket pocket. "I have something for you."

Beth suspected a kiss, maybe two. She never even saw the case until he'd snapped it open.

"This is for you. Because I love you very much and I don't want you to forget it. Turn around, okay?"

A dazzlingly bright diamond lay on a bed of pure white satin. When he lifted it out, she saw the silky smooth gold chain. In a daze, Beth obediently turned her back and felt the necklace glide around her neck, felt the touch of his warm fingers at her neck as he fastened it, then turned her around to face him.

"Do you like it?" His voice was husky now, his eyes enquiring as they met hers.

"I love it. It's beautiful. But you've already given me this ring, Gar. I haven't anything for you." She was ashamed that she hadn't even thought of it.

"I don't want anything else. If I have you, that's all I need." He tilted her chin up, flicked the single tear off her cheek and bent his head. "I love you," he whispered. Then he kissed her.

A string quartet started playing in the background, but Beth heard it only vaguely. She was too caught up in this wonderful dream. Her arms lifted around his neck and she laid her head on his shoulder.

"I love you, too, Garrett. Very much."

"And you'll marry me in spite of the invitation thing?" he joked.

"I'll marry you no matter what you do to our wedding." She smiled. Her finger gently traced the laugh lines at the corner of his mouth. "I'm sorry I've been so busy lately. I promise that we'll have plenty of time together soon. In fact, you'll probably get sick of me."

He began to slow dance her around the room. "Never."

They danced for a moment, but it was clear he had something to say. "I have to make something clear, Beth. I want us to be strong together. I don't want anything between us—not money, not people, not anything. I was the one who suggested they hold the ball here tonight."

"You were? Why?" She frowned, but kept dancing, her feet moving automatically to the pretty waltz.

"Because I wanted to erase the memory of that other time. I wanted us to have a new, fresh start here, among our friends and the community.'' He peered down. ''Is it okay?''

''It's wonderful.'' She sighed happily. ''I don't think I've ever enjoyed an evening more.''

He whirled her around and into a faster dance as the others began to trickle in and join them on the floor. Several people tried to break in, but Gar refused to let her go.

''Tonight she's all mine,'' he told them smugly. ''Go find your own sweetheart.''

''Gar, those are friends of your parents! I don't want to offend them.''

''They'll get over it.''

It was a wonderfully romantic setting, with the candles glimmering here and there around the perimeter of the room and fresh scent of flowers. Beth couldn't help but relax in the dim lighting with the heavenly music.

It was only Jordan's booming voice that disturbed her. ''Ladies and gents, we now have the pleasure of choosing our most romantic couple of the evening. I think we're unanimous in this. Give a round of applause to Miss Beth Ainslow and Mr. Garrett Winthrop.''

Beth stared at Gar, her head whirling. *They* were romantic? Ha! If Jordan only knew. But then, maybe he did know. Maybe these people were right. She thrust the doubts and fears aside and went forward with Gar to receive the chocolate cupids.

''May I inform you that Mr. Ty Winthrop, soon to be Chef Winthrop, created our wonderful meal tonight, along with the ice sculptures and the vegetable curly things.'' He shrugged at his wife. ''I couldn't remember the names.''

Everyone in the room burst into laughter.

''Ty also made these cupids. Ty, come on out here. We'd like to thank you properly.''

Clad in white from head to foot, Ty emerged from the back of the room and bowed, his face wreathed in a smile. His face turned solemn as he accepted Jordan's thanks, shook several hands and then stopped in front of Gar.

''Did you like it?'' he asked quietly.

''*You* made all that?'' Gar's eyes were huge, his tone disbelieving. ''Even the dessert?''

Ty nodded. ''Uh-huh. Next year I'm doing something flambéed.''

''Next year?'' Gar's voice hardened, but Ty didn't seem to notice. The music had started again, and several couples brushed past them in a quick-stepping promenade.

''Yep. They've asked me to do it again. This was great. I can hardly wait to start training.''

''Ty, your place is in the bank.''

Beth reached out and touched Gar on the arm, willing him not to spoil the night, especially not after his brother's wonderful success. But Ty spoke first.

''No, Gar. The bank is your place. I don't fit in there. And to tell you the truth, I don't want to. I'm sorry, but I have to be true to myself and my dreams.''

When Ty turned and left the room, Gar followed him, anger marring his handsome face. Beth followed, more worried than she'd ever been. Why was Gar so unwilling to let Ty have his dream? Did he want her to give up the flower shop? Was it unsuitable as a vocation for his wife?

"You can't give up college, training, a future, just to *cook*." Gar's voice was scathing as it rang around the kitchen. "Look at this place. Do you want to be stuck here for the rest of your life, working for someone else, scraping by?"

"Gar, don't." Beth was fully aware of the glowering looks the waiters were throwing his way. "It's his dream, let him live it."

"It's not a dream. It's a nightmare." Garrett stomped from the room.

"I'm sorry, Ty. I'll try to talk to him, get him to see."

"It doesn't matter, Beth. I've made up my mind." Ty turned away to stir a sauce that had just begun to bubble on the stove. "You'll make him happy," he murmured. "You'll be the one he invests his dreams in."

As she left, the words haunted her. *You'll be the one.* She didn't want to be responsible for disappointing Garrett. That was too heavy a burden. Could she give up her dreams for him?

She found him in the solarium, staring out the window. "I'm sorry, Gar."

"Are you?" His eyes chilled her. "You think I should leave him alone, let him pursue this stupidity, let the family down."

"How would he be doing that?" The old bitter feel-

ings resurfaced. Beth tried to squash them down, but
they wouldn't be silenced. "What's the matter, Gar?
Can't you be proud of a brother who's a chef, even if
he becomes the best chef in the world? Is that beneath
the dignity of the Winthrop family?"

He refused to be cowed. "It isn't something I'd
want to announce to the world, no. He has potential,
backing, a heritage. Why throw that all away?"

"Why keep it if it means nothing to you?" she
countered, frustration creeping into her voice.

"Don't be so quick to condemn it, Beth. Wouldn't
you rather have been raised in a home where there
was enough money to put food on the table, pay the
bills, and buy you the odd bauble?"

She gasped. "Are you going to be ashamed of me,
too, Gar? Does owning a flower shop not rate in your
book of acceptable careers? Maybe you'd rather I were
more like Cynthia, and wait around for your every
beck and call."

"Maybe I would." He raked a hand through his hair
as he shook his head. "I'm sorry! Please ignore that.
I didn't mean it."

She turned away from him slowly and moved toward the window.

"I think you did mean it, Gar. I think that in spite
of your protestations, you really do care about what
money can buy." She fingered the necklace. "That's
what this is all about, isn't it? Show me off, show off
what you can give me. Poor little Beth has come up
in the world. I made her what she is today."

She stopped then, swallowing her tears.

"I didn't mean to say that. I love you. I was just angry and disappointed."

"I know. I disappoint you. I never realized that before—"

The door burst open and Ronnie raced inside, her face flushed. "Beth, come quick. It's Dad. He's drunk and he's hurt himself."

Beth ignored Gar's comments. She followed her sister out of the room and across the hall. A thick ring of people stood around the place where Mervyn had fallen to the floor. A shattered wineglass lay at his feet, and Dinah knelt at his side.

"I've done it again," he muttered drunkenly, his smile lopsided as he stared into her eyes. "I was so proud of her, so proud. She's beautiful, my little Bethy. I wanted to show her I knew how to behave. I'm not trash. I can prove it."

"It's all right, Mervyn. You just slipped. Get up now." Dinah urged him to his feet, almost collapsing as he leaned on her.

Beth hurried to his side and swung his arm over her shoulder. "Are you all right, Dad?"

"P-perfectly all right," he enunciated clearly. "I just s-slipped."

Beth ignored the murmurs that rippled through the crowd. She was shamed, embarrassed and furious. She was lady enough not to show it, but she had to get out of here.

"You're bleeding!" Ronnie pointed to his arm where blood was now soaking the sleeve. "You must have cut yourself."

They walked him slowly out of the room with everyone watching. Beth could have cried. The town drunk and his daughters. What had changed in ten years?

"I feel funny," her father muttered. His face was ashen.

"Sit him here," Dinah ordered. She motioned for one of the waiters. "Get the first-aid kit from the kitchen. And bring a friend. I'm going to need help to take him upstairs."

"How could you do this, Dad? How could you? This was Beth's special night. Gar was trying to make her forget the last time you ruined her party. And now you've done it all over again. Drunk!" Ronnie glared at the man she'd always defended. "I think I hate you for this."

"No, Ronnie, no. Please don't hate me. I just needed a little courage. I only had one drink. Just one. I'm not drunk."

"It's true," Dinah murmured, her face intent as she inspected the cut. "He no doubt feels faint because he's lost a fair bit of blood. And because of the pressure." She straightened, her eyes pinning Beth to her place.

"He wanted to be here for you, to show you he could do this, that he could mix with these people. I knew how uncomfortable he was, how out of place he felt, but I encouraged him anyway because I thought it would help you. I wish I'd never done that."

"It's not your fault, Mrs. Winthrop." Beth glared

at the man she had called Dad. "It's his. He's always spoiling things."

"What did he spoil? Your fairy tale?" Dinah sniffed inelegantly. "Grow up, girl. Life is about reality. Sure, there are lots of snobs in that room, and yes, they were sizing you up. So what?"

"It was bad enough when they knew about the past, but now—" Beth could have groaned at the image most of them had formed.

"Now what? Now they know what you're really like? They know your father has a drinking problem? So what? They know you love my grandson. Or do you?" Her voice dropped to a whisper. "Maybe that's been the problem all along. You love respect and society's view of you more than you do him."

"Gran." Gar's voice was stern.

"She needs to figure it out now. Before it's too late to turn back." Dinah spun back to face Beth and Ronnie. "You girls have a wonderful father. He got buffaloed by some problems, but he's working them through. I suggest you two do the same. Figure out what's important to you."

She motioned the waiters close and directed them to carry Mervyn up the stairs.

"Garrett, go explain that Mr. Ainslow has cut himself and requires a doctor. Tell them to go on with the party. We'll be down later."

Gar glanced helplessly from her to Beth, but finally he went. Alone, Beth glanced at Ronnie.

"Did Ty give you the van key?" When her sister

nodded, she moved toward the entry as though her insides were frozen. "Good. Let's go."

"You can't go now! The best part is still coming." Ronnie's eyes begged her to reconsider.

But Beth had her coat on and was already at the front door.

"No, I think the best part's over," she whispered. "And it's time for Cinderella to get to work. The dream has turned into a nightmare. And it's time to end it. I don't belong here," she murmured sadly, glancing once more around the beautiful room. "I never did. Why did it take so long for me to see that?"

"Beth, Gar loves you!"

"Does he?" Beth shook her head. "I think he loves somebody I can never be—his idea of a fairy princess. Well, I'm no princess. I know that now."

Chapter Twelve

Beth peered through the swirling snow that almost obliterated the view. Some Valentine's Day this was turning out to be.

"A half a mile, they said." She pressed her foot down infinitesimally, and held her breath as the van veered slightly sideways. She righted it and continued down the finger-drifted road. "It's got to be here somewhere."

Up ahead, out of the early evening darkness, a shadow loomed, the dull glow of yellow lights signaling the farmhouse.

It took only a few minutes to carry the big white box of crimson red roses to the door, but substantially longer to listen to Bill Harrison's kind words.

"You'll never know how much this means," he murmured, checking to be sure no one was behind him. "Belinda's been so sick after the chemo that I didn't dare take the time to run in to town. Your delivery is a real blessing.'' He pulled open the box slowly, his eyes growing bigger by the moment.

Beth felt a supreme sense of satisfaction. *This is why I want to be a florist,* she told Gar silently. She'd taken the time to choose the best blooms she carried. They lay nestled in the layers of rich green fern, a big white bow holding them all together.

''You didn't have to go to all this trouble,'' he whispered, his eyes glossy.

''I wanted to. Tell Belinda Happy Valentine's from Ronnie and me, too, will you? And tell her that I hope she feels better soon.''

''I will.'' He pumped her hand heartily. ''I can see why Gar wants to marry you,'' he murmured. ''You're a perfect addition to Oakburn. You really are concerned about the people who live here. We need folks like you to provide these caring services.''

''Thanks, Bill,'' she murmured. ''Thanks a lot. 'Bye now.'' And she backed down the stairs, her heart singing through its sadness.

''Do you think maybe you should stay here for a while? Just 'til the storm eases? Visibility is getting pretty bad.'' Bill's lined forehead pleated in worry.

Beth shook her head determinedly. ''I'll keep pushing on.''

Bill had enough to worry about. She wasn't going to add to it. Besides, he needed this special time with his wife.

''I've got one more delivery to make, Bill. Then I'll hightail it home. Thanks, anyway.'' She waved and then scrambled back across the drifts to her van.

"Okay, then. But take it easy." Bill waved before closing the door.

"There's no other way to take it. Why tonight, God? Couldn't you have waited an hour or so before you threw this blizzard at us?" She muttered the words as she steered left, then right, and finally made it back to the highway. It was dangerous to stop, but she'd be okay on this side road for a minute while she checked directions.

"Three and a half miles south, left for another seven. Gotcha." She tucked the note into the visor, checked carefully, then proceeded onto the highway.

"Wonder why it has to be eleven roses?" she asked herself, musing on the odd order. "Usually they ask for an even dozen. Hey, I know. It's probably for the Parkers, they've got about that many kids!"

She amused herself by talking out loud, speculating on the owner of the oddly scrawled initials.

"I'm going to have to teach Ronnie how to print these things. Yeow!" She eased around the huge drift of snow and inched forward, intent on finding the next turnoff.

"It was nice of Bill to say such kind things, nice to be appreciated." She wondered absently if anyone could ever fully appreciate how much satisfaction she derived from her work. "This has been a very successful month. I guess the good citizens of Oakburn haven't heard the latest scandal about me. Or maybe they don't care."

Now there was a thought. She considered it more closely. Did she think about Isobel's awful history every time she went in Fenstein's to buy groceries? Of course not! She liked going there because the people were friendly and the quality was good. That was how Isobel and Marty stayed in business—they met a need.

It was the same with her, Beth decided as she clamped her lips tight and shoved her van through the mounting drifts. Her customers came into Enchanted Florist because of what she'd made of it and herself, because she gave them a fair return for their money. Sometimes she even went a little beyond fair, she mused, thinking about Belinda's hidden chocolate surprise.

She tried to puzzle it out more thoroughly, as her vehicle slipped and slid around the corner. Now she was heading east and on the last seven miles of her delivery trek.

"So in effect, they like doing business with me because of *me,* not because of what Dad did, or Gar does, or even for Ronnie's sake." She'd never thought of it that way before.

A clear patch of highway opened up as the snow blew across it. Beth accelerated, taking advantage of the clear pavement.

And because of what God had done for her.

Her worth had nothing to do with her roots, or even what she'd done. Her worth was in her value as His child. No matter how hard she worked, she couldn't improve on that.

She straightened suddenly. All her long hours, her

need to prove herself, her drive to succeed—all of that was wasted?

"Yes," she whispered, staring at the white vastness before her. "Because I am who I am due to God's grace. I never thought of that before!"

It was wonderful, exhilarating, freeing. She wasn't worthless no matter what happened, because God had given her a royal heritage.

"It's not something I've done, it's something He's done."

Her eyes widened as the knowledge seeped in. She was worthy of Gar's love, of her father's love, of God's love, because He said so. It was that easy. She could stop trying to prove herself because, in reality, all the workaholism in the world didn't matter.

She recalled what had happened earlier this afternoon. "Beth, I didn't mean I hated you working. I like the fact that you've learned to be independent, to run your own business. I'm proud of you." Gar's words had clearly penetrated the thick back door of her store. But he didn't have to yell. She was standing right inside, tears rolling down her cheeks.

"But to tell you the truth, it wouldn't matter if you were penniless and as dumb as a stump. I don't care about any of the other stuff, Beth. I care about you, what's inside you, what makes you who you are. None of that has anything to do with your dad or my brother. I love you because you're Beth. I'm just jealous of the time everything else takes away from us."

Jealous? He was jealous? Beth had scoffed at the idea.

"Go away, Garrett. I have a lot of work to do. That's what I do—work. I'm not a society deb. I have responsibilities, duties. I can't just ignore them to play with you."

The memory of her scathing remarks make her flush with embarrassment. He'd insisted she open the door.

"What is it? Can't you see I'm busy?"

His face was white, pinched, worried. "I know. And you don't want to do this in front of Ronnie. I understand."

"Don't mind me. I'm going into the cooler. Let me know when you're done." Grinning from ear to ear, Ronnie had yanked the big door shut.

"Beth, will you just listen to me for a minute?"

"I don't think there's much more to say." She'd ruined a floral arrangement because her hands were shaking too much. "I think I've heard everything I want to hear."

"I think you heard only what you wanted to hear," he retorted, spots of red on his cheeks.

Implying what? That she was too *dumb* to understand?

"Oh, I got it," she assured him, fury shooting the words from her mouth. "I got it all."

Gar's face was drawn, his eyes sad. "This isn't what I wanted," he told her quietly. "I wanted a special night, a time you would remember. I wanted you to feel on top of the world, not because you were marrying me, but because that's how God's child should feel."

She couldn't say anything.

"This thing you have about proving yourself, it isn't necessary to the rest of us. I love you. I don't know how else to tell you that. I don't care what your father did or what my father did. I don't care what people say, I love you. And the only thing I want is for us to be together." He reached up to touch her, his fingers gentle. "I love you, Beth Ainslow."

"We can't be together when there's this gap between us, Garrett. I will always be the girl from the wrong side of the tracks. I'm not your fairy princess."

His face fell, his hand dropped away from her cheek. "To me you are," he whispered. "And the only thing that's between us is what you put there. It's a barrier that only you can remove. Please think about the future. Our future."

"There is no future for us, Garrett. It's over."

"I'm not giving up, Beth. I haven't waited this long for you just to walk away. I'll be waiting, no matter how long it takes you to see the truth."

Now, as she drove along, the truth finally dawned. Even after the scene at Fairwinds, Gar wanted to marry her. To him it truly didn't matter whether her father was a fall-down drunk or a man who'd simply slipped on a bit of paper. That wasn't part of the equation. All Garrett Winthrop cared about was Beth Ainslow.

Whether she succeeded or fell flat on her face, Gar would still love her. Whether she made mistakes or didn't, whether her father started drinking again or not—none of it mattered.

Love had nothing to do with what happened outside

of her, it had to do with what went on in her heart.
Gar had loved her for over ten years, and he'd promised to keep on loving her. So would her dad. So would God.

"Why didn't I see this before?" she asked herself in frustration. "Why do I always come back to what people think of me—?"

— It was a moment before Beth felt the telltale slide of the rear wheels and knew she was in trouble. Though she fought to stay on the road, the huge snowdrift at the side sucked her off the pavement and into its arms with a welcoming *whoosh.*

Carefully she rocked the vehicle back and forth, whispering a word of prayer as the tires spun uselessly on the soft, wet snow. She kept at it, even though she knew it was futile. The reality of her situation was too dangerous to think about. But when the van refused to budge, she was forced to acknowledge the truth.

She was stuck out here in the countryside, with no help for miles.

"Great." She checked the gas gauge and frowned. She had enough to let it run for a little while, but she couldn't afford to let the tank get dangerously low. Who knew how long she'd have to wait for assistance? And would it come in time?

As the van purred, Beth suddenly realized just how dark it had become. Her headlights were buried in the snowbank. No matter how hard she peered through the windshield, she could see nothing.

If by chance someone did come looking, how would they find her?

She undid her seat belt, then eased the door slightly open. The bitter cold wind whistled in, making short work of the heat she'd built up inside. Beth forced herself out of her seat and into the snow, hoping to spot a familiar landmark, another vehicle, something.

There was only darkness, howling wind and snow that whipped and stung her bare face.

"I'm caught out here in the middle of a blizzard," she whispered to herself. "And nobody knows it."

She slipped back inside the van, allowing the blast of heat from the ducts to warm her icy fingers. When she was almost warm, she switched off the engine. The gas gauge was going down awfully fast.

I'm in trouble here, God. Big trouble. I stormed out without giving a thought to something like this. I was so sure I had to get away. She twisted around in her seat, and, with the help of the overhead light, considered the area at the back.

Only one box remained. One box with eleven pale yellow roses carefully laid inside. She lifted a floormat and arranged it over the box, hoping to protect the fragile blooms as much as possible from the cold that was seeping in.

"Ronnie will notice that I haven't come back. She'll get someone. They'll come looking. Whoever is expecting this delivery will be furious." She tried to cheer herself with the thoughts.

But deep inside she knew it was hopeless. She'd demanded that everyone leave her alone. And they had.

"Why didn't I let Ronnie put that cell phone in

here?'' she asked herself grimly. ''At least I could
have phoned for help.''

But there was no point dealing in ''ifs'' and ''ands''
now. It was too late. She'd raced off, left her friends
staring and wondering, dumped Gar and hightailed it
out of there so fast, they were probably glad to be rid
of her.

It was a pattern. She'd done it often. Run away,
ignored things, pretended she could fix them herself.
But she couldn't fix this. This time she'd really blown
it.

''What if I die out here?'' The thought made her
cringe.

''I never told Gar that it almost tore me apart to
leave here back then. I never told him that the dream
in my heart never quite died, even when we were so
far apart.''

She thought of Ronnie, working so hard to ensure
Beth was proud of her, spending hours in the shop
when she should have been out with the other kids,
having fun. Beth had wanted so much for Ronnie—
all the things she hadn't had herself. Most of all, she'd
wanted her sister to grow up carefree.

Instead she'd burdened Ronnie with guilt and obli-
gations. The knowledge ate at her, and she glanced
heavenward, her heart heavy.

''Okay, I blew it. All of it.'' She shifted, turned on
the ignition and shivered until warm air finally poured
in. ''I'm lousy at running things, including my own
life. I thought I could fix things, begin again, earn

respect and a place in Oakburn. I thought I could prove that I'm good enough. And I can't.''

She admitted the truth with a clogged-up throat. Her father's actions last night had proven that she had no control over what he or anyone else did or said. She couldn't make him into the kind of father she believed would be respectable any more than she could make Ronnie into an airhead who would abandon Beth to go have a good time.

It was the same with Gar. "I did want the fairy tale," she muttered, staring out through the snow-spattered windshield. "I wanted him to be someone he's not, to sweep me off my feet like some kind of prince. But I wouldn't let myself believe that I was worth it. I had to prove to him that I was more than adequate as a candidate for his wife."

She considered that. But why? Why do I keep getting myself into these situations? What don't I understand what You're trying to teach me, God?

The engine sputtered and died, cutting off all sound except the howl of the wind outside the van. Beth shivered, hugging her coat a little closer.

Who was in control now?

The words penetrated her brain with the clarity of a ringing bell. Beth frowned, trying to understand why she'd thought of that.

"God is in control," she whispered, reciting the only words she could remember from a song her sister often sang. "'Who makes the sun rise and set, the ocean tides wax and wane, the wind whistle or die down?''' The questions poured into her brain, demanding a response she could not withhold.

''God does.'' Beth acknowledged it out loud. ''But I've never denied that.''

Haven't you? Haven't you been trying to control everyone and everything, to make them fit your will? Haven't you just refused the gift of love God sent because it didn't fit your narrow perceptions?

Beth had never before thought of Gar's love as a gift from God, and the idea intrigued her.

Garrett Winthrop didn't put on airs, didn't pretend to be someone he wasn't, didn't even ask her to be someone other than who she was. Instead, Gar had insisted that he loved her in spite of everything she'd done. He didn't seem to care if he was in her shabby apartment at Wintergreen or dancing at Fairwinds. His love remained steady, burning brightly, enclosing her in its warmth. Wasn't that a love worth saving?

Gar didn't care if she was the belle of the ball, if she wore jeans or designer dresses, or that her father had taken a drink when he shouldn't have. He was more concerned with the important things. The person inside was what mattered to him.

That's why he'd been able to accept Mervyn when Beth hadn't. That was why he'd been able to acknowledge Denis as a part of her past life and move on. He cared about her, her happiness, her contentment.

''All I've cared about is the outward stuff, the appearances, the look of things.'' The knowledge was sobering. ''I worked so hard to be acceptable, worthy, on the same level. And it doesn't matter!''

She exulted in the sudden knowledge.

"None of it matters! God loves me in spite of who and what I am. Because he loves me, Gar thinks I'm worthy. Dad loves me because I'm his daughter, not because of what I have or haven't done. I can't do anything to improve on that."

A weight lifted off her shoulders, and Beth sagged under the freedom of it.

"I can't earn their love," she mumbled, flexing her fingers as the cold crept through her gloves. "There's nothing I can do to make them care for me any more than they already do. And all that I'm doing is pushing them away."

She bowed her head as tears came to her eyes. She remembered Gar's call to the store while she and Ronnie had been loading the last of the bouquets into the van.

"Tell him we're finished," she'd ordered Ronnie, her cheeks red with embarrassment. "Tell him to find someone who won't ruin his life, someone with less baggage. As soon as I can sell this place, we're leaving."

Ronnie pleaded for her to just listen, to give the man a chance. But Beth hadn't done that, hadn't wanted to hear it. Instead she'd filled the last order and taken off.

"Why?" she asked God. "Why do I always push love away?"

The answer stole into her heart. *You won't trust. You won't let go of the controls.*

As snow piled up on the windshield and the wind snuck in through the cracks, Beth wept for the foolishness of her life. Here she was, lost in a blizzard, because she had to run the show. It was a fitting end.

"I'm sorry, God. I always said that I believed You had good things in store for me, but I never walked the walk. All this time you've been trying to get my attention, and I've been too busy running the show." She gulped down a sob, determined to say what was in her heart.

"Okay, God. From here on in, You run the show. Whatever You have in store for me, I'll accept with a grateful heart.

"I love Gar. And though he may hate me now, I'm asking You for one more chance to tell him. He'll probably never forgive me for running out on him at the party, for shutting him out at the store, for not answering his call, but that doesn't matter. I still owe him the truth. Please, just give me one more chance."

It was cold, so cold. Beth shivered and tried to stop her teeth from chattering. How long had she been here? An hour? Two or three? She didn't know. All she knew was that she couldn't withstand the cold for much longer. Already her feet and hands were going numb in their thin coverings.

"Please help me," she murmured again. Her eyelids dropped. She was tired. So tired. Maybe if she slept just a little while.

She'd just begun the most wonderful dream when someone wrenched open her door. Freezing cold winter wind whipped across her cheeks, and Beth huddled into the seat, forming her body into a tight ball.

"S'cold," she muttered through clenched teeth. "Close the door."

"I'm going to," a dear, gruff voice muttered. Big strong arms slid under her knees and around her back. "As soon as I get you out of here. C'mon, Beth, it's time to go. This time you're not running any farther."

She felt herself being carried, heard a wheezing grunt, and snuggled closer to the warmth. "I like this dream," she giggled, rubbing her cheek against the soft wool fabric. "You even sound like him."

"Like who?" The voice was only half amused.

"Like Gar." She sighed. "He's my Prince Charming. Isn't that silly? And I'm the princess. Only I never told him how much I loved him. Wasn't that a stupid mistake? I got sidetracked and forgot the most important part. Without Gar, nothing else matters." A tear rose to her lashes, but Beth couldn't be bothered to lift a hand to remove it. Instead, she let the sadness of the dream overwhelm her.

"He was my fiancé. For a little while, anyway."

"He still is. That part isn't changing until we get married, Beth. I told you, I don't give up easily."

Beth forced her eyelids open, staring as she focused on his beloved face. She gasped, then lifted one hand to touch his cheek.

"It's not a dream—it is you!"

"It's me, all right. You didn't think I was going to leave my future wife buried in a snowbank, did you?" He tugged open the door of a vehicle Beth didn't recognize, and set her carefully on the seat. "I like a white wedding as much as the next groom, but this is going a little far.'' He laughed at her confused frown.

For several moments Beth couldn't move, couldn't say anything as he tucked her in. There was so much she needed to tell him, to explain. But it would wait. Only one thing was important.

''I love you, Garrett Algernon Winthrop.''

He grinned, a big hearty grin that did nothing to conceal the smugness in his eyes. ''I know. I've been counting on that to get us through this whole mix-up. Sit tight, I'll be right back.'' With that, he slammed her door shut.

Beth sat there and let the heat from the vents blow over her. Little by little the warmth seeped into her cold body and the dream-like trance melted away. But the storm was still raging around them, and she waited anxiously for Gar to return.

She heard him open the back door, and then he was easing into the seat beside her, his face red and wind-chafed.

''Are you okay? You didn't hurt anything when you slid off the road?'' His eyes anxiously searched her face, her body, looking for damage.

''I'm fine. But how did you know...'' She let the words die away as he leaned over and kissed her hard on the lips.

''Just relax. We'll talk as soon as we get home.''

Home? Where was home? The heat was making her drowsy and she couldn't concentrate. Instead, she closed her eyes and let it all go.

Hadn't she given it all to God? He was in charge now.

Chapter Thirteen

Gar pressed his foot on the accelerator and steered the Jeep straight through the building snowdrifts as they climbed the steep pass. His heart filled with praise as he got closer and closer to home.

Thank you, God. Thank you for second chances. And thirds. I promise, I won't blow it this time. He drove up to the door, as close as he could get, and left the engine running.

In a matter of minutes he had Beth inside and huddled in front of a fire. "Stay put. I'll be back in a minute."

As quickly as he could, he put the Jeep in the garage, picked up the flowers and walked back inside.

Beth was where he'd left her, her eyes closed. Satisfied that she was breathing normally, he poured out two mugs of the hot chocolate he'd made earlier and set them on the coffee table. Then he retrieved the flowers.

"Beth?"

She opened her eyes and blinked at him, glancing around to get her bearings. "Here? How did I get here?"

"I brought you here. You were on your way, anyway." He held out the roses. "You were delivering your own bouquet."

She stared at the flowers. "You ordered those?"

He nodded. "I'm the last stop on your Valentine run. I hope you like them. They're from the best florist in town."

"I'm also the only florist in town," she quipped, a faint smile twitching at her bluish lips. "Why eleven?"

"It's eleven years since I proposed." His eyes twinkled. "And yellow because I'm making a solid gold promise. I'm promising you joy and love. No matter what."

Gar reached out and helped her remove her coat, boots and gloves. Then he knelt in front of her.

"I love you, Beth Ainslow. When I couldn't find you tonight, I almost went crazy. Why did you run away from me? Why did you say it was over between us? What did I do wrong?"

She smiled and reached out, her soft fingers tracing his jaw. "Nothing," she whispered, tears forming at the corners of her expressive eyes. "You did nothing wrong. It's me. I've been working so hard to make myself worthy of being your wife that I forgot the most important thing." She leaned forward, cupping his face in both hands.

"I love you, Garrett. I love you more than I ever thought possible. I'm not running away again. I think I've done enough of that."

"I'm sorry your dad let you down, Beth. And I'm sorry I didn't understand about Ty. But I'm not going to let their problems come between us. Ty's old enough to find his own way. I know I can't live his life for him. I haven't done such a hot job of managing my own."

She pressed her forefinger against his lips. "Those things don't matter. I can't control my father's drinking any more than you can control Ty's future. They both have to do that themselves."

He frowned. "But isn't that what made you run away? I thought, well—" He hesitated, hating to say the words.

"You thought I was embarrassed by the scene Dad made. That's what you thought, isn't it?" She waited a moment for his nod. "In a way you were right. I was embarrassed. And I thought that his behavior, along with a whole lot of other things, disqualified me from becoming your wife."

"Beth," he gasped, "I don't care about that!"

She smiled. "I know that now. God showed me how wrong I'd been tonight when I was stuck in the van. I've been trying to mold everybody into the place I thought they should be. I guess I've been doing it for a long time."

"Why?" Gar wasn't sure he understood any of this.

"I wanted life to be the way I'd planned. When it didn't turn out that way, I tried to manipulate things and people to make it go my way. I had this idea, you see—'' she shook her head in disgust ''—I wanted my dad, Ronnie, Ty, even you, to be somebody that you're not. I got so consumed with the appearance of things, I missed...love.''

He tipped back on his haunches and considered what she was saying. The fire crackled and blazed behind him, but he focused on the small delicate woman who sat curled up in front of him.

''Did you mean what you said?'' he managed at last, aware that he was holding his breath as he waited for her response.

''About loving you?'' She smiled, her face seemingly lighting up from within. ''I've never meant anything more. I do love you, Gar. And if I embarrass you with my lower-class manners or lack of social graces, then I'm really sorry, but you'll just have to accept it. This is who I am. Beth Ainslow, born on the wrong side of the tracks.''

''Embarrass me?'' He felt a faint stirring of anger. ''When I'm with you I feel like the proudest man in the world. What does any of that stuff matter?'' Something twigged, and Gar took a deep breath. ''The only thing that would really embarrass me is if you didn't show up at the altar next Saturday.''

''Next Saturday?'' She laughed and shook her head. ''No, you mean the week after, and it's a Sunday.''

Gar shifted uncomfortably, wishing he could avoid her eyes. ''Actually, I *do* mean next Saturday.'' He swallowed. ''You remember those invitations I had dropped from that plane?'' She nodded, so he continued. "Well—that is, the, er, the printer made an error that I didn't catch. It seems everyone has been invited to our wedding next Saturday at eleven o'clock in the morning."

Gar sat there staring at the carpet, waiting for her to blast him for his carelessness. When she didn't say anything, he finally glanced up. His eyes widened at her shaking shoulders, and he got to his feet, tugging her into his arms to comfort her. How could he have been so stupid?

"Oh, Beth, honey. I'm sorry! I didn't mean to spoil everything. The embarrassment doesn't matter, sweetheart. We can get married whenever you want. The only thing that matters is that you love me as much as I love you." He stopped, took a second look and then frowned. "Beth?"

He lifted her chin and found her eyes glinting with laughter. She burst into loud boisterous chuckles. Gar sagged in relief. At least she wasn't bawling. But he still couldn't figure out what was so all-fired funny.

"I don't think it's that big a joke," he muttered when she wouldn't stop chortling.

"It's hilarious," she said, wiping tears of mirth from her eyes. "If you knew what I'd just told God, out there in that blizzard, you'd see."

"What did you tell Him?" He waited, arms looped around her waist while she regained control. "Well?"

"I told Him that I was taking my hands off the controls, that He was in charge and I'd follow wherever He led." She hiccuped a laugh. "It seems that He's leading up to the altar next Saturday."

Gar shook his head, confused by this woman and her calm acceptance of their future. "I love you, Beth, more than life itself. But sometimes you make me a little crazy. Are you saying you'll marry me next week, without all the pomp and circumstance I had planned for the week after?"

Beth sobered at that. Her eyes roved over his face, and he watched as the love lit those blue depths.

"Of course I'm going to marry you, Garrett. You're my Prince Charming. You rescued me from the snow and carried me to safety. I'm not crazy, you know! I'm not letting a man like you go."

She stopped teasing then, her eyes steady. "Nothing on this earth will prevent me from walking up that aisle next week, Garrett Winthrop. I love you and, pomp and circumstance notwithstanding, I intend to marry you at the very first opportunity. Which just happens to be next Saturday."

"Oh." He digested that for a minute and then prepared to push his luck. "And can we live here, in this house that I built for you?" He didn't wait for her response, but rushed on. "I've planned and dreamed and schemed for us to live here for so long. I've pictured you sitting in front of the fire with me, climbing the hills on a summer evening, having a picnic with our kids out by the river."

She was crying again. Gar sighed. Would he ever get the hang of this?

"It doesn't matter, Beth. Not really. We can live anywhere. As long as I have you, I don't care about any of it."

"Well, I do! I want it all. Of course we're going to live here." She fingered her ring, the garnet he'd given her, which sparkled on her finger. "I want to share the future with you for as long as we have together. And we'll live here, even if we have to shuffle things around a bit. Love is worth some compromise, don't you think?"

Gar bent his head and kissed her, a soul-stirring, heartfelt kiss that told her how much he loved her. Then he showed her all through the house, explaining every carefully thought-out detail.

Eventually they wandered back to the fire and sat down on the big hearth rug, side by side, sipping the now cooled chocolate.

"My grandmother was right," he murmured into the silence a long time later. "She said you and she were two of a kind and she was right."

"I love your grandmother, and I take that as a compliment, but I'm not sure how you arrived there." Beth shifted against his side, her hand slipping around his waist. "Explain, please."

"Dinah was the eldest of ten children. Her father was a coal miner and they were dirt poor. She always minimizes their poverty, but believe me, they were impoverished. Her mother died when Dinah was twelve."

"Okay, that's a coincidence." Beth frowned, her eyes on the flickering bed of coals. "What else?"

"Dinah took on the role of mother and raised every one of those kids until all of her brothers and sisters had left home. Then she took care of her father and made a little extra money by taking in laundry and sewing until he, too, passed on. Then, when her duty was finally complete, with no place to go and not a dime in her pocket, she looked for work." He smiled, pressing a kiss to her hair. "Dinah was a survivor, just like you."

"What else?"

"Well, she met Randolph Winthrop when she worked as a maid in his house. He fell in love with her and married her six months later, against his parents' wishes."

"Another similarity." Beth seemed lost in thought.

"They were blissfully happy. I used to watch them, snuggled together under the mistletoe at Christmas, or giggling over a box of chocolates he'd given her for Valentine's Day, and I'd think, That's how I want my marriage to be."

"They only had one child?"

"My father, yes." Gar nodded. "But they adored him. And when my father had me, they were like kids. I had some wonderful times at their house, playing hide-and-seek with Dinah in the old wardrobes and helping her in her rose garden. She never cared when I stopped over or what I wanted to talk about. She always put down whatever she was doing and listened to me. People were always coming to her for advice, and I used to wish they wouldn't so I'd have more time to have her to myself."

"You loved her."

"Yes. I still do. She's given me so much happiness. When I used to sit in church on those hard benches,

I'd look around for something to do, and Dinah would always wink at me. It was our secret wink. I'd lean down to tie my shoe, and she'd pass me a mint. She always had a mint for me, for any kid that asked."

Beth sat there, thinking about the woman who'd come from nothing and eventually inherited millions of dollars. But better than all of that, she had the priceless gift of love.

"I asked her once if she wasn't sad that she hadn't met Grandpa earlier, that they hadn't had more children. She said God had given her exactly what she needed to help her grow."

"Did a lot of her friends know about her past?" Beth couldn't help asking. The tiny delicate woman she'd met seemed so unlike a woman who'd grown up in poverty and need.

"I'm sure everybody knew. She never hid it. She said that growing up in need gave you a better perspective on what was really important. To Dinah, love was always more important, and she never lets you forget that we are all God's children." He glanced down at her. "Am I boring you?"

"No, of course not. I was just thinking how wonderful it is to have all these memories of her. She's hosted world leaders, been visited by people in high places, and yet you think of her as a warm, caring woman who took the time to play with you." She grimaced. "It's a lesson for me to look beyond what I have to what I'm giving, what memories there will be of me. It sure took a long time to learn."

She glanced down at her unusual ring and played

with it, then smiled when Gar tilted her head to look into her eyes.

"But I'm learning fast. And I think I've finally got my priorities straight. No matter what happens to us, Gar, I'm not going to forget that when it comes to loving you, nothing else is more important. I'd love to live here with you, darling. It already feels like home. This is where I want to begin our legacy of love. We can keep my place at Wintergreen for emergencies. Like tonight."

He kissed her again, his touch telling her how much her words meant to him.

When they finally broke apart, they were content to sit staring into the fire, dreaming dreams of a future filled with happiness.

"Garrett?"

"Mm-hmm." He lifted his head to look at her. "What is it?"

"What *exactly* did you have planned for our wedding?"

Gar burst out laughing, his eyes glittering. "You said you'd leave it up to me," he reminded.

Beth swallowed her frustration. *Let go of the controls,* she reminded herself.

"I am leaving it up to you. Really. I just wanted a hint. You know, an idea of what to expect."

She sighed when he shook his head.

"Oh, Beth! When will you learn to trust me?"

"I do trust you," she insisted. "I'm just wondering what kind of dress I need to get."

Gar snorted. "The dress doesn't matter. It's the

bride and groom that are important. The prince and princess are what make the fairy tale.''

Beth relaxed against his arm, her heart winging skyward. ''You're right,'' she whispered, praying a prayer for heavenly help that would see her through the next busy days. ''I love you.''

''The feeling, my darling Miss Ainslow, is entirely mutual.''

Chapter Fourteen

"**Y**ou've got to admit that it's different." Maryann nudged Caitlin in the ribs, nodding at the big heart-shaped pew markers. "He's really taken this Valentine's theme to heart, so to speak."

Caitlin giggled, juggling her daughter on her knee. "I love the canopy," she whispered back. "It's so romantic. Is it time for us to go get her yet?"

"She said she wanted a minute with her dad. I'd say that's about up." Caitlin rose, handed her daughter to the baby-sitter, and smoothed down her red-satin dress. "I have no clue where he found these on such short notice, but they're actually quite lovely."

Maryann nodded, resplendent in a matching gown. "Did you get a look at Beth's gown?"

"Uh-uh. It hadn't arrived last night when I stopped in. She was strangely calm about it all, though. Said the dress wasn't important." Caitlin handed Maryann her bouquet. "She's certainly got the right attitude."

"Let's go get her. It's time."

When they opened the door, Beth was standing by a window, studying the view. She turned and smiled, her face serene, radiant under the thin white veiling.

"It's snowing again," she murmured.

"Don't remind us! How lucky you are to be escaping it all." Maryann straightened her skirt and sighed. "You look so beautiful, Beth. This dress is perfect."

"It is rather nice, isn't it? Dinah found it. Would you believe a friend of hers is a designer?" She twirled around, sending the gossamer skirt billowing around her ankles. "And this little hat just fits. I've never worn a hat before." She sighed with sheer pleasure.

"Beth, are you ready?" Ronnie bustled into the room, her tall slim figure clothed in red velvet, just like the others. "Gar is waiting."

"Then let's not keep him standing there!" Beth picked up her sheaf of red and creamy white roses and smiled. "I'm ready."

"You look totally awesome," Ronnie breathed, her eyes teary. "I love you, sis."

"I love you, too, Ron. But if you give the Winthrops any trouble, my name will be mud." Beth grinned. "Not that I'm worrying. Dinah assured me that she and Dad will be in complete control."

"Go!" Ronnie ordered with a mock grimace. "You and Gar deserve each other."

Beth waited until Caitlin, then Maryann, then Ronnie had preceded her. Then she smiled at her father, wrapped her arm in his and whispered, "Let's go, Dad."

He hesitated a moment, his eyes soft. "I love you, honey."

"I know. I love you, too."

"I always did." He looked saddened.

Beth couldn't bear to see it on her wedding day. She squeezed his arm and grinned. "I always knew that, too. Come on, Dad. I'm ten, no eleven, years late doing this. I want to be Mrs. Garrett Winthrop before another hour passes."

He squeezed her hand, then carefully led her down the aisle. When they reached Gar, Mervyn placed his daughter's hand in Garrett's welcoming one. "Take care of her," he whispered.

"I will," Gar promised, smiling from ear to ear.

The pastor opened his book to begin the ceremony, but a resounding boom forestalled his delivery.

Beth glanced at Gar and sighed, noting the red flush on his cheekbones as he frowned at Ty. "What was that?" she asked in a hushed whisper.

"A canon. It was supposed to go off *after* our vows. Sorry, darling."

"That's all ri—"

A loud squawking of birds rang through the sanctuary. Beth raised one eyebrow at Gar.

"Doves," he whispered back. "I'm sorry, Beth. I meant to make this wedding the talk of the town, but nothing's going right. People are going to be talking about us all right."

Beth glanced upward, a small private smile curving

the corners of her mouth. *Funny,* she thought. *Very funny, Lord.*

Then she turned to Gar, her smile fixed firmly in place. It really didn't matter, she decided. Nothing could spoil the wonder and beauty of their love.

She squeezed his hand and turned to the minister. "We're ready now."

The rest of the wedding went off without a hitch. But the wedding reception had to be postponed because of the impending snowstorm. Which in turn meant that the bride and groom couldn't get away to the Caribbean.

Undaunted, Beth changed from her finery into an old pair of jeans and a warm sweater, while Gar unloaded the supply-filled car. She wandered through the house he'd built for her, amazed at the detail he'd put into each room. When he returned, she was waiting beside the fire.

"I'm sorry we couldn't fly out," he murmured, wrapping his arms around her waist. "I really wanted to spend two weeks alone with you on a tropical island."

Beth shrugged, leaning against him. "We can't control the weather, Gar. We have to take what God gives us and work with it. Besides, I'm marooned with you here, on this snowy hill, miles away from civilization. What more could I ask for?"

She was about to kiss him when the lights flickered, then went out.

"I never said a word," Gar chuckled, holding her close as the faint glow from the fire lit up the room.

Beth pulled a blanket from the sofa and spread it before the fire. When Gar was seated, she handed him a mug of steaming hot chocolate and tinkled hers against it.

"You know, when I gave up control in the snowstorm and promised God that I'd rely on Him, I never realized exactly what that meant. Two snowstorms in February, a misfired cannon, birds that won't fly away, and power that doesn't work." She shook her head. "Are you expecting anything else?"

Gar reached over and took away her mug, setting it carefully on a nearby table. He wrapped both arms around her, bent his head down and touched her mouth with his.

"It doesn't really matter, does it?" he whispered.

Beth kissed him back, a thrill of delight coursing through her. "Not a bit," she assured him softly. "Not one single bit. I love you, Mr. Winthrop."

"And I love you, Mrs. Winthrop. I've been waiting for you for ten, make that eleven, long years."

* * * * *

Dear Reader,

Welcome back to my fantasy town of Oakburn. I hope you've enjoyed my three brides and the wonderful blessings they've found, though they had to wait ten long years! Beth's courage in returning to Oakburn and facing all the problems that lay in wait for her are a reminder to me, too. I see in Beth's growth a pattern we could all follow. If we will just believe that God, our loving heavenly Father, wants more for us than we can imagine, it would be so easy to be patient and wait on His guidance. But Beth's story proves that in spite of trying to find her own solutions, God worked through her circumstances and gave her the most wondrous gift of love.

I wish you a heart full to overflowing with the love of a God who is enough.

Lois
Richer

I'd love to hear from you. Please write me at: Box 639, Nipawin, Saskatchewan, Canada S0E 1E0.

REQUEST YOUR FREE BOOKS!

2 FREE INSPIRATIONAL NOVELS
PLUS 2
FREE
MYSTERY GIFTS

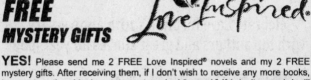

YES! Please send me 2 FREE Love Inspired® novels and my 2 FREE mystery gifts. After receiving them, if I don't wish to receive any more books, I can return the shipping statement marked "cancel." If I don't cancel, I will receive 4 brand-new novels every month and be billed just $3.99 per book in the U.S., or $4.74 per book in Canada, plus 25¢ shipping and handling per book and applicable taxes, if any*. That's a savings of 20% off the cover price! I understand that accepting the 2 free books and gifts places me under no obligation to buy anything. I can always return a shipment and cancel at any time. Even if I never buy another book from Steeple Hill, the two free books and gifts are mine to keep forever.

113 IDN EF26 313 IDN EF27

Name	(PLEASE PRINT)	
Address		Apt. #
City	State/Prov.	Zip/Postal Code

Signature (if under 18, a parent or guardian must sign)

Order online at www.LoveInspiredBooks.com

Or mail to Steeple Hill Reader Service™:

IN U.S.A.: P.O. Box 1867, Buffalo, NY 14240-1867
IN CANADA: P.O. Box 609, Fort Erie, Ontario L2A 5X3

Not valid to current Love Inspired subscribers.

Want to try two free books from another series?
Call 1-800-873-8635 or visit www.morefreebooks.com

* Terms and prices subject to change without notice. NY residents add applicable sales tax. Canadian residents will be charged applicable provincial taxes and GST. This offer is limited to one order per household. All orders subject to approval. Credit or debit balances in a customer's account(s) may be offset by any other outstanding balance owed by or to the customer. Please allow 4 to 6 weeks for delivery.

Your Privacy: Steeple Hill is committed to protecting your privacy. Our Privacy Policy is available online at www.eHarlequin.com or upon request from the Reader Service. From time to time we make our lists of customers available to reputable firms who may have a product or service of interest to you. If you would prefer we not share your name and address, please check here. ☐

LIREG07

Love Inspired

Celebrate Love Inspired's 10th anniversary with top authors and great stories all year long!

A SPECIAL STEEPLE HILL CAFÉ NOVEL FROM LOVE INSPIRED®

Opening a coffee shop was Maggie Black's dream. She just had to get a loan. Banker William Grey III wanted her to take his business class first, and Maggie agreed. After all, his velvety British accent could make even financial analysis sound interesting.

Look for

THE PERFECT BLEND

BY ALLIE PLEITER

Available July wherever you buy books.

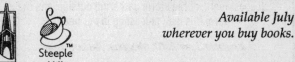

Steeple Hill®

Steeple Hill Café™

LIPBAP